Persuading Annie

By Melissa Nathan

PERSUADING ANNIE
THE NANNY
PRIDE, PREJUDICE AND JASMIN FIELD

Persuading Annie

MELISSA NATHAN

AVON
TRADE

An Imprint of HarperCollins*Publishers*

FIRST EDITION

Designed by Elizabeth M. Glover

Library of Congress Cataloging-in-Publication Data

Nathan, Melissa.
   Persuading Annie / by Melissa Nathan.—1st ed.
      p. cm.
   ISBN 0-06-059580-9 (alk. paper)
   1. Austen, Jane, 1775–1817—Appreciation—Fiction. 2. Family-owned business enterprises—Fiction. 3. Rejection (Psychology)—Fiction. 4. Revenge—Fiction. 5. England—Fiction. I. Title.

PR6064.A67P47 2004
823'.92—dc22   2003063874

04 05 06 07 08 JTC/RRD 10 9 8 7 6 5 4 3 2 1

To Mum and Dad
For everything

(except perhaps the hips.
I could have done without them.)

It was a perpetual estrangement.

Persuasion, JANE AUSTEN

1994

Prologue

"*C*ass. I'm pregnant."

Pause.

"*Pregnant?* Jesus *Christ*. How come?"

"How come? Are you insulting my looks or something?"

"I mean *how could you let this happen?*"

"I WAS LOOKING THE OTHER WAY."

"Jake."

"Hmm?"

Pause.

"I'm pregnant."

Pause.

Pause.

"I said I'm—"

"I heard."

Pause.

Pause.

"Annie, will you . . ."

Long pause.

"Yes?"

". . . tell me who the father is?"

           ★   ★   ★

"Susannah. I'm pregnant."

Immaculate pause.

Silence.

"You look shocked, Susannah."

"*Shocked?* I'm stunned, my dear. I had no idea your periods had started."

Annie opened her eyes in the dark. Nope. She knew with the certainty of death that it wouldn't—*couldn't*—possibly go that well.

Chapter 1

*C*assandra Brooke stared across the Union bar at the rugby players, her Cruel Crimson lips pursed into a thin line. Most of them didn't notice her, thanks to a rather preoccupying game involving beer and various orifices. But one winked at her so lasciviously that she felt utterly violated. She dragged her eyes away.

"I see what you mean about getting an education at college," she quipped. "I'm learning so much about men. And I've only been here an hour."

The Union bar wasn't really the ideal location for this, thought Annie, but then, there hadn't been much of a choice. Her room in halls was so small she needed an oxygen mask just to sit in it, and the canteen reminded her of boarding school, which filled her with a bizarre combination of mild nausea and painful nostalgia.

Being a campus university, situated in the middle of hills and woods, there weren't any decent cafés for miles around. At least in the Union bar, with its retro 50s diner look and extensive burger menu, they felt adult.

A rugby player belched loudly to thunderous applause.

Cass turned to face Annie so slowly that, like a gliding second hand on a good watch, the movement of her head was practically imperceptible to the human eye.

They sat motionless, Cass wishing she could feel more relaxed in such surroundings, Annie marveling that Cass could indeed do that with her head.

Annie decided this time was as good as any to speak. In other words, there was going to be no good time. She ignored the parched sourness in her mouth and forced the words out.

"I . . . I think I'm pregnant," she said.

The two old friends stared at each other across the formica table, which Annie felt gradually widen between them.

And then slowly Cass's face underwent as big a transformation as it could after choice cosmetic surgery. Gone were all signs of disdain, and in their place confusion, shock and concern. Not bad, thought Annie, impressed. She must tell her how marvelous her plastic surgeon was.

Another time perhaps.

Meanwhile Cass's mind was whirring. What to say, what to say . . . *I'll hold your hand during the op; I'll hold your hand during labor; who's the father? How does it feel? Why didn't you wait for me? Haven't you heard of contraception, for Christ's sake? You couldn't have told me this over the phone?*

Eenie, meenie, minie, mo. She plumped instead, for a simple one.

"Oh my God."

Annie looked out of the window, barely registering the acres of green grass and dense trees edging the halls of residence.

"God had little to do with it."

"It's a figure of speech."

"Mm."

"I meant to say 'Oh fuck,' but I thought in the circumstances . . ."

Annie nodded.

"So," said Cass decisively. "What are you going to do?"

"I don't know," mused Annie. "I thought I'd be sick. Cry a bit, rant a bit. Then panic-eat."

"Gosh. You've really thought it all through."

Annie shrugged.

"I might change the order."

Cass hung her head.

And who the hell was the father? Oh God, a bloody student. Trust Annie to be one of the few girls who *didn't* get pregnant at school, when at least she was surrounded by pedigree.

"Please don't tell your mother," implored Annie.

"Of course not!" retorted Cass, irritated. "It would make her go gray. And she hates that look."

"Susannah's—been like a mother to me."

Cass squirmed in her seat, moved by Annie's slow, silent tear.

They sat in sullen silence for a while.

"I assume, it's this new boyfriend of yours . . . Jack—"

"*Jake—*"

"Jake. Jake's . . . responsible? Or . . . or is it someone else?"

Annie bristled. "Well Jake was there at the time but he did have his eyes closed, so let's hope he's not the suspicious type."

Cass eyed her friend.

"Oh well, at least when you've lost everything, you'll still have your sense of humor. That'll keep you warm at night."

"Lost everything?"

"Do you think your father will give you a penny if you have this baby? Do you think my mother will ever forgive you for turning your back on your world?"

She paused to let this sink in.

"Have you told Jake?"

"No."

Well that was a start.

"Are you going to tell him?"

"Not yet."

"Why?"

"I'm only one month late."

Cass laughed with relief.

"Oh well! Why didn't you say?" she said, her voice an octave higher. "That's nothing! Once I was so late, I thought my menopause had started thirty years early. Turned out I had a virus."

"I'm as regular as Swiss clockwork."

"It's probably just tension," continued Cass, her voice staying determinedly high. "Stress. What with your exams and everything."

"I've done the test."

Cass sat rigidly on the bench, her body straining to maintain the illusion of calm at the same time as not looking over at the rugby players. Both were proving more difficult than she felt proper.

But nothing ever muddied Cass's clarity of thought, she quite prided herself on it. And she knew exactly where this discussion must lead. But how to broach the subject, how to broach the subject . . . Be subtle, be gentle, be clever. Be like Mother.

She leaned forward.

"You're not going to keep it, are you?" she asked.

Damn. That came out wrong.

Annie blinked her large eyes slowly at her friend, in the vague hope of Etch-a-sketch-ing her away.

"I mean," continued Cass, "this isn't just a cute little baby in cute little clothes, this is someone who'll turn round in eighteen years' time and blame you for everything you've ever done. If it's still talking to you then."

Annie's expression didn't flicker. She stayed silent.

"You're only nineteen for God's sake."

Annie snorted, perhaps a tad louder than she'd intended. A couple of rugby players looked over at her, visibly impressed. If she could prove that wasn't an accident they'd vote her on to the Union committee.

It was time to put forward her defense.

"Princess Diana was this age when she married Prince Charles."

"*Oh yes!*" exclaimed Cass. "You're right! And *she's* living happily ever after."

Annie frowned. She was no good at arguing, never had been. The deeper her emotions, the more each strand of argument knotted itself up with all the others in a dense mess in her head, leaving only the rat's tail end of each one visible to her. The result was that she could never follow one strand long enough to make it coherent or powerful. Instead she skipped blindly from one to another, mid-strand, confusing herself as much as the person she was arguing with. The more it happened, the more annoyed she got and the more annoyed she got, the more it happened. It was during arguments that Annie felt she most misrepresented herself. Usually while whimpering.

But it didn't mean she was wrong.

Anyway, she thought defiantly, usually she was arguing with her father or Susannah—Cass's mother and her godmother—or her two older sisters, Victoria and Katherine, Champion Arguers all. People she was doomed to lose to before she'd even begun. She had never argued with someone she loved and who loved her back. And, come to think of it, she hadn't actually had an argument for years. Maybe things had changed. Maybe the adult Annie could argue.

This knowledge made her strong.

"I'm just trying to say that nineteen's not that young," she finished, determined not to be distracted by Cass's confidence.

"Not that young?" exploded Cass. "You haven't even . . . done Australia yet! You've never been with a boy for longer than three months, you haven't even decided whether you believe in God yet, you don't even know what job you want to do. You're a baby yourself. You know *nothing*."

How dare she! Annie was suddenly livid. Cass had absolutely no idea how she felt. There was only one thing for it. It was a new tactic for her, but she'd seen others use it and she felt up to it. She would have to go off on a Tangent, into Attack.

"If this had happened last year," she said, with a firmness that belied her feelings, "with a 'suitable' boy, you, your mother and my father would have had me married off in no time."

Her chest heaved uncomfortably as she hid her hands beneath the table to hide their shaking.

"But that's different, Annie!"

Cass's pained look gave Annie a taste for victory that was totally new to her.

"Oh! I'd have been older a year ago, would I?"

Sarcasm! Was this really her? She felt giddy with the ease of it.

"You know what I mean," said Cass.

Hah! A pathetic counter, thought Annie. Truculent in defeat. And it gave her the perfect entry to another Attack.

"Yes, I know exactly what you mean. You mean that if a boy gets me in the club then it's OK if he and my father are in the same club too."

A Pun to Prove A Point! She could give lessons! And now for the Finale . . . Hit Home with a Home Truth . . .

"You're just a plain old snob, Cass."

Cass took in so much air, her lungs went blue. She was beside herself with shock and affront.

"Who are you calling plain? *Old?* I'm only two years older than you!"

"Three school years," shot Annie.

Wow! Irrelevant and personal, but a good comeback none the less. Annie hardly knew herself.

"Well, we're not at school any more," retorted Cass.

"So stop trying to talk to me as if I am."

Annie could almost hear the crowds cheering.

"And what about him? He's only my age—he's a *boy*."

"Jake's mature for his age."

Downright lie, but Cass wouldn't know that.

"Oh, don't be ridiculous. If there's one thing boys do slowly it's mature."

Bugger. Impossible To Lie To Cass. Mental note.

They sat in mutual, silent fury, both surprised and pained by their first ever row. Cass turned her attention to the rugby players, determined for Annie not to see her eyes watering.

The two rugby players were now staring hard at Cass and Annie, picturing them wearing their rugby shirts girl-style—pearl necklaces inside their upturned collars. Yep, it worked. They were foxes, all right. They barely noticed some other girls join the rest of their crowd, resulting in some obligatory guttural spitting from their friends, the mating call of modern man. Cass looked away, disgusted.

"I bet they're all gay," she muttered conspiratorially. "So far in the bloody closet you can smell the mothballs from here."

Oh no you don't, thought Annie, her bitterness emboldened by Cass's pax attempt.

"Just because these men weren't born with privilege"—she said haughtily—"it doesn't make them subhuman, you know."

A rugby player set fire to his fart.

Cass raised her perfect eyebrows into perfect arcs.

"No," she agreed. "I see they're still working their way up the evolutionary ladder to that level."

Oh great, thought Annie. Now we're just being bitchy. She felt several strands of her argument start to tangle slowly in her mind. Maybe she'd stop now. Quit while she was ahead.

They sat for a long time, both looking anywhere else but at each other. Eventually, Cass tried again.

"For goodness' sake, Annie," she implored softly. "You've only been with this . . . Jock—"

"*JAKE.*"

"Sorry, Jake—for two months. You don't even know if you love him."

Annie shook her head. Why did people always assume her emotions ranged only as far as theirs? She took a deep breath.

"Well, there you're wrong," she whispered dramatically. "That's the one thing I do know."

Cass's spirit plummeted and then swooped sharply up into anger.

"Oh well, whoopdeedoo," she retorted. "Have you heard? You can use love tokens at Kwiksave now?"

Annie looked away, her mind so muddled she couldn't even work out what point Cass was making, only that she'd had the last line and it was full of bile.

She wanted Cass to go. She hated arguing. She wanted to be with Jake. She had to be with Jake.

He'd understand everything.

"*PREGNANT? WHAT DO YOU MEAN PREGNANT?*"

She never knew Jake's voice could go so high.

"Well . . ." she started, trying to keep calm, "when a man loves a woman, he puts his—"

"PREGNANT?" he squealed again, so loudly that a passing mongrel stopped its forage for sticks in the river and looked at him eagerly, ears pricked, tongue lolling, bright eyes keen. Only when Jake joined him in panting rather heavily, did the dog scurry away.

"I said I *think* I might be preg—"

"Oh my God I'm going to be sick."

How *dare* he, thought Annie as she watched Jake bend over the edge of the river, his hair flopping into his face. That's my line.

After a moment though, Jake stood up slowly, wiped his loose curls out of his dark eyes and simply stared at Annie with an unfathomable expression. She took him in; cheekbones that seemed too strong for his soft skin; trousers that were too baggy for his long legs; and a defensive way of holding himself that made him look like he was plucking up the courage to ask for his ball back please. Poor boy, she thought.

"Sorry," he muttered, half a smile starting at the corners of his mouth. "I . . . I don't know what I'm saying. I'm not going to be sick."

Then, in one swift, sudden movement, he knelt down on one knee in front of her, steadying himself with one hand, all the time keeping his eyes fixed firmly on her face. Annie held her breath. The autumn sun broke through the naked trees, suddenly warming her to the very bone.

A fine line of sweat formed on Jake's upper lip.

"Annie," he murmured. "I think I'm going to faint."

And then he collapsed in the wet mud at her feet.

"So we're friends again?" repeated Annie into the phone.

"Of course we're friends again," repeated Cass back. "You can't get rid of me that easily."

"Thank God. I'd have felt so crap leaving on a bad note."

Whoops! Oh my God, oh my God, oh my God . . .

Bag open, cat out and frolicking gaily in the wild, Annie brainless moron.

Jake would kill her.

"Leaving?" asked Cass.

"Pardon? I think the line's going funny."

"Annie? What's going on?"

OK, quick thinking, quick thinking. Should she lie?

"Annie—what's going on?"

OK, even quicker thinking, even quicker thinking. Yes she should.

"I didn't say *leaving*, I said *heaving*."

Annie shook her head in disgust. Pathetic.

"Oh I see. As in the well-known phrase '*heaving* on a bad note'?"

Annie couldn't answer. She was too busy wincing.

Silence. Was Cass going to be big about this and just let it drop?

"I'm waiting."

Nope.

She was cornered. But wild horses would never drag the truth from her.

"All right. I'm going on holiday."

Phew—genius!

"Don't lie to me Annie, it only humiliates you."

Bugger. Impossible to Lie to Cass, Even Over Phone. Mental note Two.

Should she get self-pious?

"I can't tell you. If you love me you won't make me."

"I don't love you."

Damn. Wrong-footed again. How does Cass do that?

"Annie, of course I love you. I just want to know—"

OK, go passive—blame someone else.

"Look, he'll kill me, I just can't tell you."

"Who'll kill you?"

Damn! She was so fast.

"Never mind. Just forget I said anything."

Cass would never guess who. And wild horses couldn't drag Jake's name out of her mouth.

"It's Jake isn't it?"

Jesus Christ—she was a bloody witch.

"Have you ever thought of becoming a spy, Cass?"

"To summarize: you're leaving with Jake. In secret."

"Not exactly."

"How not exactly, exactly?"

"Well. Define secret."

"How long are you leaving for?"

Aha! Wild horses couldn't drag that one out of her. Lying hadn't worked, so she'd just keep it vague.

"As long as it lasts."

"Oh my God! You're marrying him! Just because of the baby?"

No! Wild horses couldn't, etc.

"Not just because of the baby—because we love each other!"

Annie made a drowning noise. Was her mouth actually attached to her brain? It would explain so much about her life.

Right. It was time to take control back again.

"You tell your mother," rushed Annie, "and I'll never talk to you again."

"Why the hell would I tell Mother? Please Annie. Credit me with some loyalty."

"This is our secret. It's got nothing to do with Susannah. It's between you and me."

"And Jake."

"Yes, of course. You, me and Jake."

"And the baby."

"Yes of course. You, me, Jake and the baby."

"Thank you for sharing."

"Oh SHUT UP."

Perhaps if Annie hadn't chosen that moment to change the habit of a lifetime and shouted at Cass, at least one of them would have heard the extension click off.

One Week Later

Annie hummed loudly as she packed her rucksack. The sound of gravel hitting the window of her halls room stopped her mid-hum, making it as much of a blessed relief to the student next door as it was to Annie's clothes. She rushed to the window. It was pitch black out there. She opened it wide.

"Hellooooo," she whispered.

There was movement on the gravel below. She could just make out Jake's form. Even in those ridiculously baggy jeans, even from this angle, the tilt of his head, the line of his shoulders, his unconsciously boyish stance made her stomach squirm. Or was that the kilo of licorice she'd just eaten?

"Are you ready?" he whispered hoarsely.

"Yes—how was your final final?"

"They're over! I'm a free man. I'm all yours."

"I'll be there as soon as I'm ready."

"Packed your passport?"

"Of course! Give me ten minutes."

Jake looked at his watch.

"OK. One minute later and I'll call it off," he grinned up at her. "I'm more vulnerable than I look."

Impossible, thought Annie.

"Well go away and let me pack then."

And with that, she was gone.

A minute later, a knock at the door made Annie jump from behind the bed, where she was searching frantically for her passport.

She stared at the door, as if by determination alone, she would be able to see right through it. Another knock. It must be Jake. No one else would be so stupid as to disturb her now. Maybe he knew where her passport was. Maybe he had it with him. Another knock, louder now. She rushed to the door.

And there in the doorway, heralded by an aroma of expensive perfume, stood Cass's mother, Annie's godmother.

Susannah Brooke was paying a friendly call.

Annie trembled as Susannah came in. She glanced covertly at the clock beside her bed. She had nine minutes to get to Jake so that they could get the train to Dover and from there to Paris.

Susannah stepped toward Annie and started to take off her soft leather gloves. She looked around the dusty room and, after a moment's thought, slowly started putting her gloves back on.

"Aren't you going to ask me if I'd like a coffee?" she asked eventually.

Annie was baffled. Surely Susannah wasn't here merely for a social call? Unless it was just a case of chronic bad timing. Yes, that must be it. Just bad timing. Cass would never have betrayed her and told Susannah. Just act normal and Susannah would leave soon.

"Would you like a coffee?" she asked feebly.

"No, I would *not* like a coffee!" shouted Susannah, making Annie jump. "I'd like to know why my favorite, intelligent, beautiful, talented—baby god-daughter with a life full of blossoming potential is acting like a dog on heat?"

Annie shrank on to her bed, her hand lying limply on her open rucksack. So Cass had betrayed her. Well, what had she expected? Susannah surpassed even her daughter in spy tactics. She could hardly blame Cass for this turn of events—the only person she could truly blame was herself. Meanwhile, she now had to witness her godmother's disappointment in her. She remembered why she'd hoped to be in a secret hideaway when Susannah found out the truth. No one could induce a sense of shame more successfully than her.

Susannah sighed and came over. She moved the rucksack gingerly on to the floor, sat beside Annie and put her arm around her.

"My poor Annie," she whispered and kissed her forehead. The years flew away and Annie was a child once more.

"It's been confusing, hasn't it?" continued Susannah. Annie nodded, breathing in the nostalgic smell of her godmother.

"Have you been scared?"

Another nod.

"My poor baby."

Annie glanced surreptitiously at the clock. Eight minutes.

Susannah took off her coat and laid it beside them on the bed. Susannah tilted Annie's chin up to look at her.

"I remember when I discovered I was pregnant," she smiled, her eyes warm. "It was the most wonderful day of my life."

Annie smiled.

"I was married to the man I loved and I knew that he hadn't married me for my money or the baby," she continued. "He had married me because he loved me. For better or worse. In sickness and health."

Annie froze.

"Jake is marrying me because he loves me," she ventured. She'd never so much as crossed Susannah before, so she kept her voice soft and light. Through sheer terror.

"Of course he is," comforted Susannah. "That's why he didn't propose to you before bedding you. That's why he suddenly changed his mind when he found out you had enough money to support him in Paris for a few years."

Annie stood up and walked to the other side of her room. She was now a full two paces away from Susannah. Her voice shook with the effort of defying Susannah.

"Jake loves me."

Her breathing was heavy.

"Of course he does, my darling. That's why he avoided you for three whole days after you told him the news. That's why he only proposed after you begged him to."

"I didn't beg—" breathed Annie.

"Annie, darling. A woman can only beg in situations like these."

Annie closed her eyes tight. She tried to visualize Jake. How he had come to her shaken, pale and even skinnier than usual, after the longest three days of her life and said simply, "We'll do whatever you want. I can't lose you." She tried to visualize how scared he'd looked. And she had told him then of her savings and of her plan to elope to Paris. At first Jake had been horrified, then insulted, due to a macho pride that had been so incongruous it had made her laugh. But after persuading him with all the wiles she could, he had finally been too weak to argue. And then they'd laughed with the thrill of it, both as scared as each other, yet excited by the other's sense of adventure and faith.

She tried to visualize it, as she'd seen it then, but it was fading fast.

"I . . . I . . ." she started. "I have to sit down."

Susannah rushed over to her and brought her back to the bed.

"I'll get you a glass of water, my dear."

She poured Annie some water and handed it carefully to her.

"There, there," said Susannah, rubbing her back.

When Annie had finished the water, Susannah placed the glass gently next to the clock.

Six minutes to go.

"My darling," started Susannah, her voice as soft as silk. "I loved your mother as dearly as I love you. It is my biggest sorrow that I knew her so much better than you ever did. And I know what question she'd be asking you now, at this most precious time of your life."

Annie couldn't help herself. She was so desperate for a hint of her mother now.

"What?"

Susannah imbued her words with the softest hint of humor.

"Why rush into marriage?"

Annie was stumped.

"I mean," continued Susannah. "It's not as if there's a stigma nowadays to living together—even being a single mother—so why . . . *rush* into marriage?"

Annie couldn't answer.

Susannah whispered gently, as if reading a storybook to a sleepy child.

"Are you scared you'll lose him?"

Annie stared at the lino under her feet.

"Does he have a bit of a reputation?"

Annie saw in her mind's eye that blonde bitch from Psychology whom Jake was going out with before her. And that bossy girl in last year's play. Then there was that one who'd left college to join the local newspaper. And then . . .

Susannah's voice was barely more than a whisper.

"Does eloping with you prove he doesn't love your fame and money more than you?"

Annie shook her head, trying to get the thought out of her mind.
Susannah squeezed her shoulder tenderly.

"Are you scared you love him more than he loves you?"

Annie felt her insides freeze. She'd never put it into so many
words, but . . .

She looked sadly over at the clock. Five whole minutes to go.
Ages yet . . .

"Come on poppet, wipe your tears. Men will come and go but
I'll love you forever."

Annie felt a sweet familiar weakness overcome her.

"I have to go to the toilet."

"Of course," said Susannah. "I'll wait for you downstairs in the
car. Then we'll go home."

Annie stumbled down the narrow corridor toward the ladies'
toilet.

She had to think.

Quarter of an hour later, Annie stared in disbelief at the toilet wall.

How could this be happening? She was sure she was six weeks
late. She tried to mentally flick through her diary. The sudden realization that she'd skipped a month—she'd kept doing that while
rewriting her increasingly dense revision timetable—simply added
nausea to the sudden cramps in her lower abdomen.

But the pregnancy test? Wasn't that irrefutable?

She remembered reading the bold caution at the bottom of the
instructions. Ninety-eight percent accurate.

Jesus Christ. She was a statistical blip. A two percent margin. The
test had been wrong. She'd failed the pregnancy test. Were all of
her tests going to prove as successful, she wondered bitterly, before
the sound of her own echoey sobbing told her that her body wasn't
taking this quite as well as her mind.

Twenty-five minutes later, tear-stained and hollow, she returned
to her room, as if in a daze.

The sight of Jake on her bed woke her up fast. She stared at him in shock, conscious of a bewildering change in her feelings toward him. She'd always loved the fact that he filled her tiny room, but for the first time, his presence seemed threatening.

He was holding her creased jeans in his hand. His grin froze at the sight of her.

After a moment's hesitation, he spoke.

"Don't you know you get creases in jeans if you fold them?" he said, his tone a touch too light. "You're meant to roll them."

Annie was unable to move or speak.

Eventually Jake stood up, leaving his innards somewhere near his feet. He was dimly aware that his gut felt like a black hole.

He stared at Annie, but she was unable to meet his gaze.

"Changed your mind then, eh?" he said, willing her to raise her eyes.

Annie kept her head down.

"Just like that?"

Nothing.

"And what about . . . the baby?"

Annie held her stomach and felt the pain again.

"There is no baby," she forced herself to say and started to cry silently.

Jake looked at Annie as if seeing her for the first time.

"What?"

"No . . . baby," she whispered, overcome by an unaccountable sense of shame.

They stood in silence for a while before Annie felt able to try and make it better.

"It's better this way. Susannah said . . ."

"You told *Susannah?*"

"No!" she exclaimed, self-righteously. "Cass told Susannah."

"You told *Cass?*"

"I didn't mean to—"

She broke off and they shared a horribly eloquent silence. It didn't take much silence to fill the tiny room. In fact, silence started seeping into the empty wardrobes.

Jake stood motionless, the world around him spinning. And then, he decided to take the bull by the horns.

He exploded.

"D'you think I'm some sort of toy to play around with?"

"What?"

"Thought you could chew me up and spit me out when you got bored? Is that it? Freak the crap out of me and then say sweetly 'Oh so sorry! I got my dates wrong!' "

Annie stared at him.

"It's all turned out nice and neat, hasn't it? So when did you find this out? Last week? Or was it all a lie? A trap?"

"A trap? What century are you living in—"

"Or a test? Is that it? You were testing me?"

"Why would I—"

"Or don't you like the idea of supporting me while I work my ass off trying to get a career that will support us all—when the chips are down, you'd rather be with a rich old man and save your precious money for . . . for . . . shopping? Is that it?"

Annie couldn't bear to hear any more.

"Please leave now," she said in a low voice.

He went to leave, but when he got to the door, he turned and, with his eyes down, spoke in a low, shaky voice.

"Did you get rid of my baby?"

It was Annie's turn to lose the plot.

"*Your* baby! I like that. It took you three days to even talk to me after finding out it existed—which it doesn't—and now it's *your* bloody baby. Hah! Future Father of the Year material, I don't think!"

"Oh? So it's someone else's—"

"*No!*"

"So it's mine—"

"YOURS? What am *I*, an empty VESSEL?"

"OUR baby, then?"

"There IS NO BLOODY BABY!"

They were both yelling now. Susannah was right. Susannah was always right, when would she learn? Who *was* this boy, sobbing and shouting at her?

Before Annie had time to absorb any of what they'd just said, Jake had gone, and she heard him race out of the halls and into the woods that nestled the campus halls like a blanket around a sleeping child.

2001

Chapter 2

Café Exclusive
Haverstock Hill, Hampstead
10 A.M.

"Oh shit! I'm late!" exclaimed Annie.

"What?" gasped Cass.

"I'm late!"

Cass blanched.

"*Late* late? Or just . . . late?"

Annie nodded to the clock over Cass's head.

"I didn't realize the time—I've got to go." She gulped down the last of her café latte.

"Jesus, Annie, you nearly gave me a bloody heart attack. Let's go then."

Annie stared wild-eyed at her friend. "Don't tell me you didn't bring the car—I can't give you a lift, I'm late—"

"When did I ever not bring the car? I came out of the womb in a four-wheel drive. I don't need a lift, thanks very much. For goodness' sake calm down, I'm sure whoever you're meeting will wait . . ."

"Can you pay the bill?"

Annie slapped down a fiver on the round table between them. "I know it's Hampstead darling, but one café latte still doesn't cost a fiver."

Annie was already out of the door.

"Pay me back later!" she called out.

Cass watched Annie hurl herself out of the café, knocking into a couple of tourists as she did so. What was it this time, she wondered. Had Edward Goddard finally asked her out? Was she signing up another impoverished artist for her father's company to sponsor? Or was she on one of her curious nights away when no one could contact her or find out where she'd been?

Cass caught the waiter's eye and asked for the bill.

Meanwhile Annie raced down Hampstead's Haverstock Hill.

Jesus—how did she do this every time? Every bloody time she was late. She bumped into some dithering window-shopper on the pavement in front of her and called out a hasty apology as she raced across the zebra crossing, causing a car to emergency brake.

With her flowing hair, billowing knapsack and furious speed, Annie was an intriguing sight as she swore furiously at herself all the way toward her car.

Like every driver on the road, getting behind the wheel did nothing to calm Annie's nerves. Quite the opposite in fact. No one had a right to be on her road—didn't they know she had somewhere important to be? She almost suffered turbulence turning a corner too sharply and "amber-gambled" the lights so frantically, that when a siren went off in the distance she thought it was for her. As soon as the police car sped past her, her foot hit the accelerator.

"Get out of my road!" she yelled at a Sunday driver who, complete with peaked cap, trusty Thermos and worried wife, was driving at twenty miles an hour down the middle of the road in front of her. "Why don't you just walk—you'd get there quicker and kill less people," she yelled.

Eventually, after zigzagging behind him for quarter of a mile, she risked life and limb and overtook. Ennobled by her speed, the Sunday driver found a courage he'd forgotten he had and sped up to a record-breaking thirty-five miles an hour, causing Annie to swerve at the last minute in front of him, her heart in her mouth. "Why do you think bus passes are free for you?" she yelled into her rearview mirror, before spotting a bus pulling out in front of her. She slammed on the brakes.

Just as she zipped out of a turning, a boy who couldn't have been more than seventeen almost careered into the side of her car. They both emergency braked and stared in shock and fear at each other, the blood draining out of their faces. Bloody kids! Death Wish, some of them.

As she reached the road where she needed to be, she found a parking space, zoomed into it, nudged the car behind her, cursed loudly, grabbed her bag, slammed her car door shut, locked it and rushed to the front door.

She turned the key in the lock, pushed the door open and felt almost instantly calmed by the atmosphere.

She walked into the front room. Joy was already there.

"Hi," breathed Annie. "How are you?"

"Depressed. Life is a black void of meaningless pain, thanks. You?"

"I nearly killed four people on the way here."

"Why is your life so much more interesting than mine?"

"Just lucky I guess."

"Ready?"

"As ready as I'll ever be."

They went inside to the little room, sat down on the big chairs, both sighed heavily and turned their phones on.

Annie's phone rang first. She waited for three rings, picked it up and spoke softly and warmly.

"Hello, Samaritans," she said. "Can I help?"

44a Haverstock Gardens, Hampstead Village
10 A.M.

"Did you know," called out Victoria to her husband, from behind her glossy magazine, "that men who make love frequently are half as likely to die prematurely than men who hardly do it?"

Victoria's husband, Charles, swore at himself in the mirror and then redid his tie.

The air around him chilled suddenly.

"Hmmm?" he said quickly.

Victoria spoke slowly and clearly, her vowels clipped so that Charles knew she was displeased at having to repeat herself.

"I *said*, did you know that men who make love *frequently* are less likely to die prematurely than men who don't?"

"That so?" he said, wandering into his walk-in wardrobe.

"By my reckoning," said Victoria, half to herself, half to the wardrobe, "you should be dead in a week."

Charles came out of the wardrobe holding his golfing shoes, his jowls trembling with anticipation, his small eyes blinking. "If I don't get a birdy today," he grinned, "I'll eat my Niblick."

Victoria stared at him. "I'll get the camera ready, dear," she said.

"Right you are." He looked at his watch. "Tee off in half an hour."

And he was gone.

Before the loneliness gripped her, she phoned home.

"Hhhrngh?" croaked the voice of Katherine.

"Katie darling, it's me."

"How are you, popsie?" Katherine's voice sounded as rough as a cat's tongue.

"*Awful*. I think I've got chronic fatigue syndrome. Could hardly lift my feet during my pedicure today."

"*Popsie*," consoled Katherine. "I've just been sick *three times* before breakfast."

Victoria tutted. "Not bulimia again? Weren't you seeing some-one for that?"

"No, sweetpea," said Katherine, piqued. "Sick *before* breakfast. Bu-limia would have been sick after breakfast, wouldn't it? The clues are in the words, darling. No, I have a hangover because I had such a good time last night. And then I vomited three times spectacularly, once over the chaise, once in the shower and once over Consuela."

"Oh for God's sake, Katie, *must* you give me the gruesome de-tails? I'm *ill* remember," Victoria sighed.

"Of course. How's Charles?"

"Golfing, how do you think?"

Both women grimaced. Such an embarrassment, *so* middle class.

"Isn't he going to this wretched meeting at Daddy's this after-noon?"

"What meeting?"

"You know, the one where Susannah tells us off and we all ig-nore her."

Victoria gasped with shock. "I completely forgot. I'll call Charles on his mobile. He can live without golf for one day."

"Aren't you going too, pumpkin?"

Victoria sighed.

"I would if I were up to it."

"I'll tell you all about it at the spa."

"Is Little Orphan Annie going to the meeting?"

"Probably. If she isn't out selling *The Big Issue*."

They both laughed weakly.

"Oh, how I wish I had her energy," said Victoria, and they both wheezed with lazily escalating laughter at the sudden image of Victoria wearing fingerless gloves and a duffel coat.

"That's right darling," said Katherine, "laugh through the pain."

They wheezed again.

"See you later darling. Give Daddy my love."

"Ciao."

The Ridings, Hampstead Heath
10:10 A.M.

Katherine Markham, eldest of the Markham daughters, pressed the off button of her phone and threw it down on to her silk sheets.

Fractionally slowly she inched her fragile body up into a sitting position and looked at herself in the vast mirror facing the bed.

Eyeliner smudged down her face, eyes dull and lifeless, blonde hair like a bird's nest, arms bony and limp, chest concave, expression vacant.

She lit up her first cigarette of the day and smiled at her reflection through the early morning haze.

I've still got it, she thought exultantly. I could be a bloody model.

Chapter 3

*G*eorge Markham's valet had a face so bland that George frequently forgot what the man looked like while still actually looking at him.

Mind you, George would have forgotten his own name, were it not for the fact that he reminded himself of it every morning, by glancing at the framed newspaper article that had been in his dressing room for nearly a decade. (The date had been smoothly guillotined away.) There it was in big bold letters: **George Markham, fiftieth richest man in the country** ("and it's no small country," he would point out to his valet every morning) **whose extraordinary good looks, fine business acumen and wealth has made his three beautiful daughters the most eligible women in the United Kingdom. Katherine, 20, Victoria, 18 and Annie, 16, are a credit to him.**

Every morning, while George's valet brushed down his master's suit, George re-read those hallowed words, sometimes to himself, sometimes out loud. And then his thoughts would turn to the man at his feet, polishing his shoes. Poor fellow, thought George, scrutinizing the man's features as if for the first time. Face like a spade.

Nothing was more offensive to George than bad looks in a person. It was downright rude, as far as he was concerned. He had told his assistant on more than one occasion about his own excellent plastic surgeon, but to no avail. He had explained patiently that he wouldn't even have to pay up front. George would simply take it out of his monthly wages, with a very competitive interest rate. But every morning, there the man stood to greet him, with his uniformly unimpressive features, eyes the color of duckweed. It was most provoking.

George Markham, a man of small mind and large opinions, sighed deeply. For a desperately needed early morning pick-me-up, he looked at himself in the mirror. It never failed to satisfy. Fifty-odd years on this earth had not diminished the joy he found in looking at his own features. In fact, if anything, they had served only to deepen the love he had for them.

Looking at his reflection was George's favorite hobby: it didn't stretch his attention span and it confirmed his long-held belief that the aesthetic was superior to the functional. It was his face that had got him almost everything in this world.

He smiled warmly at himself in the mirror. The ink-black of his pupils visibly swelled, reducing the liquid brown irises to a crescent-fine outline. His heart—such as it was—expanded. What style, what balance, what symmetry! He allowed himself one last wide smile—didn't want to give himself lines—before adopting his usual serene expression.

Once ready for work, George padded through his apartment. He opened his front door and breathed in the heady scent of jasmine before crunching down the gravel drive to where his limousine waited for him at the curb. Excellent exercise, walking. George insisted on it every morning if the weather was fine. One last deep breath and then into the car, which, alligator-like, darted silently away from the curb and sped off. Twenty cocooned minutes later, George was at his London office in Mayfair.

The glass door of Markhams' PR breathed open for George and he strode through the front office, nodding curtly at the blonde heads of his young staff, to the lift. Large gilt-framed posters of successful clients from the company's heyday bordered the office: a phenomenally popular novelty game that had lost its novelty within months, one of the first-ever whitening toothpastes, a Radio 1 disc jockey.

Inside the moving mirrored coffin, George brushed the top button with his index finger and, while gliding up to his penthouse office, glanced at his reflection to check that his tie and teeth were straight. They always were.

The door slid silently open.

"Good morning, Mr. Markham," greeted his secretary, Shirley, smiling warmly. "Your coffee's on the table."

"Ah well then," he greeted her back. "All's right with the world."

Shirley smiled, turned and walked as coquettishly as possible out of the room, which was not easy considering she was wearing a pleated A-line skirt and had size eighteen arthritic hips.

George eyed Shirley's retreating figure, as he did every morning. Marvelous secretary, he thought. Marvelous. Made coffee that woke you up faster than a pretty gal touching your personals.

George took his coffee, as usual, standing at his full-length window, overlooking London's hallowed streets. But today he was unable to prevent a few rather unsightly frown lines to pucker his perfectly proportioned brow.

He had a meeting at 11 a.m. with his solicitor, Mr. Cavendish, and even George knew things were going to get ugly. Which meant that his finance director—and trusted friend—Susannah Brooke should be here any minute. He glanced down at his Patek Philippe watch and noted the elegance of the long outstretched hand lying upward like the neck of a dying swan. Extraordinarily beautiful. He looked up and breathed in deeply. Ah, life was good.

He looked down again to see what time it was.

His eldest daughter, Katherine, should make it in time for the meeting, though she'd been partying till late the night before. Took after her father, that one, he reflected proudly. Might even have got herself into a glossy again, he thought with a triumphant glow. He hoped to God that this time she'd remembered to stay sober till after the photographer had gone.

There was a gentle knock at the door.

"Mrs. Brooke to see you."

Ah, Susannah! He turned to greet his old friend.

"George," greeted Susannah warmly, walking toward him.

"My dear," greeted George, allowing her to kiss him on both cheeks. They sat down, feeling safe in the knowledge that they entirely concurred with each other on every matter.

Today, however, was a difficult day for Susannah Brooke.

It had to be a day of action, something she knew George never liked taking, and it would take all her powers of patience, mental agility and rhetoric for it to go the right way.

"How are you, George?" she asked gently.

"Fine, my dear," he answered, in a deep, mellow voice that had melted many a young girl's heart, reserve and body. "I think today's going to go rather well."

"You do?" she asked, encouraged by the mischievous twinkle in his chestnut eyes.

"I do," he said firmly. "You know why?"

"No. Do tell."

"What color is this tie?"

Susannah studied the tie.

"Brown?"

George shook his head with a smug smile.

"Not just any brown. Chocolate Brown. Melted Bournville Chocolate Brown. *Exactly* the same color as my eyes. And I didn't even tell my man. It was just lucky fluke." He touched his aquiline nose with his elegant forefinger, as if to prove his point. "Always a good sign."

Susannah managed a smile.

*   *   *

Susannah had worked for Markhams' PR for well over three decades, since its heyday. And she had been a friend to the Markhams for almost as long, having met George's late wife, Caroline Markham, when both of them were nothing more than pretty young, single things in their first secretarial jobs, all those years ago.

Caroline had been lovely. Modest, beautiful, kind and intelligent— but shrewd as well, enough to know that she should demonstrate all three former qualities before the latter two. And together, she and Susannah had done very well for themselves. In fact, Caroline had excelled in the limited field open to her—for her class, era and gender. She had married her boss. Not just any boss, but chairman of the PR conglomerate Markhams' PR, millionaire George Markham.

Caroline was so universally loved that not a soul begrudged her her good fortune in making such a wonderful match. And of everyone, Susannah was the most delighted for her dearest friend, a generous reaction made easier by the fact that she had followed her only six weeks later, by marrying another wealthy man.

The two young girls' friendship had continued to blossom once they were both wealthy wives. But there the similarities in their lives ended. Susannah's husband had treated her spectacularly. He realized that he had married a clever woman, financed his wife through accountancy school, provided her with a beautiful daughter, watched her become more and more influential at Markhams' PR, and then died, leaving her more money than she and her child could ever spend, in a new life of uncompromising fulfillment. It was more than many women could have dreamed of.

Meanwhile, a different story was unfolding for Caroline Markham. The truth of it was that she had been very unhappily married. After all, it would have been too much for George Markham to have cast his eye over his typing pool, spotted the prettiest blonde, made her his bride *and* realized her worth too.

And sure enough, after Caroline's Happily Ever After ending came the shapeless, shameless sequel of real life, with no plot, little humor and a far less likeable hero.

Caroline had floated down the aisle to marry a startlingly handsome, intelligent, acerbic young magnate. Yet before their third anniversary she had finally admitted to herself the horrible truth. She was married to an irascible twat.

She slowly discovered that her husband was not, as all the lowly typists had assumed, the "brains" behind his international company. Far from it. He had simply had enough money to buy it, and ever since, his minions had had to work their fingers to the bone, untying the knots he regularly tied.

As for his acerbic wit, which Caroline had mistaken for a sharp mind, it was nothing more than a piercing cruelty he chose not to curb. He was in fact a vain, rude egotist, who had wanted a trophy blonde for a wife and it had been her luck to have been in the wrong place when he was ready to take the plunge. By the time she had fully confronted the horror of her situation she was already pregnant with her second daughter, Victoria. Two years later, Annie had been born into a loveless sham of a marriage in a last-ditch attempt by her parents to beget themselves a son.

By this time Caroline Markham was a jaded, used and lonely mother of three girls. Again she did the best thing she could do for her class, era and gender.

She did nothing.

Eventually, her early end came from an unfortunate mix of drink and pills. "A tragic accident," was the official verdict. And nothing more was said of the matter. Her three daughters, then all away from home, were told little about it, save the final fact, and were expected to get on with things. Katherine, nineteen, was staying with friends in Switzerland when she heard the news. Her first thoughts were that she would have to buy a new outfit for the funeral and that she'd miss the next ball. The disappointment of the latter surpassed the excitement of the first. Victoria, seventeen, at finishing school nearby, was distraught—or at least distracted—until she realized what this meant. It meant time, sympathy and understanding from the teachers with her school work and attention of a totally novel kind from her fellow pupils; she was a guiltless victim of circumstance, the feeble, motherless, utterly passive heroine of her own life, to be pitied, revered and secretly envied by all. She felt like a princess. Annie, fifteen, at an English boarding school she despised, was heartbroken. She had lost the one close relation she could relate closely to, and for the first time in her life, she felt truly alone. It was a feeling that was to stay with her for a long time.

Back in the adult world, there was, of course, the predictable gossip along the lines of a happy outcome for George Markham and Susannah Brooke. Their names were linked by many tabloid diarists for the first few years after their shared widowhood. But it soon became clear that George's interests lay in women who knew less of the world than he, not more, and that Susannah's interests lay in the world around her, not the men.

But that wasn't to say that they didn't find each other's company charming. Susannah still found it thrilling to meet every day with a man whose very ancestors had been King James's sycophants. George was as English as weak tea, mild weather and rabid xenophobia, and Susannah couldn't help but respect him for it. And George, full of generosity of spirit, respected Susannah for respecting him. In her work and in her most proper behavior to George, Susannah had quickly become almost as indispensable to him as she had been to his wife.

By the time Shirley popped back into the office, bringing with her a second round of coffee, George and Susannah's conversation had shifted gently toward businesslike topics.

"Mr. Cavendish is coming to this meeting, isn't he?" Susannah asked.

"Yes," sighed George. "That man worries me, you know."

Susannah went cold. "Why is that, George?" she asked softly.

"Don't tell me you haven't noticed?" he asked, unable to keep the surprised dismay out of his voice.

Susannah started to grow concerned. If George didn't trust Cavendish—whom she trusted enormously—they were in serious trouble.

"Noticed what?"

"His nasal hairs. Spend my whole time wanting to pull them out. Most off-putting."

The role of godmother to the Markham girls seemed at first to Susannah to be a role blessed in heaven. Three beautiful, wealthy debutantes with everything to live for, who would look up to her as their guide. What more could a woman bursting with maternal advice possibly want?

Three different girls, perhaps.

Susannah had had to watch each Markham girl, once so full of promise, miss all the opportunities their lives had offered them and, one by one, sorely disappoint their father. Because Susannah had greater intelligence and imagination than George and therefore a larger capacity for pain, she had felt his disappointment on top of suffering her own, larger share.

Katherine, Victoria and Annie had, in their early teenage years, been the darlings of the glossies. All three radiated a beauty that comes naturally from handsome parents and a wealthy upbringing. Susannah and George had high hopes for their future, financial and otherwise.

George's middle daughter, Victoria, now nearing twenty-eight, had married Charles Norman at the perfectly acceptable age of twenty-two.

Charles Norman came from old stock, like George, and would, one day when his father died, inherit his father's considerable estate. Victoria had done well and they all celebrated her nuptials with so much relief that it hovered dangerously near smugness.

It was only after her marriage though, that Victoria discovered the ghastly truth about her husband. Until said death of his father, Charles got nothing. Nada. Not a penny. And his father, a youthful fifty-four, had the constitution of an ox. *His* father had lived past a hundred.

The news, naturally, hit them all hard.

Susannah had had to console both George and Victoria, while feeling no consolation in her heart at all. And she was truly concerned for her poor Victoria.

In those early, shocking months of marriage it had only been the fact that Victoria liked the face of her husband that kept her sane. She was, deep down, a woman of simple tastes. Some might say, on looking at her husband's face, that she was, in fact, a woman of odd tastes. Charles's face proved that if indeed, God did lovingly mold us all, occasionally His thumb slipped.

Victoria stayed sane, but she didn't stay the same determined young heroine of her own life, with everything before her. A sense of grievance, of being wronged by the world—and especially by Charles—gradually became so much a part of her identity that few could remember her before it. She honed the identity of guiltless victim/passive heroine, which had been thrust upon her when her mother died, to new heights. Susannah watched her middle goddaughter grow more and more resolutely bitter. In time, she became Victim Victoria, Giver of Guilt to all those who cared enough to deserve it.

Meanwhile, Susannah was reduced to plotting with George different ways of funding Victoria and Charles's lifestyle. Hardly what they had hoped for her.

Charles was given a nominal role in George's company—a role which, while creating the impression that he was important, gave him little, or nothing, to do. It was a thoughtful, clever gesture from George, which gave his son-in-law self-respect and his daughter an income. It had been Susannah's idea. The young couple settled into domestic life, had their "heir and a spare" and resolutely stopped partying.

Then there was Katherine.

George's eldest daughter, Katherine, at thirty, had done enough high-publicity fundraising in her lifetime to get a one-way ticket on Concorde straight to heaven the very moment she shuffled off her mortal coil. Yet *still* she had not brought a steady investment into the family via a wealthy husband. She had had to endure the slow shame of growing world-weary in the full glare of the spotlight without her moment of shimmering, white-dressed glory. There were younger, hipper "It" girls now, who did vulgar things like write newspaper columns and reduce their high-class addictions, phobias and ailments into prurient headlines.

The fact could no longer be denied that Katherine Markham had extended even her credit on the platinum card of acceptable single life. It was growing harder and harder to maintain the angular figure and self-loathing nature that was expected of women nowadays. Her bulimia and acidic tongue were *so* twentieth century. The plain fact was that she was a has-been and her assets were crumbling before their eyes.

And as for Annie, ah Annie, where had they gone wrong with her?

Susannah endeavored not to ponder this question too often, as it pained her so much. Unfortunately, once in a while, even she was unable to control her thoughts, and it was on those occasions that she mourned the loss of her dear Caroline most.

Annie had always been Susannah's favorite god-daughter. She was more soft, selfless and giving in nature than her older sisters. But perhaps most seductive of all, because she so desperately missed the wise counsel of her mother and never received any attention from her father, Annie was far more grateful than her sisters for her godmother's attention. Perhaps this was why Susannah grew to feel that Annie was by far the prettiest of the sisters. Certainly her looks were less ostentatious than Katherine's rather obvious blondness or

Victoria's dark beauty, and for those who did pay her any attention when her sisters were in the room, they did notice that Annie's charm was the most subtle and beguiling. And then of course there was the utterly bewitching sense of loss, of steady sadness, that never seemed to leave Annie. It showed in her bearing, her manner and her voice. It made one instinctively want to stretch out and help, guide and reassure her. Annie was, felt Susannah, the ultimate in femininity. What man could resist being the one to fill the void Annie's mother had left?

Susannah had secretly hoped that the youngest Markham girl would surprise them all and, Cinderella-like, win the biggest lottery jackpot of the family. In her wildest dreams, Susannah had seen Annie marrying a titled man.

But that dream had long gone.

Susannah could have coped with almost anything happening to her three girls (except of course, obesity)—after all, hadn't the privileged suffered imprisonment, drugs, divorce, scandal, even marriage to television celebrities, without lasting financial damage? But somewhere it had all gone wrong. She didn't know how or why, but her gentle, pretty young Annie had grown up into a resolutely disappointed woman. And Susannah could barely tolerate pessimism in women. She simply didn't understand it. It didn't make any sense. It flew in the face of nature; it was base, and ugly; the very scourge of femininity. What on earth had happened?

The only glimmer of hope that came to Susannah when she thought of Annie was in the form of Markhams' new chief executive, Edward Goddard. She had seen how Edward's eyes lingered a moment longer than necessary on Annie's face, how they focused whenever Susannah mentioned her name in meetings. And, more exciting than that, she had seen that for all her youngest goddaughter's attempts at indifference, Annie's face always lit up at Edward's attention. But perhaps the most attractive thing about Edward was that Susannah had met him first and felt in the loop.

He wasn't a title, but he was the next best thing—a wealthy, distant relation to one. And the way Annie had turned out, that was all they could hope for now.

Yes, she felt sure that Edward was the catalyst for change in Annie's and all of their futures. He would bring her back home, back in the fold, for good.

"Are any of the girls coming to the meeting?" asked Susannah.

"Hmmm? Katherine is."

"And Annie?"

"Think so."

"Good."

"Why?" asked George bluntly. "Is she bringing the food?"

Susannah's dual role of the girls' guardian and, in more recent years, that of Markhams' finance director had naturally extended to caring for their widowed father too. She had indeed become the official Markham Guardian.

Over the years, this role too had become harder than she could ever have imagined.

Like Caroline, Susannah soon discovered the truth behind George's glittering career.

Many years ago, before either of the two women had even heard of him, George had been a bored young millionaire with so much more money than sense that he didn't need the sense. Indeed, sense would only have spoiled the money.

Not so anymore.

He had bought one of the top consumer PR businesses in the country, complete with its 4,000 members of staff. For him it was a buzz, a plaything, its main attraction being that it already had an office in New York. This gave him the perfect excuse to buy an apartment on Fifth Avenue with views over Central Park, while modernizing the office, no expense spared. And as chairman of such a company, he could designate himself as managing director and personally oversee the hiring of many disadvantaged, beautiful young things who hadn't had the help in life that he had.

In the past, he had been very hands-on, so to speak, with most of the female, disadvantaged, beautiful young things, and even now in his middle age, he still showed an inspirational interest in their development. He always appeared first thing in the morning, drank Shirley's excellent coffee and breezed into meetings with clients who might be impressed by the MD in their midst. His presence alone—those features again—still managed to clinch the odd deal. And although he was considerably more picky now, George still had an eye for the most deserving of his female, disadvantaged, beautiful young things. It was a life of selfless charity work.

He was blissfully unaware that his hardworking employees' buttocks clenched at the sudden appearance of him in such meetings, in dread of their esteemed boss opening his mouth and ruining everything. This rarely happened though. George had his performance honed to a tee. He merely smiled enigmatically, shook the client's hands with a confident smile, delighted that his features were having the same effect on them as they had on himself, patted his trusted employee on the shoulder and said something like "I'll leave things in your capable hands, shall I, Tom/Dick/Harry?" He would then raise both hands, palms facing the client, before humbly begging, "Please don't get up," which always resulted in said client getting up, to watch the respected George Markham leave the office. Another deal clinched, another set of buttocks unclenched.

George thoroughly enjoyed the business life.

Which was where Susannah's difficulties had begun.

By the time she had worked her way up to become the finance director of Markhams' a decade ago, the company still had the potential to claw itself back to its glory days. But in the past few years, things had been rapidly worsening and now it was in serious danger of suffering a precipitous fall in performance results and client numbers. Terrifyingly, the end had come far sooner than Susannah had predicted. The last few months had seen the company lose money faster than a fat cat with a girlfriend.

For the first time in their history, they were having to seek out clients rather than the other way around, and the company was in real danger of going under, taking George and his three daughters with it.

In its present state, George couldn't even sell his company and make enough money to maintain the standard to which he and his family were accustomed. And if they were ruined it would pain Susannah more than she could say to think that she would no longer be able to mix in polite company with her best friends.

Even more terrifying was George's behavior. He was simply ignoring the fact that the money wasn't coming in anymore at a rate to cover the speed with which it went out.

Both he and his two eldest daughters blithely went on spending. They occasionally popped on Concorde to spend weekends at the New York apartment. Otherwise they enjoyed the simple luxury of their mansion house overlooking Hampstead Heath where George occupied the ground and first floor and Katherine had the amazing penthouse apartment. They both rattled around in their respective homes, leaving vast annexes unused. In fact, Katherine was forever to be found in her father's drawing room instead of her own brightly lit, furnace-hot drawing room upstairs. While she was the first to admit that her father's home suffered from a shocking lack of interior design, the fact was that she found it far more welcoming than her own, because it invariably had her father in it.

Victoria and Charles had an exquisite, spacious four-bedroom flat near the famed Hampstead village, which Susannah was growing more and more convinced was an unacceptable extravagance, when there was so much unused room in the family home.

Annie, unlike both her sisters, had insisted on paying her own way and thanks to her mother's inheritance and her job at the nearby art gallery, had managed to secure a mortgage on a lovely two-bedroom flat with a balcony in nearby Muswell Hill—or Muswell Hell, as George called it.

As for the rest of the Markham family though, life was rich. George's beloved late Great Dane, Rufus the Great, had had a Gucci sleeping basket, collar and lead. And they all still holidayed in the best resorts, with or without Annie. Katherine and Victoria had punishing daily workouts and yoga with the very best instructors, weekly massages, reflexology sessions, manicures, acupuncture and one-to-one Pilates classes; monthly leg waxes, eyelash curls, colonic irrigation, sunbed and trichology sessions and bi-monthly seaweed wraps. If they had a headache, they popped to their cranial osteopath, a pimple, the country's best beautician, a fat day, lymphatic drainage. And then there was the morning makeup and hair session with the country's top professionals. Priceless beauty didn't come cheap.

Susannah had started to try and gently persuade George of the dangers of his excessive spending. But it was impossible to order a man whose ancestors had hacked off their servants' hands for doing less. He had proved deaf to her pleadings.

Until now. Finally, even he could no longer put off seeing the brick wall of bankruptcy in front of him.

As Susannah saw it, they had three options. They could pray for a miracle and try to sell the company to a wealthy fool with even less business sense than George; they could face reality and shut it down now before the debts outweighed the assets; or they could open their doors to some management consultants, in the hope that they could turn it around and return it to its glory days. She knew that the third option was probably a non-starter, but she just couldn't bear to give up yet. The irony was that she needed a team of management consultants in to help her work out which option to take. And to prevent this being a total waste of money, it had to be one of the best. And for that they needed serious money.

Susannah also knew that for management consultants to be able to earn their millions, she had to get George temporarily out of the picture. Much as she loved and respected the man, she knew that he could single-handedly wreck everything. He was his own company's biggest millstone.

On top of that, she knew that George was proud. He would only consent to any of this if it were done in such a way that the public would never realize what was really going on. He couldn't possibly let anyone think that *he* needed help.

This was an incredibly complex, sensitive subject.

As their conversation glided to the subject of the company, not a moment too soon—or too late—Susannah slowly lifted her briefcase on to the polished table and opened it.

"Shall we start, George?" she asked quietly.

"As long as it doesn't take too long," he said, his eyes suddenly fixed on his Gucci shoes. "Bought an E-type yesterday. Wanted to give it a turn before lunch."

Chapter 4

The family meeting was underway. Katherine and Annie had both joined their father at his office and after Victoria's emergency phone call, Charles had popped in after rushing home from his beloved golf course and flinging on a suit.

They all sat silently around the polished oval table, waiting for Mr. Cavendish, the solicitor, to arrive.

George looked across at his two daughters. Katherine, her blonde hair coiffed to within an inch of its life, her blue eyes lidded with just the right amount of smudged amber to lend them a superior air, gave him a slow, feline smile that told him Daddy was all.

With an effort, he looked away from Katherine to Annie.

Annie looked out of the window, showing George her elegant profile.

George sighed deeply.

He would never get over Annie's obstinate red hair. Never. As if she couldn't just go to the hairdressers.

It seemed that George had only recently got over the initial shock of seeing his youngest daughter for the first time. It was bad enough she hadn't been a boy, which meant that his chances of a son were now as good as lost. Four years earlier, he had been devastated when Katherine had first been brought to him, furious, pink and undeniably female. Yet it had proved impossible, even for George, not to fall in love with such a beautiful, bouncy, gurgling child—and anyway, there was still hope that his other children would all be sons. When Victoria followed Katherine two years afterward, he had become used to disappointment and had simply not expected any better from his wife.

But, by the time Annie arrived, two years later, he knew that now all chances of a son were gone. Annie personified his loss of hope.

Perhaps that explained why he had reacted so violently to the color of her hair.

"Good God, woman, what's *happened?*" he demanded of Caroline.

"What do you mean, what's happened?" she asked, exhausted, hugging her infant to her chest.

"It's got orange hair!" he exploded.

"*She* has *auburn* hair," said Caroline firmly, gently touching one of the golden curls with the tip of her finger.

"Listen here, old gal, have you been having an affair with someone uglier than death?" continued George, not knowing which he would prefer most—to be a cuckold, or the begetter of Beelzebub's daughter.

Caroline fought back the angry tears.

"She is our daughter and she's beautiful," she said in a tone he had never heard before.

"It's uglier than Himmler, woman—" he shouted, disgusted.

"*SHE!*" cried Caroline.

"All right, SHE's uglier than Himmler!"

And he had slammed the door shut after him, shaken to the core that he could have produced such a hybrid.

Twenty-six years later, Annie's hair still troubled him. It had softened into a Titian blur now, the thick curls pulled off her pale face. Of course, thought George peevishly, Annie would never lower herself to have her locks cut into a slick, modern style. If only she would have her hair highlighted, he thought morosely. Wear make-up, high heels, make an effort.

Annie felt her father's harsh eye on her and stayed looking out of the window across the streets of London.

She eventually looked over at Susannah, who gave her a tender, supportive smile. Annie's heart warmed slightly. Without Susannah's presence, her family's silent condemnation would have weighed even more heavily on her slight shoulders.

Eventually there was a knock on the door and they all looked toward it expecting Mr. Cavendish the solicitor to sidle in. When instead, Davina Barker, the new marketing director, entered the office, her neat little face showing just the right amount of concern and respect, all four of them experienced a severe change in their emotions.

"Ah, Davina, my dear!" greeted George warmly, gratified by the sight of Davina's extremely long legs in an extremely mini skirt.

She walked purposefully toward him and let him kiss her on both cheeks, tilting her head back just the right amount for him to smell the dabs of Chanel No. 5 behind her ears and see an enticing glimpse of cleavage. She pulled out the chair next to Katherine.

Katherine flashed a grin at her friend. Now the fun would begin! Davina was the only person Katherine liked who wasn't moneyed, whose family had no history and who thought Belgravia was a country. In fact she was the only paid employee of her father's she had ever deigned to talk to properly. And there was a simple reason for that. Davina was a hoot.

Davina slid her chair out and sat down, smiling pleasantly at everyone around the table, her long, straight blonde hair swaying gently as she did so. She turned to grin at Katherine as she took her little jacket off, revealing a shimmering attempt at a blouse that left nothing to the imagination. Which made sense, surmised

Annie, considering that her father didn't have one. Davina wasn't the type to leave anything to chance.

Davina looked over at Katherine and gasped loudly. "I *adore* your earrings," she whispered loudly, touching Katherine's tiny diamonds glistening in her downy earlobes. "They're *divine*. How do they make them so small? If I had a pair of those, I'd swallow them or something."

Katherine laughed with delight, feeling classier and daintier than a moment ago.

Davina took out her pad and pen and smiled over at Annie and Susannah. They smiled back.

Annie didn't need to wonder how on earth Davina had been invited to such a highly private family meeting. Susannah could only mourn silently that her Annie should be treated so obviously differently to Davina by those who should know better.

After Shirley had poured everyone more coffee, Mr. Cavendish appeared.

"Ah, Cavendish," said George. "Come on in, come on in."

Mr. Cavendish wiped his brow and took his jacket off.

"Right," he said, and opened his bulging briefcase.

"Are you gone stark, raving mad, man?" shouted Katherine. "Do you want me to get ill, ugly and fat, is that it?"

Mr. Cavendish went pale. "I am merely saying," he attempted, "that if you can manage, for just one year to do without these . . . luxuries—"

Katherine screamed and looked at her father. "Did you hear him, Daddy? *One year? Luxuries?*" She turned to Mr. Cavendish and her tone changed sharply. "Do you have any idea what happens to your colon if it isn't washed out regularly, Mr. Cavendish?"

Fortunately for Mr. Cavendish, he did not have to find out.

"Calm down, pumpkin," said George before turning sadly to his solicitor. "It simply won't do, Cavendish."

Mr. Cavendish sighed and looked at his paperwork. He didn't know how to broach the subject. Luckily, he didn't need to.

"George," cooed Susannah. "There might be another way."

"Hmm?"

"You could—temporarily—" (she twinkled her eyes and hushed her voice) "visit New York."

She let this sink in before continuing.

Katherine's eyes lit up.

George liked the idea, but wasn't sure how this was going to help.

"You see," continued Susannah slowly. "You have two choices. You could either sell your New York apartment and pour that money into the company—"

Her audience gasped. Sell the New York apartment? It was too painful to contemplate. What *was* life without its little joys?

"But that would be very obvious to the press that you are in need of money, which would be no good for the company at all. Or, we could tell the press that you have grown bored of London lately and have decided to spend time in New York. The business is expanding and New York needs your attention. You could go and live in your apartment there for six months, maybe a year. Then, as a last-minute thought, you quietly sell the wonderful Hampstead Village apartment—"

Charles started. Wasn't that where he lived? Victoria would kill him.

"And Victoria could move back into the family home with Charles and the boys—"

He relaxed. Victoria would be beside herself with happiness at this compromise.

"And we'll have put the newshounds off the scent!"

She looked around the room. Everyone's breath was held, their eyes bright.

"Just think of the money you could make on that Hampstead

Village apartment, George. Katie and Annie could go with you to New York if you wanted—to make it look more like a family decision." Susannah felt that Annie needed a break from London. Maybe New York was just the place to bring back the color in her cheeks. "Meanwhile," she continued, "Victoria and Charles and the boys would have all the space they need in Katie's quarters. With the proceeds from their flat, we'll be able to get the very best management consultants in—" she suddenly spoke faster, ignoring the sharp intake of breath that came from all around the table, "—who I'm sure will turn the company around so we can float it for millions and then you can come back to live here for good."

George looked like he was thinking very hard. He was in fact, concentrating desperately on the image of his late grandmother on her deathbed. It helped him recover himself after a sudden and all-too-effective image of enjoying Davina in New York.

Susannah continued. "I will stay in London while the consultants are here and when everything's sorted out, I'll come and join you in New York for the New Year. Until then I'll talk regularly with the New York office, and keep you informed every step of the way. Enjoy the sights while you're there! Visit your club, go to the opera, and most importantly, relax. We can't have our managing director, our chairman, having a nervous breakdown, not when we need him most. You must use this opportunity to recuperate at this time of stress. Be a guiding light for the rest of us. And of course, you can talk to us here in the office as often as usual and advise us how to run the company in your absence."

She held her breath. This moment was crucial to the survival of Markhams'.

"Yes, I—I have felt a bit peeky, recently," nodded George, thinking very, very hard of his late grandmother.

Susannah breathed out. Her relief at the ease with which this had been achieved overshadowed her surprise.

Everyone except Annie clapped their hands in excitement and started talking animatedly about the delights of the Big Apple.

Annie looked around the room, her stomach tensing with anxious frustration. She couldn't possibly let Susannah dictate where she lived. She didn't want to go to New York. She watched George and Katherine tell a wide-eyed Davina about how many society people you could see in one evening at the opera.

I'm adopted, thought Annie. There's no other explanation.

"Um," she cleared her throat. "May I make a suggestion?"

Susannah smiled confidently at Annie. "Of course, my dear."

"I would rather—if it fits in with everyone else, of course—stay here in London with Vicky and Charles and the boys, than go to New York." As Susannah's smile subsided, Annie rushed on. "I could help with the boys, I could even move in there, I could rent out my place—that might come in handy—"

"Don't see how a poky hole in Muswell Hell could help us—we're not *that* stretched," interrupted her father.

Surprised by Annie's offer, Susannah didn't even acknowledge George's words. Annie's requests were rarely unrealistic. And the occurrence of Annie asking anything with a selfish motive was so rare that it always deserved respect.

If Annie seriously meant to help Victoria, they could even get rid of Victoria's staff. She would hardly need a live-in nanny when there was a live-in sister on hand. And of course, if Annie were to stay in London, then Edward Goddard would have more of a chance to wear down her anti-romantic notions. In fact, she could ask Annie to get more involved in the business meetings—where she could keep her eye on the burgeoning relationship. She predicted an announcement by the New Year. Oh yes, it was perfect.

"My darling," she said sweetly. "That is a generous offer that makes me proud of you."

Annie hadn't finished. If the company was really in dire financial trouble, she might be able to help. And helping might ease the sense of impotence that always overcame her when she was with her family.

"And I have some savings that might be useful."

"Savings?" asked George, insulted. "What the devil have you got savings for?"

Annie colored. "A rainy day? Emergencies? A world cruise when I'm old and bored of daytime TV? Why do most people have savings?"

Susannah intervened while George stared, baffled, at his flushed daughter.

"Another unsurprisingly generous gesture, my dear. It would make your mother proud," she said. "But I don't think we've come to that quite yet." She smiled indulgently at Annie. "Keep your savings for that rainy day."

For a flash, Annie felt herself dangerously near confessing her one secret from Susannah—she realized none of them had any idea how much money she really had.

OK, she thought. Your loss. My secret. I quite liked the idea of a cruise anyway.

"But my dear," continued Susannah gently, "we may have to re-address Markhams' sponsorship of your lovely little artists."

Annie's face fell. She could easily give up her home, but not that, surely? Using a fraction of Markhams' money to transform the lives of impoverished, gifted artists had been one of the few satisfactions in Annie's life. Markhams' money had single-handedly spring-boarded three young artists on to respectable careers by funding their first exhibitions in the two years that Annie had started doing it in conjunction with her boss's gallery. For Annie, this was the only worthwhile thing Markhams had ever done. But it didn't make profits and it didn't hit the glossies, so of course, it would have to go. If she had more guts, she'd use her own money to fund the artists, but that silent, growing nest egg of hers was her protection against life and its uncertainties. It was her secret weapon.

She looked calmly at Susannah. "Of course," she said quietly. "I understand."

George buzzed Shirley. "Shirley, get your roller blades on. Prepare the New York apartment to accommodate three, book three first-class flights to New York and put Victoria's flat on the market. Oh, and call my barber, I want a trim this afternoon."

He looked smugly around at everyone as if the entire idea had been his.

"To accommodate *three*, George?" Asked Susannah as mildly as she could. "*Three* flights to New York?"

George looked over at Davina and patted her elegant hand. "Think it's high time Davina saw the New York office," he winked, touching the toe of her stilettos with his Gucci loafer. "And she can live with us at the apartment." He coughed. "Nice for Katie."

Katherine and Davina both screamed and hugged each other, while Susannah and Annie looked on, mute, helpless.

Katherine turned on Susannah.

"At least this will make up for sacrificing everything else and getting a furred colon."

Susannah forced herself to look motherly at her eldest god-daughter.

Within half an hour, the meeting was adjourned. Charles was preoccupied with returning to his game and giving Victoria the good news about the move. Once they were safely ensconced in the family mansion, she would stop resenting him for having moved her down the social ladder. This could transform their marriage. Katherine, Davina and George were preoccupied with the delights of temporarily living in New York. And Susannah was preoccupied with maintaining a bright façade. Annie alone was terrified for their future.

Chapter 5

Two weeks later, Annie felt no less terrified. She stared at the mirrored wall of Markhams' office lift as it carried her up toward another meeting. Was it the unreal smoothness of the lift or the thought of facing her family that had thrust a clenched fist in the pit of her gut?

The door slid open and Shirley appeared before her, smiling, proffering a cup of black coffee that, should Annie grow bored during the meeting, she could try to stand her teaspoon up in.

Annie jumped. She'd never got used to the fact that the lift opened into Shirley's office and more often than not, into Shirley's face.

"They've just started," whispered Shirley, her shoulders hunched for maximum volume control.

"Oh," whispered Annie, hunching in response. "Shall I wait for the interval?"

Shirley smiled a little uncertainly. "There is no interval. They'll just keep going until—"

"It was a joke."

Annie unhunched, gave Shirley a warm smile as an apology, gratefully took the coffee cup and pushed opened the heavy door with her free hand. The smell of polished wood and cloying perfume made her feel almost instantly claustrophobic.

Susannah stood at the end of the table, dressed in a sharp business suit, her hair scraped back off her perfectly made-up face. George sat next to her, his Savile Row suit so pristine it almost glowed. To his right sat Davina, pert and pretty, and beside her sat Katherine, dressed head to toe in stylish black. Beside the empty chair sat Charles, looking wistfully out at the bright blue sky.

None of them turned to look at Annie.

Just your average cozy family, she thought, as she squeezed past them all to take her seat in the far corner. When she'd sat down, Susannah paused fractionally, and recapped quickly.

"I was just explaining that we've been exceptionally lucky and managed to get the crème-de-la-crème of management consultants to come in and help Markhams' back on its feet. They don't come cheap but, well, I'm sure you'll all agree that they'll be worth every penny."

Davina was the only one who turned to Annie and smiled. Annie felt the corners of her mouth lift as her stomach plunged.

Susannah started passing around copies of the proposal from the man who was to save their future. Annie was the last to receive a copy and she watched it as it made its way around to her. She eyed it with some skepticism. Luminous lime-colored borders framed each page and at the top of every one jumped out a large, distinctive logo that looked to her like a squashed cockroach.

Then as she sat there, trapped by her family, a slow sense of significance burned its way through to her consciousness, like dynamite igniting.

First, there was merely a feeling of mild distaste at the color of the print. Next, as her eyes scanned the name that was making its way toward her, came a sense of disbelief and foreboding. And then, as the proposal was plonked gracelessly in front of her, Annie's fuse—seven years' worth of it—finally went.

She stared at the lurid lettering:

JAKE MEAD ASSOCIATES.

She stared some more at it. She blinked carefully.

Nope. It was still there.

Jesus Christ. It was Jake. Jake Bloody Mead, the boy who'd abandoned her, who let her spend her entire final year at college wondering if he'd turn up any minute, apologize, explain himself and let her continue with her life.

She sat in blank disbelief while her body did a remarkable impression of swimming away from her.

Was her family really going to entrust their entire fortunes into the hands of a pathetic, obnoxious, immature, self-obsessed *boy?* A boy they wouldn't trust her to elope with? A boy who fainted at the mere thought of making her pregnant? Who accused her of . . . ? Who ran out when . . . ? A boy who wore baggy jeans, for God's sake?

"Are you all right, my dear?" she heard Susannah ask her. "You're whimpering."

Annie made a valiant effort at a smile. She glanced around. Charles was looking longingly at the clock; Katherine was checking her nails; her father was nodding confidently, which meant he was confused. Davina was still looking pert and pretty.

Annie realized that Susannah and Cass were the only ones who even knew about her past—and Cass was the only one who even knew Jake's name. Good, she thought. That should make it easier for her to keep it a secret. And this had to stay her secret—there was no other way she'd be able to survive. She just had to keep calm, maintain a mask of serenity, a barricade against the world.

"Are you gagging, Annie?" asked Susannah, somewhat impatiently.

Annie shook her head violently.

"Would you like to leave the room?"

Yes please, thought Annie. Do you have a stretcher?

She shook her head and Susannah continued.

"Jake Mead Associates are internationally renowned for their ability to turn around troubled companies. There is a staggeringly high demand for them, so we're extremely lucky to get them at such short notice. Jake Mead, the chief exec, is proposing to give us his ten top consultants in the UK and ten in New York." She sighed. "At £3,000 a day per consultant we have about three months at the very most for this to work. Put it this way—if there aren't signs by the New Year that we're going to be saved, we'll just have to try and find a buyer."

Annie forced her frozen fingers to flick through the proposal.

Bloody stupid font, she thought. *Girly* font. Typical.

"Jake Mead and co will be living and sleeping with the company for the next few weeks," continued Susannah.

Annie's heart stopped. Oh my God, she thought. I'm having a cardiac arrest.

"We plan to negotiate that as many consultants who need to will move into what are now the two bottom floors of the family home—now that George will be in New York," Susannah went on, nodding graciously to George. "This year those floors will become a smart business apartment. When Victoria and Charles sell their place, they will be living above the consultants in what is at the moment Katherine's penthouse apartment. And, of course, so will Annie."

Annie's ears started whistling.

"We decided on this," continued Susannah, "rather than keeping those floors empty and paying for various consultants' accommodation expenses. And that way, the whole house stays in the family once they've gone. It all makes perfect financial sense."

Oh yes, it all makes perfect sense, thought Annie. We're going to hand over all our money to a twat in baggy trousers. Excellent.

"The owner of the company, Jake Mead, is most impressive," continued Susannah.

Oh you've seen his trousers then? thought Annie. Even better.

"I'm sure you'll all like him." Susannah looked at her watch. "He'll be here any minute."

There was a dull thud from the corner.

When Annie woke up, two seconds later, no one had even noticed she'd passed out.

She was vaguely aware that Susannah was still talking.

"His reputation, his previous results," continued Susannah.

His vanishing act, thought Annie . . .

"His discretion and his grasp of what we needed made him the only possible choice. It's nothing short of a miracle that we've been able to secure him so quickly. I'm sure you'll all be very pleased with what you see."

Why? Is he bringing a friend?

Just then Susannah's mobile went.

"Excuse me," she said and took the call.

She looked over at Annie.

"Oh dear," she said.

You can say that again, nodded Annie, her eyes wide.

"Apparently you were meant to meet Cassie half an hour ago at the Tate Modern." Susannah looked over at George. "Will you allow her to go, George? Cassie's been there for forty minutes."

George glanced at Annie. "Don't see why not, I'm sure this Jack Meads—"

"*Jake* Mead," helped Susannah.

He squinted at the name on his copy of the proposal while Annie's heart rate shot up so fast it almost took her with it.

"Quite so, quite so. Jake Mead. Don't see why Annie would want to stay to meet him. Can't see as she'd miss him."

Miss him? thought Annie fiercely. I'd get a bloody bullseye.

Annie didn't risk giving herself away by trying to speak, and for the first time in her life she was grateful that her family wouldn't show any interest in whether she stayed or left. She simply got up, pushed her chair slowly out from under the desk, and moved her deadened limbs past everyone and out of the door.

Once outside the office, she closed the door firmly, leaned against it and breathed very, very deeply. Deep, calm breaths, she thought. Deep, calm breaths.

Hundreds of new thoughts surfaced in her mind, but Annie knew she had to push them all to the back of it. First and foremost she had to concentrate on getting out of there.

"Are you all right, dear?" asked Shirley, suddenly beside her.

Annie rocketed out of her skin. Shit, she wished she wouldn't do that.

"Oh yes," managed Annie. "I'm just," she couldn't catch her breath. "Leaving."

"I'll call the lift for you," said Shirley, and pressed the button.

Annie stared at the lift. Jake could be in it. Now. On his way up.

The mere thought of him was having a bad enough effect on her body, God only knew what the actual living presence of him would do. She had to avoid him. She could take the stairs but they were usually locked. No one was ever encouraged to use them as they were nowhere near as impressive as the lift. She turned to Shirley.

"You know what?" she said, trying to sound relaxed. "I think I'm going to take the stairs."

"Nonsense, dear," instructed Shirley. "The lift's nearly here now."

Annie smiled. I've always hated you, she thought. Now I know why.

She tried to argue, but found she couldn't. All her energy was taken up pumping the blood around her body that she'd been saving for a special occasion.

Instead of jumping out of the window, which suddenly struck her as a wise and well-prepared plan, Annie forced herself to stay motionless, staring at the monitor above the lift, watching a tiny green cube of light smoothly and slowly ascend.

Ground floor, first, second . . .

Was it going to be empty, or was she going to find herself face to face with the pillock who'd ruined her finals and her life? The pillock she'd have risked everything for. It was a puzzler and no mistake.

Third, fourth . . .

"Are you sure you're all right, dear?" asked Shirley. "You're looking awfully pale."

I'll show you pale, thought Annie. Large window, five flights up, say your prayers, bitch.

She attempted a smile. "I need a holiday," she mouthed.

Fifth floor. The lift chimed its arrival and the doors opened noiselessly.

Using up all her energy, Annie turned to face it. It was empty.

She decided that to weep and hug Shirley might arouse suspicion, so with a great deal of concentration, she managed to propel her body forward by supporting it on one leg after the other. Walking, she remembered. She knew it felt familiar.

"Bye," she whispered to Shirley, with a weak grin on her face. She even waved as the door slowly divided them from each other. She'd made it.

Once on her own, she let out a loud moan and leaned her head against the closed door.

Oh . . . my . . . God, she thought, overawed by the size of her emotions. So much anger. All I need is a leotard and I could become a wrestler.

Then she realized that Jake might be waiting for the lift at the bottom.

Her body froze.

The lift sank slowly to the ground.

There was only one thing for it. She closed her eyes.

"Dear God. Prove you exist and let me die in here. Now. NOW."

She opened her eyes. Nope. No God. Or if there was one, He was a sadist.

She looked frantically around. Why wasn't there an exit in here? Or at least a toilet? Bloody cost-cutting crap.

She breathed deeply in an effort to regain control. Too deeply. She started seeing stars.

The lift landed her gently on the ground floor and she heard its soft chime.

She held her breath and in a last-ditch effort to compose herself, stared at the mirrored door before it opened to reveal her fate. A madwoman stared back at her.

Slowly the door silently opened.

Nothing, emptiness, void.

She almost wept with joy. Instead she walked furiously out of the office and hailed a cab.

It wasn't until she was dropped off outside the Tate Modern that she started wondering something.

What the hell did Jake look like now?

"First you persuade me this place is worth going to, then you don't turn up," Cass shouted to Annie, as Annie ran, somewhat unsteadily, toward her.

"I have the best excuse in the world," started Annie.

"I don't want your excuses," said Cass. "I want your soul."

"I left it in the lift," replied Annie, her voice vice-tight.

"Pardon?"

"Nothing. Let's go and look at lots of paintings children of three could have done."

Annie didn't have the energy to explain. Her body seemed to have run out of blood.

They wandered around the exhibition slowly, Annie taking in

little, marveling that her world map could so suddenly be wacked out of kilter.

It was a rather tiring afternoon.

Ten minutes later than expected, due to bad traffic, Jake Mead stepped out of his cab and looked up at the imposing building above him.

He straightened his Boss tie, brushed a hand over his close-cropped hair, gripped his leather computer bag even tighter and stepped purposefully into the London office of Markhams' PR.

He was ready to kick ass.

Chapter 6

The gentle rat-a-tat-tat on the door was the same as it had always been, humble yet dignified.

"Come!" called George, trying to ignore the catch in his voice and the two pricks of sweat under his arms.

His valet stood before him.

"Ah . . ." boomed George, before stopping.

Never could remember the bugger's name.

His valet—obstinately ugly as ever—coughed quietly.

"Alfred, sir."

"Yes, quite so, quite so," allowed George.

Alfred didn't move a muscle.

George grimaced. Why couldn't Susannah have dealt with this? It was her idea, after all.

"The thing is, you see," he started, and then finished. What was the thing again? He forced his brain to remember. It had all made perfect sense when Susannah had said it and the wretched fellow wasn't standing right in front of him. Luxury, expense they couldn't afford, tightening the purse strings and all that. Have to dress himself in future. It's the latest thing—some royalty even doing it now.

Ah yes. Now. How could he put that eloquently?

"All a bit of a luxury, you see," he started. "An expense we can't afford, tightening the old purse strings and all that. Have to dress like royalty now. Some of them. Hope you understand, old chap."

Alfred understood perfectly.

"Of course," said Alfred gently.

George winked at him. Splendid fellow. Sorry to see him go.

"Sir is sacking me," said Alfred.

George started.

"Oh! Well, I wouldn't put it quite like that."

Alfred gave a short smile and a curt little bow of the head. That was more like it.

"How would sir like me to put it?"

George looked at him in stunned amazement. He had no idea the man was as rude as he was ugly. Amazing how duplicitous people could be.

Alfred continued.

"Obviously, I'll have to talk to my union—"

"Your *what?*"

"My union—you wouldn't expect me to accept—"

"I would expect nothing less," shouted George. "An utter disgrace! After thirty years' loyal service, to stab me in the back like that . . ."

"Exactly my point, sir."

"What?"

"I knew you'd understand."

George swallowed hard.

"Don't force me to do something I don't want to do," he threatened darkly.

"What did sir have in mind?" answered Alfred calmly. "Wearing taupe at me?"

What? George gasped with disgust. He'd never been so insulted in all his life! *Taupe?* In mid-winter? The man was quite clearly raving. He had to get him out of his home, God only knew what he could do. He was unsafe.

What the buggering hell had happened to the buggering class system? Country was going to rot.

George furrowed his brow menacingly at his evil, double-crossing, ugly ex-valet. Alfred stood his ground.

There was nothing for it. With as much dignity as he could muster, George fumbled in his bureau drawer, eventually took out his checkbook and Mont Blanc fountain pen and, as he unscrewed the lid, sat tall in his chair. He wouldn't let anyone say he'd lost his pride at the end.

"How much?" he asked, with as much bile in his voice as possible. That should shake him up a bit. Bribery didn't become a gentleman.

"Well, let me see . . ." Alfred did some slow mental arithmetic. "Thirty years service without one day's sick leave, no pension, no holiday taken this year . . ."

George started sweating. Why hadn't Susannah warned him this might happen?

He started filling in the rest of the check while Alfred did his sums. He wrote quickly, so that his hand wouldn't shake quite so much.

Alfred managed not to smile until after he'd shut the door quietly behind him. And then he smiled so much, his features temporarily realigned themselves into some sort of order. George would have been impressed, if only his own features weren't so temporarily un-aligned at the same time.

Alfred kissed the check in his hand and headed straight out of the house for the bank. He'd learned a lot from his time with George Markham. But his most precious lesson had been to keep quiet when in the company of an idiot. He'd had no intention of staying with George once he'd heard that Victoria and Charles' spoiled little brats were moving in. He had almost resigned imme-diately, but something had told him to sit it out. And always let the idiot speak first.

It was a lesson that would help him start up his own business of valet training. And George would be his leading example to all his future students.

The gym smelled of floor wax, as usual. It was a smell that had, after four years, become synonymous to Annie with channeling her aggression. Or rather, letting rip.

She swore at herself as Daniel's size 10 swiped past her head for the third time.

"Aim at me!" she shouted at him. "Stop patronizing me just because you're a blackbelt!"

Daniel smiled at Annie as her two bunches bounced furiously up and down.

"Temper temper," he said softly and then chopped her in the face.

"I WASN'T READY!" she screamed, livid.

But Daniel had already stepped back to kick her in the stomach.

With a surge of aggression, Annie blocked her stomach, stepped back and kicked her right leg higher and wider than Daniel could ever manage. It got him in the face and he fell backward on to the mat.

Hah! thought Annie, standing victoriously over him. Female flexibility wins every time. Sex, karate and childbirth. That's what little girls were made for.

The karate instructor ambled over as Daniel rolled left and right moaning softly.

"For God's sake, Annie, you're supposed to be channeling your aggression, not killing your opponent."

Daniel blinked.

"I'm all right," he mumbled from the mat. "No harm done, mate."

Annie smiled sweetly.

"I *was* channeling my aggression," she explained. "Into his face."

As the instructor wandered off, she picked Daniel up.

"Sorry, Dan," she said. "Are you okay?"

"Ever wondered why you're single?" he asked, his hands covering his nose.

"Yeah," she said, letting go of him. "My standards are too high."

Daniel fell messily back on to the mat.

"They're average."

"New York? How *delicious*! You know Brutus had family out there, don't you? I can't believe you'd rather stay in boring old Hampstead," gushed Cass.

She looked around for a stray waiter. She was dying for a glass of wine.

Annie smiled gently. She might have expected this reception to her news.

She had never got over the fact that Cass had married a man called Brutus. She didn't think she ever would. She watched Cass catch the attention of the waiter, wondering aimlessly if she was going to have the bottle, or energy, to tell Cass about Jake today. Maybe . . . .

"Why don't you pop out and visit your folks for Thanksgiving?" continued Cass. "We'll be able to meet up—Brutus and I go out every year at that time. I know! We'll do Madison Avenue."

"I've got an even better idea," exclaimed Annie, "after I've gone bankrupt, we can *rob* Madison Avenue! Bagsie the Versace balaclava."

Cass changed the subject fast. She hated it when Annie got sarcastic.

First things first, she had a man Annie simply had to meet.

Annie sighed. Would Cass never tire of trying to match her up with some horribly eligible bore? Why did everyone assume that because she hadn't had a serious relationship since . . . for a while, she was desperate for one? Didn't they realize that as far as she was concerned, men were there to service her when she required servicing, much in the same way as a plumber was there when a leak sprung. Or, on one very fortuitous occasion, to do both at the same time.

"He's over six foot tall, built like a brick shithouse, thighs like mountains, knees like a Greek god and Brutus plays rugby with him so he's seen him in the shower—Annie, we're talking serious potential here."

Annie perked up.

"Sounds interesting."

Cass grinned.

"Deep down, you're really very shallow, aren't you?"

"It's not that deep down," smiled Annie. "I'm shallowly shallow."

"There is a slight catch though, " said Cass. "He's got a rather unfortunate manner."

Annie nodded. There was always something. "Arrogant, patronizing? Or sniveling, toadying?"

"No. *Manor.* Unfortunate manor. Two hundred acres, completely surrounded by farmland. Stinks of manure for ten months of every year. Apart from that he's perfect. Wondered if you'd like to go shooting pheasants with us all. The season's just about to start."

"So sorry," said Annie wearily. "I belong to the Friends of the Pheasants Society."

"Don't make me miserable, Annie."

"Sorry. Let's not discuss the massacre of harmless wildlife for mindless sport, shall we?"

"Let's not." Cass scanned her menu. "Right. What shall we eat?"

Over their first glass of wine, Annie explained to Cass why she was grateful not to be going to New York. She couldn't bear the thought of living at such close proximity to Davina. Katherine, fooled by simple flattery, was blind to the real motives of her "friend." But it was clear to Annie that Davina was after more than a fling with George—and Annie was concerned enough to think that there was a real danger of her getting her way. She had to keep an eye on her.

George had had many affairs—Annie felt sure that his marriage to her mother had not even put a stop to that. But, and it hurt Annie to say it, Davina knew exactly how to turn the head of a vain, foolish man like her father. God only knew what would happen if someone like Davina married him and became the matriarch of the Markham family. She was cunning and clever, putting as much effort into appearing innocent and naïve as her sisters put into being beautiful. Davina could win an Oscar for her daily performance. Annie was terrified about the schisms Davina could create within her family.

"Schisms? Why would she do that?" asked Cass.

"Your mother would be out on her ear. There would only be room for one woman in my father's life. Susannah would lose her job and probably all contact with the family. And it would be even worse for us. Your mother is masterminding saving Father's company. Davina could ruin us all."

"Jesus."

"Or what if, for argument's sake," continued Annie, "Davina and Father have children together, a whole new family of Markham miracles? What then?"

She took a gulp of her wine.

"I mean, I know Katie's not perfect," she continued, "but that doesn't mean I want to see her on the street. Without her inheritance she wouldn't last a week. And Davina is the sort of woman who, once married, would get her hands on my father's will before letting him get his hands on anything she had to offer. And where would that leave any of us? What about Victoria's boys—poor little Bertie and Harry? Their other grandfather probably has another fifty years in him yet. Until then, Charles, Victoria and the boys basically live off my father. It doesn't bear thinking about. And of course there's me. I'm fine for now, living off my pathetic gallery salary but I don't see why I should risk losing my inheritance—"

"I'm sure Mummy can sort all of this out before it comes to that. Is she aware of any of this?"

"We've never discussed it, but I'm fairly sure she sees what's going on," said Annie. "Either way, Davina is bad news for our family."

Cass pondered the predicament as they made their final menu decisions.

It was a tough one. She never knew whether to take Annie's problems seriously anymore. After that ridiculous episode when Annie had thought she was pregnant by the love of her life but actually she was just a week late and said love of life was actually an idiot, she'd learned to take Annie's problems with a rather large pinch of salt.

When they'd given their orders to the waiter, she sat back, crossed her arms and looked at Annie.

Annie took her courage in both hands.

"But there's more news. Something far worse than all of this."

"Go on."

After a decent pause, Annie explained about the management consultants moving into the flat below hers.

"They're called . . . Jake Mead Associates," she announced dramatically.

Cass's face was blank. She shrugged her shoulders. "Is that supposed to ring a bell?" she asked.

Yes, thought Annie.

She tried again, enunciating perfectly. "Jake Mead?"

Cass shook her head.

"Jake?"

Nope.

"Mead?"

Nope.

Time to elucidate.

"Immature twat you stopped me eloping with seven years ago?"

Cass stared, open-mouthed and wide-eyed. Annie continued.

"Accused me of murdering his nonexistent baby?"

Cass's mouth and eyes opened wider.

"Ran out crying, never to be seen again? Ruined my degree?"

Cass was now nodding.

"Ugly humpback with acne?"

Cass stopped nodding. "OK, now you've lost me," she said. "I thought I had him, but that last one—"

"OK, that last one was a lie."

"Oh really?"

"He didn't have acne."

"Skin as smooth as a baby's proverbial, I recall you saying at the time."

"Yeah well, I've had my eyes tested since then. And stopped speaking in clichés."

They stared at each other, their minds humming with activity. Cass didn't know where to start.

"And this hump-backed, immature, acne-ridden scaredy-cat now owns the management consultants who are going to save your father's company?"

"Yup."

"Wow. Didn't he do well?"

"He's an ass, Cass."

"Have you seen him?"

Annie shook her head. "I managed to escape—thanks to you—yesterday."

"So I've saved you from him twice now?"

"Yep. Thank you, Supergirl."

"Do you want to see him?"

"Nope. I hate him. He's turned me into a bitter, twisted old woman."

"Oh nonsense. You aren't twisted."

"Thank you."

They started to pick at their food, their excitement levels almost audibly decreasing.

"Is he married?" asked Cass.

Annie shrugged, a little too emphatically Cass felt.

"If he's not yet, it's just a matter of time."

"Yes, well it usually is."

As suddenly as Annie had wanted to discuss Jake, she now wanted to close the subject. Jake had only been mentioned yesterday and already she was suffering from thought-fatigue about him. Her brain ached.

"There's only one thing for it," Annie said firmly. She took a deep breath. "I'm going to have to meet this bloke with the knock-out knees and unfortunate manor."

Cass smiled.

"But I *won't* go shooting," said Annie firmly.

Cass poured more wine.

Annie was never quite sure why she went on Cass's excruciating blind dates with men who owned more land than chin. All she knew was that it gave Cass an extraordinary amount of pleasure, which in turn, made her feel good. She had never been able to explain it beyond that.

And to be fair, not all the dates had been disasters. Once or twice she hadn't wanted to kill herself before the entrée. There had even been one date when she'd enjoyed the meal, found the conversation interesting and, although there hadn't exactly been fireworks going off inside her stomach, a sparkler had definitely been lit. Then at the end of the evening, he'd kissed her and she'd thought she was being eaten alive.

"What was wrong with him?" Cass had asked her the next morning over the phone.

"He tried to drown me with his own juices at the end of the evening," Annie had explained. "I genuinely thought my time was up. It was terrifying."

"Oh dear."

"Still," said Annie. "Look on the bright side. I won't need to go to the dentist's for a while. My plaque didn't stand a chance."

Cass hadn't pushed the point. There were some arguments even she could not win.

Annie hadn't gone on a Cass blind date for quite a while after that. To be honest, none of the men ever really attracted her. There was always something missing. Their eyes weren't dark enough, their hair too straight, their bodies too short . . . They just weren't right.

Then, almost a year ago, she'd been persuaded to go out with another chap Brutus had been at Eton with. He was harmless enough, but he had had the infuriating habit of proffering a little cough—the sort that people usually make when they're trying to get someone's attention—every five minutes or so. Annie had spent the entire evening looking at him suddenly as if he had something of great import to tell her, only to have him grin sheepishly at her and say rather apologetically "Sorry, phlegm," while pointing help-fully at his Adam's apple. She didn't mind for herself, but it was when he had had to start saying it to everyone else involved in their evening that it had just become too ridiculous for words. The waiter had almost developed a nervous tic from it.

"Believe me, honeybun," Cass was saying. "Everything's going to be all right. All you need is a good long . . . date. Cheer you up."

Annie agreed. Why not? It had been a while. And if things went well, it wouldn't do Jake any harm to see a great hulking rugby player with the knees of a Greek god running up and down their communal stairs in the Hampstead home. Perhaps she could get him to do his exercises in the hall? In tight Lycra shorts? Yup, a date was just what she needed.

Over desserts and coffee, Annie managed to nudge the conver-sation to Cass's life. Brutus had finally persuaded Cass to go for fer-tility tests, after she had been forced to admit that two years was probably too long to wait to conceive naturally.

"How did the HGV test go?"

"HSG not HGV. I'm not trying to drive a heavy goods vehicle, Annie."

"Sorry."

"H for *hyster*, meaning 'womb,' S for *salping* meaning 'tubes,' G for o-Gram meaning 'bloody painful, invasive, humiliating experience.' H-S-G."

"All sounds Greek to me," muttered Annie.

"It is," said Cass. "Brutus says it's just like being back at school. Everything's in Greek or Latin, he feels like a failure and he keeps masturbating."

She let out a sharp jab of a laugh, her eyes darting anywhere but at Annie.

There was a pause.

"So how did it go?" repeated Annie.

Cass took a big sigh and smiled so quickly, Annie thought she might have imagined it.

"My Fallopian tubes are 'thick,' probably scarred, they don't know why because they're doctors not gods—although you wouldn't believe it the way they talk to you—I can't conceive naturally, IVF is the only option and there's only a fifteen percent success rate."

They sat in silence for a while.

"Other women have thick ankles. I have thick tubes. More wine?"

Annie nodded.

"By the way, that's I-V-F, not VIP," repeated Cass. "I for 'inhuman,' V for 'violation,' F for 'fucking hell, get me out of here.' "

"Oh honey," whispered Annie. "I'm so sorry."

"Oh I'm fine," Cass said, taking a gulp of wine. "I'm fine," she said, thumping her glass on the white linen cloth.

Chapter 7

Dr. Blake slowly crossed her arms. She looked at the clock and then back at Jake. Technically, she was supposed to take the cue from the client, but if she followed that rule with this one, she'd never have got anywhere. And it had taken her long enough to get this far.

"I sense a lot of anger, Jake," she said softly.

Jake prised his teeth out of his lower lip.

"Oh hello!" he exclaimed. "Did I wake you? Sorry—must have been the sound of the money I'm paying you to sort my life out."

Dr. Blake cocked her head slightly.

"Where do you think all this anger comes from, I wonder?"

"Well, it probably comes from sitting through twenty minutes of the most expensive silence money can buy. You must be exhausted at the end of sitting here thinking all day. Women's work is never done, eh?"

Dr. Blake nodded slowly. "How is work, by the way?"

Jake looked at his therapist. Did she never change her tone of voice? He felt the nerve in the back of his neck start to twitch.

He sighed heavily. He'd better explain everything. They only had forty minutes left now. He kept it short and neat. Dr. Blake listened to every word, nodding occasionally and looking at him with the same infuriatingly measured look of interest. But at the end, she seemed genuinely delighted.

"So you'll see her again! That's wonderful. You know what this is, don't you?"

Jake nodded slowly, a handsome grin forming on his face.

"Oh yes," he said quietly. "I know exactly what this is."

"Well?"

Jesus wept, she thought. Like drawing blood from a sodding stone.

Jake crossed his arms. "Revenge."

Dr. Blake stared sadly at her longest-serving client. She shook her head slowly at him. "It's closure, Jake. Closure."

Jake stared sadly back at her. "Oh yeah. Right," he said, his neck muscle starting to spasm. "Closure."

One week later, Jake Mead, smart, polished and calm, looked up from Susannah's organization chart and smiled at her over the large, gleaming desk. He'd never felt so determined to do a good job.

"I believe George Markham's three daughters are also directors?" he asked, his tone level. If there was one thing he had learned from his therapist it was how to keep his tone level.

"Oh yes."

"Yet I don't see them on this chart."

"Oh, they don't actually work here—I mean, those are just titles," explained Susannah. "But their role is to help and support their father when there are major decisions to be made about the business. They don't actually have a day-to-day function. George calls them in when he needs them because he wants it to feel like a family affair. One of them will be getting involved in the work with you actually."

Jake nodded, refusing pointedly to ask which one. He looked back at the chart. It was an unusual system, but not unworkable.

"And," he asked, "the chief executive officer? I'd very much like to meet him as soon as possible."

"Of course!" replied Susannah, with what Jake could only call a faint blush forming on her cheeks.

"That's Mr. Edward Goddard," she pronounced his name as though Jake should have heard of him.

He looked at her expectantly.

"He's related to an earl," clarified Susannah proudly.

Jake raised his eyebrows to express surprise and delight. "An earl?" he said. "How clever of him."

"Yes!" replied Susannah effusively.

"When do you think I might be able to introduce him to my colleagues?"

"Oh well, he's ever so busy," said Susannah.

"Of course," smiled Jake, starting to get his personal organizer out.

"Tomorrow morning?" asked Susannah. "At nine?"

Jake looked at her to check she was being serious. That busy, eh?

"Perfect," he grinned. "We'll look forward to it."

Susannah smiled.

"We're all very fond of Edward Goddard," she said coyly.

Susannah leaned forward confidently, even though they were the only two in the room.

Jake leaned forward too. He could almost smell her foundation.

"He's a bit keen on George's youngest daughter Annie," whispered Susannah, with a big grin. "And between you and me she's a bit keen on him."

Jake leaned back again and formed his mouth into a slow, smooth grin.

The nerve in the back of his neck set off again.

Closure, he thought calmly. Closure.

"How the hell is Annie supposed to compete with Agnetha?" Victoria asked Katherine. "How can she ever spoil the boys and teach them bad English, iron creases back into my clothes and break my priceless objets d'art with the same Nordic flair?" She hung her head back on the edge of the Jacuzzi and closed her eyes in bliss as the hot water pumped her thighs and lower back.

"But seriously," she said, her tone low. "How will I live without my manicures and yoga?"

Katherine smiled sympathetically, then stretched her arms out to ensure that there was no room for anyone else but them. "New York!"

Victoria smarted. She wasn't going to let that one go.

"I can't wait to move back home though," she said firmly. "Not long now."

"Why? What's so great about living at home?" sighed Katherine.

"I mean as a married woman."

That shut her sister up.

Neither Katherine nor Victoria would ever have confessed to each other, let alone to themselves, that they envied each other's lives. Happily married Victoria longed for her sister's single lifestyle, the partying, the lack of responsibility, the one-night stands.

The truth was that Victoria's engagement, wedding, marriage and motherhood had not thrilled her half as much as she had expected. And now they were over.

She and Charles had squabbled over the choice of her engagement ring—in the end, she had had to help pay for the one she wanted. One year later, on the afternoon of July 17, Victoria Virginia Octavia Markham, swamped in satin and tulle, surrounded by paparazzi, hangers on and three hundred of her closest friends and family, had smiled the radiant smile of a blushing bride. Which hadn't been easy. She was nursing a migraine the size of her father's bill, clutching a hand-sewn, beaded bag crammed with painkillers and tampons to her scaffolded bosom and dodging the surprise sheet rain.

But she'd done it.

For the first few months of her marriage to Charles, Victoria had been unbearably smug. She had done it! She had married. She had peaked. She deserved to coast for the rest of her life.

Then the news hit home of her husband's "inheritance."

Then, after their first anniversary—which Charles forgot—the truth dawned on Victoria with horror. That was it. The End. Never again would she feel that light-headed, heavy-gutted joy of the first kiss. (She wasn't thinking of Charles now.) Never again the first stuttering declaration of love, the delicious uncertainty. (Or now.) This was it. Forever. Her life was over. (Now she thought of him.)

There was only one thing for it. She had to have a baby to fill the void. A little girl she could dress in pink and call her own and pass down all her well-learned lessons, neuroses and paranoias to— someone who would really understand her.

She loathed being pregnant. The pain, the wind, the stomach, the ankles, the sexlessness. Men stopped looking at her in the street, women eyed her bloated stomach with sympathy. Then the labor—surely there should be some way around it? "I mean they've cured TB," she had said weakly to Annie afterward, "you'd have thought they'd have done something about labor." And then the relentless responsibility of parenthood. No one could ever have prepared her for that.

And to top it all, the tiny alien she produced was a *boy*. And it looked like Charles instead of her.

With all the determination of a mating salmon, Victoria fought every self-preserving instinct and got pregnant again almost immediately. Get it all over with.

"Never let anyone tell you that the first one is more special than the second," she'd told Annie, as she'd lain in bed waiting for her due date. "Believe me, the first one is a shock, the second one is a fucking miracle."

And *another* boy. She just didn't understand it. She was so feminine. How could two weenies grow inside her stomach? Nothing made sense anymore.

Right. That was it. No more babies. No more sex. No more hope.

But there was one thing that kept her going. Her older sister, not having gone through any of these experiences herself, had no idea how nightmarish they all were. She had no idea that secure, comfortable Victoria, with her two healthy heirs, longed to have back Katherine's social life, her lie-ins and her flat stomach.

And damned if she was going to tell her.

In her turn, Katherine longed for her sister's elevated status. She was sick to death of playing the singles game. All the men she met nowadays were too stupid, too young, too arrogant, too far past their prime or too full of emotional baggage for her.

Why the hell hadn't anyone decent proposed to her? She was handsome, wealthy and sharp. If she were a man, she'd have had several wives by now, let alone mistresses. But she seemed to scare men off and the older she got, the more disillusioned she became and in turn, the more terrified they became. Most of the men she met nowadays were looking for harmless young wives, which were becoming harder and harder to come by. In fact, the only direct consequence of feminism in Katherine's world had been to cause a rise in the value of harmless young wives.

She wouldn't dare confess it, but she couldn't think of anything more divine than being able to show off her own children at functions instead of her friend's or sister's. While she certainly didn't envy Victoria her choice of husband, she did envy the added kudos he had given her, simply by consenting to share his surname with her. But it wasn't just what she wanted, it was what the world expected. Katherine knew that it didn't matter how beautiful, rich or happy she was, the world expected her to show her true worth by having a man fall in love with her enough to want to share the rest of his life with her. Or at least a wedding function. And Victoria had done it at only twenty-two.

Still, thought Katherine happily, she *is* married to a troll.

In just a few days, all the plans were settled.

One week after the meeting with Mr. Cavendish, David Silver, Jake Mead's right-hand man, came to see what was until only recently George's two-floor apartment, nod in awe at the flat's beguiling views of the Heath and stare in awe at George's equally astonishing views on life.

David and Jake were to stay there together while working in London. David lived in Edinburgh and the rest of the consultants lived nearby and had family obligations. Jake had a flat in Brighton and didn't fancy commuting every morning, so it made sense to live "on site" as he called it. He could commute back home once a week to see Dr. Blake, to analyze how being welcomed into the family mansion of the woman who'd rejected him seven years earlier was helping his closure no end.

Two weeks later, George, his eldest daughter, Katherine, and the beautiful bright young thing, Davina Barker, flew first class to New York, leaving Annie to finish off their final bits of packing, oversee the renting out of her own flat and move into the penthouse apartment of the Hampstead family home.

Days later, Victoria and Charles's flat down the road was sold. All it had taken was one simple phone call made by one simple estate agent. Such flats had a waiting list without ever having to go on the market.

Since hearing that the management consultants were going to be living one flight down from her, Annie would have liked to have told Susannah she'd changed her mind about moving into the family home and stayed in her flat. But then she'd have had to reveal her reason— and she couldn't cope with Susannah knowing Jake's identity. Typically, she had good luck finding speedy tenants for her little place.

She had no choice but to make herself at home in the penthouse flat with Victoria and Charles, while Harrods' removal men came to take away George's priceless furniture into storage.

Within days, one very lucky estate agent got enough commission to be able to put a deposit down on his first flat in Belsize Park.

A regular sum of money from Annie's rent went toward the family's now joint depleted living expenses. And three million pounds, made from Charles and Victoria's flat, went straight into one of the Markhams' PR accounts, ready for when the Jake Mead Associates' invoices started arriving.

A week later, Annie stood in her newly unpacked room, overlooking Hampstead Heath, a steaming mug of tea in her hands.

As her eyes spanned the view, she smiled to herself. Maybe this wasn't going to be so bad after all.

This could be her chance to finally put the past behind her; get on with her life. It was a sign, an omen, a message.

Either that or she could kill him.

A few feet below her, Jake Mead stood in the vast echoing room that would be his temporary home soon, looking out over the heath. It was hauntingly beautiful. His eyes stopped focusing, his neck relaxed and he felt calmer than he had done in years.

They'd practically begged him to move in—and they were paying him to save their lives.

Oh yes, he thought, stretching his neck out and almost enjoying the ache. Closure doesn't come more complete than this.

Chapter 8

The door blew open, wafting Marlon inside the scruffy Samaritan office, his scarf flapping in the wind.

"Morning, all."

He walked over to behind Annie's chair, put down his old sports bag, took off his coat, walked straight over to Joy's desk and sat on it.

"How's my second wife?"

"Blow it out your ass, Marlon."

"And how's my second wife's mother?"

Joy sighed and sat back in her chair. "I left her at home with a packet of chocolate digestives and Alan Titchmarsh. She's almost deliriously happy."

"When are you going to make me the happiest man in the room?"

"You're the only man in the room, Marlon."

"Tea?"

"What's the point? I'm still going to die one day."

"Coffee then. That'll perk you up."

"Why? Does it come with jump leads?"

"For you, anything."

He turned to Annie. "Morning, Sunshine."

"Morning."

Marlon went into the makeshift kitchen, filled up the battered old kettle and got out two chipped mugs. There waiting for him was a large parcel from the *Innovative Home Shopping* magazine, to which he was addicted.

"Aha!" he exclaimed, eagerly unwrapping it. "I've been waiting for this."

His wife had long since stopped letting his parcels be sent to their home and they now arrived at the Samaritan office where there was always someone to receive them.

"Look at this, look at this!" he exclaimed, excited, his hands up in midair. He was wearing glowing white gloves, and beaming at them proudly.

"Fingered oven gloves! Isn't that just the cleverest thing? Simple, yet brilliant! How do they do it?"

Joy and Annie nodded obediently.

Annie left the office. This week Marlon's shift was taking over from hers and he always managed to come in extra early whenever Joy was in. A few calls today including one from a sex caller who, for the first ten minutes of the call had successfully fooled Annie that he was in the last death throes of emphysema.

As Annie drove back home, she wondered what chaos she'd find there today. Victoria and Charles had been quick to realize the benefits of moving in with her. Apart from the fact that she was an unpaid nanny and babysitter, she had also quickly become their referee in every debate, discussion, row and fight. She was the ballast in the see-saw that was their relationship. And although neither of them could say the words out loud, they were both equally tense at the prospect of becoming penniless. Annie was their in-house counselor.

Not only that, but Victoria assumed that any woman without children had time on her hands. Not so. Annie had filled her life to the rafters with things that made it hugely worthwhile. Try telling that to a wife and mother though. Victoria, bless her, saw her baby sister as her own personal handmaid, confidante and nanny. It was proving exhausting.

Worse than that, both Victoria and Charles made the easy assumption, like so many other people that, because Annie kept her thoughts, observations and opinions to herself, she had none.

She wandered into the flat and threw down her coat, before hearing heightened voices in the lounge.

"Give Auntie Sophie's lipstick back to her NOW."

"It's all right, he can have it to play with if he wants it."

"NO HE CAN'T!"

"Harry, stop chewing Auntie Fi's hair, it's full of chemicals."

"No it's not, I have an organic hairdress—OW!"

Annie opened the door.

Victoria's two young sisters-in-law—Charles's younger sisters—Sophie and Fiona, were sitting shoeless and cross-legged on the floor with their nephews. Both boys were laughing loudly, three-year-old Bertie holding a Bobbi Brown lipstick just out of his Auntie Sophie's reach while she tickled him, four-year-old Harry standing on his Auntie Fi's knee, looking as shocked at the handful of her thick hair that had accidentally found its way inside his mouth as she did. Both girls were clearly thoroughly enjoying themselves. It was only Victoria who, sitting on the leather sofa, looked utterly miserable. When Victoria was in a bad mood, nothing made her feel worse than being surrounded by happy people. She looked up at Annie and her eyes warmed slightly before turning hard.

"Been out shopping?"

When the group on the floor saw Annie, they erupted. The boys ran to their Auntie Annie and both Sophie and Fi got up eagerly. Annie was delighted.

Annie had always felt close to her sister's two sisters-in-law, although twenty-year-old Sophie and eighteen-year-old Fi did sometimes have the unconscious habit of making her feel like an ancient old hag. It wasn't so much their youth as their unending optimism.

"Any sign of life downstairs?" Annie asked the room in general, as carelessly as she could.

"Ooh yes," replied Fi. "Charles is down there now with Jake and David. They're moving in properly any day now. Charles says they're splendid fellows and they're all going to play golf sometime next week."

"I caught a glimpse of one of them downstairs just now," joined in Sophie. "He's absolutely gorgeous."

"That'll be David," said Annie, before thinking.

They all looked at her.

"How do you know?" asked Victoria.

Woops.

"Um. Um. I don't. I just can't imagine someone called Jake being gorgeous. Has he got three legs?" she finished feebly.

Gorgeous? Jake? Impossible, surely? Mind you, she reasoned, it was amazing what you could do with mirrors and lighting nowadays. And let's face it, Sophie did think Prince Edward was "a dish."

She calmed down a bit.

Just then Charles returned from downstairs. He was smiling broadly.

"Golfing men! And one of them's divorced so he's got a lot of time on his hands!" he exclaimed to the room, rubbing his hands in anticipation.

"Which one?" asked all the women together.

"Um," said Charles, momentarily flummoxed. "Can't remember. Ah yes I can, tell a lie. The shorter one."

"I suppose you told them you couldn't possibly play golf with them for the next year because you have two sons to look after and your wife is having a nervous breakdown due to staff shortage and no weekly massages?"

Victoria's voice almost broke as she spoke. She failed to see why Charles was still able to play golf, yet she had had to sacrifice everything that made life worthwhile. The only "luxury" she had managed to keep was her weekly appointments with her cranial osteopath. Without that, she had explained calmly to everyone at the meeting, her weekly migraines would return and she would gladly kill herself.

Charles's smile vanished.

"Oh."

"Thought not."

The awkward silence was interrupted by an eager Fi, standing by the window.

"Which one is that one?" she asked. "He's gorgeous."

Annie couldn't bring herself to walk to the window. She wasn't sure what she found more disturbing, the fact that it could be Jake down there or that Fi thought he was gorgeous.

Charles went to look.

"Ah: That one is the golfer. No, he's the bad golfer—"

"Is he the divorced short one?" asked Sophie impatiently, now also at the window.

"What's his name?" asked Victoria, who had joined her sisters-in-law.

Four women held their breath.

"Um . . ."

"Honestly, Charles," tutted his wife. "You were with him five minutes ago. What's his name?"

"Ah yes. That one's . . . David."

Annie exhaled.

"No! Jake! Yes that's right. Jake. Single, tall, bad but keen golfer. Moving in any day now. Splendid fellow."

Sophie and Fi looked at each other and grinned.

Annie felt sick.

★　　★　　★

That night in their favorite café, against her better judgment, Annie told Cass the latest developments.

"Jake's turned 'absolutely gorgeous' apparently," she scoffed.

"Oh dear."

"I don't understand it. I only dated him out of pity. He was a bespoke boyfriend rather than mass market. Trust him to go chocolate-box on me. Sophie and Fi both fancy him already."

"Really?" asked Cass. "That should be fun to watch. Like watching two toy seal pups fight to the death."

She gave a wicked grin, but Annie just sighed.

Suddenly Cass looked dramatically at her watch, landed her handbag heavily on the table, took out a little bottle, and stuffed it up her right nostril.

Annie stared at her in silence.

"Sh!" commanded Cass suddenly, and commenced sniffing. She put the bottle back in her bag. "Can you hear anything?" she asked finally.

Annie was perplexed. There was utter silence in their corner of the café.

"Nope," she whispered. "Should I be able to hear anything?"

"You can't hear my ovaries?"

Annie was completely confused.

"*Hear* your *ovaries*? Cass, it's too late in the evening to get surreal on me, what are you talking about?"

"I'm 'quietening down' my ovaries, like the nice doctor told me. You see, it all makes perfect sense—I have to get menopausal before I can have treatment to get pregnant. So when I start losing my teeth and forgetting why I've just opened the fridge door, I'll be ready to be a mother."

Annie looked perplexed.

"I wouldn't mind, but this stuff smells of dog turd."

Two hours, two portions of hot buttered cinnamon toast and

two hot chocolates later, Cass drove Annie home. Annie got out of the Land Rover.

"Cheer up, Annie," said Cass before Annie shut the car door. "Jake can't have turned into George Clooney overnight. And Markharms' PR *is* going to be all right. Trust me, I'm your fairy godmother."

Annie managed a smile.

"Good luck with the menopause," she said to Cass before closing the door.

"What menopause?" asked Cass. "Oooh! It's working!"

Chapter 9

The crunch of tire on gravel crept into Annie's dreams and the next moment, she woke suddenly. A car door far below her attic window slammed shut. Feet on gravel, the front door opening, then closing quietly. The echoing sound of footsteps on the hall stairs below loosened her bowels more efficiently than a week in Mexico.

Annie looked at her bedside clock. Six a.m.

Shit. She knew Jake was moving in soon, but she had no idea he'd come so early. Since when did he ever get up before noon?

She turned over to lie on her back. She could feel the pulse of her heart against the duvet.

Jake Bloody Mead was in the building.

He was in her home.

She tried going back to sleep, but every time she shut her eyes, she saw his face as it had been all those years ago.

After five minutes of useless tossing and turning, she reluctantly got up, feeling tired yet restless. She would be fine, she told herself as she slipped on her vest top. She would be calm, mature, serene, tranquil, sophisticated. But most of all calm. She would not give in to her anger. She was a big girl now, not the pathetic teenager whose heart he had broken.

She went to the toilet like she did every morning. See? Fine.

She brushed her teeth, while listening to the radio. Utter and complete calm. She put on the kettle just one hour earlier than usual. Serenely tranquil. Jake's eyes flashed into her mind. Totally mature. She heard his whispered "Annie" in her ears. Sophisticated. His mouth, his cheekbones, his nose, his smile. In her building. Dear God, his smell. In her building.

She felt fine, calm, serene, mature and completely in control of her emotions.

Maybe just another visit to the toilet.

Where her insides imploded.

Annie's reflection gazed reproachfully back at her.

"What did you expect?" it seemed to be saying. "You're no spring chicken, honey. Let's face it, you're more of an autumn duck."

Her skin was still butter-smooth. Her eyes bright. She examined the new gossamer lines just starting to feather the corners of her eyes. She knew it went against everything the beauty magazines said, but somehow those lines made her feel more . . . more real.

Unfortunately there was one part of her reflection that still had a girlish glow. Her skin. Or to be more precise, her "T-zone"— forehead, nose and chin. In fact, a veritable 80s revival fest was going on underneath it. How could that happen? she thought, staring at a small but fierce pimple on her chin. Spots *and* wrinkles at the same time? She could join the circus with that, surely.

Yes, she admitted it, where once there had been easy elasticity in her body, there were now comfortable curves. But still. She wouldn't go back to her teens. Yes, time had had its effect on certain parts of her body, but in contrast, her mind had grown supple, flexible and taut from the lessons that had come with each year.

She stared at herself in the mirror until she became nothing more than the sum of her parts.

I am who I am, she told her reflection gently.

And you are a feckless idiot, Annie's reflection replied.

She had found herself unusually short-tempered at breakfast with her family all week.

"Can I have chocolate for breakfast?" Harry asked.

She shook her head.

"Chicken nuggets?"

"Would you like spinach and liver?" said Annie, cutting up his toast. "Because you're going the right way about it."

Harry didn't like the sound of that. It was just like Mummy.

Annie had been up so early all week that she'd given the boys breakfast and walked them in to nursery school. Bertie was not enjoying this new routine. It was much nicer when Mummy drove them in. He practically had to jog to keep up.

"It's good for you," Annie said this morning. "Puts hairs on your chest."

It was only when Bertie started crying that Annie slowed down.

By the Friday morning, the boys' headmistress was seriously concerned by their unusual punctuality. She phoned Victoria to see if everything was all right at home. Annie hadn't returned yet.

"Of course they're happy at home," Victoria said, nonplussed into the phone. "I'm just an amazingly efficient mother."

"Ye-es. It's just that it's never happened before. We do like to keep an eye out for anything unusual in the children's routine."

"Oh well then," snapped Victoria. "I'll be sure to let you know when we start our annual Satanic abuse rituals. They might be a few minutes late for assembly that week. Thank you *so* much for the call."

Bloody private nurseries, she thought, as she slammed down the receiver.

It was still so early when Annie got back that morning that she made Charles and Victoria freshly squeezed orange juice while they were abluting. Then they all sat in silence munching their breakfast and drinking black coffee until talk was possible. Slowly, Charles and Annie stopped munching and looked at Victoria.

Victoria was staring thoughtfully at her grilled tomatoes.

"What's up?" asked Charles, his mouth full.

Victoria sighed. "I can't decide whether to eat them or not."

"Why?"

"They're full of fluid which will make me fat. But they're also full of antioxidants which are anticarcinogenic."

"Do you *want* them?"

She looked at her husband as if he was mad. "What's wanting them got to do with it?" Really, Charles could be tiresome sometimes.

They fell into silence again.

Charles went back to his newspaper and then glanced up to find his wife looking at him like he was something unmentionable on the sole of her suede Chanel mules.

"What have I done now?"

"I never said a thing."

"Then why are you looking at me like I'm a buffoon?"

Victoria picked up a slice of dry toast and stood up.

"I'm practicing."

She left the room.

Charles sat pondering on this for a moment before turning to Annie.

"More coffee?" he asked.

Annie shook her head. Then she nodded.

As Charles went to pour her another one, she shook her head.

"Yes or no, old thing?" asked Charles kindly.

Annie shrugged.

"Don't mind," she said quietly.

Charles poured her another cup, frowning in concern.

Annie stared at her coffee, as if it was some great perplexing puzzle.

She was, she knew, somewhat preoccupied of late. The truth of it was that she was terrified of leaving her own front door. Where would she see Jake first? In the High Street? In the hall? What if he kept away? What if she never saw him? She couldn't decide which scared her most.

"Ah dear, Annie. Marriage you know," Charles was saying, as he poured himself another coffee, assuming that Annie's thoughtfulness had come on from witnessing his and Victoria's regular morning tiffs. "Not as easy as it looks. Bloody hard work in fact."

Annie nodded and stared at her cup. She didn't hear another word until—

"And of course, the cherry on the proverbial . . . um . . . cupcake, is that he's not as fond of golf as the other chap. Has a handicap of seventy. The man is no less than ideal."

Confident that he'd amply proved his point, Charles sat back and started the Second Act of his breakfast.

"Isn't seventy rather poor for a handicap?" asked Annie mildly.

"Poor? It's shocking! Positively shameful!" replied Charles joyously. "The man will make an absolutely perfect addition to the family. Think he'll be ideal for Sophie. David's nice, but not the same quality, if you get my drift."

Annie thought it would be wise not to ask David's handicap.

"By the way," continued Charles, "you do know that David's invited us all down there tonight, don't you? Liked the sound of my two sisters, I don't doubt."

Annie shook her head slowly.

"Oh yes, you must join us. Don't know that David realized you live with us when he made the invite, but can't possibly have you staying up here all by yourself while we'll be down there gassing. It's not formal, so shouldn't see why they'd mind an extra one. It'll be great fun watching two top 'troubleshooters' falling over each other with my kid sisters, eh?"

Annie moved her facial muscles into a faint smile. "Yes, great fun," she said.

And then she surprised herself by wishing she could justify a facial and a seaweed wrap.

Annie sat in the Samaritan office, staring into space, waiting.

One whole day, a full twenty-four hours since Jake had lived in the flat below her and her life was still the same. Charles had assured her that he'd told David to set an extra place for her and she had decided it was the best way to see Jake again—surrounded by family so she wouldn't be tempted to garotte him.

Would he have put on weight? Gone bald? Prematurely gray?

A girl could hope.

When she had exhausted this depressing thought process, she moved on to another one. Was her father really going to lose everything? It was a terrifying prospect she could hardly bear to contemplate.

Her life really was going down the pan.

The phone rang.

"Hello, Samaritans?"

"Can I talk?"

"Of course," said Annie gently. Miming might take time, she thought.

The voice said something, or was it a cough? Annie waited. Eventually she spoke.

"I'm sorry, I didn't catch that."

"Catch what?"

"Did you . . . just say something?"

"Don't rush me!"

"I wasn't rushing you!"

"No need to get angry!"

"I wasn't getting angry!"

Shit. This wasn't going well. She clenched the phone tighter, as if that might ensure the person on the other end wouldn't hang up.

"I just need to talk."

"Well," said Annie as calmly as possible. "You just say whatever you feel comes naturally."

Silence.

"Take your time," she soothed.

Silence.

A deep sigh from the caller.

A deeper sigh from Annie.

"Oh bugger it," said the caller and hung up.

Annie sank her head on to her arms and leaned on the desk. At least my work here is meaningful, she thought. She smiled into the crook of her elbow and shut her eyes tight.

And saw Jake, laughing, his eyes twinkling, his dark curls being blown slightly by a breeze.

She lifted her head quickly and checked that her phone was still working.

When Annie got home, Victoria was trying to feed the boys. A fine splattering of organic fig yogurt was sprayed over her hair and forehead.

"That was clever!" Annie said to Victoria.

"What?"

"Holding a sieve to your face when they threw slime at you."

"What?" Victoria looked in the mirror. "Jesus Christ! Bastards!" she exclaimed and she went to wash it off, leaving her sister with the boys. She came back into the room talking.

"This is just a bloody nightmare. Why don't they give your brain an epidural to help you cope with the childhood? Doesn't anyone know that labor's the easy bit?"

Just then, another dollop of organic yogurt hurtled toward Victoria from the vicinity of her heir, Harry, so fast she didn't have time to duck. It hit her square in the eye.

Silence descended. Annie froze, almost as terrified as her nephew, who was totally unable to comprehend how that had seemed such a good idea a minute ago.

They waited for the scream. But although Victoria's mouth widened, no noise came out. Gradually Annie realized that Victoria's shoulders were shaking. She was crying. Annie went toward her, but Victoria yelled something incoherent. She stood stock still, her hands splayed as if she'd just been arrested, yogurt on her rigid face. Slowly she started mouthing something, but still no noise came out. Annie edged toward her.

"I can't hear you, Vicky," she said softly, genuinely worried.

Victoria took a deep breath and tried again. Still no noise.

"Mummy!" whimpered Harry, more terrified at Mummy's odd behavior than by her anger.

Still Victoria mouthed, but no noise came out. Then they all became aware of a high-pitched wail coming from somewhere. Annie was the first to realize it was coming from Victoria.

"I need . . ." was all Annie could make out.

"You need . . . ?" Annie repeated. "What do you need, sweetie? Help? A holiday?"

Victoria gasped in some air. "I need," she repeated—

"You need—"

And then it came loud and deep, from Victoria's very soul.

"I NEED A *MANICURE!*" she yelled, and then collapsed on her haunches, wild sobs racking her body.

"Off to bed now, Harry, I'll be with you in a minute," said Annie to her nephew.

Harry ran.

*   *   *

Half an hour later, Victoria was lying on her bed in her darkened bedroom. "I have to get ready for the dinner party downstairs," she whispered to Annie, who was sitting on the bed.

"When you feel ready," said Annie, knowing better than to tell Victoria she wasn't up to a dinner party. "You've got plenty of time."

"Fi and Sophie are coming here so we can all go down together."

"OK," said Annie smoothly.

When Charles rushed home from a golfing tournament an hour later, Annie was reading to the boys in bed and Victoria was sitting defiantly at her dressing table, in her underwear and silk dressing gown, scrutinizing her face for signs of crying. Her nose was still a bit pink and her eyes looked tired, but in a sexy sort of way. Sort of Come-To-Bed-Or-I'll-Cry-Till-I'm-Sick Eyes.

She shrugged. It had worked before . . .

The truth was she felt better now; cleansed. It was nice just to hear the word out loud. Man-i-*cure*.

Maybe one day soon.

Charles popped his head quickly around the boys' bedroom, said goodnight and left Annie to it. He almost ran into his bedroom.

He opened the door wide.

"Got a hole in one!" he exclaimed to his wife.

She stared blankly at him and then turned back to her reflection. "That's more than you do in here," she muttered, sucking in her stomach self-consciously.

Charles stood for a while, gently deflating like an old balloon. Eventually he walked across the room and leaned against the large window frame, staring out across the Heath.

Victoria opened her makeup drawer fiercely, in an ecstasy of hurt pride that he hadn't come over to kiss her. She stared unblinking at her range of foundations.

"Will you be ready in time?" she asked, her voice like ice, self-pity raging through her gut.

"Mmhmm," said Charles.

★   ★   ★

Annie dressed slowly and thoughtfully, trying to ignore the growing sensation in her stomach that today was Domesday. She had been wrong. Meeting Jake was one thing, but meeting him surrounded by her family was quite another. No, the only way she'd be able to cope with coming face to face with him again would be for her to be on her own. Preferably with live ammunition.

She'd have to make up an excuse. Say she'd been abducted by aliens. Or something.

Just as she was trying to decide whether the aliens should have one large white eye or three small green ones, a horrifying scream came from Harry's bedroom. She rushed to the room and found Harry lying on the floor by his bed, Bertie sitting next to him. Harry was in agony, Bertie ashen faced.

Charles and Victoria raced in moments later.

"What's happened?" they both asked Annie.

"I don't know—Harry, what's happened, darling?" She knelt next to him. Victoria clutched Charles's hand and he admonished himself that he should feel grateful at a time like this.

But Harry just writhed on the floor.

"Bertie darling, what's happened?" Annie held Bertie's hand. He seemed incapable of speech.

"Darling, we need to know so we can help Harry," said Annie as gently as she could. "No one's going to tell you off."

"His nose," whispered Bertie.

Harry let out another agonizing cry, his hands shooting up to his nose.

"What's wrong with his nose, darling?"

Bertie started crying.

Gently, Annie prised Harry's hands away from his nose and looked up it. She realized his right nostril was misshapen. Something was up there.

"What is it, Bertie? Be a good boy and tell me."

Bertie pointed to the fire engine that was lying next to them. Annie knew the toy well. Its ladder was missing. Oh God.

"The whole ladder, Bertie?" she asked, her voice now getting tremulous.

Bertie nodded through his tears.

Annie looked at Charles and Victoria.

"He's put the fire engine ladder up his nose," she said urgently. "I think he might need to go to Casualty."

"What?" said Victoria incredulous. "What the bloody hell did he do that for?" she shouted.

"I don't think that's important right now, dear," said Charles.

Victoria let go of her husband's hand. No one came home after a day's golfing and then told her how to be a mother. Not even Charles. Especially not Charles.

She walked up to the boys and held Bertie's arm firmly. "Why did he put the ladder up his nose?" she asked. Bertie started to cry louder.

Harry sat up and still holding his nose he said—somewhat nasally, "I wanted to see if it would fit."

"If it would *fit?* Oh!" she clapped her hands to her head in exasperation. "My son the bloody scientist!" She looked over at her husband. "He's an Einstein!"

Both boys started howling.

She turned her back on them and walked out of the room.

"It's your shift," she informed her husband as she strode past him. "Your son and heir has a hole fixation. No doubt he'll be a golfer like his father."

She slammed the door behind her.

Charles strode up to Harry and picked him up with a gentleness Annie had never seen before. Annie opened the bedroom door and Charles carried his son into the drawing room where Victoria was now pacing. She had her coat on over her dressing gown and was muttering under her breath.

"There's no way out of it, we'll have to take him to Casualty," said Charles, placing a now moaning Harry on to the sofa.

"If I'm not back in time to go to that party, I'm leaving you all," she said and bent to pick up Harry, who clung feverishly to his mother.

Two hours later, Annie had managed to get Bertie to sleep when she heard the key in the door. She rushed to the hall.

Harry was clinging to his mother's neck for dear life, and they all looked exhausted.

"What happened?"

"A nice doctor took the fire engine ladder out of Harry's amazingly big nasal orifice," said Victoria somewhat proudly. "I'll just put him to bed."

Annie and Charles stood in the hall quietly for a while. Charles looked at his watch.

"Fi and Sophie should be here in half an hour."

Annie nodded. The last thing she felt in the mood for now was a dinner party.

Victoria came out of the boys' room and shut the door silently behind her.

"Right," she said, a determined glint in her eye. "I should be ready just in time."

"Ready for what?" asked Charles.

"The dinner party downstairs at David and Jake's, of course," she said, looking at him with her practiced look.

"You can't go to their dinner party tonight! Your son needs you."

"I'll only be downstairs. I can pop up every half-hour."

"How can you even think of going to the party?"

"Well, how can you?"

"Well, someone's got to go," he replied as if this was glaringly obvious.

"Well, why the hell should it be you?" shrieked Victoria. "Why don't I get to have some fun while you do some parenting for a change? I don't believe this! Why does everything always happen to me?"

"Because you're the mother," said Charles firmly.

Victoria exploded. "Oh so that means *I* have to stay at home twenty-four-hours-a-day bringing up *your* children while *you* pop out to the office for a chinwag with my father and then on to the golf course to get a birdy in one, I suppose."

Something told Charles it was not a good moment to laugh.

Victoria was on the home straight.

"I wouldn't mind, but it's my father's money we're living off," she shouted. "So why should I be the one who has to stay at home doing all the hard work while you're off gadding about EVERY BLOODY DAY?"

"YOU are his mother," attempted Charles, trying to ignore the fact that she looked nothing like one, now that her coat was open, showing her lacy underwear and silk dressing gown. "Whoever heard of a father—"

But Victoria interrupted. She wasn't going to let Charles stop her dramatic finale.

"How can you stand there," she accused, "even thinking about going out for the evening, when your Son and Heir lies weak in his bedroom, after emergency medical attention for a fire-engine ladder up his nose?"

It hadn't quite had the dramatic impact she had hoped for.

Annie had heard enough.

"I'll stay here with him," she said quickly.

They both stared at her.

"I'll cancel the sitter and stay here with him," she said again. "I'm not really feeling up to going out tonight anyway."

"Oh would you?" asked Victoria, her tone now grateful.

"You're a brick, Annie," said Charles. "It would make our evening."

"Oh, thanks Annie, you're fantastic," said Victoria, looking straight at Charles. They were going to go out together. Like a couple. Like old times.

Charles looked straight back at her. God she looked good after a fight. All flushed and heaving.

Half an hour later, Annie stood in her room, staring at her reflection as she slowly took off her evening clothes. It turned out that the aliens saving her from going to the dinner party were none other than her family.

Meanwhile Victoria was lying, sweating on the bed. She turned her head to Charles, whose smiling face was half hidden by her dressing gown.

He wanted to say that her eyes looked alive and warm. He wanted to say that the sex was fantastic and he'd missed it. But he knew that it would probably all come out wrong.

"Hole in one," he whispered and they both smiled.

She almost said that it was a shame he didn't spend quite as long achieving this kind as he did the other. But she let it go.

Chapter 10

"*C*asualty?" repeated Sophie, "whatever happened?"

"Well," began Charles, and took a deep breath in.

Victoria interrupted.

"Your nephew decided that it was worth sacrificing his olfactory nerve so that Mummy wouldn't leave him for a whole evening. She'd been evil earlier in the day and had only read *Postman Pat* to him eight times instead of the requisite ten. Naturally she had to suffer for it."

"His what nerve?" asked Sophie.

"He put a toy fire-engine ladder up his nose," beamed Charles. Everyone gasped.

"A whole toy fire-engine ladder?" asked David.

"Oh yes," said Charles, proudly. "Doesn't do anything by half measures, my boy."

"Ow," sympathized David, remembering a long-forgotten incident involving chewing gum, a throbbing eardrum and a doctor with halitosis.

"So is he all right now?" asked Jake politely.

Victoria smiled a delightful smile at Jake. Difficult not to, really, even for Victoria.

"Oh, I'm sure he's as right as rain," she answered. "Annie—that's my sister—is staying with him and if he wakes up she'll read him to sleep. He loves that."

"Oh, does your sister live nearby?" asked David.

"She lives with us," answered Victoria. "Upstairs."

Sophie was only too glad to pass Jake a glass of water, as some food went down the wrong way.

"Oh, you'd love Annie," Fi started telling David. "She's one of the nicest people we know, isn't she, Sophe?"

Sophie nodded emphatically.

"So she lives up there with you?" David said. "She's more than welcome to pop down to our flat any time. Why doesn't she pop down now?" He was a free agent since the divorce and wasn't going to waste any time. The more women the merrier.

"Oh I doubt she'd want to do that," said Jake quietly.

Everyone looked at him.

"I mean . . . I'm sure she's far too busy to want to spend time with her father's employees," he finished quickly. "More dessert anyone?"

"She'll have canceled the sitter by now," said Victoria. "She wasn't feeling up to going out tonight. Anyway if there's one thing that Annie likes to do it's fuss over children, especially when they're sick."

"Well, we're very grateful, anyway," said Charles quickly.

There was a lull in the conversation. Victoria's tone made everyone a little unsure as to what the right thing to say was. Everyone except Charles.

"Ah yes, Annie's a brick. Now *there's* someone who'd make a good mother," he said without thinking.

Victoria glared at him, as the others all looked at their plates.

"Shall we remove to the other room for coffee?" asked Jake quietly.

The next morning was a Saturday and Annie slept in. Charles had arranged to play golf with Jake and had left the flat at seven.

Four hours later, Annie allowed herself the unusual luxury of a leisurely breakfast after slinging on an old vest T-shirt that was too small and pajama bottoms that were too big and scooping her mass of hair on top of her head. She decided rebelliously that this morning she wasn't going to shower until her body actually started to smell noxious. For the first time in living memory, Victoria was groomed before her.

Annie was exhausted. She'd been up until 3 a.m. the night before, waiting for the sound of Victoria and Charles's key in the lock. It was only after she heard it that she realized it wasn't going to help her get to sleep. She'd eventually fallen into an exhausted slumber after dawn.

"You missed a fabulous evening," yawned Victoria, pouring yogurt over her drained oats. "Except for the food, of course. I'd have thought that with-it troubleshooters would be up on their allergies. All I could eat was mushrooms and aubergine. But Jake Mead is gorgeous. I think Fi's finally met her perfect husband."

Annie's throat contracted and she put down her toast.

"Turns out he studied at your university when you were there," continued Victoria, munching loudly. "Did you ever meet him?"

Annie shook her head so fractionally that only her eyebrows moved.

"No, I suppose it's a big enough place," said Victoria, her eyes glazing over.

The front door intercom buzzed in the kitchen. Victoria walked over to it lazily.

"Hello?"

"IT'S ME," yelled Charles from downstairs, his voice reverberating around the flat.

"You don't need to shout, darling," said Victoria for the hundredth time. "That's why we got the intercom."

"RIGHT YOU ARE," shouted Charles. "I'M WITH JAKE. WE DECIDED TO GO TO THE CLUB FOR A SPOT OF LUNCH

AND A GAME OF TENNIS. NEED TO PICK UP MY KIT,
JAKE THOUGHT HE'D POP UP AND SAY HELLO—"

Victoria buzzed them up, delighted.

"Poor Fi," she said over her shoulder to a horrified Annie. "A
sports widow before she's even married the man." She ran to check
her face in the mirror.

Annie's limbs deadened. Her palms dampened. This wasn't how
it was meant to be. She hadn't got a scrap of makeup on. Her hair
was unwashed. Toxic fumes were escaping from certain regions of
her body. And her sweat glands had gone into fourth. She wasn't
ready for this.

She must get out of the kitchen. Yes, that was it, go to the toilet. Her body was stuck static, yet her insides had spurted into action, racing around and around, bumping into each other, collapsing
into uncontrollable hysteria and starting again. A complete Norman Wisdom experience was going on in her stomach. She tried
to speak but no sound came out.

She heard the front door open.

She sped out of the room.

Ten full minutes later, Annie heard the door slam shut. Thank God.
She padded back into the kitchen, humming "It's Raining Men"
fiercely to herself. She walked straight past the kitchen table and
over to the breakfast bar where the kettle was. She certainly deserved another coffee after that shock to her system. As she clicked
on the kettle, she became aware that someone was in the room
with her. She froze.

Someone coughed.

She raised her eyes and looked in the reflection of the window
in front of her. Someone had stood up behind her. Annie held her
breath and ever so slowly, turned around to face the stranger
trapped in the corner of the room behind the kitchen table.

At first she didn't even realize it was Jake.

A tall, broad man, with short, cropped hair and clear, dark eyes stared at her with a mixture of hostility and fear. She frowned. Was it him? The skin was soft, but there was an unfamiliar shadow around the chin. The cheekbones were pronounced, but they seemed to fit this man's face better than Jake's had. The legs were long, but certainly not skinny. And there was no boyish charm.

It wasn't Jake. Which meant only one thing. She was about to be hacked to death by a complete stranger in her own kitchen.

Phew. For a minute there, she'd thought it was Jake.

The man shifted uncomfortably. And with a horrified squirm, Annie realized that he looked as if he was trying to pluck up the courage to ask for his ball back please.

It was Jake.

Then he spoke.

"You must be Annie Markham."

You must be Annie Markham? The bastard was pretending that they'd never met! In her own kitchen!

Conjuring up sensational powers of self-control, Annie let him live. She then gave him a tight, short smile that didn't even reach her nose, let alone her eyes.

"Must I?" she clipped so dryly that the air seemed to evaporate around them.

They stared at each other, seeing nothing and everything.

"Aha! So you two have met!" exclaimed Victoria from the doorway. "Fabulous! Jake, this is Annie, my baby sister and *savior*. Annie, this is Jake, Daddy's troubleshooter and the entire family's savior. He's about to thrash Charles at tennis. Ah well, boys will be boys—"

"Oh yes," said Annie, her eyes never leaving Jake's. "Boys will definitely be boys."

She and Jake stared menacingly at each other, involved in an unconscious battle not to be the one to blink first.

For added confidence, Annie decided now was a good moment to place her hands with lazy confidence on her waist. With shock she realized it was flesh on flesh. Oh good God, she was in her too-big pajama bottoms. They would be happily drifting down her tummy by now. Her life had surpassed itself in degradation. Maintaining furious eye contact, she started inching her hips forward so as to feel how far down her pajama bottoms had got to. Jesus. She was perilously close to showing Jake what was strictly restricted viewing. Well, restricted to him, anyway.

She tried frantically to decide the pros and cons of pulling up her pajama bottoms in front of him. Cons: it would show loss of face. Pros: she would be wearing trousers.

Nope. She couldn't decide.

Was that gurgling noise her brain?

"Well, they say a good game of tennis is fantastic for de-stressing," Jake was smiling at Victoria, taking his eyes briefly off Annie. "Though, the state my playing's got to, I should think it'll be rather a stressful afternoon."

Victoria beamed back at his self-deprecation. So sexy in a big man.

Annie grimaced, while using the moment to hitch up her pajama bottoms.

For a much-needed shot of confidence, she decided now was the ideal stage in the proceedings to cross her arms pointedly—with a hint of accusation that only she and Jake would understand. Thank Christ. Her vest was still on. Ten years old and in dire need of a wash, but still on.

"If you *really* want to de-stress," she said softly, "why don't you just turn your back on everything and run?"

Jake turned back to Annie and tilted his head to one side thoughtfully.

Aha! The old Tilting The Head Thoughtfully trick . . .

Annie tilted her head too. Extra thoughtfully.

Deuce.

She sensed her pajama bottoms slipping down again and stopped breathing.

Victoria smiled uncertainly at them both.

"Yes. Well," she said.

Jake turned to Victoria and flashed her a wide grin. Annie almost recognized the boy inside the man.

"And I'm afraid I must run out on you now," he said tightly. "Much as it pains me to do so."

And he turned his back and walked out.

Standing motionless in the middle of her kitchen, arms crossed, head tilted thoughtfully, Annie realized two things: one, Jake Mead had grown into a pratt. And two, it was possible for hair to sweat.

She turned slowly to the kettle.

As soon as she heard the door slam she started breathing again.

"Isn't he just *divine?*" grinned Victoria. "I must phone the girls."

In the silence, Annie leaned on the breakfast bar staring blindly at the kettle. She'd like very much to make herself a coffee, but she couldn't remember how to.

Jesus Christ, she'd seen him. Been in the same room as him. Made eye contact with him. Spoken to him. Understood him. Wanted to kill him.

Maybe next time he wouldn't be able to smell her from the street.

Each time will be easier, she told herself, steadying her breathing. Each time will be easier.

Well, it certainly couldn't get any worse.

"Sophie and Fi are popping round!" cried out Victoria. "We're going to take the boys to watch Charles and Jake play tennis."

Oh God, thought Annie. It just got worse.

Annie declined Victoria's eventual invitation to spend the afternoon ogling Jake as he beat Charles at tennis. Instead, she spent her afternoon helping out at the charity shop in Hampstead High Street. Four hours of sorting the Nicole Farhi cast-offs from the Gap ones almost took her mind off the morning encounter.

But not quite. As staff and customers buzzed around her, she couldn't stop herself from fuming at the new Jake.

"You must be Annie Markham?"

Bastard! Before meeting him, she had idly wondered if they'd mention their past or if they'd both pretend it hadn't happened—but to be so distant, so cold, so estranged. And to beat her at it. In her own kitchen. She was fuming.

And she'd been in her sodding pajamas . . .

As she trudged back to the flat, she tried to judge Jake's new looks objectively.

Boy, he'd got ugly.

Not exactly in his features—they were still the same and in all fairness, the close-crop hair showed off his eyes and cheekbones to every advantage. But there was a hardness in his face now that was cold and mean. And he'd got so broad in his old age. Bulky almost. It was intimidating.

Heartened slightly by this objective study, Annie decided it was far more healthy for her to pity Jake than to hate him.

Later that evening she changed her mind.

"Jake did remember you," Victoria told her over dinner. "Not very complimentary about you though. Said you look twenty years older, wouldn't have recognized you."

Victoria was oblivious to the fact that Annie didn't have enough breath in her body to answer her.

As Charles and Victoria argued over whether it was Sophie or Fi their new friend was destined for, Annie sat silent.

Neither Sophie nor Fi was going to "get" Jake Mead, she concluded to herself as the conversation went on around her.

Because she was going to kill him first.

"And how did you actually *feel?*"

Dr. Blake was beginning to lose patience. Reticence was one thing, but plain stubbornness was a bloody pain.

Jake frowned.

"Well?" asked Dr. Blake again.

Tell me tell me tell me tell me tell me tell me tell me . . .

Jake shifted again, making ugly noises in the leather seat.

"I don't know what to say," he spoke almost inaudibly.

"Say the truth. Just say how you feel."

Jake shrugged. "Disappointed. Like it's all a big anticlimax."

Dr. Blake sighed inwardly. Oh *poo*.

"How did you feel when you saw Annie Markham?"

Another shrug.

"Like I was looking at a stranger."

Three successive images flashed subliminally into his mind—far too fast for him to understand, let alone put into words: a kiss of freckles on the back of the neck, tendrils of auburn hair escaping a hair-band, an alabaster stomach curving gently toward him.

He sighed dramatically. How did he *feel*?

He closed his eyes and pictured the scene: Annie's angry eyes boring into him so that he couldn't move. And such bitterness in her voice that he almost didn't recognize her.

"She's just a stranger."

He grimaced at the memory of what he'd said to her. "You must be Annie Markham?" Where the hell had *that* come from? Why did he always say things that actually didn't make any sense whenever he got nervous?

"No anger?"

"Oh yes, anger, but no . . . chemistry."

"Were you . . . expecting chemistry?"

"I don't know what I was expecting."

Dr. Blake nodded serenely. Ooh, she loved denial. It paid for all of Sigmund's cat food and so many beach holidays that she never needed a sunbed. Was it worth telling him? Oh yes.

"You do know there's a word for what you're going through, don't you?"

"What's that?"

"Begins with D and ends in a river in Egypt."

Jake frowned.

"D-Suez?"

She sighed heavily. "That's a canal, Jake, and thank you so much for proving my point."

Jake frowned intently at his therapist. He never understood a thing she said.

Dr. Blake wondered briefly at how such an intelligent man could be so dim. "How do you feel now?"

His voice lowered by an octave.

"Depressed," he said finally. "I've spent seven years burying myself in my career and for what?"

Dr. Blake nodded and let him go on. Clients could mock it, but she knew silence was the psychologist's most effective tool. That and a firm handshake.

"That bitch ruined my faith in women—in people. She pretends to be this wonderful person, but she's actually a manipulative liar."

Dr. Blake didn't move a muscle.

"But, you know, I'd always remembered her as being beautiful . . ."

Dr. Blake stopped breathing.

"And now—"

Jake thought again of Annie's angry eyes, the dark shadows underneath them, the sour expression of bitterness gone mad.

Dr. Blake watched his face flicker through a hundred expressions. If I had a mirror in this room I'd be out of a job, she thought.

"I've just discovered that my memory of her . . . well, either she's lost her looks or I've upped my standards. Basically, I've spent the past seven years working my ass off, convinced that every hour, every *minute* of work I did—pushing myself up that ladder, missing out on relationships, friendships, basic life experiences—was proving that Annie Markham—beautiful, gentle, perfect Annie Markham—was wrong in rejecting me. Only to discover seven years later that she's a sour-faced, hard bitch. My motivation for my entire career has . . . been flawed."

They sat in silence, absorbing this monumental psychological step. Well, Jake was absorbing it, Dr. Blake was suddenly remembering she'd forgotten to tape *Coronation Street*.

Double poo.

Sod silence, she thought. If she got home early, she'd make it in time for the last few minutes.

"How depressed would you say you're feeling now? On a scale of one to ten."

Jake stared at the carpet. He shrugged.

"Dunno," he whispered eventually.

Dr. Blake shut her pad.

"A perfect place to finish," she said with a reassuring smile.

Chapter 11

*O*ne week later, at seven-thirty in the morning, Jake, David Silver and two of their top colleagues sat working in a coffee bar near George Markham's office.

In two hours' time, they'd have their first official meeting with their new clients. They knew their plan was good. They'd spent every minute of the past week working on it. They'd go so far as to lay money on it being the answer to everyone's prayers.

Now all they had to do was convince their clients.

An hour later, Jake anticipated the usual heady sensation of adrenaline coursing through his veins.

An hour and a half later, feeling more tense than alert, he ordered his third coffee. Where the hell was the buzz?

Two hours later, on the dot of 9:30 a.m., Jake Mead Associates' four top consultants shook hands with Susannah, Charles and Edward Goddard inside George's spacious office.

Shirley came in.

Thank God, thought Jake. More coffee.

He leafed through his notes, listening to his colleagues expertly make small-talk with the clients. At just the right moment, he looked up, gave everyone a disarming, yet modest, smile and stood tall.

"Right, well," he started, rubbing his hands together to relay his company's attitude of gritty optimism.

"Oh, sorry, but we're not all here yet, we're just waiting for Annie," explained Susannah.

The coffee finally hit Jake's nervous system. Not a moment too soon, he thought, collapsing into his seat. He suddenly felt wide awake.

While his colleagues gave the slides and laptop one final check, the door opened and all except George and Jake were disappointed by the sight of Shirley with the coffee.

Behind her raced a rather jumpy Annie.

"Sorry I'm late," she said. "I got stuck in traffic."

While Annie sat down, Jake tapped his notes on the desk, making them an even neater pile than before. From the corner of his eye, he felt Edward's body language suddenly shift into another gear.

By now, Jake had carried out the silent ritual of taking in as many details about his clients as possible, seeking out the possible troublemakers and the potential allies, and always the most intriguing, the troublemakers in disguise as allies. If only they all knew how easily they could be categorized. If only they all knew how he could almost predict word for word how they were going to react to his presentation.

He took one last swig of coffee, stood up, cleared his throat, looked out at everyone, cheesy-grinned and, after the requisite dramatic pause . . . he was off.

Jake was smooth, professional and confident. He didn't falter from his script, he didn't patronize or dumb down. He joked when it was appropriate, became grave when required. He illustrated his research into his clients' world with the light touch of a geisha. He warmed them up, cooled them down, held them at arms' length, drew them in, reined them out to seduce them back. He played them like a Stradivarius.

And he didn't look at Annie once.

Until she poured herself a coffee. And with one surreptitious, sideways glance, he discerned that unlike when he'd chanced upon her in the kitchen, she was now wearing makeup. And hair combs. And a bra. But the expression was the same. Sourness, bitterness and a hint of wary suspicion. He'd seen the look before in so many of his clients' faces—the Contraception Look, he called it—and it was his least favorite look to deal with.

She probably hadn't had a man for years.

He shifted mode into serious but loving—the Parent's Voice.

"Now, let's move on to the different areas of concern for my colleagues and myself. Of primary concern to you—and therefore to us—is cost reduction." A pause before continuing. "And the first, most easy cost reduction is to reduce the head count by thirty percent."

Another pause.

"Or sack 1,200 people," came Annie's voice from the corner.

Jake eyed her quickly, sensing David's inward groan. David now owed him £50. Admittedly, Jake had been at an advantage in knowing that Annie's fragile looks belied her boldness, but a bet was a bet.

"Allow me to illustrate," he said, selecting a graph and nodding to David to turn off the lights.

As the lights dimmed, everyone turned to the graph, which illustrated this point with such painstaking detail that not one of them understood it. Not even the consultants. But it was in a fabulous shade of purple. Mauve almost, with a hint of lemon.

"Does it not occur to you," said Annie, "that the heads involved in the headcount are attached to bodies?"

No shit Sherlock, thought Jake. And I bet you think you're the first person to ever say that. Sweet.

"We *are* a company known for its heart," Edward confided to Jake.

You're a company known for its sinking revenues, arsehole, thought Jake.

He smiled an apologetic, empathetic smile. His voice was conciliatory and benign.

"Of course these are real people and let me assure you that no one likes having to put someone out of a job." Dramatic, sensitive pause. "But a large number of those redundancies are contractors who've been extended, so not all of them are going to be out of work. Secondly, many of the people who will be downsized will be IT, that is, Information Tech—"

"I know what IT stands for," interrupted Annie quietly. "And downsized."

Jake took a deep breath and continued.

"Those people will be snapped up again in no time," he mollified gently. "Thirdly, there will be people who are underperforming, forcing others to work twice as hard to cover them. And finally—" he turned to Susannah, and spoke with compassion "—we're talking about thirty percent of the staff losing their jobs so that a hundred percent can keep theirs."

Susannah nodded firmly. Beautifully put, she thought. (And beautiful biceps.)

"Seventy percent, surely."

"Pardon?"

Annie took a deep breath.

"Thirty percent of the staff losing their jobs so that seventy percent can keep theirs. Not a hundred percent."

Jake smiled.

"It will be a hundred percent of the new total staff."

Annie assumed an expression of delight.

"Oh how clever! You mean that thirty percent no longer exist at all. You've whitewashed them completely. Invisible maths!"

"*Annie!*" Susannah's voice was utterly no-nonsense. Even Jake jumped.

There was an ugly pause.

"How long do you think this company's got if we keep going at this rate?" asked Edward.

Annie, blushing in shame at being spoken to like that in public, was grateful for his thoughtfulness.

Jake managed to keep any shock out of his expression and voice at this question. Edward had been chief exec for six months. What had he been doing all that time if he didn't know the answer to that?

"To our estimation, we're probably talking a few months."

Edward nodded thoughtfully at this. He was trying to formulate something.

"Is it not possible to knock these heads off—"

"Reduce the head count."

"Reduce the head count," repeated Edward, "a bit slower. Make it a bit less traumatic for everyone. Including myself. I love my staff like . . . like children."

Let's hope you never have children, thought Jake. He opened his face into an expression of non-judgmental explanation.

"To be honest, all you do then is create a culture of paranoia—everyone waiting for their turn—and that breeds low productivity and low quality—"

"And unhappiness," concluded Annie.

Jake nodded. Were there any dangers of contesting Annie's attitude at this stage? He didn't think so. Again, he was at an advantage.

"If I may be so bold, I sense a feeling of hostility toward our role here," he spoke quietly.

Susannah shot a warning glance at Annie. Yup, he was right. Susannah was still in control.

He shot an irresistibly twinkly smile at Susannah.

"It's happened before, please, we're used to it."

He turned back to Annie, all hint of twinkle gone.

"My role here, Miss Markham, is to stop the company losing money. Not to make its employees happy." A wide grin around the room. "Believe me, if you paid me to do that, I would."

He joined in their grateful laughter.

How would you do that? thought Annie. Leave?

"Of course," interrupted Susannah quickly. "Annie understands." She sighed heavily. "I think we're all agreed then," she looked around at Edward. "A head count reduction of thirty percent."

Annie's heart went out to Edward as he nodded unhappily.

Jake took another swig of coffee, which was getting colder and more bitter.

"Then there are various costs that don't make a contribution at all to the company," he went on. "They should go."

Annie could hardly believe her ears.

She joined the others in looking up at the slide. It was more lemon than mauve this time.

"Hold on a minute!" murmured Annie. "What does AS stand for?"

Jake looked at his notes. "Artists' Sponsorship? I believe the company sponsors exhibitions."

"Yes, it does."

Jake shrugged.

"All outgoing, no income. Gotta go."

Annie stared at him, barely able to contain her anger. "Have you any idea what that money means to those artists?"

No, I'm a heartless bastard, he thought. I play the role and take the money.

Jake started chewing his lower lip, but before he replied, he was saved by Edward.

"How much money does the sponsorship specifically lose a year? On its own?" asked Edward calmly.

Jake looked through his notes, one hand over his mouth, the other loosely on his waist. Annie noticed that although he had broadened out on top, there still wasn't an ounce of fat on him. Probably on drugs, she thought.

Jake shrugged. "On its own it's negligible. So it's entirely up to you."

Edward looked over at Susannah and Annie. "I say we keep that one," he grinned.

"I agree entirely," said Susannah.

"You're the boss," said Jake to Edward. He suddenly found himself able to smile at Edward.

Jake took off his jacket, loosened his tie even more and poured himself another coffee while his colleagues changed some slides over and briefed everyone on the next stage of the meeting. Annie studied Jake as he poured milk into his second cup of coffee. When had he got all those lines around his eyes? And when had his expression got so grim? He suddenly looked up at her. It was a bold, demanding look that annoyed her, so she threw him a secret smile, intended to infuriate, before glancing with laconic approval at Edward.

Infuriated without knowing why, Jake cleared his throat and continued.

"The other primary area is to increase revenue. At the moment, as a PR company you're a Jack of All Trades. As you know, each of your departments focuses on a particular industry and what has become obvious to us—"

A graph clicked on to the wall. Ooh, magenta, thought Annie. Lovely.

"—is that one department by far and away is the biggest earning department."

Susannah beamed.

"Celebrities," she said proudly.

"Toiletries," replied Jake, pointing to the highest grid in the graph.

"I beg your pardon?"

"Toiletries is carrying all the other departments," explained Jake. "In fact Anus-Betta wiped the floor with TV presenter Marty Chuddup last year. It seems that celebs just don't come to you anymore, so you'd save an awful lot of money and bother if you stopped trying with them. However, the toiletries companies are happy to pay you top wack for what they see as a top service. So you should leverage that as your successful line of business. Stop doing things that aren't making you money."

Annie was humbled by the sight of Susannah's face. She was clearly far more horrified at the thought of losing the company's celebrity clients than she was at the thought of losing 1,200 members of staff.

Susannah wasn't just horrified. She was also terrified at the thought of having to break the news to George.

After the meeting, Annie rushed on to her work at the gallery, tension gnawing at her gut. Her boss Samantha hadn't opened up yet, so Annie was on her own. The echoing emptiness calmed her considerably.

She always loved being there first, turning the lights on one by one, seeing each painting come to life in the morning's bright silence. She stood back and took in each one. She loved the artist they were exhibiting this month.

Samantha had taken some persuasion. She'd stared at the paintings, screwing her face up into an ugly scowl.

"I don't know. There's too much . . ."

Too much what? Anger? Movement? Sensuality?

". . . *Red*."

"Of course there is!" Annie had explained. "It symbolizes blood. Women. Power."

"Oh, power, yes, I *like* it."

They stared for a bit longer. Samantha wasn't quite convinced.

"And a lot of *black*."

"Anger. The irony of post-feminism."

Samantha gasped.

"Oh, yes, you're *so* right. The *irony* of post-feminism. It almost talks to you, doesn't it?"

Annie nodded. "I see it as a symbol of women's growing alienation in a post-urban society."

Samantha gasped again and stared afresh at the picture. "Oh so do I, so do I."

They stared a bit more and then Samantha made her mind up.

"If she does a couple of female nudes I'll sign her up."

Annie smiled. Now she wouldn't have to resort to Markhams' money.

As usual, Annie had been right. Tiny red circular stickers now adorned the bottom right-hand corner of nearly all the paintings. It was enough to make up for the fact that "the irony of post-feminism" had become Samantha's phrase.

As Annie put the kettle on, she heard Samantha's stiletto heels on the parquet floor. She took a deep breath and went out into the gallery.

"Morning," she called out. "Coffee?"

Samantha stood stock still in the middle of the room, staring at one of the nudes. Her eyes were screwed up as she stared hard at the painting. Annie often wondered what Samantha actually looked like behind the peroxide and face paint. Probably quite pretty.

She stared at the painting from behind the counter. It was less bold than all the other ones, less unique and less confident. It had been the last one the artist had done and it was one of the few that still hadn't sold. Samantha spent about half an hour every day trying to decide whether it would be a sound investment for her to buy it. Eventually she turned her head toward Annie.

"I've decided," she said absently. "I'm going to buy it."

She walked toward Annie, her face grim with determination.

"Black, no sugar. You're an angel."

★   ★   ★

It hadn't taken Annie long to realize that she didn't need to actually join in conversations with Samantha. Which was useful today, because she felt rather preoccupied. Samantha's lips were moving so Annie kept on nodding pensively.

"So I said to him, all condescending, 'I'm the manager actually.' You should have seen his face. It was a study. Wish I'd had a camera. You'd have loved it. It was as if I'd just said to him 'What these? No they're false! But if you like them, you can take them home with you.' "

Samantha's raucous laughter echoed throughout the gallery.

Annie smiled on cue. "So what happened?"

"Happened? What do you think? The sod walked off. Men are fucks anyway."

Annie nodded and the two women stared out into the empty room.

"Did someone say coffee?" asked Samantha.

Annie went to the back office and put the kettle on.

"Black, no sugar. You're an angel."

Chapter 12

A few days after the delightful dinner party at Jake and David's place, Sophie and Fi decided it would be rude not to invite them back to say thank you. They also decided it would be stupid not to; it wasn't often that you found a looker like Jake living beneath your brother. Another deciding factor was that they knew they couldn't waste any time. The consultants were only here temporarily. They decided to invite them to dinner the next weekend.

Even though technically Fi had a boyfriend, of whom she was rather fond, she was not insensitive to the charms of two hunks competing over her. Sophie, on the other hand, was entirely unattached and more than ready to fall hopelessly in love. And it had better happen soon because she was beginning to develop a crush on most of the men in her life. Including the postman. In fact, particularly the postman. Something had to be done.

An evening of light entertainment was planned at their delightful attic flat in West Hampstead.

They planned an evening to look forward to. A date was arranged, the guests invited, a menu decided and alcohol stocked up.

As for Annie, she firmly believed that the more times she saw Jake, the calmer she would become in his company. So this dinner party could only be a good thing. It was necessary for her to go through, so that she could move beyond it. She was being cold-hearted, cool-headed, calm-spirited, practical, cynical, wise.

Victoria and Charles had now decided that Jake Mead would indubitably "get" one of Charles's sisters. They liked David, but he didn't stand a chance next to the looks and charm of Jake. Annie started to feel a strong sense of sympathy for David. She had always liked the underdog, but none so wholeheartedly as him.

But which sister would Jake get? This gossip became Charles and Victoria's constant conversation and as with everything between the pair, Annie became the referee.

Charles was convinced that Sophie would "catch" Jake, but Victoria was rooting for Fi. Both had their reasons. Charles didn't want Fi to split up from her boyfriend, Tony, a self-made American who had come over to Britain in the mid-90s, started up a gym and now owned a string of the most exclusive health clubs in the country. He had just opened his first golf club. First-rate fellow, opined Charles to anyone who would listen, just the chap to have in the family.

Victoria hated Tony. She detested his loudness, the way he thought her family name was "quaint" and the way he said his "a"s by opening his mouth as wide as it would go and then breathing out. It was disgusting. She didn't want Fi to connect the Markham name with some low-life American. Where was Fi's sense of tradition? Her sense of heritage? Breeding? Taste? Jake Mead, handsome, wealthy, well bred and British, could be just the man to put a stop to all that nonsense.

"If Sophie would stop hogging Jake, Fi would win hands down," she informed her husband, over their Caesar salad lunch on the day of the party.

"Nonsense. Anyone can see that the man has the hots for Sophie," Charles replied.

"Has the hots for?" mocked Victoria. "*Nobody* says 'has the hots' anymore, Charles," said Victoria. "Annie," she continued, "tell your brother-in-law he's got the brains of a chicken."

"Charles, you have the brains of a chicken, please pass the dressing."

Charles smiled at Annie. "Why is it," he said, turning to his wife, "that when an insult comes from Annie, it's endearing?"

"Because she doesn't know you like I do, dear."

Charles was undeterred.

"Well, it obviously takes a chicken to work out that if Sophie is single and Fi is in a happy relationship with a splendid fellow, Jake is going to end up with Sophie."

Victoria merely shook her head at her husband. "You just haven't got a clue, have you?" she started. "Think about—"

"Clearly not, my dear" he acquiesced, "not a—"

"I was talking rhetorically, Charles. Don't interrupt."

"Sorry."

Victoria sat back in her chair. "A man meets two delightful, one-day-to-be wealthy sisters," she expounded. "One is all over him, very obvious, the other keeps her distance. He then discovers that the enigmatic one has an equally wealthy boyfriend who has been on the scene for a while and who keeps proposing to her, but she hasn't yet made up her mind. Now, which one is the man going to go for?"

Charles shrugged his shoulders wearily.

"OK, I'll try talking to you in a language you understand," said Victoria, growing tetchy. "Listen carefully, Charles." She spoke slowly. "A golfer—that's a GOLFER—is about to take the most important shot of a tournament. The crowd is hushed."

Charles concentrated. Victoria continued.

"He has two options. He can either take it the easy way—"

"Straight down the middle?" asked Charles. "Or laying up?"

Victoria eyed him eloquently. "Don't put ideas into my head," she whispered.

Charles shut up.

"Or," she continued purposefully, "he can do something that will be a challenge to his superior skills and that will be talked about forevermore. Now, Charles, which one do you think he'll do?"

Charles took a long, deep breath, shaking his head slowly with thought.

"Which golf course are we on?" he asked eventually.

Victoria stared at her husband. "Remind me again how much you'll inherit," she asked in an ominously quiet voice.

Charles refused to give up. "Well, I'm sorry but the course makes a big difference," he said.

"It's a bloody metaphor!" shouted Victoria, finally losing her cool. "Don't you know a metaphor when you hear one?"

Charles looked out of the window.

"Charles!" she yelled, livid. "I'm talking to you. I said, don't you know a metaphor when you hear one?"

"Oh, sorry dear," he said calmly, "I thought that was a rhetorical question."

Annie started clearing the plates. As she left the dining room, she heard her sister telling her husband,

"Jake will marry Fiona. And you will have to keep paying your subscription for your wretched golf club forever."

By the time Annie returned with their coffees, both Charles and Victoria were grinning excitedly.

"We've made a bet," Victoria told her sister excitedly. "If I win and Jake gets Fi, we go on a month-long holiday to Barbados without the boys and if he gets Sophie, we go on holiday to somewhere with lots of golf courses with the boys."

"And if, by some quirk of fate, Jake gets Victoria," finished Charles, taking his coffee into the other room, "I'll be on a lifelong bloody holiday, boys or not."

Fi held the list with great concentration. Sophie looked around the kitchen and began.

"Nibbles galore."

"Check."

"Stunning Delia desserts in fridge."

"Check."

"Soup simmering in saucepan."

"Check."

"Croutons."

"SHIT! No croutons. It's ruined."

"They're passé. All oil. *Really* bad for you."

"You sure?"

"Yes."

"But Tony loves them."

"He's American."

"Good point."

"Right, where were we? Ah yes, guinea fowl ready to come out of oven in approximately an hour."

"Check."

"Honey-glazed vegetables roasting in oven."

"Check."

"White wine and champagne in fridge."

"Check."

"Two outfits revealing just the right amount of bronzed cleavage, leg and midriff."

Fi smiled at her sister.

"Checkmate, sweetie."

Ten minutes' drive away, in a bedroom on the first floor apartment of the Markham Hampstead mansion, David scanned his CDs. He grinned, picked out his "Getting Ready" album and placed it in the CD player. As the invigorating sound of drum and bass thumped its way around the flat, he went to his en suite shower.

He felt good about tonight. Ordinarily, he'd be knackered by now. They'd been working nearly every hour God gave, planning, organizing and carrying out workshops with the Markhams' staff and all he'd want to do would be to slouch on the sofa watching telly. But that life was over. Divorce had opened the door on a new life and now he was back on the scene. Out there. Running on adrenaline.

Down the hall, in his bedroom, Jake finished his fiftieth press up, wondering why they seemed so much harder to complete than usual. He must remember to tell Dr. Blake about that next week— that and the twitch in his neck. Bloody clients. Didn't they realize how knackering it was to do their job? Did they really think that a consultant wants to spend his evening with the people he spends his day having to be nice to? On the other hand, that Sophie looked up for it. Just the thought of how Annie would feel if he and Sophie got it together almost turned him on.

He flicked the thermostatically controlled shower control to freezing cold to wake him up properly and sighed loudly. Bloody clients, he thought again. And then he checked himself in the mirror, saw the tension bordering on excitement in his eyes and looked away quickly before getting into the shower.

Charles drove to the dinner party, with Victoria next to him and Annie in the back. It was the journey from hell. Annie couldn't decide what she feared most; dying in a horrendous pile-up or getting caught in the crossfire of her sister and Charles. It made the prospect of meeting Jake in ten minutes' time feel like mere child's play.

Charles drove with all the dexterity of a demented seal. One could only imagine the chaos he must cause on the golf course.

Victoria had stayed as calm as possible at first, but then two things went wrong. First, Charles started the engine and then he proceeded to try and drive.

"Charles, you're driving like a moron."

"Right you are, dear."

But gradually their good moods vanished and Victoria started to unnerve Charles as much as his driving was unnerving her. She kept tutting and gasping, holding her hands in front of her face and occasionally crossing herself—reducing Charles to an even worse state of nerves than usual when he drove.

"Careful!" she shrieked suddenly.

"What of?" cried Charles, seeing nothing on the road, but slamming on the brakes anyway. Annie tumbled forward.

"I thought I saw a cat," explained Victoria.

"Jesus Christ, woman, I'm going to need a valium when we get there."

"You need it now," replied Victoria firmly. "Did you take some Speed with your Tums before setting off?"

Charles ignored his wife, started up the car again, made a right turn and within moments was confronted by a large Volvo inescapably blocking the road. Cars were parked bumper to bumper on either side of the one-way street and thanks to the Volvo, hazard lights flashing, it was now rendered impassable. Charles hurumphed loudly. He looked in his rear-view mirror. A car had just appeared behind him. He hurumphed again. The person in the car behind him pressed his horn. Charles jumped in shock, swore, then hurumphed again. The driver behind him pressed his horn again.

"Right, that's it," muttered Charles. "I was here first," and he pushed his horn too. Nothing happened.

Charles started rocking to and fro in his seat.

"I mean, where *is* the bastard?" he said, to no one in particular, scanning the street for signs of life. He desperately wanted to get out of his car and kick the Volvo, but there was no point in doing that until he'd checked first that its driver was a dwarf. A tornado of frustration spiraled inside his stomach.

Just then a front door slammed, and someone came out of one of the flats to Charles's right—a burly young man in a suit that was as expensive as it was tasteless, walking with a ludicrously nonchalant swagger. He was practically walking horizontally. He sauntered to the Volvo and slowly opened the door, looking lazily around the street.

"He's just bloody ignoring me!" spluttered Charles. "Look at the smug bastard, he's completely ignoring me." And he hooted again.

At this, the man turned to Charles, stuck his finger in the air at him, smiled and got in the car.

"There you are, dear," said Victoria. "He didn't ignore you after all."

The man then proceeded to find a CD of his choice and put it in his CD player.

"I should bloody ram him," shouted Charles, his face now purple. "The arrogance—"

"Oh for God's sake, Charles," said Victoria sharply. "It's made us four minutes later than we were before. We'll still be the first there."

"I-I-I-" he started, livid at his wife's lack of loyalty. "He's a bloody bastard bugger," he explained to her, stabbing the air in the direction of the Volvo to clarify his point. "I bet he was a bully at school. GET A MOVE ON!" he shouted at his windscreen before hastily locking all the doors.

Finally the Volvo moved smoothly and very, very slowly down the road.

Charles was now hyperventilating, his hands taut on the wheel, beads of sweat forming on his forehead. Victoria watched him. How come he never expended so much emotion and energy on her?

Thankfully, the driver in front turned left at the next junction where Charles needed to turn right. Immediately he was driving up the backside of another car in front. When its brake lights flashed and Charles's didn't, Victoria panicked again.

"*Watch out!*" she shrieked.

"Right, that's it," said Charles, jamming on the brakes, undoing his seat belt and opening the car door. "You drive."

"Don't be ridiculous," said Victoria. "You're the man, you drive."

But Charles was already walking around to her car door. Annie had to make a move fast.

"I'll drive," she said and jumped out of the car and into the driver's seat, leaving Charles no choice but to sit in the back. Victoria panicked.

"But Annie, sweetpea, you drive like a maniac."

"Yes, but I won't divorce you after the journey."

Annie drove as slowly and smoothly as she could, forcing herself to concentrate on the road and not on the evening ahead of her. If only the others knew that of all of them, she was the one least suited to the job of relaxed driving tonight, they might have been a tad more resistant to her taking the wheel.

They were the first to arrive. They all needed alcohol badly. Victoria came into the kitchen, gulping down white wine. She was enjoying the heightened state of surviving a near-death experience and was happily telling her sisters-in-law what was wrong with the food, while Charles stood in the corner, half-smiling, nursing his nerves.

When the wine started coursing through his blood system, his blinking mechanism slowed down and that, together with his large, flat feet, which splayed out Hobbit-like from his ankles, created the somewhat unnerving impression that he was a life-size fixture, complete with its own plinth.

Annie helped Fi with the finishing touches to the meal, which was to be eaten in the kitchen-cum-dining room. Unfortunately, the activity did not help her ignore the fact that her stomach was more churned than the butter she was placing on the table.

"Where are the croutons?" asked Victoria, peering into the soup.

"How was your day?" asked Sophie deliberately.

"We haven't got any croutons," answered Fi worriedly. "Do you think we need them?"

"You're having soup without croutons?" asked Victoria, looking at her blankly.

The doorbell went.

"Answer the door, Fi," said Sophie gratefully. "It might be Tony."

Annie busied herself at the sink, with her back to the door. She heard a male voice in the hall and felt sick.

Fi came in holding Tony's hand shyly.

"Hi guys!" greeted Tony, grinning at everyone. "How y'all doin'?" He was enormous. About six foot four, square. He slapped Charles on the back affectionately, almost winding him. He shook hands with Victoria and Annie, unaware that the vigorousness of his handshake was as offensive to Victoria as it was unnerving for Annie.

Jake and David were late. Either that or they weren't coming at all. It had occurred to Annie that the poor men had been put in rather a difficult position. They could hardly refuse an invitation from clients, yet they probably had hundreds of things they'd rather do than go to a dinner party hosted by Charles's sisters. Like sit at home and hum. What if they didn't come at all? What would she do with all this spare adrenaline? She wondered if anyone had a treadmill she could borrow.

When the doorbell finally went again, Annie took a swig from her glass of wine and steadied herself at the kitchen table. Jake and David entered the room.

David was all smiles, his eyes not knowing where to alight first. On seeing Sophie, however, they decided soon enough where to land last.

Jake was more reserved. He stood rigidly, his eyes fixed firmly on his two charming hostesses as if his life depended on it, a grim grin planted on his face and a tension in his body that Annie was beginning to find familiar.

On the arrival of the two men, an unspoken tension descended upon the room. Everyone shifted slightly to fit them into the kitchen, and the dynamics shifted with them. Tony's increasing in-security with Fi caused him to bristle at the sight of two unattached men, especially one with features that were more even than his own; Charles and Victoria, now fully recovered from the horror of their journey, became alert observers; Sophie and Fi became filled with the joy of vague possibilities and Annie thought she could hear hollow drumming in her ears.

As if that wasn't enough, every person in the room was uncomfortably aware that these two men could save the Markham livelihood. Such a thought made most of the party feel grateful to the men and concerned for their own welfare. Except for Victoria. Victoria saw only that her father's employees should feel honored to be here.

Fi introduced Tony to Jake and David, rather less proudly than she had introduced him before.

"Wine?" Sophie asked Jake, with a smile just big enough to show the dimples in her cheeks.

"Perfect," answered Jake and David in unison, smiling back at her.

Oh dear, thought Annie. Neither man was here for purely business reasons and Jake was after Sophie.

She took another swig of wine.

The table seating had not been officially planned, other than firmly in everyone's minds. This led to the predictably polite yet predatory start to any dinner party. Guests moved with feigned indifference toward the evening companion of their choice when they felt the meal was imminent. Then, when Sophie shrugged her pretty, round shoulders and said "Right then, shall we eat?" various hands which had been hitherto happily clutching wine glasses suddenly shot out to the backs of chairs, claiming ownership. Gracious, grateful smiles all around indicated that everyone was happy. Except perhaps Victoria, who quite frankly, could have done better.

Sophie sat down first, followed speedily by Jake who claimed the seat opposite her. Fi followed immediately, seating herself at Jake's right, followed swiftly by Tony opposite her. Annie and David both put on a valiant performance of ignoring the fact that they had no part to play in this game of musical chairs and, smiling bravely, proceeded to sit opposite each other. Victoria and Charles were left to fill the head and foot of the table. Victoria sat huffily down at the end in between Annie and David, feeling all the humiliation of being left till last. Charles placed himself next to Jake and Sophie, feeling hungry.

Annie couldn't have found herself further away from Jake if she'd tried. Good, she thought. I can be calm here. And safe.

She was fast learning how it was going to be. She and Jake were to be in mixed company without ever mixing company. Jake was quite clearly not going to pay her the slightest bit of attention. Not a word would be spoken, not a glance exchanged, nor a reference made to allude to the fact that he even knew she was in the room, let alone that he had once been willing to share his life with her.

Fine, she thought, filling up her wine glass. That was fine with her.

As the evening progressed, Annie came to the slow realization that everyone was very, very dull. Especially when Fi and Sophie started drilling Jake on his career. It went on for what seemed like hours.

Eventually, she decided it was time to join in. It would make a nice change to hear her own voice this evening. Or in fact anyone's other than Jake's.

"He's ever so good at his job," she chimed in rather shrilly. "He's going to sack 1,200 people from Markhams."

Sophie and Fi's eyes widened.

"Wow!" they chorused.

Victoria was notably impressed.

Annie frowned and took a sip of wine. That hadn't worked.

Two minutes later, Fi and Sophie exploded into girlish giggles at something Jake said. Shit, thought Annie. I couldn't giggle like that anymore if I tried. God, they're so young. It's probably still a novelty for them to go to the toilet.

Because Jake was the center of attention at the other end of the table, he became the center of attention for the evening. Tony had started the evening competing with him, following every reference to business deals with an anecdote of his own. But he soon realized that his words were falling on deaf ears. He stopped competing and instead grew morosely and oppressively quiet. Fi and Sophie, blissfully unaware, teased, taunted and tested Jake, egged on by Charles, who found the show most enjoyable, and of course, had a vested interest.

"When on earth do you have time for relationships, eh?" asked Charles, putting into words what everyone else was wondering.

"I don't," replied Jake simply, with a short shrug.

"Oh," murmured Sophie, taking some wine to hide her disappointment.

Jake realized he'd replied too hastily. "Well, I mean, I didn't up until now," he rushed. "I mean, now that I'm working and living in the same area, my life is suddenly much simpler."

"Oh," murmured Sophie, taking some more wine to hide her relief.

Annie raised her eyebrows to heaven. Pathetic.

"Who wants to play Pictionary?" asked Fi suddenly.

There was a moment's pause as everyone took in the change of subject, before a general opinion that this was a splendid idea.

Everyone moved contentedly into the cozy sitting room where brandy, port, chocolates and the boardgame Pictionary awaited them. The rules of the game were simple. Words, phrases and sayings had to be drawn to a fellow team member who had to guess what they represented. A correct guess meant progression around the board and the first team to get around the board won. Simple, light, harmless entertainment.

Right, thought Victoria. If I don't win, I'll divorce Charles.

"Ooh! Pictionary!" she exclaimed excitedly.

Everyone shrank slightly from her exuberance.

Charles started to feel uncomfortable. Please don't let me be her partner, he started praying silently. I've disappointed her enough in life already.

"Shall we get into teams?" he asked hopefully. "Men against women?"

"Oh no," said Sophie, "where's the fun in that?"

"Ah yes," mumbled Charles in reluctant agreement. "Where indeed?"

"Couples!" shrieked Fi. "I mean, pairs!"

Tony felt hopeful for the first time all evening when Fi then proceeded to grab his hand. He couldn't help giving Jake a quick grin and was momentarily unnerved when Jake gave him a bigger one back.

"Right, Charles," Victoria said to her increasingly pale husband, "we have to win this."

"Well, it's not about winning, is it?" he attempted bravely.

Victoria shot him a warning glance. Oh God.

There was only Jake, Sophie, David and Annie left. No one was in any doubt how this would work out and indeed, all it took was one quick glance between David and Annie, a slightly more lingering one between Jake and Sophie and the teams were decided.

"Who's going to keep an eye on the egg-timer?" asked Fi. "Victoria always cheats—"

"I beg your pardon?"

"I mean—it always gets a bit—"

"I'll keep an eye on it," volunteered Charles. "Perhaps Victoria should join someone else's team so I can do it properly."

There was an outcry. Charles's last attempt to keep control of the egg-timer (three years ago now) had resulted in pandemonium and at least one broken nose. He umpired almost as well as he drove.

"No, Annie's the egg-timer watcher," said Fi firmly. "She'll keep us all in check." She winked at Annie.

"Right you are," said Charles forlornly. It appeared his fate was set.

"I'm Green," said Victoria. That was her lucky color.

"Oh damn, I wanted to be Green," said Jake, laughing. The room went silent.

He obviously didn't know the rules.

"I said it first," said Victoria, forgetting she was with strangers now.

Jake sensed the game had started already. "OK," he said easily. "You're Green. It never suited me anyway."

The others silently chose their colors and Annie picked up the dice, smiling inwardly. This game would certainly test Jake and David's professionalism.

"Right," she said calmly. "The highest number goes first. We'll start on my right and go round the circle. Victoria, throw the dice."

It suited Victoria to obey her sister so she picked up the dice, kissed it and threw it gently on to the boardgame.

Seven.

Only Tony and Fi got a higher score, so before the game had started, Victoria was champing at the bit to beat them.

Tony picked up a card which had one word written on it which he would have to draw for Fi.

He looked at the word.

Elephant.

Easy. He could do that, no sweat. He looked at Fi. If she guessed it right, he decided, he'd propose.

As Annie turned over the egg-timer and placed it next to the board on the coffee table, he drew an elephant in four seconds flat.

Fi stared at it. "Anteater."

"No."

"Badger."

"No."

"Cat?"

"No!"

Fi tilted her head. "Are you sure it's not an anteater?"

Victoria suddenly squealed and whispered to Charles. She had guessed what the drawing was. If Fi's time ran out, she'd get a score for getting it right. Charles started praying while Victoria started her usual tactics.

"Fi hon, your bra strap's showing."

"Ooh, thanks," Fi giggled. She pinged it back into place and suddenly felt gloriously self-conscious.

Tony glanced at the egg-timer. It was halfway down.

"I'll draw it again," he said urgently.

He drew it again, exactly the same, except bigger.

Fi stared at it, the tension in the room heightened.

Come on, come on, prayed Tony and he held Fi's hand tight. She smiled at him.

"Anteater," she said finally.

"NO!" he said.

"Don't shout at me, Tony."

"Sorry, honey," he said. "But it's not an anteater. I promise." He squeezed her shoulder and budged up next to her so that they were both looking at it from the same angle.

"Come on, sweetheart, try again," he coaxed.

"It looks like an anteater, Tony."

"Well, I'm sorry about that. But it's not one."

Tony couldn't bear to look at the egg-timer.

"Have you said cat?" asked Victoria sweetly.

"Um," Fi couldn't remember. "Have I?"

"It's not a cat," said Tony shortly.

"I hadn't said it was yet. Or had I?"

"Time's up!" said Annie.

Tony sank back against the sofa.

"Good try, Tony," commiserated Annie.

"ELEPHANT!" yelled Victoria, beside herself with excitement.

"One point to Victoria and Charles," said Annie.

It was now Victoria and Charles's turn.

Victoria was to draw first. She was a bloody good drawer, everyone knew that. Charles hoped to God she didn't lose her temper with him—or worse still that he didn't lose his temper with her. This could get very ugly.

Victoria picked up the card and looked at her word. *Temple*. Hah! Simple.

Slowly but surely, Victoria drew a perfect Athenian temple, complete with Doric columns and frieze. By the time she'd finished, the sand was halfway down the egg-timer. She sat back proudly and looked at her husband with utter confidence.

Charles stared at the picture dumbly.

"Well, say something!" she commanded, frustrated.

"All right. What is it?" asked Charles, stumped.

Excitement made everyone laugh.

Victoria was angry and hurt. "Well, what does it bloody look like?"

"A-a-a palace?"

"LOOK AT IT!" shouted Victoria.

"Why? Have you written what it is on the roof?" asked Charles, stressed. "This is Pictionary, Victoria, not A Level bloody Art."

"LOOK AT IT!" she repeated.

He looked at it pointlessly. "Mausoleum?"

Victoria crossed her arms defiantly.

"Pentacostal church? Synagogue?" he tried bravely.

Tony suddenly clicked. He whispered what it was to Fi and she squealed. Of course!

Victoria started to lose it.

She decided another tack. She glanced at the timer. Twenty seconds? She drew a stick man with dots for eye and a nose. She drew an arrow pointing to his temples so furiously that the pencil pierced through the paper.

Charles was even more confused now. How the hell did this picture relate to the picture of the palace?

"Headache?" he asked.

Victoria threw her arms heavenward.

Charles looked at it again. An arrow to the head.

"Murder!" he shouted victoriously.

"Don't tempt me!" yelled Victoria.

"Tempt you?" answered Charles, starting to panic now. "I'll buy you the bloody arrow."

Sophie, Fi and Tony were now openly laughing. Annie noticed that Jake and David were maintaining a polite indifference to the proceedings, although Jake's eyes were twinkling and his shoulders seemed even more rigid than usual.

"Ten seconds to go and remember—it's only a game!" grinned Annie, enjoying herself for the first time all evening.

Victoria went into overdrive. She jabbed at both pictures again until Charles in utter desperation said:

"Head Palace," he eventually tried, "and that's my final offer, you MAD WOMAN."

"Time's up," said Annie apologetically.

"TEMPLE!" shrieked Victoria, thereby preventing anyone else from guessing. "IT'S A BLOODY TEMPLE!" she screamed. "What do you think these are?" she yelled, poking at the perfect Doric columns with her pencil. "SAUSAGES?"

Charles took several long, deep breaths.

"No," he said calmly. "You don't get sausages the size of a PALACE."

"It's a temple, not a palace!" she shrieked.

Annie decided the situation needed calming down.

"Victoria? Am I going to have to confiscate your pencil?"

Victoria turned away, her face flushed, tears of anger squeezing out of her eyes.

Next it was Jake and Sophie's turn. Annie used the opportunity to study him and Sophie together intently. Sophie didn't need to try very hard, safe in the knowledge that beauty made ignorance loveable, and he indulged her every weakness and foible. It made for very boring viewing.

Finally it was Annie and David's turn. Right, thought Annie. I'm going to win. Annie picked up the card, looked at it and smiled. *Farce*.

Calmly and without a hint of hurry, she drew a stage, with curtains at the side.

"Stage," said David urgently.

Annie shook her head.

"Curtains."

She shook her head again.

"Theater."

She shook her head and continued to draw.

David watched for a moment.

"Stage."

"No."

She started drawing the set. It consisted entirely of doors, some open, others shut.

"Doors!"

"No."

Jake suddenly gasped. He'd got it. He whispered to Sophie. Riled, David found new levels of enthusiasm.

"STAGE, CURTAINS, THEATER."

Annie ignored him.

"STAGE, CURTAINS, THEATER."

She shook her head and kept on drawing.

Annie continued to draw doors. David sat staring at it, shaking his head, baffled, until suddenly it made sense. He shouted out the answer loud and clear. Annie was so grateful that she hugged him.

"How the bugger did you get that, old chap?" asked an impressed Charles.

"He used his brain," muttered Victoria.

The rest of the game continued with few upsets.

To relief all around, Victoria and Charles eventually won.

"No thanks to you," Victoria congratulated her husband.

Finally, they all sprawled out, exhausted by their efforts, staring at the board.

Eventually Victoria broke the silence. "Oh Annie, can you look after the boys Wednesday week in the evening? I've got a reserve appointment to go and see my osteopath. My migraines are getting worse. She could only fit me in at nine-thirty in the evening. Bloody ridiculous time, but I've simply got to go."

Annie smiled apologetically. "Sorry, Vicky," she replied quietly. "I've got a hot date."

"Oh?"

The entire room seemed interested, except of course, for Jake, who was quietly tidying up the boardgame.

"With Eddie the Teddie?" asked Fi.

"No," replied Annie haughtily. "That would be unethical."

"Oh! So it's unethical to shag Father's chief exec," started Victoria, "but it's not unethical to shag his plumb—"

"Yes, all right, thank you," interrupted Annie. "Why the sudden interest in my love life? Are you all too bored with your own?"

"No, we just think you're wasted being single," said Charles sincerely.

"How clever of you, Charles! To try and compliment me and insult me instead."

"Oh. Sorry."

"Anyway. The point is I can't babysit Wednesday week. I might be having a long night."

This had the desired effect. Sophie and Fi whooped and Victoria and Charles laughed. Jake read the Pictionary cards studiously.

"Obviously I'd look after the boys tomorrow if I could," Charles said, "but there's an emergency meeting at the golf club."

"Golly! Sounds important!" exclaimed Victoria. "Are you voting on whether the cucumber sandwiches should be served with their crusts on?"

Charles didn't answer.

"Bring the boys here," said Fi, anxious to stop a row. "They can join in our Pilates class and then we'll get them ready for bed to be picked up later."

"And if the date's a no-hoper, I'll pick them up and take them home," concluded Annie. "Otherwise, Vicky can pick them up after her appointment."

"Oh yes," said Victoria. "That'll be perfect for curing my migraines. Picking up two small tired boys. Thank you, team."

Charles started helping Jake clear up the game.

While Annie walked back from the kitchen after clearing away the cups, she overheard Fi and Tony by the front door.

"I'll flirt with whoever I want to flirt with," came Fi's voice. "If you can't handle it, you know what you can do."

There was silence for a while and then the door slammed shut.

And then she heard Fi say out loud,

"And it looked like a bloody anteater."

Chapter 13

Wednesday week was rather a big day. Not only was it Annie's blind date with Cass's Greek god in the evening, but in the morning it was the next time she had to sit face to face with Jake for a long period of time. The consultants were giving an update meeting after the first few weeks of their work and Susannah had specifically requested Annie's presence there. Now that George and Katherine were in New York Susannah felt it necessary to have a family presence in the room.

"It will give the right impression," she'd explained. "Try to act important, dear."

Annie was surprised at how much calmer she felt about being in the same room as Jake now that she knew what to expect: he would simply ignore her. Which she decided would be easy to deal with, now that she knew to ignore him first. While trying to act important. In fact, she'd probably be so busy trying to act important, she'd hardly have time to ignore him. She'd have to squeeze it in when she could.

Sitting between them were Edward, Susannah and David. Annie watched Jake cough a welcome cough and straighten his tie.

"Well, hello, people," he began and gave them all a disarmingly boyish grin.

Instantly disarmed, Annie frowned hard at him, as if physically trying to put a stop to the disarming process.

Jake paused for a fraction of a moment, put off by such a sudden and strong sign of hostility. Damn her. He'd show her something to frown about. He spoke fast.

"Last week we went through the 'As Is' and 'To Be' BPR analysis outputs and found opportunities for efficiency gains. The next step is simply to operationalize it." Breathe. Nod of handsome head to emphasize. "I think you'll all agree communication is the key."

Now Annie was really frowning. Was he talking English?

"Excuse me?"

Jake looked up and smiled patiently at her, making her feel like a three-year-old who'd just informed him that she had a new pixie dance to show him.

"I didn't understand a word of that."

Jake was momentarily flummoxed. The Annie he knew of old would never have confessed that. She always hated looking like an idiot in public. Meanwhile Susannah gave her a fond smile, as if her pixie dance had already begun.

"It's just business jargon, my dear."

"I understand it's jargon," replied Annie, embarrassed. "I just thought if there's any point in me being here, I might as well understand what's being said."

She looked back at Jake and raised her eyebrows, which had the unintended result of making her look half her age. Edward gave her a sideways glance—she really was exceptionally pretty. And refreshingly open about being dense. A winning combination in a girl. He was also grateful for her question—he had no idea what Jake was on about either. He gave her an encouraging smile. Annie felt as if her pixie dance was going fantastically well.

"Of course," Jake replied tensely. "That was very remiss of me. I'll try and put it into language you can understand. Um. Right. Where shall I start?"

"How about Once Upon A Time?" suggested Annie.

They all laughed. Only Jake understood that she was mocking him and not herself.

"We do tend to get carried away with our jargon," he continued. "I apologize."

Hah. One-love, thought Annie. Maybe this was going to be easier than she thought. Maybe Jake was still as readable as he used to be. Hold on, he was talking . . .

". . . So as agreed at the last meeting, we've started our Business Process Re-engineering—a . . . process—hence the title—which refers to the processes by which we get things done: re-engineering means improving them, i.e. increasing speed, quality etc."

Annie nodded slowly, her eyes fixed firmly on Jake in a vain attempt to concentrate on what he was saying and not on what she was thinking. It would be a darn sight easier if he didn't seem to be struggling so much with every word. Gosh—so many frown lines . . .

Jake frowned hard as he tried to concentrate on what he was saying instead of what he was feeling. It would help if that bitch stopped trying to stare him out. Keep going, just keep going . . . "And now, we have to . . . operationalize, um, implement all those processes that came up from the . . . BPR analysis."

There was silence. He'd finished. Annie thought about what he'd just said. Now was the time for her to say something that showed insight and intelligence.

"Ooh," she said. "Lots of processes."

Jake considered this for a moment. She'd got him there. He was in a corner. He had to surrender.

"Yes, lots of processes," he said. "Well spotted." No one could say he was a bad loser. He even managed to give her a congratulatory smile.

Annie felt her pixie dance had been a resounding success. Good thing she'd worn the pink tutu. She looked out of the window as Jake tidied his files.

Susannah leafed quietly through the BPR report.

"It all looks most impressive," she said, nodding.

Thank Christ for that, thought Jake, remembering to breathe out.

"Oh good," he said calmly. "We do feel that although it's still early days, it's remarkable to see how things have turned out. And a lot of things have come out from the staff interviews and workshops. Your staff have got some great ideas."

Susannah looked up, alarmed.

"I'm not sure I like the sound of that."

Of course not, thought Jake. What finance director ever does? And what finance director ever puts two and two together and realizes that that's exactly why they've had to approach consultants in the first place?

He smiled at Susannah and spoke gently.

"Believe it or not, staff are often the people with the best answers. They're usually the ones who know how to make their jobs more efficient."

Susannah looked dubious and Annie decided it would be a good time to change the subject. "You said—among other incomprehensible things—that communication was the key?"

David gave her such a grin of approval he might as well have given her the "thumbs up" signal across the desk. Even despite Jake's constant coolness, she could tell he was also impressed.

"I did. Thank you, Ms. Markham."

Oh prig off, she thought. Ms. Markham indeed. I've seen you in your underwear, you don't fool me. Mind you, she considered, that was a long time ago. She wondered how much he'd changed . . .

". . . So it's imperative we prevent that at all costs," concluded Jake.

Woops. Prevent what? Damn.

"Absolutely," chimed in Edward. "We don't want any nasty rumors abounding. Can't have my staff unhappy. They're like my children, you know."

Ah, rumors. Good old Edward, thought Annie, and gave him a warm grin. She was back on track.

Edward grinned back at her. She grinned a bit more. He grinned even more. Then Annie became vaguely aware that Susannah was smiling fondly at them both as if they were all in a scene from the Bible. She stopped grinning immediately. Bible smiles from godmothers were a definite turn-off.

"I said, have you had time to evaluate our BPR report or would you like to keep it a bit longer?" repeated Jake.

Edward grinned man-to-man at him. "Sorry old chap, mind elsewhere, know how it is."

"Actually, I was talking to Annie," said Jake.

"I've got a good idea!" exclaimed Edward at Annie suddenly. "We could look through it together tonight. Over a bottle of bubbly."

"Oh, I'm so sorry," said Annie genuinely. "I can't tonight. I'm . . . busy."

"Oh," said Edward, surprised at how disappointed he was. That was the last time he ever asked anyone on a first date in front of their family and his employees. "Never mind. Another time."

"Oh, is tonight your date?" Jake asked Annie.

Annie stared at him in fury. How dare he? He'd managed to ignore all signs of even hearing her talk at the dinner party, and now he was telling them all that she had a date—and in front of Edward! She stared at Jake, her eyes wide, her jaw slack.

"Oh I'm sorry," said Jake. "Was it a secret?"

Annie's eyes continued to widen and her jaw to drop. She only regained control of her facial features when it occurred to her that she probably looked like a guppy.

Edward seemed to visibly back off. "Oh well then. Another time."

Annie could almost feel Susannah's disapproval freeze on her shoulders.

Right, she thought, so furious at Jake she forgot to blink for whole minutes. That was it. It was War.

* 　 * 　 *

Jake shook Susannah's hand, holding the eye contact, grin and handshake even longer than usual. Every second counted.

"Most impressive," said Susannah. "Keep up the good work."

"We do our best."

As he left the office for his car, he let out a long, deep sigh. He opened the car door and slid in behind the steering wheel. Once in the cool of the car, he leaned heavily on the wheel.

"Don't ever do that again," he told himself, his hand jerking up to his twitching neck. "Don't *ever* let her get to you again." He screwed his eyes shut. "Don't fuck this up because of her."

Then he sat up, put the key in the ignition and drove away.

"And then she just told me she didn't love me anymore. And get this—she'd never really loved me—she'd tried to, because I was so hopelessly in love with her—that was the word she used, hopelessly—but she'd always felt more like a sister to me than a girlfriend—no she didn't say girlfriend, what did she say—oh yes, lover. More like a sister than a 'lover.' A sister! Three years and she'd always felt like a sister toward me. Of course, she hadn't mentioned that when I'd bought her the villa in Tuscany. Or screwed her senseless while we were moored at Monte Carlo. Now, don't get me wrong, I love my sister as much as the next man, but that doesn't mean I want to shag her brains out. Oh God, sorry. Bad taste, sorry. But what I want to know is, if that's how she behaves with someone she feels sisterly toward, what the hell does that say about her pratt of a brother? Between you and me I always thought there was something fishy going on there. Now, there was a thoroughly irritating twat, let me tell you. If he'd have got into Eton—which he wouldn't—he wouldn't have lasted a bloody week. Anyway, to cut a long story short, owch. Bloody owch.

"Thought of suicide, of course. But hate the sight of blood, can't tie knots and not good with pills, even when I take them with

Ovaltine. Amazed how anyone does it, to be honest. And frankly, as my old man always said, it's the coward's way out. More importantly, who'd look after the manor? Anyway, cut a very long story very short, life goes on, doesn't it. Yep, life bloody well goes on and on and on and you get used to the hellish dump that is your world and slump from one meaningless day to the next, safe in the knowledge that death will inevitably release you from this sham of an existence.

"And then Cass suggested I meet you, so here we are."

Annie smiled weakly at Angus over their untouched dinner. The blind date was going about as well as she had expected.

"Would you like to see the dessert menu?" asked the waitress.

Only if it comes with ear plugs, thought Annie morosely.

Angus clapped his hands together in anticipation.

"Ah yes, the perfect end to a perfect evening." And on that witticism, he toasted Annie.

She smiled at him briefly. Go on, she thought, as he winked at her over his wine. Ask me something about myself. Anything. It's been two hours. I don't even mind if it's personal. Ask me what my bra size is. Ask me if I like to talk dirty during sex. Anything.

"What I don't get," started Angus, "is that I could—and did—give her everything. I mean, everything. In fact, what could she possibly get without me that she felt she couldn't get with me?"

Insomnia? reasoned Annie.

"You know, the thing about women . . ."

Oh do tell, thought Annie, perking up slightly. I don't know any women. So much to learn, so little time . . .

"I don't think they realize they're doing it, it's sort of beyond their control. They're prisoners of their hormones. I don't really blame them, I suppose, it's what makes them so endearing . . ."

I'm going to kill Cass, thought Annie, and immediately felt better.

An eon later, Annie saw the waitress finally bringing over their desserts. She gave her a wide, expansive smile. One step nearer to freedom. She watched Angus tucking into his bread and butter pudding and tried not to be depressed by the fact that there was a mother out there who loved him.

Light years later, they stood outside the restaurant.

Angus clapped his hands together again.

"Nightcap? My place?" Another wink.

God, Annie hated winkers.

I'd love to, she thought, but I'd have to shoot myself afterward.

"I'd love to," she said, "but I have to go and pick up my nephews for my sister."

"Oh." Angus was surprised.

"She's got a migraine," explained Annie apologetically.

She almost changed her mind when Angus touched her lightly around the waist, told her how wonderful he had found her company and then shyly but surely gave her a remarkably effective kiss.

Am I being rash? she wondered idly, enjoying its effects.

Nope, she concluded finally. He might start talking again.

Instead, she nipped over to Fi and Sophie's flat to pick up the boys. She hoped they hadn't been too much of a nuisance. Or weren't too exhausted. It was now eleven o'clock.

She stood outside their door massaging her temples and trying to remember how life had felt before she'd met Angus. Was I happy then? she wondered. It all seemed so long ago.

When the door opened and Jake stood in front of her, her mind, which Angus had left numb, was now blown.

They stared at each other for a while.

"Hello," she said finally, deciding it was as safe as anything else to say.

"Hello," he replied.

"It's Annie Markham," she explained helpfully. "I've just been on my date. Perhaps you could inform Reuters?"

Jake blinked at her. He had absolutely no idea how to play this.

He'd been prepared all the other times. And surrounded by people. Luckily Annie started talking again.

"Can I get to my nephews or are you on sentry duty?"

Jake opened the door and stood aside, keeping his eyes anywhere but on her.

"They're upstairs."

"Oh well done. Communication is the key, they say . . ."

Amazed at how swiftly her feelings could change from boredom to fury, Annie had no choice but to walk past him.

She felt stupidly self-conscious climbing the dark, narrow staircase in front of Jake. As she went, she kept her eyes fixed on the stairs, focusing on the royal blue carpet, aware that Jake was keeping a steady two paces behind her. Good, she thought. It's where he belongs.

Fi's voice came down the stairs.

"Who is it?"

Annie decided to let Jake answer that.

"It's um—"

In one swift movement, she turned and stepped down so that her face was level with Jake's. He almost jumped.

"It's ANNIE," she hissed at him, her breathing heavy. "A-N-N-I-E. Annie."

This close to him, she noticed that his eyes hadn't really changed at all. Except that she'd never seen them this startled before. After the slightest of pauses, his expression changed from startled to sardonic.

"Ah yes," he whispered slowly, "how could I forget?"

What the hell was that supposed to mean? The idea that Jake might actually think that he had a right to be angry with her was so new to Annie that she just stared in open bewilderment at him.

Neither of them knew how long they stood like that before Fi appeared at the top of the stairs.

"Hiya, Annie!"

Annie and Jake jumped away from each other and Annie ran up the stairs.

When she reached the flat, the boys were fast asleep on the drawing-room sofa. Everyone was in there with them, all staring at Tony, who was standing motionless in the middle of the room, on the phone. Annie had clearly interrupted some very important transaction. She felt conscious of Jake behind her as he finally followed her into the room and went straight over to the sofa.

Tony seemed about as tense as her. His whole body was rigid and his eyes were fixed in the mid-distance as if he was concentrating so hard, he couldn't possibly focus as well. Annie was about to greet everyone, but realized they were all fiercely watching Tony.

Suddenly Tony took the phone away from his ear, pressed a digit on it and placed it back to his ear. Sophie and Fi held their breath. No one said a word. He did it again. And again. Now he closed his eyes in thought and did it again. Suddenly, he started clicking his fingers furiously at Fi and in a flurry of activity, she picked up a credit card on the coffee table and, almost dropping it, passed it to him. Frowning in concentration, he pressed a large number of digits into the phone, his shoulders hunched and the tip of his tongue protruding from his lips. Silence.

And then finally, a serene beam burst on to his face and he breathed a deep sigh of relief. Everyone joined him and with a flourish, he put the phone down and said proudly,

"Six tickets to see tomorrow's screening of *At Home With My Llama*."

The others grinned and calmness descended on the room. Tony turned to Annie, seeing her for the first time.

"Hi, Annie," he said. "You are coming to see the film with us tomorrow, aren't you? Of course, I can always cancel—I've got a spare hour tomorrow to call the cinema . . ."

Annie shook her head quickly. She didn't want to see a grown man cry.

"Sounds great," she lied.

"How was the date?" asked Fi.

"Awful. I'd have sent up a flare, but it was a non-smoking restaurant."

"Oh dear."

"Anyone else interested in Available Angus? Body the size of a brick shithouse, brain the size of a split atom."

"What's his number?" asked Fi.

"I'll ask him. He's still paying the bill."

Tony coughed loudly.

"Well, we're meeting at the cinema tomorrow at eight," he told Annie. "Don't be late."

"I'm never late," said Annie.

It was Jake's turn to cough.

"Won't be long!" came Sophie's voice from her bedroom.

"I'll go and get the boys' stuff," whispered Fi and she left the room, followed swiftly by Tony.

Suddenly Jake and Annie were alone in the room with only the sleeping boys as distraction. Annie glanced over at Jake, but he was determined to act as if she was invisible. She was beginning to find his immaturity infuriating. She paced the flat.

Meanwhile Jake, seemingly unaware she was even in the room, was rifling through some magazines that were on the coffee table, whistling gently under his breath. Right, she thought. She crossed her arms and started wandering around the room humming just as loudly. Jake stopped whistling, leaving her off-key on her own.

Worse, she was humming "Tie a Yellow Ribbon Round the Old Oak Tree."

There was a rustling on the couch.

"What's that noise?" asked Harry, waking up. "Where's Mummy? I'm scared."

Ever so gently, Annie knelt down by Harry's head and started to stroke his hair.

To say that Jake was unmoved by the sight would have been unfair. And untrue. The sight of Annie Markham, her golden hair tumbling down her back, her soft skin luminous from the effects of good food and drink as she soothed her nephew, moved him quite significantly. He felt repelled.

Jake didn't have long to wait for Sophie. She entered the room, looking young, fit and very pretty. With his eyes scanning her skin-tight outfit, Jake replaced the magazine on the coffee table.

Sophie beamed over at Annie.

"We're out clubbing," she squealed. "It was the first window Jake could spare me this week because he's been so busy."

"Don't wear him out," said Annie kindly. "He's not as young as he was."

"Yeah well, some things keep a man young," replied Jake, grinning meaningfully at Sophie.

Annie smiled conspiratorially at Sophie. "Like immaturity and a younger date," she confided.

Sophie giggled and then stopped.

Annie wished them both a happy evening and explained to Sophie that if she kept Jake in the shadows, no one would notice his age.

She watched them go and then glanced over at the magazine Jake had been reading.

"How to get over your ex!" screamed the cover.

Meet him in seven years' time, she thought ruefully as the door slammed shut so violently it almost came off its hinges.

Chapter 14

That evening, Charles leaned back in his leather armchair, and took a sip of Laphroig. He felt very much at home. Sitting in the oak-paneled club lounge with four of his best golfing buddies was quite simply one of life's joys. The meeting had been far more important than even he had realized.

"They don't stand a chance, you know," his friend, Bill, was saying. "They'll realize that if they want anarchy they can go to another club and that'll be the end of it. This is a respectable, traditional place and a few sex-starved young'uns aren't going to change that. Over my dead body. All we have to do is work at convincing the rest of the club." He took a gulp of his brandy.

"Mind you," said Marcus wistfully. "Wouldn't half add some color to the place, don't you think? Women playing golf, eh? Little skirts . . . short socks . . . and whatnot?"

Marius and Edgar exploded.

"Heresy!" cried Marius.

"Cut off his head!" shouted Edgar.

"Find him a prostitute," said Bill.

They all laughed into their drinks and Charles joined in happily. Then he pictured Victoria in a tight Pringle sweater and crossed his legs.

★　　★　　★

The next day Cass woke early. She always woke early. Six-thirty a.m. to be precise. It was as if her body was on a natural alarm clock. Her first conscious thought, as always, was that the silence might burst her eardrums. Brutus was sleeping soundly next to her.

She got out of bed quickly, padded through the bedroom-sized wardrobe and selected an outfit for the gym, humming determinedly to herself. She gave her bikini-beautiful body the once-over in the mirror. Taut long limbs, slender torso, long, narrow waist, full breasts. And thick Fallopian tubes.

In the car, she put on bright, poppy music to provide her with skim segments of escapist romantic fiction and friction. It worked less and less these days. The gym was large, warm and welcoming. Cass handed in her membership card to the receptionist, and the young girl looked at it and then smiled a waxy smile and called Cass by her first name, which always irritated her. Surely she'd know her name by now without having to glance at her card—she'd been coming for five years.

She went via the pool so that she wouldn't have to walk past the crèche.

Inside the enormous air-conditioned aerobics studio, two other immaculate women were already there, waiting for the instructor. No one looked at each other or spoke a word. They all stared at their own reflections, the room stark with resounding silence.

Cass looked at the reflections of the other women, trying not to eye their stomachs. Both women had generous, rounded bellies and she forced her eyes away from them and hoped to God the instructor wouldn't be too late.

Five minutes later, there was a full class and a loud, bossy instructor who barked out instructions and kept telling them to "make it worthwhile." Cass bounced and strained with all her heart to the loud pounding music, but the silence was always there in her head.

By the time she was back home, Brutus was sitting up in bed, focusing intently on a syringe in one hand, and tapping the air out of it with the other. Without a word, she climbed on to the bed, and got on all fours. A quick tap on the backside and a sharp jab of pain. Then, thank God, a soft kiss.

Half an hour later, she and Brutus breakfasted, talking about everything and anything except what was on their minds. Then, while he was out playing rugby with friends, she went shopping.

Dinner was now always in front of the television, regardless of whether or not there was anything they wanted to watch. They used to listen to music together and read, but now music seemed to depress Cass.

Later, she lay in bed, as usual, picturing her unborn children, their laughter echoing behind a heavy glass door she couldn't open.

Meanwhile the silence in her life—where there should have been mewling, puking, spewing, crapping, gurgling, squabbling, laughing, shouting, crying—was always there, threatening to drive her mad.

As Annie parked her car around the back of the cinema, she thought about all the things she'd rather be doing than joining Tony and Fi, David, Jake and Sophie on a stupid film outing.

Baking, she thought. She'd always wanted to learn how to bake.

She sat behind the wheel, watching people rush by in the rain, finding it almost impossible to muster the energy to leave her car. She was late, the film had probably already started.

A knock on the car door startled her.

She looked at the window to see the grinning face of David.

She smiled and opened her door, touched when he held the umbrella over her head.

"You must be knackered," she said to him, as they sped to the warmth of the cinema. "Are all your meetings as fun as yesterday's?"

"Oh no. Some are quite boring."

"Aren't you exhausted?"

Once inside, David grinned at her as he closed the umbrella. "That's exactly why we need to get out," he said. "To forget all about it."

They queued to pick up their tickets.

"Shall we get the tickets for the others?" asked Annie.

"No need. Instructions were to meet inside if possible. If not, we'll meet up in the bar on the corner afterwards. We'll probably find them all inside. Jake left early to pick up Sophie."

The small cinema was already filling up. There were only a few seats left, and David and Annie chose two seats in the middle of the back row.

Annie scanned the cinema for Tony and Fi, hoping desperately not to spot Jake and Sophie while she was at it. She was relieved when she found none of them.

And even better, it looked like no one was going to be sitting in the two seats smack bang in front of her. Feeling smug and cozy, Annie lowered herself in her seat.

"Want any grub?" asked David. She shook her head. "Won't be a tick," he said and forced twenty people to stand up and let him out.

Annie sat still, letting the warmth of the cinema envelop her. Maybe this wasn't going to be such a bad evening after all. She needed some good escapism.

Just then, half of the row in front of her started tutting and one by one, stood up slowly. Two latecomers were coming to sit in the seats in front of her. She hated it when that happened.

It was Jake and Sophie.

Annie hunkered down further in her seat. They sat right in front of her, so close that, if she had wanted to, she could have burned Jake's neck with a cigarette end.

God, she thought, his neck muscles were like train tracks.

Sophie opened a packet of chocolate and offered one to Jake. He shook his head. Sophie took one and placed her head briefly on his shoulder.

Hussy, thought Annie.

"I wonder where the others are," murmured Jake.

Sophie finished her mouthful. "Probably won't be here for ages. Pity. It would have been fun to sit with Annie."

Jake looked at Sophie. Annie shrunk back in her seat. She hoped to God the lights dimmed before David returned.

"Why Annie?"

Sophie shrugged.

"She's just . . . fun. I dunno," said Sophie, offering Jake some of her fizzy drink. He declined.

"Fun in what way?" he asked.

She shrugged again and sucked on her straw.

"Nice. Funny." She thought about it. "Fun."

Gee thanks, thought Annie. Let's hope they don't ask you to write my obituary.

"This is Annie *Markham* we're talking about?" asked Jake.

Annie fought the temptation to kick his seat.

"Yes! Annie. Annie Markham—you know, the one you met—"

"Yes, I know."

Annie raised her eyebrows, impressed. So he does know who I am.

"I just don't think of those words to describe her."

Annie's hand flexed into karate chop position. I could kill him from here and be out before the adverts.

It was Sophie's turn to look wonderingly at Jake.

"Why not?" she asked innocently. "She's lovely."

Annie's hand relaxed. Ah, sweetheart.

Jake grunted and took off his jacket. Annie held her breath as he threw it over the back of his chair. It touched her knee. Sophie opened her toffee pecan ice cream.

"Don't tell anyone," she said, as she prised the plastic spoon out of the lid, "but me and Fi always wanted Charles to marry Annie instead of Vicky."

"Oh yeah?"

"Mmm," answered Sophie. She started to look around the cinema.

"What happened?"

Sophie edged closer to Jake. Jake edged closer back. Annie edged closer to both of them.

"Well, Charles tried to get off with Annie at a family party once, but she wasn't interested."

Annie frowned. Charles? Get off with her? Were they talking about the night when he spilled his drink down her front? And then offered to get it dry cleaned? She'd always wondered why he'd seemed so insistent. Nice technique.

"When was this?" asked Jake.

"Years ago—just before he and Victoria got together, in fact," answered Sophie. "I was only a child at the time."

Annie shook her head. Did you hear that? She was only a child! She still *is* a child. You should be ashamed of yourself.

"We decided that Susannah Brooke didn't approve. Have you met Susannah?"

Jake nodded.

"She's like a mother to Annie," continued Sophie. "You know Annie's mum died when she was young? They were very alike— really close apparently. They say Annie's never really got over it."

Annie felt a sharp stab of pain hearing that period of her life dealt with in such a matter-of-fact way. Wasn't everyone that close and similar to their mother? And did anyone ever get over it? She tuned quickly back into what Sophie was saying.

"Well, Annie does everything Susannah tells her. Apparently . . ."

Sophie edged even closer to Jake now, leaving Annie no choice but to move dangerously close to them both to hear what she was saying. She kept her eyes down. She could smell Jake's aftershave. Probably the only thing about him that hadn't changed since college.

". . . Apparently Susannah saved Annie's life by stopping her from running off with a money-grabbing student when she was at college."

Annie gasped in horror and then smacked her hand over her mouth. Neither Jake nor Sophie noticed the noise. Jake was listening too intently to Sophie to notice anything.

"Want some ice cream?" asked Sophie, holding out her spoon to Jake. "It's toffee pecan. Delicious." He shook his head.

"Can you imagine how much nicer our life would be if Annie was our sister-in-law?"

Jake didn't answer.

Annie was fit to burst. It took all her self-discipline not to knock their heads together. Is that what everyone thought about her? Is that what really happened? She got so confused when she thought of that time that she sometimes forgot, herself.

No—it wasn't Susannah who'd persuaded her not to elope, it was Jake who'd given her no choice. He'd run out on her for God's sake! Without ever letting her explain that she'd made an honest mistake about the baby. He had done everything to prove Susannah right. Sod Susannah—he had proved *all* parents right. Young girls need to be kept well away from stupid young boys.

It was all Annie could do not to butt in and say her piece. Rocking in her seat helped.

In desperation for something to do, she started to search frantically for David. If he came in before the lights dimmed, she was done for. They'd know she'd heard everything. She turned to the door and saw David standing there grinning at her. He waved a bucket of popcorn the size of a pedal bin. As he walked toward her, she turned to look at Sophie and Jake. Sophie was brushing some invisible fluff off Jake's shoulder. Annie felt torn. Half of her wanted to break Sophie's arm, while the other more lenient, forgiving half wanted to break Jake's head. It was a tough one. Instead, she turned back to David and grinned maniacally. Any second now, he'd spot Jake. She had to keep him from looking at him. She didn't take her eyes off David and felt her grin stick to her face. As he reached the end of the row, the lights started to dim. Thank God, she thought, and dropped the grin.

As the adverts started, she lowered herself further into her seat and then kicked Jake's. He didn't notice.

Annie wondered why the familiar advertising jingle didn't start up. Instead an image of a red rose pulsed on the screen to the sound of a heartbeat. And then the words:

Fi, I love you. Will you marry me? Tony

There was a baffled silence in the cinema, followed by a muffled scream. Sophie joined in. Eventually, the entire cinema was cheering and chanting for Tony. Eventually, flushed and delighted, he stood up to take a deep bow. After some clapping, Fi joined him. They kissed and sat down again. Then came adverts for popcorn and the lights came up again.

"Shit!" whispered David urgently in Annie's ear.

"I know," whispered Annie just as urgently back.

"I forgot my drink."

And he was off.

Annie was now sitting bolt upright in her chair looking for Tony and Fi. People were shouting congratulations at them. Sophie was laughing with delight. But Annie was trapped. She couldn't go to Fi and Tony because then Jake and Sophie would realize she'd been sitting behind them . . .

"I can't believe it," Sophie was squealing to Jake. "I thought she'd keep saying no."

"Keep saying no? Has he proposed before?"

"Oh God yes, every month for the past year," giggled Sophie. "He must have realized that our Fi needed more persuading than that. I can't wait to congratulate them—but I'm too embarrassed to go up in front of everyone."

Jake stared at Sophie.

Annie sat looking at his profile. Eyelashes like a bloody girl's. And that's his best side too.

"How could she possibly refuse him when she actually wanted to marry him?"

"Oh, that's Fi all over," grinned Sophie. "Daddy doesn't like Tony, and Fi, bless her, can't make a decision to save her life. This is the girl who goes into Starbucks and says 'Coffee please. You decide.'"

"But this is hardly the same thing," insisted Jake. "This is the person you're going to spend the rest of your life with."

Sophie turned serious. "I know," she said solemnly. "We're totally and utterly and completely different. No one ever tells me what to do. If I like a man, I like a man."

Annie grimaced as Sophie and Jake locked eyes. Eat your heart out, *Love Boat*.

"You seem to know your own mind very well," murmured Jake.

Annie snorted behind him. Of course she knows her own mind! Hardly difficult when it hasn't finished growing yet.

Sophie's eyes dropped to take in the handsome curve of Jake's mouth. She nodded and smiled, her shoulder now touching his.

Harlot, thought Annie.

"I even know what wedding dress I'm going to wear," whispered Sophie.

Oh yeah, that'll get a red-blooded man panting for more. Describe your wedding dress. Hah! You should give lessons, little girl.

But to Annie's astonishment, Jake didn't turn and run. Quite the opposite in fact.

"You seem very sure of yourself for someone so . . . young," Jake whispered slowly.

Oh dear. Annie didn't like the sound of that. She knew that tone of voice. She searched frantically around the cinema. Was now a good time to set off the fire alarm?

Sophie inched her shimmery lips nearer to Jake.

Oh God! Not that! Not here! Not now!

"I'm not that young," she whispered seductively. "I'm twenty-one next year."

Twenty-one! Next year! That makes her twenty. Possibly even nineteen. Just. Barely past eighteen. It's practically child abuse for God's sake.

Annie went rigid as Jake let Sophie the child-whore kiss him.

To her relief, the light around her suddenly dimmed and her heart failed.

Thank God, she thought. I'm dying.

She waited for her life to flash before her, but the stubborn image of Sophie molesting Jake kept taking center stage. Oh! Absolutely typical. Hogging her limelight to the end. Is there no end to this man's solipsism? (Is it possible to die so angry? she mused.)

Then she became dimly aware that people to her left were standing up and tutting. The cinema was now pitch black.

She wasn't dying after all. The film was about to start and David had returned.

Shit.

The film was an instantly forgettable lightweight comedy. But it was not a forgettable night. Fi and Tony had got engaged, Sophie and Jake had snogged and David and Annie had eaten their entire bucket of popcorn in under four minutes. David was going to phone the *Guinness Book of Records* in the morning.

Annie was exhausted. She couldn't quite believe that she'd had to witness everything. Still, at least she knew for a fact that Sophie had been the one who'd started it. In fact, if her eyes didn't deceive her, Jake hadn't seemed all that interested. Not as interested as he used to be anyway . . .

Once out of the cinema and in the bar, her mind was whirring. She was livid with Sophie for reducing the death of her mother into a character footnote. She was furious with her for telling Jake that cock-and-bull story. She was steaming with Jake for believing it. She was livid with David for a) fancying Sophie and b) not being man enough to beat Jake to it. And she was mad with herself for not having had enough foresight to have bombed the cinema.

All in all, a normal evening out.

While Annie's mind hurtled chaotically into the stratosphere, Tony spent the evening being loud and ecstatic at Fi's final answer to his proposals. They had already decided to get married in six months' time. Fi beamed happily at everyone for half the evening until it suddenly dawned on her that she was now on a diet.

"Drinks are on me tonight," commanded Tony to all and sundry.

Good, thought Annie and ordered a double vodka.

An hour later, she was propping up the bar with David. Both as determined as each other not to spiral into depression after witnessing Sophie lean her pretty blonde head on Jake's shoulder throughout the entire film, they had both hit upon a subject rich in opportunity for them to shine like beacons of intellectual excellence for the wondering world around them.

"*Magic Roundabout* was shite," David was shouting at Annie. "Only good thing about it was the theme tune."

They then sang the theme tune to the *Magic Roundabout,* as many before them had and many after them would. Annie didn't notice Jake joining them to get a round in.

"*Bagpuss* was the best," she was saying. "Especially when the mice made chocolate biscuits."

David nodded sagely.

"Good point!" he exclaimed. "Henceforth, I shall call my first-born Mice."

"*Mr. Benn,*" came a voice behind them. It was Jake.

"Ooh!" squealed Annie. "As if from nowhere, a stiff in a suit appeared."

Jake stopped himself from saying that he wasn't wearing a suit.

"*Mr. Benn* was a top program," he said briefly. "Who wants a drink?"

Sophie piped up from behind him, in an attempt to be seen and heard.

"I loved *Rainbow*," she said confidently.

"You what?" said David.

"Oh yes," rushed Annie, feeling the ground sink beneath Sophie's feet. "I think I remember that—"

"That was wank!" exclaimed David, outraged. His time of indulging Sophie was over. "Bungle and Geoffrey were fucking retards for nancy nappy-wearers. Now *Bagpuss*—he was the dog's bollocks."

"We had *Bagpuss* too," said Sophie quickly.

"No!" said David dramatically. They all hushed. "You had *Bagpuss* repeats."

Point made. As Sophie accepted defeat, he rammed home his victory by managing to get the pint glass to his mouth without spilling any of his drink.

"You know what I think?" said Annie quickly. "Kids today don't know what they're missing. Teletubbies? Load of toss."

Sophie's face flowed into a grateful grin and Annie almost looked up to heaven. Her near brush with death had taught her that however angry she might be at the world, it paid to be nice occasionally. I hope You saw that, she thought silently. Otherwise You're for it.

An hour later, she drove home with her knuckles white on the wheel.

Chapter 15

"Coffee, anyone?" asked Marlon, interrupting his own humming.

Joy and Annie nodded. "Cups or mugs?"

"Needle," said Joy, holding out her upturned arm. "All the veins are good."

Marlon stopped undoing his coat. "Better than good, they're heaven. Can I smell them?"

Joy looked up from her magazine. "When are you going to leave me alone, Marlon?"

"When are you going to leave your cat and move in with me?"

Joy sighed loudly. "I don't have a cat, Marlon. Not all single women have cats, you know."

"Excellent! Then no one will get hurt when you move in with me."

"Except your wife, of course."

"Oh, she's very understanding."

Joy, still reading her magazine and chewing her gum, held up her middle finger at Marlon, as he strode across the threadbare carpet to the kettle. He saw the finger, looked over at Annie and smiled.

"You see, Annie, if anyone ever asks you, it's the subtlety I've fallen for. The sheer unmistakable sign of a lady."

Joy slowly looked up at Marlon. "When exactly did you decide to make my life hell?" she asked him quietly.

Her roots were showing, her black bra showed through her poly-ester blouse, her stomach bulged becomingly over her lap, her thin an-kles shone through her sheer black tights. He stared at her, enraptured.

"When I started dreaming of you instead of Sunderland football club."

She turned away from him in mock disgust, before he could see that she'd smiled too.

"Anyway, I'm not here for my shift," he said, when it was obvi-ous they weren't going to ask him any more questions. "Just came to pick up my latest parcel."

He went to the large brown-papered object by the kettle. "Just what I've been waiting for!"

Annie and Joy sat back and watched as he opened his parcel.

"Look at that!" he said, proudly showing them a four-inch mir-ror. "Bloody ingenious."

"It's a mirror, Marlon," said Joy.

"Yes, but how much of yourself can you see in it?" asked Mar-lon smugly.

"Too much," answered Joy, before turning back to her magazine.

"Full length!" cried Marlon. "Full length! Only four inches high. Bloody ingenious! How do they do it? It's bloody magic."

Joy sighed loudly. "And you say Cynthia doesn't appreciate you? The woman must be crazed."

Marlon didn't hear her. He was too busy looking at himself full length, in his four-inch mirror.

The phone went and Annie picked it up.

"Hello, Samaritans?"

"Hello, Avon calling. Have you ever thought of having your face buffed?"

Annie was losing patience with these time-wasters. She went straight to the point.

"Are you feeling suicidal today?" she asked in a soft, caring voice.

The line went dead.

Marlon brought two instant coffees over and placed them in front of Joy and Annie. He perched, as usual, on the edge of Joy's desk and sat smiling at her.

He didn't smile for long.

"How's Cynthia, Marlon?" asked Joy.

"Hmm? Oh, fine."

Joy sat back in her chair and crossed her arms.

"What does she look like, Marlon? Tell us."

"Oh, all right I suppose. In a sort of 'married-to-the-wrong-man' sort of way."

"How many sons has she borne you?"

Marlon paused.

"Three."

"And how many hot dinners has she cooked you?"

"You're beginning to spoil my fun, you know."

"Well, perhaps she wouldn't see it as fun, Marlon."

Marlon glanced over at Annie before getting up.

"I've never met such a beautiful spoilsport in my life," he said grumpily to himself before leaving.

The door slammed behind him, leaving Joy and Annie in silence.

Eventually Joy spoke, her voice low.

"You'd think that being reduced to a married man's sordid, extra-marital fantasy would put you off him, wouldn't you?" she said.

Just then they heard the key in the front door. They looked up at the clock and realized their shift was nearly over. Neither of them knew who was taking over this week and they sat in silence trying to gauge who was walking in, putting their coat on the chair and approaching the phone room. They were pleased to see the face of Carol poke around the door. Just then the phone went. Annie waved at Carol and picked up the phone.

Joy whispered to Carol.

"Hello love, how are you?"

"Thought you'd never ask," grinned Carol. "My sinuses are playing up, I've got a verruca the size of a two-pound coin just next to my bunion and if I don't have my varicose veins done soon my legs are going to explode."

"Hello? You're through to the Samaritans," repeated Annie as softly and invitingly as she could into her phone.

Carol started handing out hand-made cookies to Joy and Annie as she talked.

"My Irritable Bowel Syndrome has turned into Now-I'm-Really-Angry Bowel Syndrome, my hot water tank burst last night, my eight-year-old got suspended from school for punching his teacher in the knee and our landlord's upped the rent."

"Are you masturbating?" asked Annie into the phone.

Carol and Joy glanced over at her, as she politely but firmly finished her call.

"And it looks like I've just missed some fun," finished Carol, taking a bite of cookie. "Typical."

Half an hour later, Annie and Cass sat in the farthest corner of the Coffee Cup, hidden from the world, arguing.

"I will never go on one of your blind dates again. Never. Four hours of mind-numbing hell," Annie was saying. "Four hours. I nearly ordered arsenic with my coffee, but if I'd have keeled over in front of Angus, I wouldn't have been found for weeks."

"Hold on, young lady. I only told you that he looked like a Greek god," said Cass. "I never said he was good company. Can I help it if you're shallow enough to date a man without checking if he's got anything worth talking about?"

Annie refused to argue. Especially when she was only going to lose.

"That's the last blind date I ever go on," she said firmly. "I've absolutely had it with them."

"You won't have to," replied Cass. "Mother overheard two of the secretaries talking in the office toilets today. One of them said that Edward Goddard's fallen head over heels in love with you. Everyone knows it."

Annie's eyes lit up. She crouched suddenly close to Cass, whispering urgently.

"Did I tell you Sophie pounced on Jake last night?"

Cass frowned.

"Not quite the reaction I expected," she said. "But we can work on it."

"Edward Goddard is everything Jake Mead isn't. Sensitive, caring, blond—"

"—Interested—"

"Sensitive."

"You already said sensitive."

"Well, he's *very* sensitive."

"By the way, any news on our friend in New York, Davina Barker? Has she made any inroads into your father?"

Annie groaned. She had spoken briefly to her father regularly every day. In the first few days, every time he had used the word "we" in reference to their various outings, she had asked "who's we?" and every time, he had answered impatiently, "Me, Katie and Davina, who else?" Slowly the answer became "Me, Katie and Davvy" and now, to Annie's horror, the answer was invariably "Me, Davvy and Katie."

Things were not looking good. Annie was beginning to think she ought to go out there for a long weekend at least.

Annie filled Cass in on Tony and Fi's engagement plans and after some meaningless chat, Cass filled a pause.

"I'm having my eggs collected tomorrow," she said dully. "Putting them all in one basket and all that."

Annie nodded. She knew better than to interrupt.

"They're going to sedate me," continued Cass, "probably to

stop me asking stupid questions—check that my ovaries are big enough—did you know your eggs had to be big enough? Nope. Me neither. Then Brutus does his all-important job, thanks to a choice magazine, and they put his . . . and my . . . together and we wait to hear if they've mated. Isn't it just too romantic?"

"I'll be thinking of you, hon," said Annie quietly, crossing her fingers under the table.

"Don't just think, pray," ordered Cass, trying to smile.

Watching Edward lean over and whisper something in Annie's ear, Jake ran the tip of his tongue along the inside of his mouth. The ulcer tasted pleasingly bitter.

What was it he hated so much about Edward? He tried to figure it out.

Edward laughed at something Susannah said and Jake noticed that the second Susannah turned away from him, Edward stopped laughing. Jake glanced away quickly, before Edward could catch him spotting it.

Then Edward looked around the room and, giving everyone the same charming smile, he asked if anyone had anything to say.

"My door is always open," he explained, his voice so low it was husky.

Jake transformed his smile into a pleasant one when he realized Edward's eyes had rested on him.

"Thanks, Edward," he said, affecting sincerity. "We appreciate it."

Edward simply nodded thoughtfully at Jake. Oh dear, thought Jake. He knows I'm on to him.

Edward then turned to Annie and, in front of everyone, gave her a long lingering look that said much more than was strictly called for in a morning business meeting.

Annie hadn't been so obviously "clocked"—by someone Cass hadn't set her up with or by someone who'd come to fix the leak—for as long as she could remember, especially with witnesses, and the effect it had on her was staggering. Her body's natural air-conditioning experienced a temporary power-cut and she had a mini-meltdown. Her cheeks warmed, her eyes sparkled, her body glowed and, intriguingly, when Edward's eyes momentarily flick-ered to her lips and back to her eyes taking in everything in be-tween, her erogenous zones started mustering, yawning and blinking in the light.

She felt as if her body, aware that her mind had important deci-sions to stay behind and make, was nonetheless skipping ahead into the sun with all the reckless abandon of a child.

She smiled back at him, aware that her whole body was blushing.

Jake decided it was high time the meeting was adjourned. He had important work to do.

"Right," he said, snapping shut his laptop. "I think that's every-thing."

Everyone packed up their stuff and for the first time, Annie was unaware of when Jake had left the office. She was overwhelmed by a surge of reckless optimism that hadn't hit her since her teens. She wanted to join Greenpeace.

The optimism lasted well into the afternoon. The gallery was quiet today—it was always quiet—but never before had Annie seen the paintings with such focus and insight. She even phoned the artist and left a message telling her how wonderful her work was. She looked out of the large glass frontage and smiled happily at the gray day. She'd forgotten how intoxicating hope was.

When she got home, not even Victoria's news brought her down.

"We're all off out tomorrow night—the sitter's booked so you can't say no," rushed Victoria excitedly.

"Where?" asked Annie happily. She was free tomorrow.

"We're going out for a meal. Jake and David will come straight from work so we're going to a restaurant near there. It was Sophie's idea—she's booked it already."

Annie smiled. Ah, poor Sophie. Throwing herself at a sap like Jake. Would it be presumptuous to invite Edward along, she wondered?

"Do you mind putting the boys to bed tonight?" asked Victoria. "Only I've booked myself in for a Shiatsu. Charles is at his wretched club, so why shouldn't I treat myself too?"

"Good for you," said Annie warmly. "We can watch *101 Dalmations.*"

"Only once," said Victoria. "Don't spoil them. Harry's been naughty today. He pulled the music teacher's wig off. Gave him an angina attack."

Annie gasped.

"It's all right. It's only Mr. Matthews. He was half dead anyway."

Brutus and Cass picked up the phone together from other ends of the house.

"It's good news," said the voice at the other end. "You have six embryos. Would you like to come in tomorrow morning for the embryo transfer?"

By the time Brutus ran downstairs to Cass, she was already crying.

"Darling," she whispered, through the tears. "We're going to have an embryo transfer."

By the time they all arrived, the restaurant was crowded and cozy and Annie got herself a seat in the far corner. Her steely determination to cope with the Jake/Sophie situation made her feel stronger than ever in Jake's company. At least now she had something tangible to confront and deal with. It was almost better than being ignored.

From the corner she could watch and enjoy, without being too caught up in the action. And no one here was taking any notice of her anyway: Victoria was on a high, simply because she was out mixing with adults and Charles was on a high because Victoria was in such high spirits. Admittedly, Victoria hadn't taken the news too well about Fi and Tony, but she had clearly got over it. She even smiled maternally over at the happy couple as they whispered and canoodled by the fire. She and Charles were now at least united in agreeing that Jake and Sophie were a good thing. Otherwise they might lose Jake for good. Jake was everything they'd ever looked for in a suitable match for their sister. Handsome, rich, powerful and owner of a BMW. Annie sat by David, watching the evening progress before her, feeling like a fly on the wall; distanced, invisible, with 360-degree vision. And feeding off the discarded remnants that the beautiful people left behind.

David was finding it hard to keep his eyes off Sophie and, as the evening progressed, Annie found herself sympathizing with him so much that she started entertaining him with anecdotes, compliments and harmless flirtation. It was actually beginning to work as they found themselves giggling together in shared, mild hysteria.

While doing so, she caught an involuntary glimpse of herself in the restaurant mirror on the other side of the room. She barely recognized herself. The glowing winter fire lit up her pale complexion and enhanced her rich coloring. She felt more attractive than she had in years. She grinned to herself. Good old Edward. Amazing what he'd done for her already.

Deep in conversation with David, she experienced a sympathy dip in her stomach for him when Jake laughed at one of Sophie's jokes. She hadn't heard that laugh for a long time.

"Wow," she said to David. "I didn't know your boss could do moose impressions."

David snorted into his wine.

Annie suddenly realized why baddies always seemed to be having so much more fun than goodies. Each dig at Jake gave her a delicious, piquant twist that put the traditional feel-good factor in the shade. Grinning wickedly to herself, she pictured Edward in her mind's eye and enjoyed the rest of the evening wondering whether his eyes were brown with hazel flecks or hazel with brown flecks. When she accidentally glanced over to Jake and found herself being coldly scrutinized, she found it easy to give him a quick, almost complicit grin and look away before he had time to react.

Jake hadn't intended to rest his eyes on Annie, but they had defied him as usual. She really was looking gorgeous tonight. If you liked that shrewish look. He looked back at bright, bubbly, blonde Sophie and gave a reassuring smile, unsure of exactly whom he was reassuring. Thank goodness Annie had turned into a cold, selfish, shriveled up old hag. Otherwise he might be in trouble. Sophie reached up and kissed him.

"How's the work going at Markhams'?" Annie heard Victoria finally ask Jake, over their coffee.

"Fine thanks."

"Are you boys going to save us?"

The table went quiet.

"I certainly hope so," replied Jake without a glimmer of a smile.

"I'm sure you've got all the help you need," added Charles. "Edward Goddard's one of the best. He's related to an earl, you know."

They all glanced over at Annie who looked down to hide her grin and flushed cheeks.

"Shame his high connections couldn't teach him how to be a chief exec," said Jake bitterly into his coffee.

Concerned by Jake's unprecedented unprofessionalism, David interrupted the embarrassed silence that followed.

"We usually find that the top men are the ones least in the know. Just part of their job," he said feebly. "We'd have been surprised if it hadn't been the case, to be honest. Shows he's doing it . . . um . . . well . . ."

Annie stared at Jake.

"I expect Edward's a bit too sensitive for the job," she said pointedly.

Jake looked up at her.

"Something like that," he replied quietly.

The atmosphere was dulled for the rest of the evening and once the bill had been dealt with, they made their way back to the car park.

Tony and Fi were only too happy to wander through the streets until they found a cab and left the others as soon as they could without being rude. Jake had a two-seater and so could only give Sophie a lift home, but David had kindly offered to give Annie, Charles and Victoria a lift.

On their way, the six of them passed a narrow, long, dark cobbled alleyway, which had the rare quality of looking as inviting as it did terrifying. They could just make out uneven walls and an old pub on the corner, which wouldn't have looked out of place in a Sherlock Holmes adaptation.

"Ooh look," squealed Sophie. "Isn't that amazing?" She pulled on Jake's arm like a child. "Let's go down there."

"No way," replied Victoria, horrified. "It looks terrifying."

"Where's your sense of adventure?" asked Sophie. "You've got boring in your old age."

"I'm not old and I've always been boring," shot Victoria. "And it looks horrid."

"Annie, come on, *you're* good fun," coaxed Sophie.

It almost worked. But Annie looked down the alleyway and either it was her vivid imagination or she sensed some movement at the far end. No way.

"Sorry, Sophie. I'm going to have to fight nature on this one and actually side with my big sis."

"Gee thanks," said Victoria.

"You're all so boring! Oh, come on. Doesn't anyone want some fun?" asked Sophie in a little-girl voice, looking at David and Jake imploringly.

David shifted uncomfortably but said nothing. Annie felt for him. Politics made it impossible for him to race down a darkened alley with Sophie until his boss made a decision. David looked up at Jake.

"Jake? What you wanna do, big guy?"

They all looked up at Jake.

"Come on, big guy," repeated Sophie, in a whisper. "You'll protect me, won't you? What's the point of living if you don't take risks?" She laid her chin on his chest and looked up at him with her baby blues.

Victoria snorted.

Jake looked across at where the snort came from. Victoria was his client, after all.

"Hey, don't let us stop you getting killed," she said sweetly.

Charles grinned at him sheepishly.

"We'll wait for you out here."

Sophie and David both looked at Jake eagerly. It was clear that the decision lay with him.

Annie, feeling very much the outsider, eyed Jake wondering which way his iddy biddy brain would go. What would he do? Would he side with the more responsible people in the party, who were also his clients, or would he fall for the silly charms of a twenty-year-old and try to impress his colleague? Hmm, a real teaser, that one.

Jake caught her eye. He also caught the wry smile on her face. Bitch.

He looked down at Sophie.

"Of course I'll protect you," he murmured, holding her tight. "And you're right." He looked back up at Annie. "What's the point of living if you don't take risks?"

Annie tried to find him ridiculous, but instead felt her eyes well up.

David and Sophie whooped like children.

Without further ado, the three of them edged their way into the alley, and within moments Charles, Victoria and Annie couldn't see them anymore. Good, thought Annie. She started squinting into the dark. She was absolutely positive she could sense movement at the far end of the alley.

They all heard a sudden noise.

"What was that?" whispered David.

None of them stayed long enough to find out.

Sophie squealed with the excitement of a child being chased and ran back toward the others, followed swiftly by David and Jake.

"That was so exciting!" she squeaked to the anxious Charles, Victoria and Annie. "I'm all shaky!"

"You can't see in front of your hand in there," said David, pretending that he wasn't "all shaky."

Jake couldn't bring himself to look at Annie.

"Right. Let's get home," he said, moving them all away from the alleyway. He felt almost as stupid for humoring Sophie as he did for shaking. And he didn't like what he'd seen in the alleyway.

But they weren't going home yet. There was comforting of Sophie to do on the part of Charles and David, and dissecting and recounting on the part of Sophie. Sophie was in her element and she wasn't going to have her spotlight dimmed by a spoilsport. An adventure had happened! She'd been frightened of the dark! There had been a nasty noise!

While everyone fussed loudly around Sophie the Adventuress, Jake and Annie momentarily glanced at each other. Annie looked away quickly. She knew that the "risks" comment had been directed at her. She would have liked to congratulate him—walking four feet down a dark alleyway had really shown her how misguided she'd been in her life. But she knew her voice wouldn't keep steady.

Meanwhile, Jake was utterly thrown by his feelings. Was this what he'd come to? Putting himself and others into danger just to annoy Annie? And why did he keep letting her affect him so much? In the pitch black of the alley, he'd suddenly seen things clearly.

The fuss around Sophie continued. Charles was genuinely worried for his sister—she was sensitive, she shouldn't put herself into risky situations like that. Look how much she was shaking. David was able to use the opportunity to put a friendly arm around her shoulder as they laughed together over how silly they'd been. Victoria delighted in scolding them all.

Annie and Jake looked back to the now silent alleyway.

As Annie spotted something glinting on the floor, Sophie screamed.

"My bag! I've lost my bag. My Chanel bag!"

Another adventure! Sophie in the Spotlight Again.

"It's all right," said Annie firmly. "I can see it."

Partly to get away from the nonsense going on around her, partly to get away from Jake, Annie rushed toward the gilt trim shining in the dark. It didn't look too far away.

"Don't go back in there!" yelled Jake, petrified.

Annie sped faster. She didn't need him telling her what to do. He'd more than proved the criteria for his decision-making powers, thank you very much. She raced even faster when she realized he was coming after her.

Almost instantly she couldn't see a thing. It really was pitch black in there. Only the sound of Jake's breathing told her she wasn't alone. At least, she hoped it was Jake's.

"Can you see it?" asked Jake, his voice by her ear. She had to stop herself from grabbing hold of him for fear. Victoria was right. The alleyway was terrifying. She focused on the trim of the handbag glinting at her feet and bent down slowly toward it. She grabbed the bag.

Her skin turned to ice.

Instead of grabbing an incredibly expensive, tiny, chic purse,

Annie had grabbed what was on top of it. Which could only be described as a hand. A very hairy hand. A giant, very hairy hand. The hand of a hairy giant. A monster, maybe.

Annie's body prepared for fight or flight mode. Which meant she stopped breathing and thought she was going to faint.

"What's wrong?" whispered Jake in her ear. She could feel his warm breath on her neck.

"Is that you?" she whispered back.

"Of course it's me."

"I mean . . . is that you holding the bag with me?"

Silence.

"No."

Silence.

"I'm the one next to you who now has to change his trousers."

Silence.

A small whimpering noise came from the direction of Jake.

"That was me."

"Thank you."

Before Annie could decide what to do next, Jake grabbed hold of her around the waist and tried valiantly to whisk her behind him.

Furious, Annie fought him off, her legs midair, her hand firmly on the hand. The hand wasn't letting go of the bag.

"Get off!" she yelled.

"You heard!" shouted Jake. "Get off!" He kept his grip on Annie as she kept her grip on the hand and the hand kept its grip on the purse.

"No! You!"

"What do you mean me?" yelled Jake. "I'm helping!"

"GET OFF!"

Jake and the hand leapt back in shock and Annie was thrown into the middle of them.

"Oh God, Annie! Sorry! You frightened me! Move!"

Annie and Jake could just make out the enormous shadow of a man in front of them. He was big. Very big.

It was clear Annie couldn't move.

"Right . . . now . . . Annie," said Jake. "Just . . . stay calm . . ."

Annie stepped forward and kicked the shadow in the groin.

"And then kick him in the groin. Perfect."

They heard a moan in the dark. The shadow tried to punch her, but she blocked his arm with her right hand, attacked him with a roundhouse kick—made all the more effective by her DM boots—followed by an elbow in the neck. He was down.

"Jesus Christ," mumbled Jake. "Remind me never to attack you in a dark alleyway."

Annie started jogging on the spot, exhilarated beyond belief.

"Come on!" she yelled into the darkness at the shadow writhing on the floor. "Call that a fight? Come and get me!"

Someone punched her in the face.

Damn. There were two of them.

The force of the hit walloped her backward into Jake, and they both stumbled to the floor, Annie landing on Jake.

"Some men don't like being teased," Jake's squashed voice came from underneath her.

Right. That was it. Livid at being so humiliated, Annie jumped up, yelled the karate attack, which terrified the attacker almost as much as it terrified Jake and, with her aggression suitably channeled, chopped the attacker in the face.

He staggered and fell but she knew it was only a momentary reprieve.

"Quick! Run!" yelled Jake, as he stood up, grabbed her hand and pulled her out.

"The bag!"

"Forget the bag!"

He practically scooped her off her feet again, and they raced toward the light. But the attacker was fast. They could hear him getting up and starting to run after them. Just before the end of the alley there was a sharp turn to the right. Once they made it past there, they should be safe. After that there was only about three yards before the light—and the attacker was a good four yards behind them. Once they hit the light and people and traffic, they were home and dry. They just had to reach it before he reached them.

The pounding of his size thirteens got nearer and nearer.

It felt like he was right behind them now. Annie could almost imagine him reaching out and pulling her hair. She must get it cut.

They turned the corner.

The attacker was about one yard behind, still to turn the corner behind them.

They weren't going to make it.

Then, to her astonishment, Jake pulled her sharply into an invisible alcove at the side of the alley and held her against the wall so tightly she was completely hidden and protected by him. She also couldn't breathe. Her face was hidden in his neck and she tried to pull away but his hold was too tight. They stood, clamped together, their breathing jagged, their hearts pounding into each other's ribcages.

She heard the attacker pass them and felt Jake release her slightly. They stared at each other in the dark as they listened to his footsteps. And for one pure moment, the world as she knew it stopped. There was only her and Jake.

The man reached the end of the street and, after a few moments, cursed dramatically.

They heard Victoria's sharp voice.

"I hardly think that was necessary."

And then they heard him run away.

Jake and Annie both started to heave with suppressed giggles, holding on to each other tightly to stop the shaking. As the stifled noise of their laughter grew dangerously loud, Jake held her tighter again, burying his mouth in her hair. The shock of it stopped her laughing immediately. They both knew there was another attacker in the alleyway—the one Annie had kneed in the groin. Had he run the other way? Was he still there? Was he dangerous?

The sound of Sophie's high-pitched whine hit them at the same time.

"Where's my bag?"

"Oh my God," muttered Jake. "She's in the alleyway. You run while I get her."

"No—"

Jake held her firmly by the shoulders. His voice had lost all of its formal pride. It was the Jake she remembered who spoke to her now.

"Please, Annie. Run."

She ran.

Jake went the opposite way to Sophie in the alleyway and grabbed her by the hand.

"Hello!" she said happily. "Are you having fun without me? Did you find my bag?"

Jake looked on the floor. No bag. No shadow. It was time to leave.

"No," he said. "Let's go."

Suddenly, Sophie was swiped around the head with her bag, and the first attacker raced past them, into the light and away.

Sophie the Adventuress started wailing. Jake soothed her as he tried to drag her out of the alleyway. Once he hit the light and the others, he let go of her hand, numb with shock.

He didn't notice the looks on everyone's faces as he ran toward them. Nor did he notice that Sophie wasn't keeping up with him. All he noticed was that Annie was mouthing something at him.

He slowed down and his body came to a halt as his brain slowly tried to unravel some meaning from what his eyes saw. They were all staring past him at Sophie and shouting.

He turned around in slow motion. Sophie was stumbling toward him, her body wracked with sobbing. Before Jake had time to react, she slumped in an untidy heap on the pavement. And landed on her head.

The others sped toward Sophie, shocked at what they saw. By the time they reached her, Victoria and Fi were already sobbing in loud, ugly gasps.

Charles tried to speak, but the sight of his sister was too much for him.

"Blood!" he kept saying. "Blood!"

Typically useless, thought Victoria, who started screaming.

In a shaky voice, Annie started telling Tony to take Fi, Victoria and Charles away. He tried to, but Victoria was too busy screaming. A crowd was now forming around them.

Jake moved slowly toward the group, trembling all over. There was a look of such terror on his face that Annie thought she might start crying too. He looked down at Sophie, unconscious and white on the ground. Sure enough there was a horrifying red puddle by her head.

"Oh God," whimpered Jake, "Oh God." He looked up at Annie. "What shall we do?"

"We need an ambulance," said Annie urgently. "Do you think we can carry her? Or should we leave her for the ambulance men?"

She stared intently at Jake. He stared back.

"Ambulance men," he repeated.

"It probably looks worse than it is," insisted Annie before turning to Victoria.

"Stop screaming!" she yelled. "Tony! Take her and Fi away NOW."

They obeyed. Charles started whimpering next to Annie.

"We need an ambulance," said Annie to Jake. "Can I borrow your mobile?"

Jake fumbled in his jacket for his mobile and with an unsteady hand, gave it to Annie.

She looked at the phone.

"How do you use it?" she asked, perplexed, panic starting to clutch at her chest.

"Um," began—and ended Jake.

Annie looked up at him. They stared at each other, both growing dimly aware that the sound of a siren was getting closer.

Chapter 16

It was 2 a.m. and Jake, Charles and Annie were sitting, muscles aching, in Jake and David's drawing room. Jake had insisted on Sophie being brought here. He would look after her until she felt a hundred percent better. Sophie lay sleeping soundly in his bed.

Sophie's wound had, as Annie had predicted, looked far worse than it had been. She had knocked her temple on a sharp piece of bad paving and had only been unpleasantly concussed. In truth, the punch to Annie's face had been worse and was only now turning into an ugly welt across her left eyebrow that was starting to throb. She held an ice pack to it in her left hand, which had gone numb from the cold.

The shock had left them all exhausted. Victoria was sleeping upstairs.

Charles, David and Jake now sat with Annie, trying to decide what to do next.

"I must tell Mum and Dad," said Charles.

"Of course," said David.

"They'll want her at home with them."

"No," said Jake firmly. "This is all my fault. I should have—I shouldn't have—"

"It's OK, mate," soothed David. "She's all right. Just a bit of concussion and a nasty shock. The doc said nothing a week of daytime telly wouldn't cure."

"Are they saying her brain's been damaged?" asked Annie.

"I'll look after her here when I'm not working," Jake said firmly. "It's the least I can do."

"I'll help you out there, mate," joined David.

Annie started to nod, but stopped when she thought her head was going to explode from the pain. She was only slightly concerned that Jake and David's attention might wander somewhat from saving Markhams'. She reprimanded herself quickly for such an ungenerous thought.

"I'll call Sophie's office first thing tomorrow," she whispered. "Tell them what's happened. Send in the doctor's sick note."

Jake looked up at her.

"Thanks," he said quietly. "How are you feeling?"

She managed a small smile.

"Like I've been in a fight," she whispered. "Cool."

She stood up slowly. "I need a hot drink. Anyone want one?"

Three pairs of eyes looked up at her gratefully.

She walked heavily into the kitchen and turned on the kettle. Standing in the dark, she tutted aloud at Sophie for having caused this all. There was knowing one's mind and then there was being a spoiled little madam. Feeling immediately guilty at her thoughts, and at her sudden intolerance of Sophie, Annie decided to help her. As soon as she'd phoned Samantha and got a few days off from the gallery, she'd spend her days just sitting with Sophie until Jake and David got home to be with her.

The kettle boiled and Annie poured boiling water into the teapot.

She then carried the tray back through the darkened hall and just as she reached the door, she realized she'd forgotten the milk. She stopped outside the door, trying to decide whether to take the tray in and then go back for it or turn back now. Her brain cells seemed to be damaged. But the sound of Jake's voice made her suddenly alert.

"She's more reliable than any of us put together," came his whisper through the door. "And totally and utterly in control. Underneath that fragile exterior she's stronger than all of us. You should have seen her beat that bloke to a pulp. Terrifying."

She heard the others murmur their assent.

"What I'm trying to say is, if you want something done properly, ask Annie. And she only lives one flight up. She's the only one I trust. I know she's working and Victoria's at home, but—and no offense, Charles—I'd just feel safer if we asked Annie to keep an eye on Sophie."

"None taken," replied Charles. "I couldn't agree more."

So, thought Annie wearily, leaning her head against the door— and then jabbing it away when pain shot through it. I'm the perfect carer for Jake's new, young, injured girlfriend. How touching.

She opened the door.

"Who wants a nice cup of tea?" she said, wondering why her insides were glowing as much as her forehead.

Annie let Edward lean forward and brush her bruised forehead with his lips. It was an unusual way of getting a taster of things to come.

He sat down on the sofa beside her, his arm outstretched behind her back.

"What time are you popping down to see Sophie?" he whispered.

"About half an hour."

Edward started to caress her hair gently. Maybe an hour, she thought.

Edward looked at her for so long that she started to worry that someone had turned his power button off.

"Shouldn't you be at work?" she asked eventually.

He sighed and moved away, wiping his hand over his face.

"To be honest, it's all changed so much since those bloody management consultants have been there," he said. "Not getting quite the same enjoyment out of it as I used to."

Annie would have frowned if it hadn't hurt like buggery.

"They have to do their job," she said softly.

Edward gave her a kind smile.

"You're so good, Annie Markham. The world would be a better place if we all gave each other the benefit of the doubt."

This time she did frown. "What are you saying? Don't you think they're doing their job properly?"

Edward shook his head slowly.

"That's not the half of it," he said softly, almost to himself. Then he slowly stood up. "Don't you worry your . . . battered little face about it."

For want of anything better to do, Annie smiled up at him.

"I wondered . . ." he started, "if we might go for dinner some-time? When you can nod without painkillers, of course."

Annie's smile grew. "That would be lovely," she said softly. "I'd like that."

He gave her a wide grin. "I'll call you when I'm in the office with my diary."

As he left, Annie wondered if it was old age or the recent blow to her head that stopped any squirm of excitement build up in her stomach.

She closed her eyes.

And was back in the alley, in Jake's arms.

She stood up slowly and went to get her bag. She was popping down to see Sophie again today. To be honest though, she didn't know how many more days she could do it. Sophie had spent the last two days talking non-stop about Jake. She didn't care about the age gap and had always liked Older Men. They were so much more experienced than Young Boys.

Annie had nodded slowly, trying hard to push the image of Jake holding her in the alley out of her mind.

And then, as soon as it had started to get dark outside, which it did earlier and earlier each day, Annie had been so conscious that Jake might come home that she had been tense enough to bring on a now familiar evening headache. When David had turned up instead of Jake, as he invariably did, it had been an effort not to be bad-tempered with him, such was the letdown she felt. This couldn't go on. Jake and Sophie were clearly an item. She had to get used to it.

She picked up her bag and her door keys before looking around the room. Just as she went to turn the light off, the phone went. It was Susannah.

"Darling, how are you?"

"Oh, nothing a good holiday couldn't help."

She really wasn't in the mood right now for a business update.

"Ah, well, my dear, I might have the perfect solution. Edward is taking a trip to the New York office to update George on his change of tactics since the management consultants have helped out—"

Oh yes? thought Annie. Why hadn't he mentioned it? Or was that why he had suddenly made a move on her after waiting so long?

"And I think I may join him out there in a few weeks. I wondered if you'd like to pop out before me. Do you the world of good, a change of scenery."

Annie mused on the possibility. She didn't much like New York—too noisy for her tastes. Then she thought of Sophie and Jake. Downstairs. She was owed weeks of holiday from the gallery—and she could even do some important research in SoHo. Yes, time off was due to her.

"And of course, if you go out there soon," continued Susannah, "you can update me on all the business developments. Be my little New York spy. You're the only one I really trust. So you'd be really helping me out."

"I'd love to," Annie said firmly into the phone. "Sounds great."

"Wonderful!" exclaimed Susannah. "Victoria and Charles are going too—with the boys. A family holiday."

"Wonderful," murmured Annie into the phone, her head starting to throb.

Chapter 17

"**H**i, Annie, d'you fancy a bit of tender loving care this Sunday?" asked Cass over the phone one evening. Her two weeks' waiting to hear whether or not her embryos had survived were driving her mad. She had to go out.

"I'd love it," answered Annie. "But we were going to go to the Heath and then tea in Hampstead."

"We?"

"Victoria and the boys."

"Oh."

"Would you like to join us?"

Cass thought about it for a moment. She couldn't think of anything worse.

"Yes thanks, that would be lovely."

Victoria was the center of attention. Her figure was at its prime—she knew it—and her eyes were sparkling with youth and vitality. Men were casting her approving, animal glances wherever she went.

It was wonderful, but she wasn't remotely interested. She was being chatted up by a charming ex-boyfriend whom she knew had never stopped loving her. He couldn't take his eyes off her flat stomach. Somehow they both knew that tonight—just tonight—

they could do what they wanted. And they both wanted the same thing.

"Shall we stay for one more drink," she was asking him now, knowing full well what his answer would be, "or shall we go back to my place?"

He gave her a smile that should have come with a government health warning and leaned in close enough for her to feel his warm whisky breath on her cheek.

"Can I play on my Nintendo?" he whispered in her ear. "Bertie's woken me up. I think he's done a wee-wee in bed."

Victoria felt her body being dragged, lifelessly, away from her dream. She opened an eye.

Harry was hopping from foot to foot beside her. The room was pitch black.

"Mummy, can I play on my Nintendo?" he repeated. "Bertie's woken me up. I think he's done a wee-wee in bed. He's crying. Can I play on my Nintendo?"

Victoria's eyelid collapsed back down again. She didn't even have the energy to cry. Please God, she thought to herself. I'll never eat a whole chocolate cake in one go again as long as I live. Just get this child out of my room.

"Mummy?"

"What time is it?" she asked him, her voice rasping and hoarse.

He looked at her digital alarm clock. Lots of bright red lines.

"Um," he said hopefully.

Victoria dragged her head to face the clock. She groaned loudly.

"Have you woken me before five in the morning just to ask if you can play on your Nintendo?"

"Um," said Harry hopefully, again. Didn't sound too unreasonable to him. He'd waited for hours already.

"Come back when I'm awake."

"When?"

"When you've finished college."

She drifted back to sleep, but her ex-boyfriend had gone. The noise of a four-year-old shifting from foot to foot next to her head was still there.

"Harry," she croaked.

"Yes," replied Harry quickly.

He leaned in to her so as to hear her soft whisper better.

"Be a good boy and leave home."

Pad pad pad pad next to her head.

"Mummy?"

"Ugh?"

"Can I play on my Nintendo?"

"Ask your father."

"I can't."

"Why?"

"He's asleep."

Somewhere, somehow, Victoria found the energy to start crying.

"*I* was asleep, you wretched child!"

"But you aren't now."

"And whose fault is that?"

"Can I play on my Nintendo?"

Victoria motioned him to come nearer and whispered in his ear, still with her eyes shut.

His ear was a centimeter from her mouth. She breathed in his sleepy-child smell.

"Go to your father and shout *Fore* in his ear. Loudly. He'll be very proud."

Harry didn't move for a moment.

Then pad pad pad pad next to her head.

"Mummy, can I play on my——"

"YES!"

The padding went away. Ah bliss! At last. Silence . . .

Victoria was back at school. All the desks were in a circle, which was unusual. The English teacher cocked her head to one side and stared fixedly at Victoria. Well, one eye did. The other one stared fixedly at the hockey pitch. Victoria never knew whether or not her teacher was looking at her. Slowly but surely Victoria turned her head to look at her schoolmate. Her schoolmate had slowly but surely turned her head to look at her.

"Victoria," commanded her teacher. Victoria's schoolmate breathed an audible sigh of relief.

"What does Othello really think of Cassius?" asked the teacher.

Victoria's mind went blank. Othello? Cassius? She could almost hear the vaults of her brain echoing shut. Luckily her schoolmate leaned close to her and whispered in her ear. To her amazement, the teacher didn't seem to notice. Victoria listened carefully to what her friend had to say.

"Mummy, I did a wee-wee in my bed," she said clearly.

Victoria repeated the words out loud and to her horror, the whole class started laughing at her. She opened her eyes quickly.

Paddity paddity pad by her head.

"Mummy, I did a wee-wee in my bed," came the voice again, full of heart-wrenching remorse.

Without letting her mind catch up with her body, Victoria heaved herself out of bed, picked up Bertie and carried him into his bedroom. He buried his head in her neck and started crying.

"It's OK," she whispered. "Wee-wees are fine. It's only when you kick your brother in the neck that Mummy gets testy."

After she'd stripped his bed and washed Bertie, she realized there was nothing for it. He was wide awake.

Oh God, why wasn't Annie awake yet? It was all very well Annie helping in the day, but it was the nighttime that was the bugger. It was pure genuine torture, nothing less. If they ever wanted to get information out of a spy, they should just make him look after two boys under five for a few months. Anyone can be a mother when they're wide awake. Charles didn't have a clue how hard it really was. Why wasn't he awake yet? She'd tutted loudly enough to wake the devil. Why the hell was she awake? It wasn't even six o'clock yet and she was sitting on the floor, leaning against the wall, reading a book about a teddy bear's knickers to her youngest son for the third time. The rest of the world was asleep—she was totally alone. Her eyes felt like they were being dragged down by sandbags, her body seemed to be on a different time clock from her brain. It was like jet lag without the tan.

The book dropped to the floor. Her breathing mingled with Bertie's. Sensing that her son had grown heavier in her arms, she managed to prise open her eyes. He was asleep. Carefully, she lifted him, ever so gently, into his bed, dreading the moment when he'd have to leave her arms because that was when he usually woke up and started crying. No, he was fast asleep. She allowed herself one brief moment to watch him and marvel at the way he breathed in and then out, before turning away from his bed and tiptoeing out of his room. She could catch another hour in bed before the boys woke properly.

She inched his door open, her eye still on her sleeping son. She crept, cat-like, out of his room. She shut his door silently and turned around without making a sound.

She came face to face with Harry.

"Mummy, my Nintendo's broken. Will you play racing cars with me?"

Later that day Cass and Annie strolled wearily down Hampstead High Street behind Victoria who was pushing the double buggy like she was in a marathon. They had all spent a blustery hour on the Heath.

Cass and Annie would have been happy to have gone to the usual Coffee Cup, but Victoria didn't like it there.

"The chairs are uncomfortable, there's never enough room for the boys and the food is uninspired, Bertie not NOW," she had explained.

Cass and Victoria had never really hit it off but they both promised to be on their best behavior today, for Annie's sake.

"I hear all business meetings with the chief exec are going well," grinned Cass at Annie as soon as they all sat down at the café table.

"We-ell," answered Annie hesitantly. She looked over at her sister who was telling Bertie that if he whined once more she was going to return him. He was still under guarantee.

"Edward seems to be worried about the way things are going—" she attempted.

"You know what I mean. Mum said there's so much chemistry in the meetings she needs a bunsen burner and some goggles."

Annie allowed herself a quiet, glowing smile. She'd forgotten how nice it was to have her ability to attract confirmed.

"Have you heard?" interrupted Victoria. "There might be wedding bells soon?"

"Ooh goodie," said Cass. She loved gossip, especially happy gossip. "Who?"

"Sophie and that Jake Mead."

Annie felt the room shoot off in the distance, leaving her in a dark thumping vacuum. Cass put her hand near Annie's on the table and gently probed Victoria.

"But they've only been together for a couple of weeks. How do you know?"

"Mummy—" said Bertie.

"Well," started Victoria, ignoring Bertie. "Apparently Sophie phoned Fi last night and asked her how she would feel about doing a double wedding." Victoria grinned and sat back proudly.

"Oh my God," said Cass.

"Mummy, can I—"

"Jake was besotted with Sophie even before the accident," rushed Victoria. "And it's all got very intense since. He's not getting any younger and she's as keen as anything. You often find older men having whirlwind romances. They've sewn all their oats and recognize the right woman when she comes along. It's so romantic—her being so weak and everything. I knew this would happen. I said so as soon as they met."

Annie was too worried about her sudden double vision to worry about contradicting her sister.

"Mummy, I need—"

"I'm talking, Bertie. See? Mummy's lips are moving and noise is coming out. Be a good boy and stop whining, or I'll cut you out of my will."

She turned back to her captive audience. She hadn't expected the news to have had quite as dramatic an effect on Cass as it had.

Then she grimaced and sniffed. She looked disapprovingly at Bertie.

"Bertie," she said in a tone you could cut stone with, "have you done a doo-doo in your pants?"

Nope, thought Annie, through the humming in her ears. That'll be me.

Victoria rolled her eyes, picked up a bag full of spare trousers and underpants and took him off. What was going on with Bertie? He seemed to potty-train so well. Was he going to have to go back into nappies? She didn't think she could bear it.

Cass and Annie sat in silence, one stunned by the news, the other stunned by its effect on her.

Finally Cass spoke.

"Be fair to Bertie," she muttered. "If Victoria was threatened to be cut out of her father's will for whining, she'd probably crap herself too."

Annie saw Cass's lips move but just heard noise.

Ten minutes later, Victoria was back. She plumped herself down on her chair, not looking at Bertie.

"Would anyone like a small child?" she asked. "Going free? Once potty trained, now regressing—particularly if you abuse it by attempting to have a life of your own?"

To her chagrin neither Cass nor Annie laughed.

"Are you sure you should talk about Bertie like that?" asked Cass, winking fondly at Bertie. "I'm sure he's the cleverest boy in the world so he can understand every word you say."

Victoria smarted.

"Thank you, Cass," she replied. "I don't need to be told how to look after my own son." She let him go and he hurtled straight into the waiter's knees. The waiter smiled painfully and kept on walking. Bertie busied himself opening a closed pram at the table opposite.

Victoria suddenly felt thunderous. How dare Cass invite herself along and then make her feel like an idiot. How come she always did that? How dare she? What did she know about motherhood? After all, Cass had had years of carefree, selfish, moneyed irresponsibility compared to her own quagmire of responsible, budgeted motherhood.

Meanwhile Cass could barely think for seething. She had forced herself to come out with Victoria only because the prospect of staying at home, waiting for her body to accept or reject the embryos inside it, was too much for her to bear. Every morning for the past two weeks, she'd woken up waiting for a timebomb to go off in her body. She could hardly breathe for worrying about losing this potential baby and this . . . this . . . spoiled girl had two beautiful, healthy boys she seemed to hate.

Annie was so horribly aware of how they were both feeling that she could almost hear their thoughts, like broken glass in her head. She sat back in her chair, knocked out by all the different emotions going on inside her. Sometimes she felt as though her skin was made from a different texture to other people's. It was more porous, as if every millimeter of her body soaked up other people's seeping emotions. Sometimes, like now, there were so many people under her own skin, there was barely enough room for her. But today her own pain only added to it, so that she felt weighed down by it all. The perfect mood for lunch out with the girls.

"Are you ready to order?" asked the waiter.

No, none of them was ready to order. He'd come back in a moment.

"It's bloody hard being a mother you know," said Victoria in a brittle voice.

"Have I said it wasn't?" asked Cass.

"I don't get a moment to myself. My life isn't my own anymore—"

"Have you ever had their salmon steaks here?" asked Annie. "They're surprisingly good."

"And I haven't slept a whole night through for more than five years."

"Neither have I," said Cass, unimpressed. "Brutus snores and I have a small bladder."

"Or perhaps their steak tartare?"

"Small bladder! Until you've had a baby you don't know the meaning of a small bladder," scoffed Victoria. "Try three hours' sleep every night for a few months. You'll dream of only having to put up with Brutus's snoring."

"I never said I have to put up with Brutus's snoring. I like it. I obviously don't need as much sleep as you do."

"Ooh look, they've got gnocci!"

"And then there's the Repetitive Game Syndrome. If I've played racing cars with Harry once I've played it with him three thousand times. I'm telling you, motherhood is the most boring job in the world—and at the same time, the most responsible job in the world. Like pairing God's socks."

"I'm sorry," said Cass finally, slamming her menu down on the table. "But did *I* make you pregnant?"

Victoria was nonplussed for a moment.

"Don't be disgusting," she muttered.

"Well, did I?"

"Of course not," Victoria tried to scoff.

"Well then," said Cass. "I'd *so* appreciate it if you didn't try and make me feel guilty for your choice of motherhood."

Victoria was speechless with fury.

"Are you ready to order?" asked the waiter.

"NO!" they shouted in unison.

It had been a brainwave of genius proportions to bring up the subject of New York. Annie felt sure it would be the one subject on which Cass and Victoria would both agree. She was right. And at the same time it might actually cheer her up. Well, two out of three wasn't bad. All tension was temporarily swept under the carpet, while the two women shared numerous memories, hints, vital names and facts about the city.

"That's arranged then," said Cass. "I'll see you there for Thanksgiving."

"Excellent!" said Victoria. "We can all get outfits there for the double wedding."

Annie's stomach burrowed into the floor.

One short week later it was all arranged. Annie, Charles and Victoria were off to New York that week, to stay with George, Katherine and Davina in the family apartment on the Upper East Side overlooking Central Park, until the New Year. Annie couldn't get there fast enough.

Harry and Bertie would stay with Charles's parents and then join them all out there for the fortnight lead-up to Christmas.

Tony and Fi were already out there, meeting Tony's family and buying wedding clothes and a trousseau. Cass and Brutus would come over with Susannah for Christmas. Edward had already flown out for the first of many meetings with George.

They would all be there together for New Year. By which time, Cass would be two months' pregnant with her triplets.

Chapter 18

Annie looked up at the clock from her bed. It was 5 a.m. She yawned silently, anxious not to disturb Joy who was on a call in the room next door. It had been an exceptionally quiet night—the longest call being from someone who was beside themselves with hurt and anger after being rejected by the Samaritans as a possible volunteer.

When Annie first started doing her regular nightshift at the Samaritans, it used to worry her that she found it so much more pleasurable waking up there than at home, but now she just accepted it as part of her perverse nature.

She didn't tell any of her family—not even Cass—about her work at the Sams. She knew they wouldn't understand. They'd think she was a do-gooder, instead of just another shallow person selfishly trying to find meaning in their otherwise utterly meaningless life. The Sams brought Annie what new shoes brought to Victoria: a short burst of feel-good factor that inevitably wore off almost immediately. In fact, Annie felt better about her life the worse the caller's predicament was—go figure, as Tony would say. She felt like a frustrated child when the callers didn't fall over themselves to thank her for her wonderful listening skills. "You're very clever, aren't you? You've really helped me, you know . . . I think you're wonderful . . . Ooh, now that's a good question . . ."

If only all these sad, desperate people knew when they called the Samaritans, *they* were helping *her* . . .

Nope, there was nothing selfless in her being a Samaritan.

But try telling that to her family.

She knew that she'd miss this place more than anything else about her life in London. It was a weird thought that the next time she'd wake up here it would be a new year.

She stretched her arms behind her head and then looked out of the window, allowing her mind to do its usual morning jog, while half listening out for the phone. Why was she feeling so spectacularly low this morning?

She decided to mull it over, give it time, think it through thoroughly.

At first, it was just an uncomfortable presence in the back of her mind, like the unnerving sensation that creeps up on you just before you realize there's a two-foot-wide spider in the corner watching you dress. And then the irrefutable fact of it grows so undeniably real that suddenly, without even swiveling your eyes in their sweaty sockets, you know, not only that the spider is there, but that it's smiling. And now you have a simple choice. Either you can run away as fast as the wind—probably thumping into the doorpost on the way through blind terror—or you never move again.

And so it was with Jake. Finally, with a sinking heart, Annie understood that, like a two-foot-wide smiling spider in the corner watching her dress, her feelings for Jake were an irrefutable fact of her life. Hot-tempered, proud and immature. And under her skin more than a swollen tic. He was in her bloodstream, flowing through her veins, pumping into her heart and out again, breathing life and purpose into her nerves and fibers. Like depression, she realized, love had nothing to do with rational thought or mental control. It was an emotional virus that entered and left the body of its own accord. And she'd been playing host to it for a long time.

And she had a simple choice. She could run like the wind or never move again.

Defeated, she bent her heavy head down. The ugly truth of it was that it was irrelevant how imperfect Jake was. What mattered was that he felt the same about her as she did about him.

Which, seeing as he was about to marry into her family, seemed unlikely.

Her simple choice became simpler still.

She had to run away as fast as the wind.

Thank God she was going to New York in a matter of days. She realized that the only way she could cope with Jake marrying Sophie would be for her to stay out there.

Exhausted by too many emotional truths in one morning, she looked up at a poster advertising the Samaritans. A woman sat on a park bench on her own, surrounded by people out together feeding the ducks, pushing children on the swings, kissing. The woman's face was a picture of silent, aching despair.

Depressed? Lonely? Let down? Confused? Heartbroken? asked the poster.

Yep, thought Annie. Thank you for clarifying. Oh well. At least I'm in the right place.

Her mind tortured itself by dwelling on nasty thoughts. Sophie and Jake were probably already discussing their table plan with Fi and Tony. Would she have to go on the top table? The wedding would be in a grand hotel, Harry and Bertie would be page boys. She would be chief old maid. Would she have to get a special dress for that role?

How was Jake supposed to save her family now, when he had wedding plans to make? Hardly professional, was it, to get emotionally involved with his client's family—when they were paying him three grand a day to give them his all? Typical. (How well anger temporarily obliterated pain, thought Annie, as she got out of bed and went to clean her teeth. Angrily.)

When she came back into the room, feeling fusty from three hours' bad sleep, she found Joy sitting bolt upright in her chair, blinking wearily up at the ceiling.

"How was your shift?"

Joy rolled her head around slowly. "The usual. The odd pervert, a couple of depressives, one mad man and a double glazing rep."

"A good night then."

"No complaints."

"Coffee?"

Joy turned to her. "Shit. You look terrible."

"Thanks."

"What happened to you in the night? A visitation from the Ghost of Christmas Past?"

"More like the Future."

"Well, let me make the coffee. I'm not leaving you alone with a kettle flex."

Annie sat down in the silent room and curled up in her chair. When the phone rang, it seemed harsher than usual.

"Hello, Samaritans." It came out as a guttural expletive.

There was a pause and then someone spoke quietly and hesitatingly.

"Oh. I . . . I thought I was phoning for a pizza."

Oh dear. Her irate foghorn tone must have put them off. Some people were so touchy.

"And . . . how are you feeling?" Now she sounded impatient.

A pause. "Hungry."

Click.

Good, thought Annie. No room for empathy or sympathy today. Body and mind too full of pain.

As she was replacing the receiver, the phone went again.

Let's see if she could do better this time.

"Hello, Samaritans . . ." (Impatient, angry, cold.)

She gave Joy a smile as a strong coffee was dumped on her desk.

The person on the other end was trying unsuccessfully to get a grip of themselves. They were crying noisily. They were male.

"Take your time." (I'm not listening anyway. *You* think *you've* got problems.)

This only seemed to make the crying worse.

"I'm here now." (I'm still here. And getting bored.)

The crying increased in volume.

Eventually, it subsided somewhat.

"Sometimes it's hard to start, isn't it?" (Go on, hang up on me. You know you want to.)

The crying turned into howling.

Annie closed her eyes, listening to every nuance of pain at the other end of the phone. The caller was now trying to say something. It sounded like "Give me a song." Surely not?

"I'm sorry, I can't understand what you're saying." (I'm a Samaritan, not a mind reader.)

More crying.

"Take deep breaths." (Take one really deep one.)

"Shin for a Long!" said the voice, definitely angry.

She frowned into the phone.

"Shin for a long?"

"NO!" shouted the voice, furious. "Cynthia's GONE!"

Annie kept frowning.

"Left me," continued the voice. "I woke up to find a note, a bloody Dear John note," and the crying started up again.

Joy yawned loudly from her seat in the corner.

"Cynthia?" asked Annie.

Joy stopped yawning.

"My wife, who do you bloody think? God, Annie, get a grip! It's me who's in trauma, not you!"

How did the caller know her name? Annie was stumped.

"I woke up early this morning, because my shift starts at eight, thought it was a bit quiet, realized that Cynthia wasn't in bed, went downstairs, found a bloody note on the kitchen table. She's taken the boys. Left me for a bloke from work." And the crying started again, only this time it was much weaker.

Annie's jaw dropped. It was Marlon.

"Oh my God, Marlon, I'm so sorry."

"Oh thanks. That's all right then. I won't kill myself because although my wife and boys have all LEFT ME, Annie Bleeding-Heart Markham feels sorry for me." Big sniff. "And there I was thinking my life was over."

Oh shit, anger. Annie knew what that meant. Big pain.

She let him sniff noisily into the phone. She looked over at Joy.

She suddenly saw Marlon in her mind's eye, wandering blithely into the office, wearing a stupid scarf, grinning inanely, harassing Joy, who pretended she hated it but lived for every line. Annie knew that the memory of that would have sustained her in New York. Why did this have to happen now? Couldn't it have waited a week until she'd gone?

She was only slightly surprised at how quickly her thoughts had turned to self-pity. She really was a crap Samaritan.

"Come into the office now, Marlon. The kettle's just boiled."

Silence.

"There's a parcel here for you."

Nothing.

"We've got chunky KitKats."

Cynthia had never let him keep chocolate in the house. Bad example to the boys.

"Thanks," said a muffled voice.

She put the phone down.

Joy stared at her.

"Cynthia's left Marlon. He's in a bad way," said Annie to the room, picking up her bag and coat.

Joy's internal organs jump-started. No jump leads required.

"I'm just popping out to get chunky KitKats."

Joy nodded.

"Bring me a dozen."

"Ooh! Look at that!" exclaimed Joy in confused awe, holding up a very odd contraption to Marlon and Annie. Unable to tell exactly what it was, she read the blurb that came with it, putting as much exhilaration into her voice as was humanly possible. "A Spinal Rack and Neck Stretcher!" She looked over at them both. They both stared back at her. "Wow!" she said, not altogether unconvincingly.

Marlon was unimpressed. He looked terrible. His eyes were sunken into his face and his skin had turned a soggy yellow.

Joy put down the contraption and sat next to him. He didn't seem to see either of them properly. He didn't eat his chunky KitKats, though their presence strangely soothed him. Until Joy ate them all.

The three of them just sat for a while, Annie and Joy holding one of his hands each, while he sobbed intermittently. Every now and then he'd say "She's been having an affair for ten months," or "Even the boys have met him," or at one point, "I bet he's got more hair than me." Then he turned to Joy and seemed to focus for the first time.

"Joy, please accept my sincere apologies for playing with your emotions so ungallantly all these years," he said gravely, before sniffing.

"Don't be silly, Marlon."

"It was shameful of me," he said, shaking his head.

Joy nodded, as he started crying again.

"I understand, Marlon," she whispered. "You're all right."

The phone went.

The three of them stared at it.

"I'll get it," said Annie.

"No, I'll get it," said Joy.

"No, I'll get it," said Marlon.

They both looked at him as if he'd just announced he was pregnant.

"Let's hope it's a good'un," he said, giving his nose a final blow that by some miracle didn't blast his head off. "I need cheering up."

"Hello, Samaritans?" he said, a catch in his voice.

The caller hung up. He put the phone down slowly.

"OK," he said, pointing to the phone, his voice cracking. "Now *that* I take personally." And he started to cry again.

As Joy made Marlon a hot sweet tea in the unfamiliar setting of her own kitchen, he suddenly found himself overwhelmed by an awkwardness caused purely by her presence. It hit him what he'd miss most about Cynthia.

Cynthia—who by some fluke had agreed, in another time and life, to share his name, his address and his children, had given him courage. Courage like he'd never known in his life before. Courage to look in the eye the woman he was born to meet. Courage to hold a proper conversation with her. Courage to actually flirt with her.

Now Cynthia was gone, he had no one to close his eyes, kiss passionately and pretend was Joy. He had no one to help him pretend that flirting with Joy was harmless fun instead of walking the precipice between life and death, hope and despair, something he found impossible to do without blushing and getting tongue-tied. With Cynthia gone, he had no safety net against rejection, no daily reminder that it was mad to hope for your dreams to come true.

As Joy placed the drink gently on the table in front of him, he couldn't even look up at her.

Now that Cynthia was gone, Joy was lost to him.

He started weeping silently again.

★   ★   ★

It was their last night in London for a while. Victoria lay awake in the dark, her eyes wide open. Charles was taking off his trousers, jumping as he lost his footing, and placing them hurriedly on the back of the chair. Some change fell out of the pocket and he didn't bother to pick it up. Now he was undoing his shirt buttons at some speed, humming breathlessly to himself. His shoes banged noisily into the wardrobe door and his underpants slid to the floor at the foot of the bed.

She knew the signs.

Charles wanted sex tonight.

She lay with her back toward him, thinking a silent mantra. Not tonight, not tonight, not tonight.

She didn't have a headache. It was only sex with Charles that gave her headaches. She just couldn't face having to lie there pretending. It wasn't that she didn't particularly like what was going on, she just couldn't concentrate when Charles started busily kneading away, like a baker on his first loaf of the day.

Not tonight, not tonight, not tonight, she prayed, closing her eyes firmly.

She stopped breathing, waiting for Charles's shy, sly touch. Any second now. She just couldn't face it.

He hurrumphed loudly.

"Night then," he said as he rolled over and promptly fell asleep, a knack that she'd always envied.

Victoria lay there, listening. Was it a trick? Was he playing hard to get?

Nope. He was out cold.

With horrendous clarity, Victoria suddenly realized what was going on.

Charles no longer found her attractive.

A large tear slid down into her ear, causing her to go temporarily deaf.

She was alone in the world.

*   *   *

Charles closed his eyes. He was Nick Faldo, Victoria was his cad-
die and the boys were in the crowd. He took a perfect swing—
thwack! The crowd gasped as one, and the ball flew—like
magic—up, up, up into the clear blue sky and . . .

It was morning.

Chapter 19

Just days before Annie was to go to New York, she stopped visiting Sophie with the excuse that she had too much pre-trip organizing to do. Her forehead now looked much better, and she studied it every morning in the mirror watching it change from smudged aubergine to a subtle blend of sunflower and lilac.

She didn't seem to be suffering from any signs of shock after the attack apart from extreme weariness. And the recurring image of Jake holding her, tight and breathless in the pitch-black alley was becoming as tiresomely effective as a naff advert. Every fifteen minutes there it was; a perfect, freeze-frame image to remind her how crap real life was.

Bizarrely, at the same time, the incident had given her an inner confidence from knowing that she could protect herself in the worst possible situation. She had bought a mobile phone though, since the attack, now convinced that it was a potential life-saver in emergencies.

She had heard through Victoria, who was popping downstairs to see Sophie at least twice a day, keen to "look after" Sophie, while trying to glean as much pre-wedding gossip as possible, that Sophie was scared to go out. Jake was having to go out and get her anything she needed apparently, though always when she was being looked after by David.

How sweet, thought Annie. How whirlwind.

Victoria soon gave up visiting Sophie, however, as she grew more and more peeved when Sophie refused point blank to talk to her about Jake and the wedding.

Every second, Annie waited for the official news of Sophie and Jake's engagement.

The news could come from anyone—Sophie, Fi or Tony. All of them would think that she, together with Victoria and Charles, would be delighted to hear of a second wedding. She was steeling herself for it every minute of every day. Thank God she was going to New York in three days. Physical distance from Jake was just what she needed. Physical distance from her life would be even better, but you can't have everything.

"What will Mummy do without her darling boys?" Victoria asked Harry and Bertie dramatically when she kissed them goodbye.

"Shop?" answered Bertie.

Victoria grinned. "That's my boy," she said and felt a speed-bump jolt of excitement in her gut. Fifth Avenue! Madison! Broadway! The opera! Crap TV! Lie-ins! No doo-doos! She might burst with excitement.

The dreaded call didn't come and Annie found herself leaving England without having to pretend to anyone that she was delighted about Jake's forthcoming nuptials.

However, this did nothing to make the flight more bearable.

Susannah and their father had forbidden them from going first class and they had had to slum it in business. Annie had tried to persuade them that "Cattle class" was sufficient but was shouted down most unceremoniously. There was cost-cutting and there was torture, Victoria had cried. The safety video came on, and over piped music a soft female voice calmly explained what they should do "should the oxygen supply fail."

"Pray?" suggested Victoria to Annie next to her, who had gone an impressive shade of almond white. She hated flights.

Typically, a fitful toddler was seated in the row in front of Victoria, Charles and Annie.

"Look!" ordered its desperate mother, after it had cried non-stop for ten minutes. "Sweeties!"

The baby looked. It seriously considered the sweeties.

"Mmmm," encouraged its mother emphatically.

The baby seriously considered its mother's noises. Then it thrust the sweeties into her face and screamed till it went puce.

Victoria made up for all the people who had ever tutted at her when her boys had cried in public. She tutted for England. She almost rubbed her upper gum off.

"Should they allow babies in business?" she asked Charles twice very loudly.

"Yes, dear," he replied just as loudly, before undoing his seatbelt, kneeling down by the baby's seat and showing it his Silly Face. It not only shut up the baby, but most of the customers and staff.

Annie looked out of the window and watched the clouds obscure her view of diminishing streets and cars.

When the food arrived, Victoria realized she'd forgotten to ask ahead for a vegetarian meal. Sod it, she thought, I'm trapped. I'll have to eat whatever they give me. The feeling of relief was enormous.

It was beef. She turned to Charles.

"If I get BSE, will you shoot me?"

"I promise."

The flight was only seven hours long, and for Charles and Annie, it went very quickly. For Victoria, who chose to watch *The Horse Whisperer*, it felt like ten. Eventually, they arrived at JFK Airport at five in the afternoon. Shirley had arranged for a car to pick them up and take them straight to George's apartment. Victoria grew more and more excited as they drew nearer. This was more like it; this was where she belonged. Big cars, big buildings, big people. She breathed in the air and felt dizzy with excitement.

Here she was at last. The city of high risk, high speed, high cho-
lesterol and low toilet seats. And no children hijacking her sense
of self.

As they drove over the Queensborough Bridge, the Manhattan
skyline hit the horizon. Victoria felt the stirrings of excitement. It
was all out there, just out of reach, happening without her. She
could hardly wait to get out there and shop. Then the limo turned
a sharp right and they were facing a rundown tenement block.

Charles felt increasingly detached from all that was going on
around him. The city was so different from his own traditional
country background—not a golf course in sight—and he couldn't
help but be aware of how happy Victoria was in these surroundings. Could he ever make her happy?

"This is where it all starts," Victoria was rapturing. "We're just
pale imitators—you name it, it started here—aerobics, jogging,
roller blading, skinny latte, the internet—"

"Date rape, yardies, gridlock—"

"Shut up, Charles."

Annie was merely feeling as distant from her family as usual. She
sat in the car, eyes barely registering the changing scenery, ears
barely hearing Victoria's commentary. The break from Jake was
only serving to make him more vivid in her mind. She could see
him now, touching the back of his neck, chewing his lower lip . . .

His constant presence was so real, that if he'd stepped out from
behind one of the buildings now she'd only wonder what had
taken him so long to get there.

She was also desperately worried about Marlon and Joy. But
when she remembered that she was driving toward Edward, she
was delighted by a small but unmistakable twist of excitement in
her stomach. Wow! Was Edward going to be her cure?

Although George Markham told everyone that his apartment was on
Fifth Avenue, the entrance to it was technically on the corner of East

63rd Street. This caused a lot of confusion for first-time visitors, but George resolutely refused to bow down. As far as he was concerned, most of the rooms of the apartment overlooked the park. It felt like a Fifth Avenue apartment, so it was a Fifth Avenue apartment.

The smile from the doorman's face had just the right balance of blankness and obsequiousness to make Annie giddy with homesickness; Victoria with happiness. He helped them with their luggage and pressed the button in the elevator for them. "How civilized," sighed Victoria, closing her eyes with pleasure as they whizzed up to the penthouse apartment.

"Darlings!" exclaimed Katherine in the vast lobby.

"Pumpkin!" squealed Victoria.

The two sisters ran to offer each other their cheekbones and hugged without any bodily contact. Katherine welcomed Annie and Charles by turning her face away from them, allowing them graciously to kiss her powdered cheek.

She then led them into the drawing room, where her father and Davina sat self-consciously on separate sofas, pretending to read large hardback bestsellers. George pursed his lips into a smile.

"My dears!" he said and slowly got up.

Victoria ran to him.

"Daddy!"

"Pumpkin!"

Annie reached up and gave him a peck on the cheek.

"Father," she said calmly.

"Annie," he returned.

Davina hung back and when spoken to, made all the right noises and facial expressions. She was absolutely delighted to see them at last. Yes, wasn't the apartment beautiful. Of course, they must be exhausted and famished. She couldn't believe they'd finally got there—now the family was complete.

She was deferential yet hospitable, delighted yet humble. And Annie was surprised at how hostile she felt toward her. It seemed fully reciprocated. There was a new hardness in Davina whenever her cool blue eyes turned her way. Maybe it had always been there, and she was just noticing it for the first time, a new perception from having had a gap from Davina's company. She couldn't put her finger on exactly what was different—all she knew was that somehow, Davina's hard eyes made her feel more homesick for Joy and Marlon than her family's indifference to her.

With great effort, Annie returned all the right noises and facial expressions, hoping that she was as good an actress as Davina. What a waste of energy. And energy was so hard to come by at the moment.

The apartment was as luxurious and intimidating as they had all remembered. One entire side of it was floor-to-ceiling windows, providing stunning views over Central Park and beyond to the elegant, exclusive buildings of the Upper West Side. Specks of life were out there, jogging, roller-blading, power walking, strolling, and invariably just out of sight, mugging. It felt like the center of the world.

The plan was to spend the first evening enjoying an informal dinner together at the apartment. It would probably be the last evening they'd all spend in, let alone together—New York had too many restaurants, bars, clubs and theaters to waste staying in. But for now, the flat was enough of a novelty for everyone to want to remain together. And Victoria, Charles and Annie were too tired to go out.

They sat down on the sofas, while Davina busied herself making them all drinks and passing around the canapés, and George busied himself showing off about their exploits in New York.

"We've dined with the Houselmans twice," he started. "Spectacular place they've got, although I prefer our views, and we met Hollywood star Ginnie Salamon at the theater last week."

Victoria gasped. "Isn't she dead?"

"Almost," replied Katherine.

"What's she like?"

"Fat!"

"She's tiny!"

"The woman has a stomach you could sleep on." Katherine took a gulp of her bourbon and ice. "And her bottom! If she ever does a period piece, she won't need a bustle."

"Sounds perfect," muttered Charles quietly into his gin.

"Wasn't she beautiful though?" asked Victoria.

Katherine shook her head. Bones jarred from the sudden movement. "Too much makeup," she grinned and sighed. "It was wonderful to meet her. Oh and then there was Amanda Mortimer. I never realized how tacky that woman was—I swear, you could smell the Charlie on her."

"Oh my God, how disgusting!"

"I didn't know it had a smell," said Victoria, astonished.

Katherine looked at her sister as though she was mad.

"It's a perfume, darling, of course it's got a smell."

"Oh the perfume! Oh I see. Oh, how common."

There was a pause in the conversation.

"Can we do Bergdorf-Goodman's tomorrow, Kate?" asked Victoria.

Katherine looked over at Davina.

"We've rather done it to death, haven't we, darling?"

I see, thought Annie. And I thought we were all on a budget. She hadn't really expected anything less, but the knowledge that her family had been busy spending money they couldn't afford concerned her greatly.

Davina looked at Katherine innocently.

"I'd be delighted to go again," she said to both sisters, her expression a study in artlessness.

"Annie will go with you," said Katherine.

Annie and Victoria glanced at each other, nonplussed.

"Actually I was thinking of going to the Guggenheim," said Annie quietly.

"Oh," said Victoria. "Do they do couture there?"

Annie maintained eye contact for as long as possible to make sure Victoria wasn't joking.

Victoria maintained it back.

Nope. She wasn't joking.

"It's a museum of modern art," Annie said finally.

There was silence.

Annie looked hesitantly around at her family. Five pairs of eyes stared unblinking at her. She felt as if she'd just announced that for her next trick she would snort all the canapés up her nose while standing on one leg whistling "Abide with Me" and wearing a duck costume. Mind you, at times like these, she felt tempted to do that just to ease the tension.

"They've got an exquisite gift shop," she added, rather weakly.

Her family let out their breath as one.

She sat down, suddenly overcome by jet lag.

"You're more than welcome to go together—without me," Davina was saying, her mouth and eyes round with innocence.

Doesn't she get a headache pulling that face all day, thought Annie.

George coughed suddenly and ran his hand through his thick hair, trying not to smile at the thought of everyone going shopping except him and Davina.

"I'm sure you'd love to go with your sister," finished Davina.

Katherine ignored Davina completely and said,

"Oh what the hell! We'll all go again—I don't suppose it will harm us, will it, Davvy?"

Victoria was delighted and Annie was impressed by Davina's act of being thrilled by the decision.

Katherine was genuinely glad to have her sisters there with her. In two months she had progressed from feeling the town was full of eligible men to knowing that there were only two who were remotely acceptable, one of whom was more in love with his car than any woman, the other who had a back hairier than his head. Must she always compromise?

But now that her sisters were here, she could enjoy the status of Weary Expert through their eyes. Nothing made being a know-all as much fun as having witnesses.

The chef suddenly appeared to announce that dinner would be ready in exactly forty minutes.

Conversation was abruptly called to a halt.

"Time to dress for dinner," announced George.

Annie was surprised to find that her memory of the apartment had been unnecessarily harsh. Her suite really was beautiful and she realized that if she wasn't happy to be here, at least she wasn't miserable. Deliciously thick cream carpet sank beneath her bare feet and the proportions of her room were so pleasing as to make her feel that despite her unhappiness, all was right with the world. She'd never before appreciated the power of proportions. She unpacked her clothes, had a quick, invigorating shower and then lay on the bed, wearing only a toweling robe.

So many people out there, she thought, barely able to hear the taxis hooting miles below. Every now and then a siren halted midway through its call. She sighed. Poor poor Marlon. Poor, poor Joy. But more importantly, poor me.

She must get access to a computer so that she could e-mail them straightaway.

She must not get maudlin. This was her new life.

Edward Goddard is here in this city. He thinks he's in love with me. I am lovable. I'm safe and warm and clean in an ugly world. I have nice hair.

Then she stretched out on her bed and slowly closed her eyes. And saw Jake, breathless and urgent, in a dark London alleyway.

She opened her eyes quickly and stared at the ceiling.

★   ★   ★

Charles was ready first. He wandered into the drawing room and stood looking out at the view. He didn't hear Annie come in behind him.

"Pretzel?" she asked, for want of anything else to say, picking up a bowl of snacks and offering him some.

"Hmm? Oh no thanks," he said, stroking his paunch lovingly. "Don't want to spoil my appetite."

"No of course not," said Annie, putting the pretzels on the coffee table.

They stood staring down at the view together in silence.

Davina was next to join them. She went straight to the coffee table.

"Pretzel?" she asked immediately, in a tone far more conducive to spoiling an appetite than Annie's. She held them enticingly close to her bronzed chest.

"Oh why not?" said Charles, taking a handful. "Whet my appetite."

Annie refused the offer, shaking her head mildly.

"Have you been enjoying yourself?" she asked Davina.

"Oh, I've been having a wonderful time," Davina replied, holding the pretzels so close to her chest they gave her an even more impressive cleavage. "Of course," she rushed, "I've also been liaising with the office constantly, talking to the consultants back in Britain, keeping your father up to date." She smiled sweetly at Annie. "Must earn my keep."

Annie smiled sweetly back and couldn't think of a thing to say.

Just then George appeared. He stared obediently at Davina's bosom.

"Ah pretzels!" he bellowed.

Davina walked forward to him with them still in her hand.

"Never resist a pretzel!" he announced to the others, as he took a handful. Annie wasn't sure if this was a statement or a command.

Katherine was close behind him and she went straight to the drinks cabinet where she poured herself a Scotch.

And then Victoria came in behind them. She was rather flushed with all the excitement of being in New York and had paid extra attention to her makeup and hair tonight, in a desperate attempt to take the attention away from her body.

"Right!" said George, on seeing his daughter appear. "Dinner time!"

They all trooped into the cozy fourteen feet by fourteen feet dining room. Placecards had been left on the empty plates.

Once everyone had found their places, they stood for a brief moment waiting for George to sit down.

"You look—you look—*lovely,*" said Charles across the table to his wife. The sentence had started off as a simple, open, honest expression of sentiment. So why had it grown embarrassing as he'd said it? His embarrassment made him self-conscious and his self-consciousness made him ashamed.

Victoria looked up at him stunned.

Is this what her family did to Charles? Terrified him into paying her empty compliments that made him blush?

"What do you mean *look* lovely, Charles? Are you saying it's all an act?"

"I-I-I—" Charles was baffled.

Katherine laughed. Oh, she'd missed her family.

"No, I—"

"Oh God, Vicks," scoffed Katherine. "Don't go paranoid on us, just because you've put on weight."

Charles felt his wife's humiliation.

"So what if she has?" he asked heroically, ready to confess the depth of his feelings for his wife as never before. But a sickening gasp swept around the table. It would have taken a stupider man, even than Charles, not to realize that he'd just made a boo-boo. Something had to be done. And fast.

"What . . . what I mean to say is," he said, his sweat glands making their presence known to him, "is . . . is who wants to be a cold, hard, skinny bitch?"

Victoria stared at him, too surprised to reply that that was her ideal of womanhood.

Charles turned suddenly to Katherine.

"No offense, Katherine," he said quickly.

Katherine looked surprised.

"None taken, Charles."

Davina started to blow her nose loudly.

"I mean—" continued Charles, his sweat glands now making their presence known to everyone.

"It's all right, Charles," said Katherine, starting to take offense. "You know what they say . . . Sticks and stones may break my bones, but at least I'm not *fat*."

Davina started coughing into her handkerchief, her eyes watering.

Charles was lost. He had absolutely no idea what to say. How come he always started off saying the right thing but ended up blubbering offensive crap? Why was it such a long and tortuous journey from his brain to his mouth? He looked desperately at his wife. She couldn't meet his eye.

Annie didn't know who to try and save first. She looked over at her father to see how he was reacting. He was checking his reflection in the silver knife.

"Well," hissed Victoria finally to her husband. "I may be fat but at least I don't have a face like a palsied chicken."

Davina dropped her fork and dived under the table to retrieve it.

And with that, Victoria rushed out, leaving them all to a delightful, informal family dinner.

"It's not that I don't love him," said Victoria through her tears. "I just . . . I just want to kill him."

"Yes," said Annie. "Sometimes it must get like that."

"No, not sometimes," said Victoria in a low voice. "All the time."

"Ah."

"Hatred is so exhausting, Annie. Resentment and hatred. Disil-

lusionment, resentment and hatred. No wonder I'm tired all the
time. He's just so . . . so . . ."

". . . Enigmatic? Most men are."

"Enigmatic?" scoffed Victoria. "The only thing enigmatic about
Charles is his driving. He thinks indicators are for girls. No. He's
just insensitive to my—"

"Demands?"

"Needs."

"Oh."

Annie looked out at the night rain. If only Victoria could
learn to become responsible for her own happiness, instead of
blaming poor Charles all the time. It could change everything.
Annie was starting to see that if she had taken responsibility for
Jake all those years ago, instead of handing it over to Susannah
on a plate . . .

Maybe she could get Victoria to see that taking responsibility for
her own life was a viable option. It would take sensitive handling,
but it could be done.

"What would make you happy?" she asked eventually.

Victoria considered the question seriously.

"A husband who did everything for me."

Maybe not.

Annie wanted desperately to go to sleep, but she knew that Victoria needed cheering up. Charles had gone out after dinner and
wasn't back yet.

"How about tomorrow we do a bit of shopping and treat our-
selves to coffee in Greenwich Village?" suggested Annie.

Victoria grimaced. "Why would I want to go to Greenwich Village?" she asked.

"All right, coffee at The Waldorf then."

Victoria sniffed. "You go," she said. "I want to stay in tomorrow.
Go to your precious Gluggenstein shop."

★   ★   ★

Later that night, Annie found the apartment office: she was tired and it was dark but she managed to turn the computer on and log on to the internet.

She wrote a quick note to Joy and then one to Marlon, asking how they both were, giving her address and, should they ever need it, her phone number. She clicked on send, turned off the computer and left the room.

Chapter 20

Annie stood on the sidewalk, her teeth chattering with the cold, facing a winter splendor that was Central Park. She had been here a week now and had been stunned to discover that in the few years since she'd last visited, she had changed enough to like this city.

She'd walked to the heaving, bustling theater district, where people spoke so loudly in the street that she kept thinking they were about to start hitting each other, then all the way back to the Upper East Side with its shiny brass fire hydrants and glossy dog walkers clutching their even glossier dogs.

For the first few days, she had felt horribly self-conscious, as if a neon sign shone from her forehead broadcasting the fact that she was a tourist. She felt convinced that everyone else shared a common understanding of the way of the world. They understood how the subway worked, how the grid system worked, how the language worked, how the money worked. And she was on the outside looking in.

But that feeling didn't last long. Gradually things became clearer. And in fact they became even clearer than they had been at home. Nothing here was left to chance or was left unsaid. Every public building stated boldly how many people it could hold, every street was one way and everyone spoke from the heart without embarrassment or shame. She began to wonder how she'd survived in London for so long, in dangerously overcrowded public buildings, filled with people who were so repressed they were all waiting to go home and grow their ulcers in peace and quiet.

The Christmas decorations were the same as at home and the Bing Crosby seasonal songs bursting forth from the shops into the streets reminded her of London. But everything else was larger, louder and faster here. It was as if someone had turned up the volume and fast-forwarded reality. She felt invigorated.

Tomorrow she was having the first catch-up meeting with Edward and her father, so she could update Susannah back home on how everything was going. It would be the first time she'd seen Edward since he'd visited her at home. He'd left a message on her answerphone explaining his visit to New York—"to check everything was going to plan in the Big Apple" and his voice had been full of affection.

She was somehow feeling more optimistic about the outcome of her father's company. She didn't know why—it was as if the size and focus of New York had simply sharpened her positive emotions. Life seemed to be happening to her again.

She pulled her coat and scarf tight around her body and strode to Central Park where she watched the roller bladers, cyclists, scooters, joggers and walkers speed over and under the manmade bridges, personal stereos and mobile phone attachments glued to their ears. No wonder Americans find England quaint, she thought. She felt positively anachronistic sitting there with her unhampered feet and ears. She might as well have worn a corset.

Just then her new mobile phone went off and because she was a tourist, she didn't feel any sense of embarrassment whatsoever. That was, until she took off her mittens and started to use the thing.

"Annie, you'll never guess!"

"Hello?"

"The second wedding, you'll never guess who it is!"

"Who is this?"

"Annie? Is that you?"

"Yes, who is this?"

"It's VICTORIA, for Christ's sake. Annie, it's not *Jake* and Sophie—it's David and Sophie! Can you believe it?"

"What's David and Sophie?" asked Annie, too cautious to believe her ears.

"The second wedding—Sophie's engaged to that short, divorced management consultant! Can you believe it?"

No, she couldn't.

"I said, CAN YOU BELIEVE IT? Jesus, you know how to spoil good gossip, don't you?"

"No, I can't," laughed Annie. "I can't believe it."

Annie screamed into the phone with delight. Well, she didn't want to spoil Victoria's good gossip.

"I CAN'T BELIEVE IT!" she yelled, laughing.

"I *know!*" Victoria started giggling.

"He's so *short!*" squealed Annie.

Victoria had instant hysterics.

Annie had forgotten how easy it was to make Vicky laugh.

"He's a management consultant! She'll never be able to move in polite society again."

Vicky choked.

"He's not Jake!"

They whooped with laughter.

"He's the Other One!"

"Sophie's choice!" roared Vicky down the phone. "Did we need any more proof that the girl has the IQ of a rabbit?"

Annie exploded on cue into hysterics. No one in the park even looked at her. God, she loved America.

"He's now my brother-in-law." Victoria was suddenly serious. "Fuck."

"I'll be home in a mo," said Annie quickly. "You sound like you need cheering up. Thanks for the good gossip, sis."

The sun broke through some cloud and Annie was suddenly bathed in winter warmth. Jake wasn't going to marry Sophie! This amazing fact warmed her right through and she started running home. Then suddenly it occurred to her that Jake was still as estranged from her as ever and, worse still, might now be heartbroken.

She stopped running suddenly. And the sun hid again behind a cloud the size of Manhattan Island.

When she arrived home, she found Victoria on the phone to Fi. Charles was out. It was indeed going to be a double wedding in the New Year. Probably Easter. Fi was delighted—she thought David was wonderful. Tony already adored him.

As soon as Victoria got off the phone, she started talking nineteen to the dozen. Annie managed to glean how the David and Sophie story had happened.

During the very early stages of Sophie's recovery, while Jake was out at work all the time and David was always around in the evenings, Sophie had realized with exquisite horror that she was with The Wrong Man.

The poor young girl had said nothing, hoping against hope that the problem would somehow solve itself. And it did, spectacularly. Jake's hours were so long that she fell out of love with the Company Boss. And then fell in love with David.

The End.

"And they're both determined to marry immediately!" finished Victoria.

"And how do you feel about it now?" asked Annie.

"Better," said Victoria firmly. "There's something stubborn about Jake that I didn't notice at first. Not nice to have that in the family. God knows where it might end. Oh no. She made the right decision after all. Good girl."

Annie grinned openly at the way her sister's sheer selfishness had helped her find life's silver lining.

But how was Jake feeling? She had to know.

"Shall we do Madison Avenue?" Victoria asked excitedly. "I've got to get an outfit for the weddings. Katie and Davina are there already—we could meet them for coffee—I could give Katie a ring on her mobile—" she was already at the phone.

E-mail. Annie could e-mail David. Congratulate him. Ask how they all are. Hint at Jake.

"You go ahead," she instructed Victoria. "I've just got to do something."

She went to her bag and found David's card. His e-mail address was at the bottom. She went straight to the office. She gasped. The view over the park was spectacular. The tops of the trees made a russet and yellow carpet, undulating toward the splendor of Upper West Street. The silence was almost moving. Next to the window was a small, unobtrusive intercom speaker interconnecting all the rooms—there was also one in the hall, the drawing room, the kitchen and her father's bedroom. They used to have an intercom system in their London home, but they had got rid of it a few years ago when her father had had the place redecorated. They had all preferred life without it. After all, what was the point of being able to afford a place big enough to lose each other in, if you couldn't lose each other in it?

She tapped in David's address and started typing a message. After much deleting and swearing, she read the final version. It was chatty, informal and polite. Interested without being inquisitive. Chirpy without being ecstatic. She re-read it once more and clicked on the Send icon.

Then she spotted that she'd had two messages. One from Marlon and one from Joy. For some reason, she clicked on Marlon's first.

Darling one!

What a nice surprise! How nice of you to think of me! How's New York?

I'm having a nervous breakdown. Everything's meaningless
without the woman of my dreams.

How are you?

Marlon

Oh dear. Annie replied immediately. It wasn't as easy as she
thought it would be. How can you listen sympathetically on e-
mail?

She typed in that time helped.

Well, that was one of life's biggest lies. Time didn't help—it just
made you older.

She deleted.

She typed in that she loved him and would always be there for
him.

That was more about easing her guilt about leaving the country during his biggest crisis than helping him through this bad
patch. And she wasn't coming back, so it was hardly true.

She deleted.

She typed in that Joy would always be there for him.

But she knew that Joy had feelings for Marlon that he couldn't
return. She didn't want to put either of them in a painful position.

She deleted.

With a big sigh, she started her fourth version.

Marlon

New York is great. My family is mad.
I love you.

Annie

Now for Joy's message. She clicked it open.

OK, when he flirted with me it was an insult. One long bloody insult. An insult to my self-respect, to my intellect and to my clothes sense. Not to mention to his wife.

Now he's stopped and I want to kill him.

It's like he's gone into himself. I can't get through anymore. And do I really want to? Can you imagine how painful it is trying to help the man you love get over another woman? No, of course you can't, you pretty young thing.

How's New York? How's your family?

Write soon

Love
Joy xxxx

Annie started to type in that time helped.

She deleted.

She typed in that she loved her and would always be there to help.

She deleted.

She typed in that maybe there was something more to Marlon's flirting—maybe, who knew?—Marlon had latent feelings for her? . . .

She deleted.

She typed in that what gave Joy the right to think she had a fucking autonomy over feelings? Yes, she *did* know how painful it was to help a man get over another woman, since she asked . . .

She deleted.

She started again.

Joy

New York's great. My family's mad.
I love you.

Annie

She turned off the computer and stood staring out at the view for a moment.

A voice made her jump.

"Hello there, you're not working are you?"

Charles was standing behind her, his face more lugubrious than Eeyore's.

Annie smiled enough for two at him.

"Where've you been?" she asked, her voice bearhug warm. "Haven't seen you for ages."

"You're the only one who's noticed," he said morosely. "I've just been mooching, nothing special. Not over enamored of the place, must admit."

"Fancy popping down to SoHo or Greenwich Village for a coffee?" asked Annie.

Charles perked up. A village, he thought. Sounded almost like home.

Charles stared uncomfortably at the waiter's nipple, which bulged underneath his skin-tight T-shirt.

"It's pierced," explained Annie, when they'd finished their order.

Charles nodded thoughtfully. He wondered what the boys at the golf club would say about that. He realized with some surprise that he didn't give a damn.

"Everything I do is wrong," he mumbled. "I can't do a thing right. I don't know *how* to do anything right, because I don't know what she wants anymore."

A T-shirt-clad pierced nipple temporarily obliterated his view of the world. When it had gone, there was a café latte in front of him on the table. Magic.

"Have you talked to her?" asked Annie.

Charles snorted and then shook his head.

"I'm going back home," he said with a final push of energy. "Got a flight late tonight. We need some distance. I miss the boys. I'm doing no one any good being out here."

Oh my God, thought Annie. Make or break time. She knew there was no point in trying to change his mind. What could she do? In desperation, she heard herself say to him,

"E-mail her, Charles. Regularly, I mean."

E-mail could be profound. You could say things on e-mail without blushing. You could slice through all the hurt and embarrassment of social interaction and experience the essence of pure communication. She thought of the e-mails she'd sent Marlon and Joy. Well, you couldn't do worse than Charles did in person.

Charles looked at her thoughtfully.

"Hmm," he said, his voice so low it sounded like distant thunder. "If I remember."

"Thought I'd go back home," Charles told Victoria.

Typical, thought Victoria. Just when things were getting exciting. She raised an eyebrow.

"Miss the boys, miss golf, miss, well, you know, miss being . . . me . . ."

"Are you saying I don't miss the boys? And as for missing being you, now you know how I feel being a single parent twenty-four hours a day."

"New York just . . . I'm not home . . . it's . . ."

Oh, what the bloody hell was he trying to say?

"Charles, must you always obfuscate?"

"Must I what?"

"Why can't you just talk to me in plain English? Sharing a language is one of the few things we actually have in common."

"Not sure I agree with you there, actually."

What did he mean by that? That they had more in common than that, or less?

She suddenly felt lonely.

"Will you come back with the boys?"

Charles shrugged.

"Oh great," said Victoria, finding her breath unexpectedly heavy. "I'll be a single mother again."

Charles didn't answer.

"Fine. Give the boys my love." She felt an unexpected pang. "Tell them I'm looking forward to seeing them."

Charles waited for Victoria to come to kiss him.

She left the room quickly.

Chapter 21

Annie woke feeling bright and bubbly. She was to sit in on the first of Edward's updates with her father, make notes and relay them back to Susannah at home. Adrenaline surged through her body at New York speed. A quick walk around the park, hot coffee and a bagel and then the meeting at eleven. Excellent.

Even though it was only eight in the morning, the manic park exercisers were all out in force already. Annie had to dodge them as she took in the morning views and sounds. Occasionally people actually smiled at her, some said hello or "morning," others asked her how she was, wished her a good day.

She sat at her already favorite bench, munching her bagel and sipping her hot coffee, until she felt too cold to stay still any longer. Then she made her way back to the apartment with a bounce in her step. Was it New York that was doing this to her, or the feeling of hope from Edward's attention or the news about Jake? Either way, she felt as though her life was starting up again.

She couldn't quite equate the fact that Jake being newly single made her feel good, which in turn made her feel good about Edward. What was going on there? Did she need Jake to become free and available again to realize that she really was ready to move on? Did this prove that she was now ready for Edward? Of course! That made perfect sense. If Jake had been with Sophie, she'd have felt that being with Edward was "making do." Or was she still kidding herself? Was Jake pining for Sophie and was she coping with that by turning to Edward? Oh God, brain ache. Don't try and work out the confusing signals, work on the facts.

The facts: Edward was interested. Jake wasn't. Act on the facts and you can't go wrong, she told herself. Go for it with Edward. Forget Jake. She spotted the Walk sign and started to walk confidently across the road. Where she was almost run over by a stray taxi.

Edward had suggested popping into her father's apartment for the meeting, rather than making him come all the way to the 52nd Street office. Annie was initially disappointed—she'd been looking forward to dropping in to the nearby Museum of Modern Art afterward—but after a friendly chat with the doorman whom she had grown to like very much, she decided it would be nice to have Edward in the apartment. She wondered briefly if he liked art as much as she did. And which period would be his favorite? Was he a Pre-Raphaelite man? Or an Impressionist lover? A modern art fan, maybe? Or possibly portraits were his thing.

As she closed the apartment door behind her, she could hear voices in the lounge. She glanced at her watch: 10:30 a.m. It couldn't be Charles, he had already gone home in the dead of last night to catch the first flight he could get. It couldn't be Edward, he wasn't due here for another half an hour. Who was it? Before taking off her coat and scarf and checking her reflection in the hall mirror, she popped her head around the corner of the door, her eyes alert.

There stood Edward and her father, enjoying an early morning coffee.

"Ah, Annie, m'dear, do come in," said George warmly.

Annie walked into the room, choosing to enjoy her father's warmth and ignore the novelty of it. Her father was clearly keen to create a happy family atmosphere in front of Edward. Maybe Edward could do the whole family good, not just her.

She was grateful that her cheeks were flushed from the walk, because she knew that if they weren't, the directness of Edward's gaze would have had too obvious an effect.

"Hello, Edward," she said, taking his outstretched hand for a formal handshake.

"Hello, Annie," he replied, holding her hand as firmly as her gaze.

Annie was enjoying the experience so much, she didn't even mind Davina joining them with a notebook and pen at the ready.

"I'm so sorry," gushed Davina, glancing quickly at her watch. "Am I terribly late?"

Edward and Annie turned to her reluctantly. For all her profound apologies, Annie could sense that Davina was put out by Edward's early arrival.

"Good God no, my dear," assured George, patting her on the shoulder. "Better late than never, eh?"

Annie was surprised at how curt Edward seemed with his pretty, blonde, leggy marketing director. In fact, all Davina received from her chief executive was a negligible nod of the head.

Annie looked at Edward afresh.

Until now, she'd felt fairly sure he was an unusually sensitive man. Now though, she had her proof. Just like her, Edward had clearly picked up on the clues that Davina was untrustworthy. Clues that were as nebulous as fluffy, white, sun-blocking, rain-holding clouds. Annie was getting fonder of Edward by the minute. More than that, she felt for the first time in years that she had an ally. Slowly, drip by drip, the ice-cold sense of loneliness that shaped her life was starting to thaw.

"I would have got here earlier, actually," started Edward, ignoring Davina's hint that he had come before his appointed time. "Only I couldn't find the apartment. I thought you actually lived *on* Fifth Avenue—"

"Righty ho then!" exclaimed George loudly. "To the office."

Once inside the office, they all acted efficiently with each other. Impressive performances all around, thought Annie. All nearly as good as Davina.

Edward gave his business strategy update, interrupted only by George's occasional grunt of approval and Davina's less and less frequent questions.

Annie watched with delight as Davina's usually successful self-deprecation collapsed on Edward's deaf ears.

George nodded gravely at Edward every time he looked his way. Clever chap, good stock, nice face. Didn't understand a bloody word he was saying.

When Edward finished, George gave a long deep sigh.

"All sounds very impressive to me," he said, glancing straight over Annie at Davina. He sighed dramatically and wiped some imaginary dirt off the edge of the table and then thumped it, as if sweeping the meeting away.

"What say we to a morning drink?"

Edward grinned widely and started packing up his stuff.

Annie watched him, aware all the time that Davina in turn was watching her. She turned to her suddenly, delighted in shocking her into an unprecedented natural reaction. Davina blushed and looked away sharply.

As Edward finished packing, Annie suddenly remembered why she was here. To report to Susannah. Woops. The way she'd been concentrating, all she could probably tell Susannah was what color suit Edward was wearing and that she only thought of Jake twice during the meeting. Pathetic.

"Um, Edward—"

Edward shot her a charming smile.

"I don't suppose you have any, erm, anything in writing I could send to Susannah from this meeting, do you?"

He unclicked his briefcase.

"Of course."

Davina gave a little cough. Annie almost looked under the desk for a hiccuping Chihuahua.

"Perhaps we could arrange another meeting when Susannah gets here?" suggested Davina.

"Surely this is simpler," argued Annie, her smile fixed.

Davina returned the smile. "Of course."

They hated each other. It was official.

Without taking his eyes off Annie, Edward delved into the front pocket of his case and handed Annie a disk.

"Would you like me to add some of my latest marketing strategy to that?" asked Davina, her hand outstretched as Edward gave Annie the disk.

Annie turned to face Davina. What *was* going on? Was she suddenly trying to impress her? Or George? Or Edward? Was she actually trying to pretend that she was earning her keep by fulfilling her job description rather than her father's fantasies?

To her relief, Edward seemed totally unimpressed.

"I'm sure if Annie wanted that, she'd have asked for it," he said smoothly.

Davina tried to smile, but was unable to meet anyone's eyes.

"Of course," she said. She turned to George.

"Then I guess it's time for that drink," she grinned.

George seemed to wake up.

It was the nearest Annie had ever seen Davina get to losing her cool.

She was mightily intrigued. What had she just witnessed? Had Davina sensed the silent understanding between Edward and herself? Could she tell that they could see through her? Was she suddenly worrying for her safety now that they were both here?

As her father and Davina left the room, Edward started to close down the computer.

"Ooh look," he said, looking at the screen. "You've got a message."

"Have I?"

"Yup."

"Re: Congratulations!" he read. "Sounds interesting." And he gave her a warm smile.

"Are we still on for our date?" he murmured, his hand still on the mouse.

"Yes," she said. "That would be lovely."

George's voice called Edward from the drawing room.

"Tomorrow night?" asked Edward quickly.

Annie nodded, placing her hand on the mouse with his.

"I'll pick you up at seven. Enjoy your e-mail." And with that he whisked off to her father.

Annie sat in the chair. "Enjoy your e-mail." It was a long time since anyone had cared whether she enjoyed anything, she realized.

She double clicked, feeling foolishly special. Whatever was in this e-mail, it already held sparkling significance for her.

It was from David. The message was warm, direct and concise. And written by a moron.

Dear Annie

Thanks for your message! I'm so in love with Sophes I can hardly breathe!! Isn't she just the most beautiful, gentle, kind, brave girl in the world?

Tell Charles not to worry about Jake. The old bastard is absolutely fine about me and Sophes. Couldn't be happier. Said she was too good for him anyway. And who am I to argue with the boss?!!

Hope you're all well—we should be out there soon.

Love to all
David

Annie read and re-read the message. So Jake was only too pleased, was he? Hmm. Somehow, that didn't ring true for her.

Had Jake lied to David? Or lied to himself?

She had absolutely no idea. She couldn't pretend to know Jake anymore. And that hit her almost as badly as the news of his impending engagement to Sophie.

Ah, poor, poor Sophie. Doomed to a lifetime of being called Sophes. Thank God she had the IQ of a rabbit.

Annie closed down the computer and went to join her father, Davina and Edward for their drink.

Chapter 22

For their first date, Edward and Annie made a compromise. She chose where they ate, he chose where they drank afterward.

She chose what they talked about, who won which discussion, where they sat and when they smiled. He chose when they kissed.

Sweet Basil was a small café in the center of Greenwich Village. The food was good, but not as good as the jazz. While her family enjoyed the splendor of dinner jazz at Café Carlyle on the Upper East Side, Edward and Annie watched as an amazing fourteen-piece jazz band squeezed themselves on to a stage barely big enough for four. Against all the opulence of a pine-clad wall, they burst into life-affirming music and Annie's world briefly harmonized around her.

She looked over at Edward and found his bright eyes were on her, an affectionate smile on his handsome face. God, I'm gorgeous, she realized.

They made their way back to the Upper East Side, where Edward had discovered a tasty bar where the only light they used was candlelight. After half an hour, Annie's eyes adjusted and she was able to drink her drink without spilling it. It was the perfect nightcap to a perfect evening. And the alleyway advert hadn't appeared once. She looked at Edward—or rather his shadow—and found herself hoping that he was the concluding chapter to the Jake saga in her life.

When the taxi dropped Annie off at her apartment, Edward hopped out to see her to the door. They played the private space game—stared at each other for the appropriate nano-seconds and went in for the final kiss. It was almost too perfect.

Half-smiling, Annie closed her eyes and savored the momentous moment.

And then the alleyway advert started.

Behind her eyelids, as she felt Edward's lips touch hers, she saw Jake, inches away from her in the dark alleyway.

Bugger.

Twenty minutes later, as she brushed her teeth, looking at her reflection in the mirror, Annie realized that she couldn't ever imagine Edward losing his cool like she'd seen Jake do countless times. She couldn't imagine Edward falling for the likes of a twenty-year-old flippertygibbet who would prefer a man who called her Sophes. She couldn't imagine Edward running out in tears if she ever had to break bad news to him. He was solid, dependable, trustworthy.

Mind you, try as she might, she couldn't imagine Edward in an alleyway either.

She stared at herself in the mirror.

"But I can work on it," she told her reflection.

"Thank you for sending me the disk, darling," said Susannah over the phone. "It all looks fine to me."

"Good," said Annie.

"I suppose I ought to show it to Jake, but I don't really see the point."

"What do you mean?"

"My dear, I'll be honest with you. Jake Mead Associates have until the end of the year to sort Markhams' out and I don't think they're going to make it."

Annie's throat clammed up. So! Mastermind Jake Mead had

failed them all. They were ruined. It came as something of a surprise to Annie to discover that she'd have preferred him to have proved her wrong than right and actually saved them all. Was this, in fact, her punishment for putting her petty squabble before the family's need? No, probably not. She didn't believe in Divine Justice. Thank God.

So it was just bad luck that Jake had taken their money and had failed to use it to save them.

"I'm sorry, my dear, but . . . we're losing just as much money as ever. In fact, since Jake Mead has come in, we're losing more than ever before."

Annie couldn't think of anything to say. Well, anything to say that wasn't offensive.

For once, Susannah felt herself unable to console Annie. For once, she was truly terrified for their future.

"Please," said Annie eventually. "Just give that disk to Jake. Who knows? It might be our last chance."

Susannah sighed down the phone.

"He *was* our last chance," she said finally. "But OK. Why not? I'll give it to Jake."

Over the next week, when Annie wasn't thinking of the business, her family's inevitable bankruptcy, Davina's next move on her father, Edward's next move on her, or Jake in a bloody London alleyway, she spent her time wandering the streets of New York.

The Christmas countdown was in full swing and despite everything, Annie found herself carried away by the exhilarating atmosphere. New York was a city that assailed all her senses. She had forgotten how pungent its aromas were. She'd step out of a building and *wham*! Hot chocolate-roasted peanuts. Madison Avenue— expensive perfume. Central Park—horse dung.

Victoria and Annie's first shopping trip together was to be their last. While Victoria sighed longingly over some square-toed diamante-strapped, $425 sandals, Annie discovered Madison Avenue Bookshop next door. Victoria found her half an hour later, upstairs, sitting by the floor-to-ceiling window overlooking Sulka, Jaeger, MaxMara and Joseph, reading Jane Austen.

Victoria had not bought the shoes. This hit Annie hard. They really *were* in trouble.

She looked up at her sister. Victoria was looking mistily out of the window at the exclusive boutiques.

"Look at that view. It's beautiful." Her voice cracked with pain.

They agreed to meet back at the apartment, and both went their separate ways, hugely relieved to be alone.

Two hours later, a peroxide-blond assistant was showing Victoria a piece of silk that looked like it had been caught in a mangle.

"This is walking architecture," he accentuated. "You'd be wearing Art."

Victoria nodded in awe and tried not to care that she couldn't buy it.

Then, after a quick bite to eat, when she was safely away from Annie, Victoria kept finding herself in children's boutiques. And then once inside them, she kept finding herself guided, as if by a supernatural force, to the powder-blue sections—for four- to five-year-olds. And then she kept having to rush out before the tears came. Oh God, she missed her boys so much it was a physical ache.

Not long now, she kept telling herself. They'd be back soon—with or without Charles.

And so she wandered around the shops for hours, trying to whip up some enthusiasm for "walking art and architecture," but she just grew wearier and wearier. And the Americans. They were so friendly. All she had to do was open a road map and some stranger would appear by her side offering advice, without a by-your-leave. Didn't these people repress anything? It was enough to drive one mad.

And did they mean it when they said, "Hihowyadoin?"

Was she supposed to smile, answer, ask them how they were

doing in return or just ignore them? It was a language she didn't
understand. And the noise. If she heard one more siren, she was
going to go mad. She just wanted to be home, with the boys, with
Charles, with her family . . .

Just before her feet and emotions became too painful to bear,
she arrived back at the apartment. No one was there. She made
herself a big whisky, turned on the television before remembering
that every channel was rubbish, went into her room, shut the door,
sat on her bed and, to the sound of wailing sirens, howled.

Meanwhile, Annie was busy discovering her own New York.

She sought out silence and there was plenty of it once she knew
where to look. If she was feeling spiritual, all she had to do was
turn a sharp right angle away from the buzz of Fifth Avenue and
wander inside St. Thomas's Church, to gaze at the altar in wonder.
She could hop out of a taxi on 40th Street, plunge herself into the
echoing halls of the public library and sit on one of the exquisitely
carved wooden seats at one of the exquisitely carved wooden tables and lose herself in words for a day. Or she could stand in any
of the many museums and find herself transported to a world ripe
with silent meaning.

She spent many day-long outings with Fi hunting for wedding
dresses, while keeping an eye out for something that might suit Sophie. But when she was invited to join Fi and Tony on one of their
many wedding ring excursions, she was glad it was on the day they
chose to try the diamond district, New York's Hatton Garden, and
not Tiffany's. She had stood in a shop, looking out at the street, her
back to the sound of exaggerated cries from the vendors, and spotted a cat sleeping in the window of Gomez bookshop. The next
day she returned and was transported into a world of literary bliss.
You just had to know where to look for the silence.

When Edward had any free time from the office, he spent it
with Annie. She tried not to notice that it didn't concern her in
the slightest that he had hardly any free time.

*   *   *

Susannah was now in New York and her ever-present joy at Cass and Brutus's news about the triplets made her uncharacteristically positive about everything—except Markhams' prospects.

"I can't pretend, Annie," she said at an informal catch-up meeting over warm mulled wine in the foyer of The Waldorf, "I'm really worried."

Annie had updated her on everything she'd picked up so far and Susannah had taken it all in with a sorry face.

"How long do you think we've got?" asked Annie, the old terror resurfacing fast. Susannah sighed. "Who knows? The consultants have been with us for three months now and we don't seem to be getting anywhere. We brought them in to save us, but the money that was pouring out of the organization before they came is now hemorrhaging out at an alarming rate. I simply don't understand it. All the figures add up, we're not doing anything different, yet we have more and more money going out."

They sat in glum silence, watching the happy, wealthy hotel guests buzzing around them.

"I think we're going to have to let the consultants go," Susannah said finally. "First thing in the New Year. We simply can't afford them. Then we'll see if *we* can sell the business, but I won't pretend we'll get very much for it in this state. It's a sorry business, Annie, my dear. A sorry business."

Annie's body tensed. Jake would be out of her life again. For good this time.

She stared miserably at her cold mince pie, aware that Edward had suddenly become less attractive.

Later that evening, Annie checked her e-mails. Again, one from Joy, one from Marlon. This time she clicked on the one from Joy first.

Hi

How are things there?

You'll be pleased to hear Marlon is getting better. I take him out twice a week—just to get him out of the house. Oh, Annie, you should see it—Cynthia took everything. Even the photos of his boys—there are dark shadows all over the walls.

Occasionally he goes into himself and I can't get through to him—but I make sure that every time we see each other, we spend at least a little time talking about Cynthia. For God's sake don't tell him, but I do this for entirely selfish reasons. The faster he gets her out of his system, the faster there'll be room for me.

It's odd without the flirting. More real, more serious. More frightening.

Mother's got hemorrhoids and Carol says hi.

J xxxx

Annie smiled. She clicked on to Marlon's.

Light of my life!

How's New York?

I'm feeling a new man. Strictly between you and me, I'd rather be feeling a new woman, but the woman I'd like to be feeling won't stop bloody talking about Cynthia.

Bloody Samaritan.

I miss the boys.

Love
Marlon

Blimey, thought Annie. Marlon was over Cynthia! Marlon wanted Joy! If only they both knew . . .

And she could solve it all with a few taps on her keyboard.

What should she do? Tell Marlon that Joy was interested? Tell Joy that Marlon was interested? Or leave well alone and let it happen of its own accord? Should she be in such a position? Should she influence their future? Should she use her inside knowledge to give joy to those she loved? Or should she let them be masters of their own destinies and find out for themselves?

What to do, what to do . . .

She thought of Susannah and Cass and how they'd interfered with her life, positive that they were doing the right thing. She clicked on the reply icon.

> Dear M and J [she wrote to both of them]
>
> Everything's fine here. Business going down the pan. Family collapsing round ears. New York lovely.
>
> Love you
> Annie

She sat back and sighed heavily.

Why was every communication open to misunderstandings, complications, tangents? Why couldn't people just say what they meant? Why was it so difficult to be honest? When did we lose our childish honesty that made playgrounds such a heady combination of heaven and hell?

She sat staring into space.

The crude buzz of the intercom interrupted her thoughts. It was Victoria.

"Are you all right in there?"

Was she all right in there? No, not really. Life was a constant losing battle between meaning and worthlessness, gain and loss, communication and estrangement.

"Annie? Are you all right?"

"Yeah. Fine thanks," she said before something in Victoria's tone made her ask, "Are you?"

"No," gasped Victoria. "I've just had some terrible news."

Annie stood in the kitchen, frowning in disbelief at her sister. Victoria was holding on to the breakfast bar with one hand, her other still on the phone.

"What do you mean 'they're not coming back'?" asked Annie incredulously.

Victoria shed all pretense at not caring about Charles and the boys and started sobbing like a baby. Annie had to concentrate especially hard as she stuttered her explanation.

"Th-they're h-aving s-such a g-g-good t-time at h-home w-without m-me," wept Victoria, "and G-grandma and G-grandpa h-have g-got a . . ." she sobbed a bit more, "a *b-bouncy c-castle*."

She started wailing.

"But what about Christmas?" asked Annie, seriously worried.

Victoria looked up, her eyeliner smudged so much and her face so downcast that she looked like a badly drawn pierrot.

"If Ch-charles f-feels l-like it."

Then Victoria hugged Annie so hard, Annie thought she might not live to see Christmas herself. Suddenly Victoria stopped hugging her as her body became totally overcome by sobbing. Annie watched in horror as her sister's sobbing slowly turned to retching. She rushed her over to the sink.

To the relief of both, nothing happened and Victoria's sobbing slowly subsided into muffled whimpering.

They stood at the sink, Annie's arm firmly around Victoria.

"Does Charles know how you feel about this?"

Victoria shook her head and then rested it on Annie's shoulder.

"What did you tell him?"

Victoria blew her nose.

"I told him he could do what he wanted."

Oh for God's sake. Annie wanted to shake her.

"Is that what you feel, Vicky?"

Victoria thought for a moment. And then started sobbing again.

"Oh dear," said Annie. "What are we going to do with you?"

"What shall I do?"

"Isn't it obvious?"

Victoria shook her head.

Annie held Victoria by her shoulders and stared at her in the face. Victoria could hardly keep eye contact.

"I think it's time to be honest with your husband," said Annie.

That stopped Victoria in her tracks.

"What do you mean?" she whispered.

"I mean tell him how you feel about him. And the boys."

The two sisters stared at each other in the silence.

"I never thought of that," murmured Victoria, hope in her voice.

Dr. Blake couldn't believe her ears.

"Are you sure about this?"

"Never more sure."

"When I said closure, this wasn't quite what I had in mind."

"It wasn't quite what I had in mind either."

"But then you were thinking more revenge, as I recall."

He laughed.

"Was I?"

"As I recall, yes."

He shook his head at himself, smiling all the time.

Dr. Blake felt a bitter taste rise up in her mouth. She always hated this stage. It was like releasing an animal she'd nursed back into the wild. Part of her hated to see them go; part of her knew this was what her job was all about; part of her knew she'd miss them; part of her resented their sudden independence; and most of her was terrified at her loss of earnings.

So many parts. No wonder she talked to herself.

She looked at him with a quizzical smile.

"And this is all because of what 'hit you' in that alleyway?"

It was a low trick—manipulating him back into victim mode. She knew what she was doing, but couldn't stop herself. It was just happening so suddenly—she hadn't had time to prepare herself.

Jake nodded happily.

"Does that make . . . *sense* to you?"

Stop it right now! Stop it! Acting like a spoiled bitch instead of his psychotherapist. Well, I'm not his psychotherapist anymore, am I? He's chucking me. I can be as bitchy as I like. OK, stop talking to yourself, it's getting spooky.

Jake shook his head, grinning like a fool.

"Nope, I suppose it doesn't make any sense," he said. "But then nothing you said to me made much sense either. And this was far quicker and considerably cheaper."

Ouch! Get those claws in.

"Most alleyway transactions are, Jake."

Jake stared at Dr. Blake in shock. Did he detect a change of tone in her voice? A hint of bitterness maybe? Scorn, even? Was there a real person in there after all? He looked at her critically for the first time. She was much smaller than he'd pictured.

Typical—she only shows it when she knows he's leaving. Women were so bloody contrary.

He beamed warmly at her for the first time in seven years across the large, silent room.

Oh my God, she thought. He's really good looking. Out of his bloody tree, but really good looking. (Mind you, what more could she hope for in her line of work?)

She gave him a sad smile back and stood up. "Have a good trip."

Jake stood up too. Should he kiss her goodbye? Shake her hand? Hug her? Cry on her shoulder like a child?

She turned away and walked behind her desk before he could do anything. Safely there, she gave him a warm grin.

"I'll miss our sessions, Jake. I do wish you the best of luck."

"Thank you."

He almost added "You too," but sensed that it wouldn't go down well.

And, after seven years of therapy—followed by closure of a spectacular kind, Jake Mead turned and walked out of Dr. Blake's office for the last time.

Chapter 23

The day started bright, cold and fresh. Cass and Brutus would be arriving in the city later that afternoon and Annie's eagerness to see them lifted her slightly from her dip after Susannah's dire prediction of the family's future. Cass's pregnancy was going well so far.

Annie was to see them all at the Metropolitan Opera House that night. Her father, Katherine, Victoria and, of course Davina, were joining them and she had invited Edward. Tony and Fi were also coming after a day of sorting out their wedding list and Sophie was due to arrive today with David. Annie felt comforted by the thought of seeing them all.

Verdi's *Otello* meant little to any of them except Annie, but the extravagant beauty of the opera house and the idea of sitting in a box were enough to coax her family into coming.

"The good news is I managed to get us two boxes, the bad news is it's slightly restricted view," Annie had warned them when she'd bought the tickets.

"Restricted view?" her father exclaimed. "What's the point of going if people can't see you?"

"No. Restricted view of the stage. Not of you."

Her father was looking forward to it immensely.

Annie was tempted to pop into the office, but knew that she could do nothing to help. Instead she had a day designed specifi-

cally to boost her spirits. First, meeting up with Edward in the
park before he went to work—for requisite ego-building in nice
surroundings—then lunch with a newly arrived Sophie—gossip,
good food and any info on Jake she could wangle—followed by a
pleasant afternoon on her own, wandering around The Frick
Museum—solitude and art.

In between, she would pop back to the apartment, as usual, to
check whether or not Charles had sent an e-mail to Victoria.

Central Park had become Annie's friend. She had started jogging in it after experiencing one too many nights of fitful sleep.
Her body was missing the regular exercise from karate and she discovered that a morning jog gave her the perfect chance to get her
thoughts in order before the inevitable worries started creeping in.
And it meant that on the way home she could buy a freshly baked
doughnut, warm out of the oven, before the queues started.

After a hot shower and change of clothes, Annie was back out
in the park. Today was not as cold as yesterday, and the weather re-
sembled a dazzlingly bright autumn day in London, the sky's blue
interrupted only by speeding white clouds, the trees boldly bare.
She stood under the gothic arch of the Hansel and Gretel-style
building that housed the information center, staring ahead at the
skaters on the ice rink twirling against a backdrop of naked trees
and the monolithic buildings beyond.

Leaning against the railing, watching people wandering past, she
noticed that umbrellas were suddenly blossoming. When the rain
turned to hail, she pushed up her collar and smiled as the skaters
vanished within moments.

Motionless, she watched the world go by.

Shoulders suddenly hunched, faces down, everyone was rushing by, trying to dodge the rain. Then suddenly she spotted a pair
of long legs under an umbrella that made her stomach somersault.
If it hadn't been impossible, she'd have sworn it was . . . just then
the umbrella was blown temporarily away from its holder's face. It

was! She watched as the figure disappeared temporarily behind some bushes to the right of her view. She ran to the right of the building and waited, breath halted, to see if he would come up the hill toward her, or if he had taken the other route and was gone again.

After what seemed like hours, the figure appeared again, running now, straight toward her.

Conflicting emotions raced for supremacy inside her body so fast that she had to act quickly before the wrong one won. She ran out from under the building into the rain, straight into his path.

"Jake!" she exclaimed, the cold rain pricking her cheeks, tingling her hair and feet.

He started, stopped in his tracks, stared at her and seemed struck dumb, while a rainbow of expressions flickered over his face.

Try as she might, Annie couldn't work out a single one of them. Happiness at seeing her? Shock? Fright? Relief? Boredom? Adoration? Gratitude that he wasn't going out with Sophie?

Impossible to tell.

Suffice to say he didn't rush into her arms—which as far as she was concerned, was a bit of a letdown.

So. He was still in love with bitch whore Sophes, eh?

"Hi," he managed eventually, his hand flying to the back of his neck. Could she tell he'd just been thinking about her?

Hi.

One syllable, opposite of low, thought Annie. But what did it *mean*?

She had no option. She had to keep him talking until he'd used enough syllables for her to be able to decipher any emotion behind his words. She hadn't been a Samaritan for nothing.

What should she say now?

You remember that time in the alleyway . . . About that baby . . . I hear Paris is nice this time of year . . .

"What are you doing here?"

"Getting drenched," he suddenly grinned, as if coming out of the effect of a stun gun.

"Here, you're getting soaked," and he held the umbrella over both of them. It was a relatively large umbrella, but it still meant squeezing up a bit.

Annie was so unused to Jake actually being decent to her that she was now totally confused. It was a context she hadn't worked in for too long. If he was deliberately trying to confuse her she'd have been impressed. But was he?

Was he trying to wrong foot her? Or rather, make up for lost time? Had the alleyway incident stayed with him too? Or did the new surroundings of New York simply eradicate everything that had gone on before and they could start again?

Or did Jake just have an umbrella and not want to see a girl get wet?

He'd only been here for a matter of minutes and already she had brain ache.

The hail was actually hurting them now and unless Annie got inside Jake's jacket—which did occur to her—this was going to become seriously unpleasant. She gestured for them to run under the canopy of the building. They stood there for a bit, watching the sudden downpour.

She had to know how Jake felt about Sophie's engagement to David. And why was he here? There was no time to waste. The conflicting emotions were still in there, battling away. Pride, anger, hurt and resentment were busily battling for victory over Warm Interest. *Quick*.

"I mean, what are you doing *here*? In New York? I thought all the important stuff was being done back home."

Ask about Sophie. Listen and nod, then ask about Sophie . . .

Jake shrugged, leaning against the railings, looking studiously at his umbrella as he furled it up. What was he going to say next, she wondered. Can I have my ball back please?

"Susannah called us in London. It sounded pretty serious, so I decided to come out. I flew in last night. I was just on my way to the office."

Annie was suddenly terrified. She had no idea Susannah was going to do this. Was she going to let them go?

She didn't have a moment to lose.

"Is it about . . . the money that's hemorrhaging out of the company?"

Jake looked at her. "If it is, Susannah hasn't mentioned it."

What? Why weren't they telling him anything? How could he help Markhams' if he didn't have all the information? Didn't they trust him? Was it a bad sign that he was here? Were they going to sell the company immediately? Without telling her? And what did he feel about Sophie?

"Oh. Well, she's very worried about it. Very worried."

"You mean . . . the *vanishing* money?"

Oh, so he *did* know.

"Yes," she said, relieved. "Susannah hasn't got a clue where it's all going. Have you?"

He shook his head. "I've only just been alerted to it by one of my colleagues," he said quietly. "We're looking into it now. I . . . um, I think I may have an idea where it's going. We're doing all we can as fast as possible, I promise."

She couldn't help the grin. Jake was her ally once more! Her knight in shining armor. Who ran out on her seven years ago, without warning . . .

Keep talking, keep talking.

"Oh thank God. Have you told Susannah?"

"Not yet. I don't think she'd take it too well."

"You must tell her."

"Must I?"

"Yes. She thinks she can't afford you anymore."

Jake stopped breathing. He had to ask.

"You want me to stay?"

What did that mean? Did he want her to want him to stay? Or was that her just wanting him to want her to want him to stay? Or was she just going mad?

"I want you to save us."

"How long have I got?"

What did that mean? How long have I got to save your life? Or how long have I got to be with you? Or how long have I got to live? Was that buzzing sound her head?

"A week. The New Year. Then she'll let you go."

"Jesus," he whispered. "Thanks."

Right. Now, Sophie . . .

"We think there may be an inside leak actually," said Jake suddenly. Yes, it was worth risking everything. He couldn't have kept a secret from her now if he'd tried.

Annie gasped. She spoke before thinking. "Oh don't be ridiculous."

Stung, Jake shot back.

"I'm not being ridiculous. I'm being thorough. I'm doing what I'm paid to do."

Oh, so this was purely business then. Victoria was right. He was a stubborn bastard.

"Who would be a leak then?" she asked disdainfully. "My father?"

He looked away from her, watching the rain.

Oh fine. Not talking now. How mature.

She tried another tack. "Look, I'm meeting Edward here any minute—"

"Oh yeah?" He stayed looking at the rain.

She stared at him. There was no need to be so rude. After all, she'd sat behind him and Sophie all the way through that wretched film and never once said "Oh yeah?" to him in that tone of voice.

"Yeah," she replied, making up for lost time.

Warm Interest finally lost the battle. In fairness, it had put up a good fight. Piqued, she indulged the victor.

"I hardly think you're in any position to have a problem with that, do you?" she accused bitterly.

Jake suddenly looked straight at her.

"As a matter of fact I do."

She couldn't believe her ears! She'd be damned if she was going to let those stupid dark eyes boring into her have any effect on what she said or did. Anymore.

"What the hell's it got to do with you who I go out with? If you haven't forgotten, we're not going out with each other any-more, on account of you running out and leaving me—"

"It's got nothing to do with us going ou—"

"Oh right. This is just friendly advice is it?"

Jake exploded.

"*Friendly*! How can I be friendly? You lied to me about having my baby, then said you'd elope with me, then changed your mind at the last minute—"

"I didn't lie to you—or change my mind—"

"Oh, what? So you knew all along that you'd dump me, did you?"

"I MADE A MISTAKE! I THOUGHT I WAS PREGNANT AND I WASN'T. I'D ONLY JUST FOUND OUT WHEN YOU CAME INTO MY ROOM. AND IF YOU'D STUCK AROUND TO FIND OUT, YOU'D HAVE DISCOVERED I WAS AS UPSET ABOUT IT AS YOU WERE."

Phew. Glad she'd got that off her chest. About time too.

She felt strangely light, as if she might blow away in the wind.

Jake stared at her in stunned silence. Too much information. Unable to compute. Focus, talk, breathe. When he finally spoke, his voice didn't seem to be coming from his body.

"Annie. All I'm saying is . . . be careful who you trust—"

"HI THERE!"

They didn't hear what the voice was saying at first, only that there was one, and it was obliterating their conversation.

Jake and Annie both looked to where the voice was coming from and saw a tall, slender shape standing in the light. They assumed the man was a mad stranger. Then Annie remembered. Edward! She then experienced a sinking feeling that was so profound she feared her womb had prolapsed.

Edward seemed delighted to have found them together, yet conscious that delicate feelings needed to be soothed. He smiled warmly at them both before coming forward and shaking Jake's hand so firmly, Annie worried for his shoulder socket.

"We were just about to share a soggy bagel and double-strength, half-spilled coffee," continued Edward, holding up a wet paper bag. "Care to join us?"

"I'm sorry," said Jake softly, staring fixedly at Edward. "I only like dry rye and decaff. Otherwise . . . obviously, hard to resist . . ."

Edward laughed.

Jake then gave Annie a short, blunt goodbye without meeting her eye, turned to Edward and said, in lieu of goodbye, "Edward." And then he turned up his collar and ran off into the rain.

Edward and Annie stayed there until the rain finally came to a halt fifteen minutes later. Both Central Park and the rain soon lost their appeal as Annie got colder and colder. She just wanted to get back to the apartment and take off her soggy clothes. Have a hot bath. Close her eyes and marvel at what she had managed to finally say out loud to Jake. It was a truly momentous day.

And not only because of what she'd said. But because she finally realized that adverts are always better than the real thing.

When Annie reached the apartment, Victoria was still in the increasingly lengthy process of getting up. She was sitting in the drawing room eating a chocolate-flavored children's cereal, her finger flicking through the TV channels, her eyes glazed over. Annie, restless and on edge, went into the office and turned on the computer. Yep, there was a message.

She pressed the intercom button and buzzed Victoria.

"There's an e-mail for you," she told Victoria.

Victoria jumped in shock at the voice to her right. She turned, brushed aside the curtain and looked at the little gray box. The red light was flicking, showing that it was on.

"For me? Are you sure?"

"Yep," replied Annie into the office intercom. "From Charles."

They swapped rooms. Annie went and sat in the drawing room, looking out at the park, feeling shell-shocked and depressed. She sat in the silence for a while until an ugly buzzing came from the intercom.

"Annie! I need your help!"

It was Victoria from the office.

She found Victoria sitting staring at the computer, her hand over her mouth. Her eyes were watering.

"You OK?" asked Annie.

Victoria nodded.

"How do I reply?"

Annie clicked on the reply icon and a space appeared for Victoria to tap her message into. She didn't mean to pry but she couldn't help but catch the first few words of Charles's message.

My lovely Vicks . . .

Victoria sniffed loudly while looking for the D key. She hit the E key instead.

"Shit," she muttered. This might take some time, thought Annie.

"Shall I leave you to it?" she asked.

Victoria nodded.

Annie closed the door behind her. Good old Charles, she thought. He'd remembered.

*   *   *

Feeling shaken, stirred and swallowed in one, Annie left the apartment and headed for the Russian Tea Room to meet Sophie.

The fondness the two women felt for each other was now exaggerated greatly by the new fact that Sophie was engaged to David.

"Oh Annie," Sophie grinned, as soon as they had ordered their food. "The poor boy was damaged, that's the only word there is for it. I don't like to say this about anyone," she said happily, "but David's ex-wife was a complete and utter bitch. He says I've restored his faith in women."

Annie smiled. How could Jake have compared?

By the time Annie got to The Frick Museum, her mood was buoyant again. She had told Jake what she should have told him years ago. It was over. She always felt better when surrounded by paintings and sculpture. It was as if heartache and fear didn't exist in a world of such speechless truths.

Unlike the other museums in New York, this was just one very wealthy man's art collection and it had a unique, eclectic feel all its own. Constables overlooked Rodin figures. The soft pastels of Whistler nestled amidst the dark forbidding Rembrandts. Annie was able to forget her chaotic thoughts and absorb herself in another world within moments.

And then, while staring at a Whistler woman, it suddenly hit her.

The woman's body was turned away from Annie, but her gaze was direct and assertive. The woman had purpose, direction, hope. Everything she felt she lacked.

That was it!

Standing staring up at the picture, Annie decided she would phone her financial adviser this afternoon and find out exactly what her savings were.

She could hardly concentrate on the rest of the exhibition. For the first time in her life, she knew exactly what she wanted to do with it.

Today was getting more momentous every second.

*   *   *

The next day found Annie in SoHo, map in hand, walking purposefully from gallery to gallery. She knew down to the last cent what she could afford and what was out of her price range. She also knew her art and knew what she loved.

It took her all day, but finally she found a painting that she loved and wanted to own.

The brush strokes were large and free, the colors bold and bright. It had light and life and meaning and Annie stared at it, savoring the moment. The painting held an unmistakable message that pierced through the confusion of her life and clarified her world.

And it had a really nice blue in it.

She recognized the name of the young artist, and although the painting wasn't cheap, Annie knew that one day it would be expensive—if not priceless.

Exhausted but happy, she took the painting straight to her room and placed it on the bed, leaning against the wall.

She knelt in front of the bed, placing her elbows on it, as if to pray, and stared intently at her new painting; her new beginning.

Back in North London, Charles walked quickly into his club, his collar turned up against the bitter winter cold. The gang was there, sitting in prime position by the log fire and he went over to join them.

"You're late, they've already started the counting," Edgar said accusingly.

"Sorry," said Charles. "Couldn't get a babysitter for the boys."

They looked at him in silence.

He coughed.

"Wife's in New York with the family," he explained.

They continued to stare.

"It's not looking too good," primed Edgar. "There's far more

Trotskies than we thought. If we're not careful there'll be chintz curtains in here before you can say Fore. Every vote counts, men."

They shared a drink, toasted Tradition and then went into the clubroom to vote.

Charles could hardly grip his pencil, his hand was sweating so much. He looked behind him and checked that none of the gang was anywhere near.

He closed his eyes, bit his lip and slowly but surely, put a big black cross in the square.

After all, what was life without progress?

Chapter 24

Annie could hardly wait until tonight. Now that she'd managed after all these years to get everything off her chest to Jake, a painful chapter in her life had finally closed once and for all. She could really start to enjoy herself for the first time in years and it started now. Edward had decided at the last minute to stay in New York for Christmas—his family were scattered all over the globe and Christmas had never been much of a thing for any of them. Annie's own family had been only too delighted to welcome him into the heart of their celebrations. And although she had experienced a temporary blip in interest toward him when she'd thought Jake was out of her life, all that had changed now. Edward suddenly seemed the answer to all her prayers. Sane, safe and steady.

Who knew? She might even beat Jake to the altar after all . . .

The only fly in the ointment was that Davina would also be staying for Christmas. Annie had carefully avoided any show of interest in Davina's plans because she knew that her own feelings would show through too clearly. So she'd been grateful when her father brought the subject up a few weeks earlier.

"Annie, will you be sharing Christmas lunch with us?"

Annie looked at him in some surprise. As opposed to what? she wondered.

"Of course, Father," she said.

"Splendid," he murmured. "Splendid. I'll tell the chef."

To Annie's even greater surprise, Davina had turned to her and beamed.

"I'm so pleased you'll be with us. It wouldn't be a proper family Christmas without you."

Annie stared at her and turned to her father. Beaming proudly, he patted Davina on the hand.

"Davina's parents are in Switzerland this year. Skiing."

"I'd rather stay here anyway," said Davina, before adding with gentle humility, "You're all family to me now."

George beamed.

Annie marveled that she wasn't sick there and then.

No one else seemed in the least worried that Davina had become a permanent member of the family. In fact, Victoria was in an infuriatingly good mood. The boys were due out within days and she spent every spare moment checking her e-mails for messages from Charles.

Annie had invited Edward to the apartment for pre-opera family drinks. All were delighted to see him and, apart from Katherine, who kept a condescending distance, they all welcomed him like a long-lost family member. Annie felt as if the jigsaw pieces of her life were finally slotting into place.

Davina was probably the only person who seemed cautious with Edward, and Annie was pleased to see it. It made Edward's presence all the more welcoming.

Annie couldn't wait to see Cass and Brutus, who had arrived safe and sound in New York that day. Sophie, David, Fi and Tony were also going to be at the opera. The presence of Cass always soothed her and she felt the new couplings of Charles's sisters would somehow be the Epilogue to the Jake chapter of her life. As the drinks started to drag, she found herself champing at the bit to get to the opera.

★　　★　　★

She wasn't the only one champing at the bit to get to the opera. Jake squirmed in the corner of the taxi, wishing David and Sophie would stop smooching beside him. He should have arranged to meet them there. This was hardly what he needed on his way to Annie. The howling wind outside didn't help either. It lashed against the car, making him feel even more vulnerable than he already did. He tightened his jacket around him, but it didn't keep out the ice in his gut.

What Annie had said to him in the park—or rather, yelled at him across the park—had taken just long enough for him to walk about four feet away from her before sinking in. Dear God, she'd made an honest miscalculation—a mistake. All those years ago, she really *had* thought she was pregnant. And she'd come back into her room in halls shaking and scared after finding out the truth, needing him and he'd . . . Oh God, it didn't bear thinking about. All those wasted years . . . He could see her face now, all uncertain and young. And like a great bellowing idiot, he'd simply yelled at her. When she'd needed him most.

Why couldn't this bloody taxi go faster?

"Jake, you all right, mate?" asked David.

"Yes. Of course I'm all right."

"Only you're grinding your teeth. We can hear you above the gale."

Jake looked at David, unconsciously clapping his hand to the back of his neck.

"I'm fine."

Annie's taxi journey would have stretched the patience of a saint, so it was hardly surprising that Annie felt tense. For a start, they must have met the only taxi driver who had never heard of the Metropolitan Opera House.

"Ze Mexicaan Owffal whaat?" he said in an indistinguishable accent.

"Metropolitan Opera House," she repeated slowly, trying to keep the impatience out of her voice.

The taxi driver nodded.

"Ze Mexicaan—"

"No. The Met—"

Edward interrupted.

"The Lincoln Center please."

"Aaaah! Ze Nincum Center! Why deen't yow saay?" he laughed and promptly got stuck in a jam.

They all rushed, heads down through the increasingly strong wind, to reach the warm building. No one was looking up in wonder at the stained-glass windows tonight.

Annie was the first into the theater foyer and she ran up the red-carpeted staircase where she stood smack bang in the middle, staring down expectantly at all the doors.

The others moved slowly up to join her and as she watched them approach, she noticed properly for the first time that no one in the entire place—not even Katherine—was as beautiful as Davina. And Davina had really pulled out the stops for tonight. Wearing a silk scarlet ballgown that flowed gracefully around her perfectly curved body, she stood out from the crowd. Was this her future stepmother?

Susannah, Cass and Brutus arrived first. Someone somehow had opened a valve on Annie's feelings. She was almost overwhelmed with warmth for Cass and hurtled through the crowd toward her.

Cass was looking well—and most importantly, the happiest Annie had seen her for a long time.

"Can I touch the bump?" asked Annie foolishly.

"You want to touch my bottom in public?"

"The bump with the babies in it, stupid."

"Why of course."

As they all went to find their seats, Annie suddenly caught sight of the others. As she ran toward them, she ignored the presence of

a large shadow in the background. Good feelings were on a winning streak tonight.

Then over David's welcoming shoulder, she came face to face
with the shadow and couldn't help but notice that it was in the unmistakable form of Jake's body. Topped by his face.

She froze.

What the hell was he doing here? And what the hell was her
body doing freezing?

Chapter closed, chapter closed . . .

And then, to top it all, while she was greeting David, Jake smiled
at her. If she didn't know him better, she'd even have said that the
smile had a hint of nervousness to it.

Was he spying on her? Spoiling her evening with Edward on
purpose? Deliberately trying to confuse her? Still in love with Sophie? Keen on opera?

She turned abruptly away.

It didn't work.

"Look who I managed to persuade to come," insisted David.

Jake stepped forward toward Annie. He could do this. He
would do this. He would talk openly to her for the first time in
years with no misunderstandings. No bitterness, no bile. Just
sweet conversation. And he'd start with a subject that had made
Britain what it was; a subject that meant nothing and glossed
over everything. He would talk about the weather. He grinned
hopefully.

"Windy tonight!" he exclaimed, rather louder than he'd hoped.

"Are you?" replied Annie, unimpressed.

"No, I meant—"

Bugger.

"Isn't this a big surprise?" laughed David.

"That's one word for it," said Annie dryly, amazed at how fast
anger could resurface.

"Did you even know he was in New York?"

Jake kept his voice low. He was worried it might tremble otherwise. Instead it came out like Wenceslas snow—all soft and even. "Actually we met up in the park this morning."

"Oh!" exclaimed David. "There goes the surprise then."

"Oh, I wouldn't say that," said Annie, straight at Jake. "I'm amazed Jake's here."

Jake spoke earnestly and his eyes held Annie to the spot. "I thought we could—maybe, *should*—start where we left off—"

Did she hear that right?

If Annie hadn't felt Edward's comforting arm around her shoulder just then, she might have been unable to stay upright. She leaned into Edward's body for support. Thank God for Edward. Oh dear, she was so confused.

"Jake!" greeted Edward loudly, stretching out his hand. "Delighted! You must be following us."

Jake smiled politely, but didn't take his eyes off Annie as he shook Edward's hand.

"That's right," he said.

There was an uncomfortable pause. Jake held Annie's gaze. Edward held her shoulder. Annie held her breath.

She had no idea how the situation would have ended, if it hadn't been for an interruption from an unexpected quarter.

"Hi there, Jake," said a delighted Davina, over Annie's right shoulder. "We met in London, just before I came out to work here with George."

And Jake was as struck dumb as Annie by the delectable Davina openly flirting with him. She was playing no games. The message was clear. She wanted him and she wanted him bad. Annie turned away to stop herself from launching her body at Davina's throat.

As Edward guided Annie toward their seats, Annie cursed the fates. Just when she thought she was getting over Jake, Davina had to prove her wrong.

So many reasons to hate one person.

But what about Jake? Had she just heard him right? Did he really want to start where they'd left off? Was he talking about the park this morning, or . . .

She didn't dare think it. But why else would he be here?

She turned around and caught him chatting to Davina. Davina burst into girlish laughter. When Jake's eyes caught hers over Davina's head, she looked abruptly away and grimaced. Oh no. Not again.

Thankfully, Jake hadn't managed to get seats in one of the family boxes or with the others who had seats in the orchestra, but Annie heard them all arrange to find each other in the bar during the intermission.

At that instant, the bell rang telling them that the opera was about to begin.

As Annie took her seat next to Edward, she scanned the auditorium frantically for where Jake was sitting. She couldn't find him anywhere. Was Davina molesting him somewhere? Was no woman safe with that man?

Annie and Edward were sharing a box with Cass and Brutus, to the left of the auditorium. Edward edged toward Annie, who had moved her chair to the end of the box in a failed attempt to give herself more space. He kept whispering sly observations about the audience into her neck and then laughing conspiratorially. She had no choice but to respond with a polite smile. The smaller response he got, the larger his movements became.

She could hear Davina's affected laugh piercing the hub of pre-opera gossip. She was determined not to look to where the laughter was coming from. She wouldn't give her—or Jake—the satisfaction. Instead, every time Davina laughed, she edged closer to Edward. If she could, she'd have sat on his lap.

Just as the orchestra started tuning up, she couldn't help but look out at the auditorium once more. Then just as the crystal chandeliers started floating majestically upward and the lights to dim, she locked eyes with Jake. He was sitting practically opposite them, his eyes fixed darkly on her and Edward.

Flustered by such an honest look, she looked down at the electronic titles in front of her, for want of anything else to look at.

Her hand shaking slightly, she pressed the button on the titles. Orange electronic lettering shone out. *Otello. Act One.*

Edward had decided to share Annie's screen with her, which meant sitting very snug so as to be able to see them.

The curtains went up. There appeared to be about 300 people— 300 rather large people—on the vast stage. They burst forth into an explosion of sound that was even louder than the sound effects of a storm around them. They seemed to sing a whole song in one long breath. Annie looked at the titles to see what they were singing about.

Thunder!

Edward inched closer.

Their position at the side of the auditorium meant they missed much of the action. The turmoil going on inside Annie's head meant she missed the rest. She had to get to Jake. Find out what he really meant. She just had to be with him.

After the slowest forty-five minutes of Annie's life, the curtains whisked down. Annie wanted to speed away from Edward, through the heaving throng.

But the opera singers were taking their intermission bow. She couldn't summon up the energy to clap. The audience gave them an ovation and Annie could almost feel Jake standing up, amid the crowd in front of her.

As soon as the stars of the show vanished behind the thick curtain, Annie sped off, leaving Edward stuck behind a mass of people.

Jake was waiting at the bar, with David, Sophie, Tony and Fi. Annie quickened her pace.

She stopped near him and watched him approach.

Was this it? Was he going to tell her he'd got her wrong? That he'd made the biggest mistake of his life running out on her like that? Was he going to say that he wanted to give it another try? Was she going to say yes?

Was she ever going to breathe properly again?

Jake was so close they were practically touching. But he was a different man from the one before the opera. He spoke with a repressed urgency she remembered all too well from London.

"Please ignore everything I said," he said curtly. "Both this morning and before the opera. I didn't know what I was saying."

What?

Annie started breathing again. Badly, but it was a start. Her body was experiencing more highs and lows than a British Bank Holiday weather forecast.

It settled on her good old friend, anger.

"*I-ignore* it?"

"Ignore it."

"Ignore *what*, exactly?"

"Well done."

"No. I meant it. Ignore *what*?"

"The bit about trusting—you can trust who you like. You were absolutely right. It's got nothing to do with me."

Oh right! Her head started pounding feverishly. Not so much can I have my ball back please as can I take your heart out and squelch it . . .

She tried to keep any hurt out of her voice and stay calm. After all, she was at the opera.

"Oh right. I see," she squealed in a voice uncannily like Minnie Mouse. "You want to give us your blessing now?"

"Well. Maybe not my blessing—"

"Your congratulations?"

"Not really—"

"A big friendly hug all round?"

"No, not especially—"

"Does this mean you'll be Edward's best man? Only, he's been meaning to ask you for weeks—"

OK, now she was overdoing it.

Jake bristled. "It's clear you and Edward are more serious than . . . I thought. I had no idea. I wouldn't have—"

"What? Played with my feelings?"

Woops. Gave the game away a bit there. So much to think about, so much to hide . . .

Jake kept his head down as he spoke. "I was letting my . . . my feelings get in the way of my job. I thought I was being purely professional, but I now realize I wasn't."

Time to cut to the chase.

"What are you actually trying to say to me?"

He looked up and stared at her.

"I'm so sorry, Annie. Sorry for everything."

And with that he ran out.

Again.

Annie stood paralyzed, watching him go.

"Care for a drink?" asked Edward, suddenly at her side.

She shook her head without turning toward him, her soul expanding, her heart free-falling.

Chapter 25

Annie stared, stunned, as Jake pushed his way out into the cold, wet night. For the second time in her life she felt the lack of him slowly fill her. A stinging sensation swelled at the back of her eyes.

He really was a pillock sometimes.

"Davina's in the drinks queue giving it all her charm—shouldn't expect she'll take long to catch the barman's eye—what would you like?"

Annie turned to find that Edward was speaking at her. And now he was smiling at her. Now he was gently touching her elbow to guide her back into the throng. She let it all happen, too shell-shocked to keep up with Jake and His Amazing Vanishing Act, Part II.

For some unknown reason, she hated Edward with a vengeance.

Dazed and confused, Annie reluctantly returned to the bar. With each step that she took with Edward, the possibility of gearing herself up and running after Jake shrank until, by the time she entered the bar, she was convinced, like a long-battered wife, that calmly staying put was simply her fate.

When they got there, the queue was nowhere to be seen. Instead, a mass of people were crowded around something or someone on the floor.

To her horror, Annie realized that her family was in the center of the huddle. She pushed her way through the crowd and almost fainted at the sight of Brutus and Susannah holding Cass in their arms as she bled on the bar floor, her hair soaked in sweat, her stark face pulled more by terror than pain.

"Which is the nearest hospital?" a voice shouted.

"St. Luke's Roosevelt," answered another voice. "Or 113th and Amsterdam. It's a Level One."

"Do St. Luke's. It's quieter."

"How long'll it take?"

"Ten mins max. Straight down Columbus."

Good God, thought Annie, suddenly desperate for a good old British accent. Why didn't anyone speak English here?

An ambulance arrived in moments and a hysterical Susannah and ghost-like Brutus went in the ambulance with Cass, Annie following in a taxi. To her surprise Victoria wanted to join her. Her father, Katie, Davina and Edward, unable to help, went back in to watch the second half of the opera.

"You will be all right, won't you?" whispered Edward to her as he squeezed her hand.

"Yes of course," rushed Annie, grateful for his concern and even more grateful that he wasn't coming with her. "Go back and enjoy the opera."

She waited for the calm clarity of thought that had overcome her when they had been attacked in London to click into place again.

Then when she realized it wasn't going to happen, she really panicked.

An enormous sense of being out of control threatened to engulf her. It was as if she had used up all her reserves of control and her body just couldn't cope this time. She and Victoria didn't speak a word in the taxi, partly through shock and partly through the terror of being driven by a complete maniac.

Their taxi driver was determined not to lose sight of the ambulance for them and Annie suspected that he had been waiting for such a command ever since he got his license.

As they swerved past a red light, causing several incandescent drivers to blast their horns and swear at them, Annie was grateful that at least if they crashed, they'd have an ambulance on hand in seconds.

"Good God, look at that!" pointed out Victoria, as they passed St. Paul the Apostle church. "They've stone-clad that church! Don't they have *any* sense of style?"

Why wasn't her family normal? Why couldn't Victoria just be there to give support?

When they got to the hospital, Annie realized how accurate the television program *ER* was. She felt as if she was looking through a shaky, hand-held camera, the words everyone spoke somehow feeling unreal, yet horribly real at the same time.

Cass was whisked away within seconds, Susannah and Brutus both desperately holding on to her, as if somehow that would help. Annie introduced herself as a friend of Cass's to a nearby doctor, who told her in no uncertain terms that he didn't care if she was Father Frigging Christmas, she couldn't come with him into the OR.

There was nothing for them to do but wait. Annie sat on the plastic chairs provided and stared blindly up at the television screen. A woman was making mince pies.

"And don't forget—keep paying attention to that oven," she was instructing firmly, as she finished decorating her pies with pastry cut-outs of holly leaves.

"Sod the oven, lady," muttered Victoria to the television. "Pay some attention to your roots."

Annie's eyes glazed over. A Christmas cake and ten gingerbread snowmen later, Brutus and Susannah appeared by her side.

"She's asking for you," Brutus told Annie.

Annie stood up suddenly. She must have seemed unsteady, because Susannah and Brutus both put out a hand to hold her.

"She hasn't lost all three," said Susannah in a voice that seemed a long way away. "They think she's only lost one."

"So far," whispered Brutus. "A couple more weeks and it would have had a chance to live."

A nurse appeared behind them and offered to walk Annie to Cass's room.

She stood outside the door for a while. Finally, she saw her hand push it open.

Cass was lying still on her back, staring blankly at the ceiling. Her face was a shade similar to the green pillow she was lying on; her hair in thin, damp strands fanning her face.

Annie tiptoed next to her. Cass didn't seem to hear or see her.

Annie touched Cass's hand. Cass didn't move.

"Cassie," she whispered, bending down, so that her head was near to Cass's.

At the sound of Annie's voice, Cass turned her head away toward the wall, her lips trembling.

Annie stared at the back of her friend's head, not knowing what to do next. She could see that Cass was trying to say something, but the effort seemed to defeat her.

Silently, she crept around the bed until she was facing Cass. She bent down, stroked Cass's damp hair and kissed her on the cheek.

Cass's lips were moving, but no noise came out of her mouth.

When Victoria finally left Annie at the hospital, she was desperate to e-mail Charles about what had happened. It was hardly surprising that she failed to notice a familiar-looking Barbour in the hall cloak cupboard, in her rush to get her coat off and log on.

As she rushed past the drawing room door, a fleeting image of Charles sitting on the sofa barely registered in her brain before she reached the office. Once inside the office, she pressed the button on the computer and stared at the screen. She frowned. That was odd. She could have sworn—

"Hello."

She spun around. Charles was standing in the doorway.

Inexplicably, she felt tongue-tied.

"Cass had a miscarriage," she finally blurted out.

"Oh," said Charles.

Victoria needed a hug. "In the interval."

"Oh dear."

And a kiss.

"I was just about to e-mail you."

"Poor Cass," said Charles, his hand on the door handle.

Victoria noticed how his fringe flicked pleasingly across his eyes.

"How are the boys?"

Charles smiled. "A handful," he said proudly.

"Don't I know it?" said Victoria.

"Yes. I, er, I, er . . ." God, it was so much easier on e-mail. "I picked them up from Mum and Dad's as soon as I got back. Missed them. Discovered . . . well, truth is, discovered it's not quite the same when you have them twenty-four hours a day. I think I've seen enough doo-doos to last anyone a lifetime. Except my own, of course. I haven't had the time."

Victoria didn't know what to say. Charles was ruining her victim role for her. Typical.

"I brought them here," Charles continued. "They're in bed." Victoria felt her whole body fill up with warmth. She didn't mind the tears. Charles, bless him, pretended not to notice and continued in the same level tone.

"They were almost unbearably excited at the prospect of Christmas and New Year with Mummy. You won over the bouncy castle, no contest. I-I thought when we get back home, we could get some help. With them. Maybe not full time, but just something. And I thought it was worth me coming back with them," he said softly. "For . . . for . . . New Year. And, of course, the chance to have a crap in peace."

Victoria laughed.

"Good."

Charles let out a deep sigh. He didn't want to risk anymore words.

"Are you coming to bed?"

Victoria nodded and slowly, they walked to their bedroom.

They lay there in the dark, both too scared to move. After a while, Victoria realized that Charles wasn't going to make the first move. Dear God, did that mean she'd have to? After what seemed like forever, a small voice sounded in her ear.

"Kiss me."

She didn't know what to say. She didn't know what to do.

"Where?"

"In New York, stupid. What do you think I came back for?"

"But—"

"Kiss me, woman."

For the first time in her life, Victoria didn't wait for his touch. She closed her eyes, pretended she was someone else and discovered her husband, gently, slowly, deftly. Charles lay there motionless, his eyes alert in the dark, his breathing heavy.

Victoria found she loved his smell, she loved his softness and most of all, she loved the new sensation of being in control. To her astonishment, she discovered she was as moved physically as emotionally by her husband's vulnerable body. When he could no longer contain himself, Charles gently pushed her on to her back. But Victoria resisted, pushing him back down.

Her days of taking this lying down were over.

"You do know I love you, don't you?" murmured Charles into the dark.

There was silence. Then eventually,

"Yes. But I've forgotten why."

★   ★   ★

Meanwhile, Edward had come back to the apartment with George, Katherine and Davina and was doing a superb job of calming everyone down. George and Katherine, though not as fond of Cass as Annie was, were both thoroughly shaken by what they had seen. It had been most traumatic. George was frantically pacing the drawing room.

"There was absolutely nothing we could do," Davina tried to soothe him.

"No, you're right, of course, as usual," he replied, shaking his head anyway.

"We would have only been in the way," finished Edward, his piercing eyes focused briefly on Davina.

"Oh absolutely," agreed George. "Absolutely. Still . . ." he sighed loudly and covered his eyes with a tired hand. "Tragic . . ."

They all nodded. He continued, in a world of his own.

". . . all those people having to see it happen. So *public*. And at the *opera* too."

Katherine landed heavily on the sofa and started crying. Davina was next to her in no time.

"Try not to think about it, darling," she told her. "She's in the best hands now."

Katherine wiped her hand over her face and leaned back in the sofa. "Her face—it was so horrible."

"I know."

"I'll have nightmares for months. I'm incredibly sensitive to images."

"I know."

In one rapid, smooth movement, Edward was on the other side of Katherine.

"Shhh, it's over now."

Katherine nodded, sniffing loudly.

"Be brave, darling," whispered Davina urgently.

As Katherine put her head in her hands, Davina and Edward caught each other's cold eyes over her head and instantly looked away.

Chapter 26

*C*hristmas Day was not quite what Annie had expected. She was woken early by the sound of two young boys racing through the apartment, giggling and whispering so loudly they could be heard in Rockefeller Center, followed by the sound and smells of cooking going on in the kitchen. George had decided against going to a hotel for lunch, it seemed so impersonal somehow, and Susannah had convinced him it was a horrid waste of money. It had been far cheaper to pay the chef double rate for the day. Susannah, Brutus and Edward would be joining her family—and of course Davina—for traditional Christmas lunch. But it would now be a muted affair.

Annie dressed quickly before grabbing an apple for later and going straight to the hospital. Perversely, she was glad to have something so important to take her mind off Markhams'. When she got to the hospital, she found Brutus and Susannah in the corridor outside Cass's room. They looked even more shaken than yesterday. For one heart-stopping moment, she feared that Cass herself might be in danger. But it wasn't that.

"She's lost another one in the night," murmured Susannah, holding limply on to Annie. "They don't hold out much hope for the third."

Annie looked through the window into Cass's room. Cass was hidden behind two nurses who were attaching her to a drip and filling in forms at the end of her bed. When the two nurses moved, Annie stayed looking at Cass. When Cass's eyes met hers, they stared silently at each other for a while, before Cass closed hers and turned away.

If Harry and Bertie had only known how much effort everyone was making to keep their first New York Christmas a jolly, light-hearted affair, they would have been bowed down by the weight of gratitude.

Brutus did not come to the lunch, Susannah did but left soon after. Annie, however, stayed at home. She didn't want to return to the hospital. She was beginning to feel that somehow she was making things worse for Cass.

When everyone had finally gone to bed, Annie ran herself a bath and slowly sank her head back into the still water, too exhausted by a sudden onslaught of painful memories to move.

Hot water flooded into her ears, soaking up her brain so that all she could hear was the sound of liquid, swirling in the crevices of her mind. Water gushed in and out of every nook and cranny of her memory and reason, rinsing through fixed opinions, dislodging overworked hurts and washing musty judgments. Seven years' worth of self-identity, stuck in silent, forgotten waters like the *Marie Celeste*, stirred slightly—but just enough to give Annie a new view of herself, of Jake, of Cass.

And then when it felt as if her waterlogged mind might burst her skull, she lifted it out of the water, so that all she could hear was warm silence and a slow, dripping tap.

Staring at her big toe as it leaned on the tap, she faced up to the painful realization that she had always wished deep down, that one day Cass would understand how she had felt about losing someone she really cared about. It was only just dawning on Annie that although she had never knowingly blamed Cass for interfering with her elopement by telling Susannah, in her innermost heart, she had.

She also realized that if Cass hadn't had the knack of needling exactly what she wanted out of her, Annie's life would be very different. Likewise with Susannah. Annie wondered at herself. What on earth was she doing—at twenty-six years old—spying on her own father's business because her godmother had asked her to? Why wasn't she going to the meetings for herself? Why was she letting her godmother tell her to "*act* important" at the meetings when she *was* important? She was a director and daughter of the managing director, for goodness' sake. And why had all this only just occurred to her?

There were no two ways about it, Susannah had been running her life. And it wasn't a life that gave her much joy.

And Cass knew. Which was why she had tried, unsuccessfully for the last seven years, to make up for Susannah's intrusion and find Annie a mate. They weren't so much blind dates she'd been going on for the past seven years, they were guilt offerings.

And she also now knew why all those blind dates had been doomed to failure from the start. And why poor Edward felt more like an A Level discussion paper than a lover. *Edward Goddard Is the Answer to All Annie's Prayers. Discuss.*

The vision of Jake telling her he was sorry before stumbling out of her life again had been sweet torture every time she'd shut her eyes. He was there with her all the time—so what was new? But she simply didn't have the energy to deal with it at the moment.

Half an hour later, as Annie lifted her body out of the bath, she was almost overcome by a feeling of cold air enveloping her body, a feeling of such lightness she felt giddy.

Later that evening, she stayed in at the apartment, too weary to leave, yet wishing desperately that her family would leave her alone. She sat in the drawing room with her father, Katherine and Davina and, with a new, disturbing focus, she saw that Davina had carved out a role of monumental importance to them both. In every circumstance, every situation, only Davina knew how to soothe each one, only she knew what to say to calm them. Davina stroked their egos with the same evenness and patience as a punka wallah wafting a fan over his master's head. It didn't need much of an imagination to see that in the privacy of George's bedroom, she merely swapped one sort of stroking for another.

Thus, Davina had become the only person ever to stand between George and his darling eldest daughter, Katherine. Annie had never seen her father show such frustration with Katherine as when he felt Davina was showing her more attention than she was showing him. Davina had achieved what Annie had always thought was impossible; she had caused a rift between father and his favored firstborn. To her desperate frustration, Annie could see no way to solve this puzzle. Insight did not always come with solutions.

Tired, but somehow cleansed, Annie felt Joy and Marlon were due another e-mail. She popped into the apartment office and logged on.

Annie

I'm falling further and further the more I see him. And if he doesn't stop talking about that bitch one of us will have to die. There's only one thing for it. I'll have to stop seeing him.

J

And then Marlon's . . .

Annie

Saw the boys at the weekend. The She-Devil will let me see them every weekend. I'm overjoyed, but of course it means me and J is now out of the question. I want to spend every minute of every weekend with the boys and how can I possibly ask her to take that on?

I'll have to stop seeing her. It hurts me too much.

M

Annie had had enough. If she couldn't sort her own life out, she could at least sort out theirs. She clicked on to both of their names at the same time and started tapping.

Life's too short. If you don't both seize the wonderful gift life offers you with great big fat fistfuls, you could spend the rest of your life regretting it.

You have a choice. A life of lonely regret or happiness with some pain along the way.

You choose. I love you both.

A

She stared at the message for ages. So easy to dispense advice. So difficult to take it.

Should she, shouldn't she?

As soon as she'd clicked on the send logo, she felt better.

When, just before ten o'clock, Edward appeared, Annie was so weary that she simply felt grateful to see him. He was a friend, an ally. She'd deal with the other aspect another time.

He came in to sit with them all and after a while, she needed to get out of the stifling atmosphere.

"Would you like a hot drink?" she asked Edward.

He nodded and they both went into the kitchen.

While Annie started warming up some milk for hot chocolate, Edward started asking her what she thought of Davina.

She shrugged. "I think she's blonde," she said, trying to smile.

Edward didn't return her smile. "I think you see what I see," he said quietly.

Annie looked at him as he stirred the milk. "Oh yes? And what's that?"

"That she's cunning. And out to get what she can." He was about to say something else, but the kitchen door swung open and Davina appeared.

"Are you making hot chocolate?" she asked winningly.

Annie nodded.

"Would it be too much trouble to ask you to put some more milk in? Your father and Katie would love one too—with a bit of whisky added of course."

Annie gave her a short smile. "No problem."

Edward went to the fridge and passed Annie another milk carton. Davina didn't look like she was going to leave, but then she was called by an impatient George. For a second, it looked like she was struggling in her mind as to whether to stay or go, but with a sudden dazzling smile, she left the room.

Edward walked purposefully over to the intercom and turned it off.

He stared significantly at Annie.

"I wonder who suggested hot chocolate for all?" he asked eventually.

"What do you mean?"

"Our blonde friend did, of course," he replied. "She knows we're on to her. She doesn't like us being alone where she can't check what we're saying."

Annie was just about to ask Edward what made him feel that he had any right to be as worried as her about Davina's entrance into her family, when he answered it for her.

"You may have noticed that I feel great loyalty toward your family," he said quietly, walking around the kitchen counter so that he was standing next to Annie. He leaned against the counter by her side.

She said nothing but kept staring at the warm milk. She wasn't interested. In fact she was more interested in the milk than in him.

"You haven't noticed?"

She simply nodded.

"Have you wondered why?" he was whispering now.

"Not really," she answered. "I've been a bit preoccupied to be honest."

"Of course."

Bubbles of heat appeared around the edges of the milk and as Annie went to turn the gas down, Edward's hand was on hers.

"Annie—"

The kitchen door swung open and Davina was there again. Annie had never been so pleased to see her. Edward made a point of not moving, but Annie jumped a mile.

"Sorry! Was I interrupting anything?" asked Davina innocently.

"No."

"Yes."

"Only, Katie's getting a bit desperate for her hot chocolate. Would you like a hand?" and she started getting the mugs out of the cupboard. Edward watched her silently as she stretched up to reach one of the top shelves. He didn't offer to help. Ignoring him expertly, Davina busied herself measuring out the cocoa and chatting to Annie.

"Isn't it funny? As soon as you tell yourself you want a hot chocolate, suddenly you need it instantly? It's good for the nerves, though, isn't it?"

Annie, exhausted, nodded and half-smiled at Davina's gentle babbling. God, she talks crap, thought Annie. And she does it so well.

Davina put all the mugs on the same tray and carried them out into the lounge. "Coming?" she asked as she pushed open the door with her backside and held it open for them.

Edward and Annie had no choice but to walk past her out of the kitchen.

Chapter 27

Cass was waiting for scan results and was getting restless and bored being stuck in bed all day. Annie now stayed with her as much as she could. Cass was able to look her in the eye now, and they didn't speak much, but it was clear that Cass was glad she was there.

Whenever Edward was able to get away from work, he insisted on coming with her. For support, he said, but she really didn't need it. In fact, she much preferred going on her own.

Jake was keeping to himself now. He didn't see any of the crowd anymore and certainly didn't bump into Annie in the park or at the opera. Apparently he was at the office all the hours God gave.

Good. She couldn't cope with him right now. It was typical of the bad timing of her life—now that she resolutely knew how indisputable her feelings for him were, she'd terrified him off. Just the thought of him made her so tense that she'd have probably spontaneously combusted at the sight of him.

One day, on a rare occasion that Annie was at the hospital on her own, Susannah walked her slowly along the dragging corridor toward the exit.

"Well, it's nice to see that something good has come out of all this tragedy," said Susannah quietly, an affectionate eye on Annie's profile.

Annie knew she was talking about Edward. She smiled weakly.

"Edward *is* very nice," she allowed.

"My dear, a little dicky-bird tells me that the 'very nice' Edward has a very nice surprise question to pop on New Year's Eve."

Annie looked at Susannah in alarm. Encouraged, Susannah continued.

"We could be looking at more than two weddings next year . . ."

At the hospital door, Annie felt positively virginal as Susannah kissed her on the forehead.

"Your mother would be very proud."

As Annie walked out of the hospital, a blast of cold air hit her and along with it, a realization that was colder still.

She should have stopped listening to her godmother years ago.

The next day, something odd happened which, were Annie not already emotionally confused, would have made her so. But she was simply too exhausted to be able to dissect meaning from events for herself anymore.

As she was walking into the hospital with Edward by her side, she saw Dr. Hastings at the end of the corridor walking toward them. Dr. Hastings, an English obstetric surgeon who had been living in New York for the past few years, was one of Annie's favorite doctors in the hospital, partly because the woman didn't treat her like an absolute idiot.

She was pleased to see her. Now she could ask her how Cass was, without being in earshot of anyone else.

But as she drew nearer, she saw that Dr. Hastings did something funny with her body. She seemed to squint at them both from the distance, then jerk her body upward in shock, stop mid-walk, almost turn back and then change her mind.

She kept walking toward them, only far slower than before. Before Annie could even turn to Edward, he had gone—double backed on himself and turned a corner. Vanished.

By the time Dr. Hastings had reached her, she seemed to have recovered her equilibrium. She told Annie in her usual measured tones that Cass was unchanged, although every day that the baby survived was a day working in its favor. Just as they finished their conversation, she stopped herself.

"Annie, can I ask you a really weird question?"

"Of course."

"Was that man you were with just now—was he Eddie Goddard?"

"*Edward* Goddard," corrected Annie. "Yes, that's right. Why? Do you know him?"

Dr. Hastings snorted. "Yeah," she said. "I know him all right."

And Dr. Hastings walked off.

Annie shrugged her shoulders and went to see Cass.

Jake looked down upon the eerily quiet streets of New York from the twenty-fourth-floor offices of Markhams' PR. He had sent all the other consultants home early. He quite liked the feeling of being the only one in the city who was working the evening before New Year's Eve. Except that he had one day left to find evidence of where he was sure the vanishing money was going. Just one day to save Markhams' PR. One day to persuade Annie Markham he was worth loving.

And he was absolutely sure he could do it.

Susannah had been blunt with him. They simply couldn't afford his company anymore. They'd have to go. They would be trying to sell Markhams' in the New Year. He knew what that meant. In the state it was in now, the owners would hardly make anything. The Markham family would never recover. He had to do something. He couldn't ruin Annie's life twice.

He sighed deeply and delved into his computer bag. There was Edward's disk that Susannah had handed him a while before.

What was it he didn't trust about Edward? Was Edward dangerous for the Markham family? Or was he just a tosser who was after Annie?

No, Jake was convinced Edward was dangerous.

And it was his professional integrity telling him so. Years of experience in the field. His insight. Perception. Intuition. A gift, some might call it.

And, of course, raging, thumping jealousy that made his skin crawl.

If only he could work it out. He slid the disk into his laptop for the hundredth time. He was *not* going to give up on this.

He clicked open the files for Markhams' PR spreadsheet for the Profit and Loss Account and Cost and Revenue Projections. The graph silently zoomed into focus, all bright colors and pretty pictures.

Yep, all the figures were present and correct, down to the last penny. Jake frowned and shook his head. He just didn't understand it. The company had a black hole in it, a vacuum through which all the money was being sucked. The fact that the situation had worsened in the past few days convinced him he was right about where it was going. He just had to find proof.

He closed the file. There were numerous other files on the disk but all of them were password-protected. He didn't know where to start, so he started tapping in anything that came to mind.

An hour later, he'd got no further. He hadn't managed to open one of the files.

He rubbed his eyes, stretched, yawned and leaned back in the office chair. His thoughts, as usual, moved to the last time he'd seen Annie. That bloody fiasco of an evening at the opera.

He saw her again, sitting in the box with Edward, letting him whisper into the nape of her neck, his lips touching her tendrils of hair—

He stood up suddenly. Walked to the window.

He pictured Edward leaning forward to shake his hand, a wide grin on his open, bland face.

And then, for some unknown reason, he visualized Davina squeezing herself past Edward and introducing herself to him. What was all that about? He pictured how she'd flirted with him— as if there was an audience watching her every move. And for the first time he remembered Edward's reaction to her.

His body jolted almost before his mind did.

Hold on a minute . . . Yes! There was something about the way—

That was it!

He raced over to his computer again, double-clicked on the top file and then tapped in a new password.

He held his breath as the screen blinked slowly.

And then there it was in black and white before his very eyes. The black hole of Markhams' PR.

At last. He had his evidence.

Chapter 28

Marlon sat in the kitchen, thumping his fingers unconsciously on the table. New Year's Eve and all was well with the world. He would be seeing his sons regularly next year and he'd got Cynthia out of his life.

The New Year was going to be a good one, he told himself for the tenth time that morning.

He'd canceled Joy that morning over the phone. She'd been surprised but kind. He knew she was hurt, but he just couldn't keep it up anymore. The stories about Cynthia, the illusion that he was in pain. The pretense that Joy was just his best friend. And now that he'd have the boys to look after in the New Year, he couldn't waste his energies on anything else. They deserved more than to feel shunted around from one unwilling parent to another.

Right. To work.

He switched on the kettle and, to silence the emptiness that echoed in his ears, he turned on the radio.

Two minutes later he walked his coffee into the front room which doubled as his study. He tidied up the sofa and switched on his computer.

Ah, Annie had sent him another nondescript, indecipherable e-mail. How nice.

He clicked on.

He read it once.

And then again:

Life's too short. If you don't both seize the wonderful gift life offers you with great big fat fistfuls, you could spend the rest of your life regretting it.

You have a choice. A life of lonely regret or happiness with some pain along the way.

You choose.

I love you both.

A

Jesus. It was all or nothing with that girl.

With a nasty shock, he realized she'd sent the same e-mail to both of them. So Joy had received the same message. What could that mean? Did Joy know how he felt? Thank God he'd canceled her! He'd never be able to look at her in the face again. What did Annie think she was doing?

He started replying to Annie, but his hands were shaking so much above the keyboards, he couldn't get beyond *Daer Anie* . . .

The knock on the door made him jump so high he almost fell off his chair.

He stretched to the window and looked through the net curtain to the front door.

There stood Joy. As she looked over, he let the net curtain drop.

Oh bother, now she'd seen him, she knew he was there. What was she doing here? Was she going to be angry with him for sending Annie e-mails about her? Was she going to demand for him to be turned away from the Samaritans for stalking her?

Maybe she hadn't seen her message yet. Maybe she was just popping round to see if he wanted anything from the shops . . .

She knocked again. Louder this time.

He knew he had no choice. He walked, like a prisoner to his execution, toward his front door. Thankfully it was a very short walk.

He opened the door.

He stared at Joy. Her eyes seemed more bright than usual, but it was an edgy brightness.

"Marlon."

"Joy."

They looked at each other a bit more.

"Are you going to invite me in or do I have to use force?"

"Do come in."

Now he was really terrified.

They stood in the hall, aware that the small but significant movement from terraced street to narrow hall had done nothing to ease the tension.

Maybe it was just a lighthearted social call . . .

"I take it you got the e-mail."

Oh Jiminy.

"I just found it."

"I take it that's why you canceled me this morning."

Was that pain and embarrassment behind her abruptness? His heart went out to her. It almost killed him to know he'd hurt Joy.

"No—"

"First you flirt *shamelessly* with me for five years. Then you use me as a well-padded shoulder to cry on when your wife leaves you. Then you cancel me—no excuse—just because some silly girl in New York seems to have got it into her head that I can't take—"

"I love you."

His voice was brittle with fear.

"What?"

"I love you."

It was surprisingly less terrifying to say the second time.

They stared in shared disbelief at each other.

Marlon felt ashamed.

"Sorry."

Joy's smile was slow and full. Her voice was suddenly full of tenderness.

"About bloody time," she whispered.

Later that evening, toes entwined under the warm blankets, they toasted the New Year in together and thought of Annie with more gratitude than she'd ever know.

December 31st started sluggishly in New York as if, aware that it was the last day of the year, it just didn't have the energy to do it all over again. Annie knew the feeling. She lay in bed, too tired to get up, too wired to sleep. Scraps of information whizzed and whirred around her brain so fast that they met, fused and sparked, creating entire new worlds of emotion. The Big Bang was going on inside her head. Unsurprisingly, she was getting a headache.

The sound of a phone ringing interrupted her thoughts. Safe in the knowledge that no one else in the apartment would bother to answer it, she forced her body out of bed and over to her phone, beside the chaise longue.

"Annie, it's me," whispered Cass urgently.

Annie's heart stopped for a beat.

"My God," she croaked, wide awake, "are you all right?"

"Yes—"

"Sure?"

"Yes—"

The baby's all right?"

"Yes—"

"Have you had your test results yet?"

"Yes, everything's fine—"

"What's up?"

"Annie! You have to come in and see me."

"I was going to. I've only just got up—"

"Yes, but you've got to come in soon, before my mum gets here or Edward. It's very important."

"Why? What's happened?"

"We can't tell you over the phone. We have to tell you face to face."

"*We?*"

"Just get here. Quick."

And the phone went dead.

For some reason Annie was terrified. What the hell was so important that Cass had called her specially? And who was "we"?

Annie convinced herself during her shower that "we" was Jake and Cass. They were going to elope and they needed Annie to put Brutus and Susannah off their trail.

Fumbling frantically for her clothes, she changed her mind. Jake had told Cass that Annie had been obsessed with him for seven years and he'd had enough. He would be waiting for her with cameras from the *Ricki Lake Show* to humiliate her into closure.

In the taxi on the way to the hospital, she changed her mind again. Jake had confessed his true feelings for Sophie—he had been in love with her all along—to Cass, and Cass wanted Annie to spike David's drink and give Sophie concussion again—

The taxi arrived at the hospital.

She ran into Cass's room and saw straightaway who "we" was. It was a big disappointment.

Dr. Sarah Hastings was sitting in the chair next to Cass's bed and Annie's entrance interrupted their deep conversation.

"Thank God! I thought you'd never get here," started Cass.

"Is this going to be a big shock?" asked Annie, sitting on the other chair by Cass's bed. "Because I'm not very good with shocks."

Cass sighed deeply.

"I don't know."

"Oh dear."

Dr. Hastings spoke.

"I think you should know something that might—might upset you," she said.

Oh no, thought Annie. Jake is a Mafia boss, using the screen of consultancy as a front . . . No, wait! He's a *woman*, like in that film—

"It's about Edward."

Who? The stunned, baffled expression on Annie's face seemed to worry the other two.

"Oh dear, this might be even more difficult than we thought," whispered Cass. "Be gentle with her," she told Dr. Hastings. "Pretend you're telling a much-loved patient that they're dying."

Dr. Hastings nodded. "Eddie Goddard is an ex-convict who's embezzling money out of your father's business."

"Jesus Christ!" exclaimed Cass. "Remind me not to come to *you* if I'm dying."

Annie was mute.

This meant she *shouldn't* marry him, right?

She turned slowly to Cass.

"It turns out that—" started Cass.

"Back in England, before I specialized, I did a stint as a doctor for Pentonville Prison," interrupted Dr. Hastings, "Eddie was one of the inmates there."

"Plain old Eddie Goddard," interrupted Cass again. "His parents were rich, but certainly not related to aristocracy. He went to Eton so he had all the right contacts but went totally off the rails and once his parents lost all their money in some hideous investment cock-up, he used all his old contacts for his own illegal aims."

"But why—why me?" asked Annie.

"It's just part of his trick," explained Dr. Hastings in the same tone as she would explain that someone prefers two sugars in their tea rather than one. "He gets inside a company and steals from within. And if possible, he screws the prettiest girl in the company. But he had a bit of a thing about you. I'm afraid that was my fault."

Cass and Annie stared at her.

"I used to bring him in *Hello* and *Tatler*. There were pictures of you all over his cell walls. In fact, I was very jealous."

"Jealous?" repeated Cass and Annie, shocked.

"Yes, jealous," sighed Dr. Hastings. "We had a very short-lived fling. I couldn't help myself. A moment of madness." She looked down at her hands as she mumbled this.

Annie and Cass both suddenly felt sorry for her.

"He can be very persuasive," murmured Annie reflectively.

"And totally convincing," added Cass.

Dr. Hastings shook her head. "That's nothing. You should have seen him in his prison outfit. Buns of steel."

Cass and Annie blinked.

"Anyway, as soon as he came out of prison, he actively sought you out," continued Dr. Hastings to Annie.

Annie put her head in her hands.

"So, let me get this straight," she said weakly. "He hasn't got management experience?"

Cass gave a deep sigh.

"Annie, the man's a convicted crook," she said slowly. "Nothing he has ever told anyone holds any water." She paused.

Annie waited for her answer. Clues weren't enough anymore.

"No. He has no management experience."

Annie shook her head and finally spoke slowly. "So while we've been hoping that he can save us from ruin, *he's* the one who's been ruining *us*."

Dr. Hastings and Cass looked at her sadly.

"The more keen he is on you, the more money he's been swindling out of your father's company. It heightens the chase for him."

They all sat in silence for a moment, letting their minds catch up with this latest piece of information.

"Are you all right, honey?" asked Cass quietly.

"No!" whispered Annie, exasperated, hot tears stinging her eyes. "I'm not all right. I'm furious with Edward. I'm furious with my-

self for enjoying his company and friendship and flattery so much
and . . . and for falling for his lies. I'm terrified of what he's done
to the company and all of our futures. I'm angry with you, Cass—
yes I am—and your mother, for always trying to influence my
thoughts. Why couldn't you both just leave me alone?"

She slumped in her chair.

"And I just don't know who to believe anymore," she mumbled
finally.

She took a deep, deep sigh, that seemed to reach her toes.

"Happy New Year."

For the first time in Annie's experience, Cass was speechless.

That was *it*, she thought furiously, as she stormed back to the apartment. She was *sick* of other people trying to tell her what to do,
who to be, who to be with. She didn't trust anyone anymore, least
of all Cass and Susannah. She could only trust herself. That was the
last time she would ever let anyone influence her decisions.

When she got home, she was relieved to find she was alone.
Her family were all out at a champagne luncheon at the Houselmans. They would be there for hours yet, before coming home to
change for the New Year's Eve celebrations at The Plaza Hotel
down the road.

She lay on her bed, exhausted. She was just about to phone Joy
in London for a heart-to-heart, when the phone rang. She
stretched out to answer it.

It was Jake. She was almost as unnerved by this as by his almost
desperate tone.

"Can we talk?"

She couldn't have been more shocked if he'd asked "Can we
rumba?"

"Of course."

"Where's your family?"

"Out."

"How long for?"

"Hours." She frowned. "Why?"

"I can't say over the phone. We'll be there in a minute." And he hung up.

She sat up on the bed. What was all this with the "we" again? What the hell was going on? Why was her body acting as if she was about to make a parachute jump? As if she didn't know. How long had she got before Jake arrived? Was there time to put more make-up on? Was there time to—

The door buzzed.

Standing with Jake was a bulky man in a pastel puffa jacket with thin legs in black jeans. He looked like a rather ugly stick of cotton candy. Jake introduced him as a policeman and she forgot his name immediately.

"We'd have been quicker," explained Jake, "but I thought you were actually *on* Fifth Avenue—"

"Come in."

It didn't matter how much she kept thinking she was in control of her emotions, the sight of Jake always left her body in mild shell-shock. Ice-cold hands, hot head, stomach of blancmange.

She was surprised that there was still some residue anger left over from the last time she'd seen him when he'd walked out on her again. And now she had no fall-back position. She could hardly draw herself up to her full height and say to him chillingly, "Don't you know I'm about to be engaged to an ex-convict who's swindled my whole family?"

Didn't quite have the right ring to it.

They walked into the drawing room where Annie sat down to stop her legs from trembling.

"I'd offer you a drink," she said, "but I don't think I'd get much of it in the glass."

"That's OK," said Cotton Candy Cop happily. "I don't drink on duty. But Jake could make you one."

Jake found the drinks cabinet and poured Annie a stiff whisky.
Duty? Did he say duty? This was a *duty* call?

"So you know about Edward? Or should I say Eddie?" she asked.

Cotton Candy Cop and Jake looked at each other.

Jake handed Annie her drink and sat down next to her. He stopped himself from putting his arm around her.

"You knew?"

"I found out about half an hour ago."

"Who from?"

"My friend Cass is in hospital. Her doctor knew Edward—Eddie—when he was in prison."

"So they're not gonna tell anyone in your family?"

Annie shrugged. "I can tell Cass not to if you want."

"Is she good at keeping secrets, this friend of yours?"

Jake looked away.

Annie shrugged. "I haven't told her any for a while."

"Well do me a favor," said the cop. "Tell her to keep this one. As soon as possible."

"OK."

Annie looked defiantly at Jake. Typical that he was here to tell her the bad news about Edward. He gave her a short smile.

"How are you?"

Annie shrugged with as much defiance as she could. It was nothing a fourteen-year-old truant wouldn't have been proud of.

"Fine."

"Whaddya know about this 'Edward' guy?" asked Cotton Candy Cop.

Annie told them everything she'd just been told.

Cotton Candy Cop turned to Jake.

"All yours, pal."

Jake took a deep breath.

"OK," he said deliberately and took a disk out of his jacket pocket. "I have the evidence that could put Edward away for quite a while. This is the disk he gave you to send to Susannah. He . . . he must have had other things on his mind when he handed it to you because there were other files on that disk that he certainly wouldn't have wanted you to see." Jake came to a halt.

He sighed. Why did he have to be the one that broke the bad news to Annie? "Edward has been embezzling money out of your dad's company slowly but surely since he first joined as chief exec. At first, he thought there was more than there was, so as soon as he realized there wasn't much to play around with, he got to work quickly. Then when we came in, he upped the speed. And we're fairly sure he must have overheard me trying to tell you not to trust him that day at the park, because ever since then he's practically finished the company off."

Annie barely had the energy to nod.

Cotton Candy Cop nodded his head in Jake's direction and gave a big cheesy grin.

"And this guy knew all along. Whaddya think of that, eh? Clever guy!"

Jake kept his eyes down as he spoke into his chest.

"I'm afraid at that stage it was nothing to do with being clever."

"Ah, you English—you're so modest!"

Jake continued. "But he couldn't have done it alone. He had to get someone in there first to help shoehorn his way in. Smooth the way if you like. And then keep it smooth while he did the important stuff. His PA, so to speak."

Jake paused. "Annie, we know who his accomplice is."

Annie looked at Jake. His eyes softened as he spoke.

"It had to be someone who could tell him things about the family so he knew all the right buttons to press. Someone who had infiltrated the family. Someone who also had access to the company's files."

Annie gasped. "Ohmygod!"

Jake nodded.

"Davina!" they both said together.

"That's how I was able to find the evidence," said Jake, his words tumbling out. "I knew there was something fishy about them at the opera, but I just couldn't put my finger on it. There was a lot of hostility between them and yet . . . they seemed to be communicating without talking. And although she was flirting with me, she was thinking of Edward. Basically," he paused. "Well, basically, she reminded me of me." He shrugged, and Annie was too stressed to notice the deep blush deepen across his cheekbones. "I realized they must have been involved with each other at some point. And then it dawned on me. They still *are* involved with each other. But they're having to keep it a secret. The name 'Davina' was Edward's password to a file that showed me everything I needed to know."

With effort, Annie closed her mouth and blinked. Both at the same time. While breathing. Multi-tasking.

"So *that's* why she hates me so much!" she whispered. "She's been jealous."

"You were datin' Edward, weren't you?"

Annie grimaced.

"Sorry, hon, but we need to know everything," insisted Cotton Candy Cop. "Were you sleepin' with the guy? Givin' him pillow talk?"

Jake stood up.

"This is between you two, I think. I'll leave you to it. I have some e-mails to be getting on with anyway. Can I use your office?"

Cotton Candy Cop wasn't letting him get away that quickly.

"I'll be outta here in a little while," he said. "I'll call you on your mobile for a rendezvous."

"OK," said Jake, already halfway out of the room.

Annie directed him down the hall.

When he had gone, Cotton Candy Cop leaned forward. "He's a handsome guy, ain't he?"

"Who?"

"Edward."

Annie nodded absentmindedly. Had Jake just admitted that while he was flirting with Sophie he was thinking of her?

The cop started putting her in the picture.

Davina Barker had been working with Eddie Goddard for over a year. He had sought her out when she had first started working for Markhams'. She had at first only been flirting with George for obvious reasons, and enjoying the attentions of a wealthy man and the prospects that all that had entailed.

But when Edward got to her, she hadn't stood a chance. She fell for his charms and started to risk everything she had achieved so far by siphoning off small amounts of money from the company into Eddie's offshore bank account.

And then the perfect opportunity presented itself for Eddie to move in. The job of chief exec came up. By now, he knew through Davina exactly what would impress George. All he had to do was turn up at the polo club for a couple of months, mention his distant connections, and hey, presto. He got the job. Now he could oversee Davina. And, once he was in, and didn't need Davina as much as before, he made a move on Annie Markham, whom he'd always fancied. Simple.

It all made perfect sense to Annie now. The more Davina had fallen for Edward, the more she was losing interest in her own far slower game with George. And the more interest Eddie had shown in Annie, the more jealous Davina had grown of her.

Annie also knew that Susannah had trusted Edward absolutely, enough to tell him things he didn't strictly need to know—and Susannah knew exactly how Annie felt about Davina, thanks to Cass's dutiful updates. That was how Edward knew to appear to mistrust Davina whenever he was with Annie. Meanwhile, Davina knew, via Edward, that Annie was on to her. No wonder Davina hated her.

Annie felt all the air had been punched out of her. She couldn't trust anyone anymore. And the nearest she'd got to being in a relationship with a man in seven years had actually been the biggest sham of all. She'd been utterly and totally duped.

"He win you over?" asked the cop eventually.

"Who?"

"Edward."

She shook her head.

"Nope. I didn't tell him anything," she said in a flat voice. "The truth is I was using him just as much as he was using me."

Cotton Candy Cop nodded.

"You didn't tell him anything about the business?"

Annie shook her head. "I liked him as a friend, but I never really trusted him," she said. "I thought I did, but in hindsight, I didn't tell him a thing. I told Jake more about the business than I ever told him."

She would have been ready to say more—is that why she had mentioned Jake? But the cop wasn't interested. He was already lifting his bulky frame into a standing position.

"OK, lady," he was saying. "I gotta get this disk down to the station. All you gotta remember is not to tell anyone about the true Eddie Goddard and Davina Barker. That clear?"

Annie nodded. That seemed easy enough.

Then she remembered.

"My family are expecting an announcement tonight."

"Between you and him?"

"Who?"

"Edward."

"Yes."

"Jeez. I thought you said you were using him?"

"Well, I was, but I didn't really realize until . . . recently. And then once I'd realized, it was sort of too late. And I didn't have the energy to say anything. Look, all you need to know is that I've been told that Edward's going to propose to me tonight, and as far as my family is concerned, I'm going to do the right thing. As usual."

"Which means?"

"They thought I was going to say yes."

"And were you?"

"No. I was going to refuse him."

The cop smiled at her.

"Sounds like you been goin' through your own little drama here."

"Nothing I can't handle."

They smiled briefly at each other and Annie's smile got briefly wider. Relief—and a new sense of freedom—flooded over her.

"Good girl. So all you gotta do is keep up the act. Just keep pretendin' like you're about to pop his ring on your finger and we'll all be fine. Don't tell a soul the truth. You hear? You confide in any of your bosom buddies and they might start treating them differently and then we lose these two slippery characters. D'you understand? This ain't no schoolgirl secret to blab to the first person you see, OK?"

"I'm not a schoolgirl."

The cop smiled.

"Good. I gotta go before your folks arrive. What you doin' tonight, sugar?"

"I was going to stay here for drinks with everyone and then go to the hospital to see Cass and Brutus. Then after midnight I was going to join all my family—and Davina and Edward—here. They were all going to the New Year's Eve party at The Plaza."

The cop nodded gravely.

"Now listen to me very carefully," he said. "Don't do anythin' that might arouse suspicion. Stay for the drinks and then go to the hospital as planned. Treat everyone as normal—especially Davina and Edward. We need those two to be at The Plaza waitin' for us. Preferably after midnight, when everyone's had the best part of the party. Just sit pretty." He grinned. "That shouldn't be too difficult, should it?"

Annie tried to stand up, but he was already leaving the room.

"I can see myself out," he shouted from the hall.

After she heard the door slam behind the cop, Annie sank into the sofa, drained.

When the doorbell went, she was poleaxed by indecision. Who could it be? Could it be Edward? Was he going to surprise her more than he could imagine by proposing now, before the party? What if he'd seen the cop just leaving?

She didn't want to answer the door to anyone. Ever again.

Then she remembered what the cop had said—act normal. Pity she couldn't remember what normal was. She thought hard and finally decided that normal people would probably answer the doorbell.

She got up and answered the doorbell.

And there stood Susannah.

"My dear," said Susannah, walking straight past her into the drawing room. Annie had no choice but to follow her.

Susannah twirled around and faced her. She was grinning rather manically.

"I just wanted to see you on this rather special day. How are you feeling, my dear?"

Annie chose not to speak.

It was a clever move, influenced largely by the fact that she was unable to.

Act normal, act normal . . .

Susannah changed her expression to one of fond devotion. She looked like she was constipated.

"I can't help but worry about you," she said softly. "You're so much like your poor dear mother. She was never very good at making her own decisions either."

That did it.

Annie shut her eyes. She just wanted Susannah to go away. Why did she always confuse her so much?

"Don't do that, Annie, it will give you lines," said Susannah impatiently. "I shouldn't think Edward likes lines."

Annie opened her eyes. Too right. Especially vertical ones running down his suit.

"You know I only want you to be happy—" continued Susannah.

"No you don't," whispered Annie before she could stop herself. There was silence.

"What?" Susannah's voice was full of steely hurt.

"Sorry, Susannah," said Annie, with careful softness to her tone. "I think you *think* you want me to be happy, but you confuse your own happiness with my own."

Act normal, act normal . . .

It dawned on Annie that a normal person—one who wasn't still mourning the loss of her mother and her lover and had lost sight of her own mind in the grief—would have said all this years ago.

"And the result has been that you have single-handedly made me unhappy for the past seven years."

Susannah's voice was like a hacksaw.

"What are you talking about?"

Annie felt years of pain rise up to her chest. The anger at being abandoned by the two most important people in her life, let alone being duped by Edward—all of it was being redirected toward Susannah.

And Susannah deserved it. Annie realized that Susannah had done exactly to her what Davina and Edward had been doing to her father's company for the past year. Using insider information to extract exactly what she wanted, not caring about the empty shell she left behind.

"I may have been young," she whispered, "but you knew exactly what you were doing. You confused me, you turned your own daughter into a spy—"

She ignored Susannah's gasp of shock.

"—to get inside me so that you could press all the right buttons.

You thoroughly undermined all my confidence so I ruined the most important decision of my life."

Susannah looked at her as if she had finally lost the two remaining marbles the family had pinned their hopes on.

"You're not still harping on about that pathetic college incident, are you?" she demanded.

Annie shook her head to get Susannah's voice out of her ears. How did she always make her feel that her emotions were wrong? How could emotions be wrong?

Susannah was still talking.

"That time you thought you were pregnant, only to discover you were one month late through student stress? Did you need any other proof that you were too young for marriage?"

Annie felt her back straighten. She was not going to be confused this time. She would win this row. She felt a lifetime of tangled thoughts slip undone inside her head. She could see every strand of thought clearly for the first time in years.

She took in a deep breath. "The right man doesn't always come at the right time. So Jake came too early for me—does that mean I deserved to lose him?"

"Jake?" exclaimed Susannah. "What does Jake have to do with it?"

"He was the 'money-grabbing student' I was going to leave with."

Susannah went pale with shock. Words failed her. *Jake?* She realized that if Jake had been in the family all these years they might not be in this dire predicament. She'd certainly never envisaged the student to be anything like Jake. If she'd known . . . her mind was almost bursting with too many thoughts at this new piece of information.

Annie was satisfied. She'd certainly never seen Susannah look so discomposed. She continued.

"You terrified me into taking the safe option. You actually convinced me that he was only with me for the money and that I was trapping him for all the wrong reasons. How could you do that? When I trusted you so much! You used your knowledge of me against me—against my own happiness. And you're still doing it. You confuse me all the time. How can you?"

Her breath may have run out, but her words hadn't. They were tumbling out, together with the tears, with a force that almost scared her. She couldn't look up at Susannah; she just had to keep going.

"When I told him that I wasn't leaving with him, he left me. Went out of my life. Just like that."

Annie caught her breath. "And I've never been happy since."

There was silence. Annie's voice dipped with pain.

"I've been *grieving* for seven years. Everything I've done since has been a coping mechanism. And you—who profess to know me and love me so well—you haven't even noticed—"

Susannah didn't respond.

Annie sank back down into the sofa and buried her head in her hands.

Finally she looked up at her godmother. Susannah was looking in shock at her.

"I did notice," Susannah eventually whispered. "I just didn't know what to do about it."

They stared at each other in silence for a while.

The phone's sudden ring made them jump. They both stared at it. Susannah picked it up.

Annie watched her on the phone, her mind full of discordant, soured thoughts.

Susannah put the phone down, her hand shaking. She turned to Annie.

"It's Cass," she said. "She wants us both. It's urgent."

"Oh my God."

"Coming?"

"Of course."

When they reached the hall, Annie was almost as shocked as Susannah by the sight of Jake standing there. She had completely forgotten he was in the apartment.

And from the look of him, he looked just as shocked to see them there. They all jumped at the sight of each other and then stared dumbly for a while, their mouths opening and shutting like goldfish.

"Jake was just doing some e-mails from here," Annie finally explained to Susannah, resenting her need to explain. But Susannah was uninterested in anything but Cass.

"We're just going to the hospital," Annie told Jake. "Cass has—"

"Yes I know," said Jake.

"Oh."

"I overheard. Um. From the hall."

"Oh."

"I've just got one more e-mail to do. Could I—"

"Just shut the door behind you," finished Annie and they left Jake standing in the silent apartment lobby. He stood quite still after they'd gone, his chest heaving, his eyes damp. But one part of him was the most relaxed it had been for years. He stretched his neck out and put his hand to it. Not a single twitch. In the silence he closed his eyes and grinned so wide it almost hurt.

Behind him in the drawing room everything was still. Except for the tiny red light flickering in the growing dark, on the inconspicuous gray intercom.

Chapter 29

By the time Susannah and Annie had reached the hospital, Cass was feeling much better. She'd had a nasty fright and had thought she was losing her last baby. But she wasn't.

The doctor was the most positive she'd ever been.

"Every day longer that the baby stays inside her is good news, and it's beginning to look like a survivor."

Annie insisted—for the first time—that she go in to see Cass first. She took Susannah's quiet approval as a sign that her words hadn't soured their relationship for good.

Once with Cass, Annie made her promise not to tell her mother the truth about Edward. Cass agreed immediately and Annie knew then that the tables were finally turning.

"You do love me, don't you, Annie?" asked Cass quickly.

"Of course," answered Annie, stunned. "We all do."

It had been the most she'd been able to say. Too many new thoughts had surfaced about Cass. They'd looked at each other for a moment, before Annie had said she had to go. Now was not the time. She returned to the apartment exhausted with only five hours to go until the worn-out year was dead and gone.

Annie's family had already returned and after making the right noises, she had locked herself away in her bedroom. Tonight was to be the biggest performance of her life.

She studied herself in her bedroom mirror, about to dab on some makeup, and tidy up her hair but, to her surprise, she had a Fonzie moment. Perhaps it was a trick of the light, perhaps it was the way the glass caught her at that second, perhaps it was because she had just got so much off her chest—whatever it was, she looked beautiful.

If only her insides were as balanced as her features.

When she finally wandered into the lounge, ready to go back to the hospital, the sight that hit her eyes was quite mesmerizing. Everyone was dressed in such finery that she felt like Cinderella and almost wished she was going to the ball instead.

When the buzzer announced the arrival of Edward, she acknowledged all the knowing smiles of her family, didn't look at Davina and went to answer the door.

Edward was standing at the door in a tux, holding a single red rose. He looked deeply gorgeous and he knew it.

He bowed and handed her the rose.

Unable to do anything else, she took it.

"OW!" she yelled.

She'd caught her thumb on a thorn.

"Oh, Annie!" exclaimed Edward, taking her thumb in his hand and kissing it, closing his eyes in apparent bliss.

Annie thought she was going to retch.

When he went to kiss her, she closed her eyes and saw Jake. No change there then, she thought bitterly.

Back in the drawing room, Annie sat down quietly on the sofa and decided to take some chips. She realized she hadn't eaten since breakfast. As she dug her hand deep in the bowl, she spotted a piece of paper lodged underneath it.

ANNIE

It was Jake's handwriting—she'd know it anywhere.

He'd left her a note there. She wiped salty hands on her leg, desperate to open the note.

"Are you all right?"

It was Davina.

Annie almost jumped out of her skin. Davina mustn't know that Jake had been here earlier.

"You look rather pale," she said, an attempt at affection in her voice.

"She looks absolutely perfect," said Edward, sitting down beside her. "Pale is beautiful."

Davina managed a micro-smile before turning her golden brown shoulders away from them both.

Edward wasn't going to move away, so Annie held his gaze while moving the crisp bowl on top of the letter. She glanced down at it briefly when she took another few crisps. It was completely hidden. She must pick it up after they'd all gone to the party.

They were waiting for David, Sophie, Tony and Fi, before leaving and of course, they were late. Annie couldn't possibly leave before the others—she had to get hold of that letter without Edward and Davina seeing—but it was getting later and later and she knew Cass would be getting worried.

After what seemed like an eternity, the door eventually buzzed.

"Sorry we're late, everyone," David explained amid the throng. "We couldn't find it. We thought it was actually *on* Fifth Avenue."

After loud greetings followed by even louder farewell noises, Annie finally closed the door on the last of them and raced to the lounge, her heart pounding in her chest.

ANNIE

She could hardly open it fast enough, her hands were shaking so much.

The phone made her jump and she stuffed the letter in her coat pocket and answered the phone. She wouldn't have been able to read the note with any distractions.

The voice on the other end was hardly recognizable.

"Annie, it's Susannah. Please come to the hospital now. Cass needs you."

"What's happened? Has she lost the baby?"

Susannah's voice was breaking. "She says she needs you."

Brutus's eyes were dark and hooded. But when he saw Annie, he managed a smile.

Cass's room was dark when Brutus finally opened the door for Annie.

"She's fine," he whispered. "But she seems to think she has to talk to you."

Cass looked up immediately and tried to get out of bed.

Brutus rushed forward. "Get back into bed, darling. Annie's not going anywhere."

He gave Annie a brief smile before leaving them in the darkness.

Cass forced herself to sit up and, staring determinedly at Annie, patted the bed.

Annie sat down facing her friend. Cass was much calmer than she had expected.

"It's about the baby," she started.

"It's all right, isn't it?"

"Not that baby."

Oh. Annie shifted on the bed. She spoke quietly and with a voice full of affection.

"That baby didn't exist, honey."

Cass shook her head.

"It did to you."

"You were—*we* were so young. It was so long ago."

Cass sighed.

"I don't know where to start—" she whispered.

"You don't need to—"

Cass put her hand up.

"I never thought about how you were feeling. Not once. Now I know how you felt."

"Don't be silly—this is different . . . we were children—"

"I never told Mother about the elopement. You do know that, don't you?"

Annie was stumped. Her voice lowered.

"It doesn't . . . matter anymore."

"It *does* matter. I never told her. She was listening in on our phone call. I had no idea she was going up to college to get you until you came back home with her. By then I thought you'd just changed your mind. But it was all my fault for forcing you to tell me your secret. If I'd been a real friend I'd have trusted you."

Annie didn't know what to say.

"You must forgive me."

"Of course I forgive you."

"No, *really*. Now. It's so important to me. Will you ever forgive me?" Cass's voice was barely audible.

Annie moved forward on the bed and hugged Cass. She wanted to say that there was nothing to forgive. She wanted to say that it was too long ago to remember. She wanted to say yes.

But all she could do was cry.

An hour later, Annie left a sleeping Cass in her room. Susannah went in to sit by her daughter for a while, and Annie sat with Brutus.

An hour and a half later, Susannah wandered out of Cass's room. Susannah was going home to bed and insisted that Brutus come home too. He needed rest. They all did.

She looked at Annie. There was less affection in her eyes, but a new hint of respect, and Annie was surprised to find that after all the years of fearing the worst, she had survived her godmother's disapproval.

"Do you want to pop in and say goodnight to Cass?" asked Susannah, and Annie popped her head around the corner of the door.

Cass was lying down again, and when she saw Annie, she smiled.

"Aren't you going to the party?" asked Cass. "With your family . . . and . . . with Jake?"

Annie gasped. Jake's letter! She'd completely forgotten!

Cass's smile widened.

What time was it? Annie checked her watch. Twenty to twelve—less than half an hour before the cops go for Edward and Davina.

With rather unbecoming haste, Annie waved Susannah and Brutus into a cab and tore Jake's letter out of her pocket. She started pacing the sidewalk back home. She knew she could get a taxi at any time, but for now, she needed the air.

ANNIE

She opened the typed note quickly. And stopped walking.

I can't bear it any longer. I can hear everything your'e saying through the intercom—and it's like a dagger in my soul.

have I ballsed it all up?

Oh god the years I've wafted. And then when I see you again—I act pathetic and proud, resentful and angry. But Annie you must know, I've never loved anyone except you. Just becuase I don't know how to deal with my feelings doesn't mean they weren't there. Overpowering me all the time.

I;ve been such an ifiot.

And then in the alleyway I realized my feelings for you hadn't changed a bit—why do you think I came to New York?

Come to The Plaza tonight! Meet me at the clock tower in the ballroom at midnight.

If you're not there I'll understand that you can't forgive me and I'll get on the first flight back to London tomorrow morning. This is the last time I'll bother you.

Oh god but if you're there. . . .

I love you

Jake

Sorry aobut the fyping; I'm a tad tense.

Annie gasped, cried and laughed all at the same time, before re-
alizing that she only had fifteen minutes to get to Jake and then
she started running too. She frantically scanned the street for a
cab. There were loads, but none of them would stop. Of course!
What idiot would try and get a cab at quarter to midnight on
New Year's Eve? Anyway, the chances were that if she managed to
hail a cab, she'd only end up in a traffic jam. It wasn't worth the
risk. She could run it in just about fifteen minutes if she kept up
a good pace.

She had to go down Columbus, cut across Columbus Circle and
then go all along Central Park South, alongside the park. Easy.

She picked up her pace, her heart flying.

As she headed down Central Park South, an enormous bang
exploded to her left. Stunned, she looked—without stopping
running.

An exquisite firework cascaded down over the bare trees of the
park and a thousand celebrating New Yorkers went "Oooh!" as one.

Her heart leapt in her chest. She looked at her watch. Midnight.
New York had started celebrating. Oh God, she had to get to Jake.
As she ran the rest of the way, her eyes on the glorious party in the
sky above her she didn't know that she was out of breath, or that
she was giggling like a teenager.

Five minutes past midnight and she was now only yards away from
the hotel.

Would Jake have waited? Or was he still the impatient boy he'd
been seven years ago?

She raced into the hotel entrance and was suddenly struck by a
sense of dismay.

Everyone was in ballgowns and tuxes, hugging each other and
kissing.

She pushed open the heavy door and walked straight into a
bouncer.

"I'm sorry, madam," he said, looking her up and down. "Invitation only."

"I've got an invitation," insisted Annie, "I just didn't know I'd be coming. I *promise*. You *have* to let me in."

But the bouncer wasn't having any of it.

She looked furtively around to see if any of her family were down in the foyer. There were several parties going on in different rooms, and one was nearby. To her delight, she picked out a bulky form that she recognized. Oh God, what was his name? Butz? Putz?

"Officer Klutz!" she yelled above the noise. "Officer Klutz!"

Somehow, something made the cop look over. He raced toward her.

"Did I forget to tell you I'm undercover?"

No, she thought.

"I have to see Jake," she was almost crying. "Please tell this man that I'm invited."

Officer Stanowski—she knew there was a "K" in it—turned to the bouncer.

"Pick on someone your own size, buddy," he said and gave her a wink.

She almost hugged him, but she was in a rush.

"Where's the ballroom?"

"Go in the elevator, first floor, turn right, follow the corridor, you can't miss it," said the bouncer.

Annie raced for the elevator and almost ran on the spot waiting for it.

She was out of it before the door had finished opening and racing down a thickly carpeted corridor that didn't seem to have an end to it. When she finally reached the end, it turned abruptly right, and more red-carpeted corridor stretched out forever. Only the increasing noise of a party helped her run now, as she panted for every breath.

When she finally reached the enormous ballroom, there were so many people, all she could see was the massive clock above their heads and loads of balloons. It was now almost ten minutes past midnight. But where was the clock tower?

As four hundred inebriated, wealthy New Yorkers saw in the first few moments of the New Year, she was overcome by panic. She started to squeeze herself through the mass of bodies, hoping to God that luck would be on her side and Jake would still be there. She couldn't lose him again.

Suddenly she saw him.

He was standing directly under the clock, staring at the floor, despite the hedonistic party atmosphere around him. Of course! The clocktower was under the clock! Now who was the ifiot?

Annie hurled herself in his direction. Despite being buffeted mercilessly by the partying crowds around him, Jake was standing stock still, his eyes on the floor, his hand massaging the back of his neck.

"Jake!"

He couldn't hear her.

"JAKE!"

He still couldn't hear her.

"JAKE!"

Nope. Still couldn't hear her.

At last, she was by his side.

The crowd was so loud that neither of them could hear themselves think, let alone actually communicate with each other. But that didn't matter.

They looked at each other for a moment.

And then, slowly, instinctively, deliciously, Jake and Annie hugged the breath out of each other and refused to let go, while everyone around them started deliriously hugging anyone in sight.

As they were almost knocked over by the crowd, they kissed away the pain of too many years, hot tears mingling on their cheeks and down their necks.

As the sound of "Auld Lang Syne" rang out around them, Annie knew that she was finally forgiven.

Chapter 30

The New Year was only ten hours old, but for some, it felt as if time had stood still.

People were talking in the streets and greeting each other with kind wishes for the New Year. In Central Park, for the first time since Annie had been in New York, there was not one single jogger. Instead, star-struck lovers wandered aimlessly around, grinning stupidly at each other and a group of excited roller bladers performed their first show of the year.

Jake and Annie never saw Edward and Davina get arrested, in fact, they didn't see much else except each other that evening. They stayed at the party until the early hours of the morning and then wandered the city, feeling part of it and yet, at the same time, like voyeurs, set apart by their superior happiness.

Jake was holding Annie as if he'd never let her go again. "I swear, in that alleyway, I nearly lost it and snogged the life out of you."

"If it hadn't been for the seven-foot bloke running after us."

"Yes."

"And your girlfriend being there."

"I'd spent the entire evening thinking I hated you, when in fact I was a seething jealous idiot because you were with David and I was stuck with Sophie."

Annie's voice was hushed.

"How could you think I'd lie to you about having your baby?"

"I told you in that incredibly well-crafted, well-typed note. I was an ifiot. A mad ifiot. A *young,* mad ifiot. Will you be able to forgive me?"

"Yes. You believe me now?"

"Of course."

"How could you leave me—just not come back?"

"I kept thinking I would come back and every time I tried, my body seemed to back out. I just couldn't face the rejection. And the longer I left it the harder it got. I just buried myself in my work. Will you be able to forgive me?"

"I already have. Forgiving you about going out with Sophie might take longer. What was all that about then?"

"Well, I thought it was about getting my legover, but it appeared to be to get over you. Revenge. Pure and simple. That's what hit me in the alleyway. That and the fact that my whole life after walking out on you had been one long act of revenge—on myself, for screwing up my life so spectacularly."

They watched the park in silence for a moment.

"So what about golden boy then?"

"Edward?"

"Yeah—Edward Goddard, relation to an earl, crook and swindler."

Annie thought about it for the first time.

"Confusion. Revenge. Anger. Loneliness."

"And momentary bad taste."

"And momentary bad taste."

Jake grinned. "I can live with that."

David and Sophie were overjoyed for their friends, although Sophie felt mildly dissatisfied at not being the heroine anymore. And she was to stay convinced forever that Annie had been a rebound thing for Jake. Poor Jake. He'd obviously been more hurt than she'd imagined by her rejection of him.

Tony was only too delighted.

"Look what I started with all this pairin' up stuff!" he announced to all and sundry, hugging his Fi to him.

Far be it from Jake or Annie to inform them that they had had the head start on all of them by seven years.

Susannah took the news stoically. She had realized that something like this might happen, although perhaps not *quite* as speedily. As for George and Katherine, they were somewhat preoccupied with the horrifying revelations about Davina and Edward.

In fact, neither George nor Katherine were to ever fully recover from the hurt caused by Davina. Their pride was damaged beyond repair and they never allowed anyone in their inner sanctum again. They were to live a boring but safe life.

Thanks to Jake's evidence, the police found the offshore bank account that all the money had been siphoned off into, and Markhams' PR did not suffer anymore than it already had.

On Jake's advice, George and Susannah let the consultants do what they could with the company, while living off a substantially reduced income. As soon as possible, they sold it and then reinvested wisely. The Markhams would never be as rich as they once were, but they weren't going to go under.

A few years later, Jake, as one of the family, was able to dispense more advice and, thanks to his sound investments, the Markhams' lifestyle became far more close to how it used to be, if not exactly up to the same standard.

George and Susannah agreed that it was good, sound advice. And they were both relieved, that in having such a man married into the family, they could sleep at night knowing they were in safe, trustworthy hands.

In time, Victoria learned to be sensitive about winning more golf club cups than Charles. And he was truly grateful for her help with his swing—her swing was extraordinarily beautiful, it brought him out in goose bumps every time he saw it.

And there were more than goose bumps when they played in the married doubles tournament every summer. Summer had soon become their peak season, in more ways than one.

But neither Charles nor Victoria could ever have predicted the shared pride they were to feel at their sons' growing prowess at the game. All Victoria had to do was pretend that their skill was from their father and Charles's happiness was complete. And all Charles had to do was pretend he didn't know she was pretending.

They were all very happy together.

As for Cass and Brutus, their daughter, Bella-Anne, was their pride and joy and it was thanks to their excellent parenting that she didn't grow up a spoiled little madam. And, of course, it helped that when their excellent parenting became too much for little Bella-Anne, she could visit her godmother Annie, who always gave her a ready ear, unconditional love and infinite wisdom. And never tried to push her into anything.

Meanwhile, Annie finally invested her savings into her own gallery a walk away from her home with Jake. And so she began a new life of being her own boss. It surprised no one as much as her that the gallery, her family and her happiness with Jake thrived.

Epilogue

Central London Samaritans
8 a.m.

Annie walked into the office as fast as she could, which was slightly faster than a stoned tortoise. With some effort she sat at her desk.

"Hiya," said Joy. "How's our god-daughter?"

"It might be a godson," corrected Marlon.

"Don't insult her, they can hear everything by this stage, you know. They can *do* everything at this stage."

"Well then, she could start by carrying me," said Annie.

Annie bent down to pick up the toy in her bag and start wrapping it. It was Bella-Anne's fourth birthday today and Cass would kill Annie if she wasn't at the highly elaborate tea party she was putting on.

Annie's mobile went off. Damn, she always forgot to turn it off in here.

"Hi, Annie, it's Phoebe from the gallery."

"Hiya, I can't talk for long."

"OK. You know that piece you got in SoHo about five years

ago? Well, a man just came in and offered a million. Thought you might like to know."

Annie grinned as she felt the first familiar twitch of pain in her lower back.

"Thanks, Phoebe," she said, keeping her breathing steady. "Don't answer him just yet. I'm going to be incommunicado for a day or two."

There was silence for a beat.

"OK," said Phoebe, managing to keep any excitement out of her voice. "Speak to you . . . afterwards."

"Look after the gallery."

"I promise."

Annie quickly made another call.

"Hello, Jake Mead?" came a deep voice.

"Hello, Jake Mead," she smiled. "Ready for number two?"

"Oh my God, when?"

"Only just started. It'll be hours yet. Pick Sam up from nursery, phone Cass or she'll kill me for not being at Bella's tea party and I'll meet you at the hospital as soon as my shift's over."

"Right."

"By the way, we got an offer on the Marvello—the one I got in New York that time."

"How are you feeling?"

"Did you hear what I just said?"

"I heard a lot of noise that wasn't about how you were feeling."

"Jake, we're talking about a lot of money."

"Good. Breathe deeply. I'll be there as soon as I can."

Annie turned off her mobile and tried to rub her back. Joy came over silently and took over with older, expert hands.

"Did you say number two?" asked Marlon. "What the hell are you doing here, woman? We're not doctors. Stop massaging her and call an ambulance."

Annie and Joy grinned as Marlon started hopping from foot to foot.

"Were you a Morris dancer in another life?" asked Annie.

"Or a robot?" asked his wife.

Just then Annie's Samaritan phone started ringing.

"Oh my God, she's taking calls while she's in labor!" shouted Marlon. "Someone do something."

"Well, answer the phone for her then," ordered Joy.

"What and miss all the fun?" screeched Marlon.

Annie grinned up at Joy and leaned over to pick up the phone.

"Hello, Samaritans?" she said softly into the phone.

And as the backache temporarily dulled, she closed her eyes and saw Jake there, smiling at her.

Acknowledgments

A sincere thank you to my local Samaritan Center for allowing me into their wonderful world.

Thank you Kirsten Edwards and Michael (Baf) Barrie for his karate expertise. I'm still waiting for the demo.

Thank you Andrew, as ever, for getting the food in, dealing with the builders, paying the bills and nodding quietly while I ranted. And for generally making my life a joy.

Thank you Mum and Dad, for buying me the biggest *Thesaurus* in the world. As you can probably tell from reading this book, it served as a wonderful doorstop.

Thank you marvelous Maggie at Ed Victor, for your unending support, chirpy optimism, great company, amazing contacts and fantastic taste in restaurants.

And thank you, Gillian, at Piatkus, for your invaluable editing skills. And for being firm when I needed it, kind when I needed it and most importantly, knowing the difference between the two.

And thank you so much for all the letters I've received from people who read and loved *Pride, Prejudice & Jasmin Field*. You have no idea how each letter helps soothe the ego of a paranoid neurotic.

Next time, please send a copy to my mother too. It would save so much on postage.

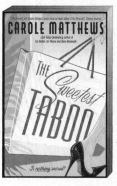